DEATH RATTLE

The Guns of Samuel Pritchard

DEATH RATTLE

THE GUNS OF SAMUEL PRITCHARD

SEAN LYNCH

PINNACLE BOOKS
Kensington Publishing Corp.
www.kensingtonbooks.com

KENSINGTON BOOKS are published by

Kensington Publishing Corp.
119 West 40th Street
New York, NY 10018

All Kensington titles, imprints, and distributed lines are available at special quantity discounts for bulk purchases for sales promotions, premiums, fund-raising, educational, or institutional use. Special book excerpts or customized printings can also be created to fit specific needs. For details, write or phone the office of the Kensington sales manager: Kensington Publishing Corp., 119 West 40th Street, New York, NY 10018, attn: Sales Department; phone 1-800-221-2647.

ISBN-13: 978-0-7860-4493-1
ISBN-10: 0-7860-4493-4

First printing: July 2019

10 9 8 7 6 5 4 3 2 1

Printed in the United States of America

Electronic edition:

ISBN-13: 978-0-7860-4494-8 (e-book)
ISBN-10: 0-7860-4494-2 (e-book)

*This book is dedicated to my son, Owen,
who is fond of westerns.*

PART ONE
SOLDIER

Chapter 1

Atherton, Missouri, October 1863

Samuel Pritchard quietly eased back the hammer of the Hawken rifle. He didn't want the telltale *click* to spook the flock only thirty yards from where he and his friend David "Ditch" Clemson lay concealed behind a fallen tree.

The rifle belonged to Ditch's father. The Pritchard family owned a similar weapon, but Samuel was rarely allowed to take it out, and never on a school day. Thomas Pritchard was a practical, hardworking, and devoutly religious man. He was also a man who didn't like guns and believed his son's time was better spent working at the family's sawmill or devoted to his studies at Atherton's only schoolhouse. Had he known seventeen-year-old Samuel cut class with Ditch to go hunting along the Missouri River, he'd have been more than displeased.

The boys were in the mile-long stretch of woods between their families' properties, the Clemsons' humble cabin and horse ranch, and the Pritchards' prestigious, two-story home. Thomas Pritchard was known in Jackson County as a wealthy man.

Young Thomas Pritchard started out cutting and freighting wood along the Missouri River by himself, shipping it to Kansas City by barge. Before long he had a crew of local men working for him and was able to provide a solid living for his beautiful wife, Dovie, and their two small children, Samuel and Idelle.

But as the children grew, and the Terre Haute & Richmond, and Madison & Indianapolis railroads began pushing west, lumber was needed like never before. Thomas invested in a steam-driven saw, and then another, and soon his modest business was booming. When the war started, the Pritchard Lumber Company added government contracts to its burgeoning list of clients. That's when the money really began rolling in.

Pritchard placed the rifle's front sight on the neck of a large tom, intending for a head shot. A .54 caliber ball could do a lot of damage. He wanted a clean kill and as much of the bird's meat intact as possible.

Though only a few days shy of his eighteenth birthday, Samuel Pritchard was very big, like his father. He stood well over six feet and, also like his father, possessed a powerful physique born from a lifetime of cutting, loading, and hauling lumber. Thomas Pritchard took pride in the fact that his son was one of the strongest youths in Jackson County. Had he known Samuel was also one of the best rifle shots, which he didn't, he'd have been furious. Skill with a gun was something the elder Pritchard frowned upon.

Most of the men in the county, some even as young as Samuel, had already volunteered and gone off to fight on one side or the other. Ditch's older brother Paul was a Confederate volunteer, and last anyone heard was serving with Shelby's Missouri Iron Brigade somewhere in Arkansas.

Those who hadn't volunteered had been conscripted by the Union. The Enrollment Act, passed the previous March, required all males age twenty and above to join the Federal army. Thomas Pritchard hoped the war would end before Samuel attained conscription age. Should the war still be raging, however, he had more than hope to keep his son from participating. Thomas Pritchard had a plan.

Though Samuel didn't know it, it was his father's intention to buy out his enlistment. This practice was legal, and would be carried out by paying a local family to have their son enlist in his place. There was no shortage of impoverished families with boys of eligible age in Jackson County who would welcome the cash money Thomas Pritchard would pony up to keep his own son out of harm's way. If that didn't work, Thomas had a backup plan; he could pay to have Samuel's enlistment commuted. This would be far more expensive, but could be accomplished by direct payment to the district provost marshal who headed the local Federal enlistment board.

The Federal district provost marshal, hotel and saloonkeeper Burnell Shipley, also happened to be Atherton's mayor. An easier man to bribe didn't live in Jackson County.

In the meantime, Thomas Pritchard was careful to remain neutral. He refused to publicly take sides and kept his family, especially his son, from doing the same.

Tensions were high along the Missouri River since the "War of the Rebellion," or the "War of Northern Aggression," as it was called, depending on which side you favored, began. Folks in Jackson County were split down the middle into which camp they fell, with the greater number of rural residents siding with the South, and the majority of Atherton's townsfolk aligning with the North.

There had been feuds, raids, gunfights, and even murder, sometimes between members of the same family who'd chosen different camps. Such was life in the border states during the war, and it was Thomas Pritchard's goal to remain as nonpartisan as a man could be in such volatile times. A big part of his neutral posture was keeping his son Samuel away from guns.

Before the war, it was rare to see men wearing side-arms. Though hunting rifles were common outside of town, and widely employed, a man wearing a pistol openly on his belt within town limits, who wasn't a lawman or soldier, was a peculiar sight.

Now most men sported pistols, and not just in the country. Just about every fellow walking the streets of Atherton was heeled. Consequently, the last thing Thomas Pritchard wanted was for his son to become known as a skilled shot. Such a reputation, in these hair-trigger times, could get a man, or teenage boy, killed.

Pritchard took in, and let out, a slow, easy breath. Steadying the rifle's front sight on the gobbler's head, he gently placed his finger on the trigger. He had to make the shot count. The only ball, cap, and powder the boys brought were in the gun.

He was about to squeeze when the sound of gun-shots rang out. There were five or six of them, off in the distance. The flock of turkey before him spooked and scattered.

"Damn," Pritchard cursed at the missed opportunity. He lowered the rifle's hammer and the boys stood up. "Who fired off all those shots?"

"I don't know," Ditch answered, "but look yonder." He nudged Pritchard and pointed over the tree line to the east. "Smoke. It looks to be comin' from where those shots came from."

"That's our place," Pritchard said, dread creeping into his voice.

"I know," Ditch said.

The boys started running.

Chapter 2

Pritchard and Ditch approached the edge of the woods bordering the Pritchards' property at a full sprint. Ditch had taken the Hawken back, and both boys were out of breath from their all-out run. Pritchard was in the lead, as his much longer legs and greater strength gave him speed over his medium-sized friend. The smell of burning wood, and the increasing glow of flames as they neared, urged them onward.

Pritchard reached the woodline first and halted. Ditch skidded to a stop on his heels. Both stared in horror at the scene before them.

The Pritchard home was fully engulfed and sending a billowing trail of black smoke skyward. There were riders, six of them, wearing gray reb coats and cloth masks under their hats. All had pistols. Some wielded torches.

Pritchard was taking it in, frozen and aghast, when Ditch grabbed his arm and pointed to the big sycamore off to one side of the house. There, hanging by the neck from a rope looped over one of the big tree's stout branches, was his father. One of his boots had fallen off. He swung slowly back and forth.

"Pa!" Pritchard gasped. He started toward him. Suddenly there was an explosion in his head and everything went hazy. The last thing he remembered was seeing the ground jump up toward his face.

Pritchard blinked, and his vision came back into focus. He was on his back, looking up at the sky. It was late afternoon, and the sun had begun to dip below the tree line. He carefully sat up. His head throbbed.

"Shhhh," Ditch cooed, his hand over Pritchard's mouth. "Stay quiet. There's a couple of 'em still out there."

Pritchard realized he was no longer at the edge of the woodline. Ditch removed his hand.

"I ain't proud of smackin' you in the noggin with a rifle butt," Ditch whispered, "but I ain't gonna apologize. We both know I can't take you. If I'd let you run out there, you'd be swingin' in that tree next to your pa."

Pritchard slowly nodded. "How long have I been out?"

"Couple of hours. I drug you back into the woods, so's we wouldn't get seen. Your house is nothing but a pile of ashes."

"Let's go look."

"You ain't gonna get stupid again, are you?"

"No," Pritchard said. "I've got my wits about me now."

Ditch picked up the Hawken, and both boys crept silently again to the edge of the woodline. What awaited them was exactly as Ditch had described. The house was a smoldering black heap of charred wood. The barn was intact, but the doors were open, and all the horses gone. All but two of the gray raiders had departed.

The remaining two horsemen had dismounted and tied their animals nearby. One, sipping from a bottle and chewing a blade of grass, sat with his back against the sycamore tree where Thomas Pritchard's body still hung. The other stood next to him, leisurely smoking a pipe. Both had removed their canvas masks. That a dead man swayed overhead seemed to bother them not in the least.

"You didn't see any sign of my ma or Idelle, did you?" Pritchard whispered, angrily wiping back tears he hoped his friend Ditch didn't see. He was almost afraid to ask the question.

"No sign of them," Ditch assured him.

"Ma took Idelle into town to do some shopping this morning," Pritchard explained.

"It's just as well they weren't home," Ditch said. Neither wanted to think about what would have transpired if his mother or his nine-year-old sister, Idelle, had been present when the riders arrived.

"Why are two of them still here?" Pritchard asked, pointing to the graycoats. "Why didn't they take off when the rest of the raiding party left?"

"I figure those two were left behind to get you when you came home." Pritchard absorbed his friend's words. "Maybe your ma and Idelle, too.

"Aren't they afraid of a posse coming?"

"Nope," Ditch answered. "They ain't afraid of no posse. Look closer. Recognize either of 'em?"

"Yes." Pritchard squinted. "I know them both. The one smoking the pipe is Bob Toole. He works at Shipley's hotel. The other one is—"

"—Glen Bedgley," Ditch finished. "Deputy Glenn Bedgley. Don't forget, Shipley doesn't just own the town. He owns the town marshal and the county sheriff, too. Still think they're afraid of a posse?"

Pritchard shook his head. "I don't get it. Toole and Bedgley are both Union men. Hell, Toole runs the enlistment board for Shipley. Why would Union men be dressed like Confederate raiders? And why would they kill Pa and burn our house?"

"I don't know for sure," Ditch whispered, "but I can guess. My dad says Shipley's using his position with the government to take over everything he can get his hands on. Remember last winter when he took over the riverside loading docks, claiming they were vital to the Union cause? And the train station? And how he took over the livery stable and the stockyards this past spring?"

"I do," Pritchard said. "Pa said Shipley tried to buy out the sawmill last year, but he refused to sell."

"I wouldn't be surprised if Shipley had his eye on your family's mill all along," Ditch went on, "especially since your pa never took sides with the Union. I'll bet he's in town, as we speak, declaring the sawmill a 'vital resource to the war effort,' and commandeering it for the 'Great Cause.'"

"I get it," Pritchard said. "By dressing his men as reb raiders, Shipley can blame the raid on folks who lean with the South. Not only will that cover his tracks, it'll rile up every Union gun in the county."

"That's how I figure it," Ditch said. He put his hand on Pritchard's shoulder. "I'm powerful sorry about your pa."

Ditch and Pritchard were silent for a long time. Pritchard again fought back tears. They watched the sun slowly fall and kept their eyes on the two Union men, dressed in rebel gray, lounging beneath Thomas Pritchard's dangling body.

"What do you aim to do?" Ditch finally asked.

"First, I'm gonna kill those two murderin' bastards," Pritchard said. His tears were gone, replaced by narrowed eyes and a set jaw. "Then I'm going to cut Pa down from that tree and bury him."

"Then what?"

"Then I'm going to pay Burnell Shipley a visit."

Chapter 3

Pritchard and Ditch crept across the lawn toward the two men in gray coats. Ditch held the Hawken at the ready, with the hammer back. Pritchard grasped Ditch's skinning knife in his left hand and a hatchet in his right.

It was dusk, and full dark was only minutes away. The flickering firelight from what was left of the Pritchard home, and the crackling of still-burning embers, cast dancing shadows and covered the sounds of their movement.

The two boys carefully circumnavigated the property and emerged from behind the sentries. The Union men were by now both seated and looked to be dozing, though one held a pistol loosely in each hand.

Pritchard picked up a hatchet from the woodpile near the barn as they made their way around the yard. He tried not to look above the two gray-coated men, at his father's hanging body, but found he couldn't keep his gaze from drifting up. The best he could do was stare at his pa's dangling feet, one bootless, while keeping the two men below in sight.

Suddenly Ditch and Pritchard were upon them.

Bob Toole saw the boys first. He cried out a warning, started to rise, and went for the pistol stuck in the wide belt around his gray reb coat.

Pritchard brought down the razor-sharp hatchet and sliced off Toole's right hand in one clean swoop, as he tried to draw the Navy Colt. He followed up by ramming Ditch's knife, hilt deep, into the hotel clerk's chest.

Deputy Glenn Bedgley, his guns already in hand, struggled to get his fat body to his feet. As he clumsily rose, he thumbed the hammers back on his pair of 1858 Remington .44s. He was bringing the weapons to bear on Pritchard, at point-blank range, when the .54 caliber ball fired from Ditch Clemson's Hawken rifle entered his stomach. Bedgley dropped the pistols, screamed, clutched his midsection, and fell forward onto his face.

Ditch set his rifle against the tree as Pritchard examined the downed men. Bob Toole was dead, his sightless eyes staring up at nothing. Pritchard extracted the blade from his chest and handed it to Ditch.

"Cut down Pa, will ya?"

"Sure, Samuel," Ditch answered solemnly, taking the knife.

Pritchard kicked Bedgley over onto his back. The bearded deputy was conscious and still clutching his stomach. His face was contorted in agony. He looked up at Pritchard looming over him.

"You're in a heap of trouble, boy," Bedgley grunted, straining to get the words out. He punctuated his sentence by spitting blood.

"And you're gut-shot," Pritchard said. "You won't see morning."

"Get me into town," Bedgley ordered, "to the doctor."

Pritchard ignored him. He tossed the hatchet aside and picked up Bedgley's dropped revolvers. He had never before held a pistol. The weapons were heavier than he anticipated.

"Give me a hand, will ya?" Ditch called out. He'd cut the rope and was struggling with Thomas Pritchard's large, heavy, body.

Pritchard lowered the revolver's hammers, stuck both guns into his belt, and helped his friend lower his father to the ground.

"Looks like he put up a fight," Ditch said, pointing to the skinned knuckles on both of Thomas Pritchard's hands. Pritchard parted his father's shirt and saw several gunshot wounds on his torso.

"As much fight as one unarmed man can put up," Pritchard said grimly, "against a pack of armed cowards." He took some solace in hoping his father might have already been dead when they hanged him.

"Get Toole's gun," Pritchard told Ditch.

"No thanks," Ditch said. "I ain't takin' a gun out of a dead man's fist." He pointed to the dismembered hand, still wrapped around the Navy Colt. It lay several feet from Toole's body.

"Safest way to take a gun from a man is when he's dead, I reckon," Pritchard said. He picked up the detached hand and pried it from the gun. Then he tossed the hand aside and examined the pistol. Holding the weapon up to the fading firelight, he checked the load.

"Only four unfired," he announced. "Toole shot Pa at least once." He spat on Toole's body, tossed the gun to Ditch, who reluctantly caught it, and walked back over to where the deputy lay writhing.

"How about you, Deputy?" Pritchard said, examining

one of the Remingtons in his belt. The revolver was
unfired, and all six of the chambers in the cylinder were
still loaded. The Remington revolver was designed
with safety notches between the cylinder's charge
holes. This meant the pistol could be safely carried
with all six chambers fully loaded. Everyone knew only
five chambers in a Colt's cylinder could be loaded, if
the bearer didn't want to shoot off his own foot.

The second Remington, however, had only four
cylinder holes still charged, and the barrel was black-
ened with burnt powder. "Looks like you put a couple
into Pa, didn't you?"

"Go to hell," the deputy hissed. He turned his head
and vomited blood.

"Who else was riding with you?" Pritchard asked.

"I ain't tellin' you nuthin'," came the reply. "If you
know what's good for you, you'll get me on a horse
and into town to Dr. Mauldin."

"Where're my ma and sister?" Pritchard said. "They'd
have been home before dark unless something was
keeping them."

Deputy Bedgley's face broke into a lewd grin. "Your
ma is at the Atherton Hotel. Right about now, I'm
guessin', she's getting the high hard one from Burn
Shipley. Your little sister is probably watchin', so she
can learn how to take it when she gets old enough."
He cackled and spat more blood. "Course, there's
some say she's old enough to take it now." His voice
trailed off into tortured laughter.

Pritchard reached over and took the knife from
Ditch's belt. He knelt over Bedgley and held the shiny
blade in front of the deputy's eyes.

"You'd best think against that," Bedgley said, all the mirth instantly gone from his voice. His eyes widened from pain to terror.

"This is for my pa," Pritchard said. He thrust the knife into the deputy's bulging abdomen, just above the pelvis, and started carving upward. Bedgley howled and weakly tried to grab the knife. Pritchard easily slapped his hands away and continued slicing.

"Don't look for Pa when you get to hell," Pritchard said. He stopped cutting when the blade reached breastbone. He withdrew the knife and stood up.

Deputy Glenn Bedgley twitched, his eyes rolled back, and he began to make gurgling noises from deep within his throat. Blood bubbled from his mouth, and the sound of choking, clucking, and gasping increased. It sounded like he was drowning in his own blood. He convulsed once, ceased moving, and died.

Neither boy spoke for long seconds. "I never saw a man die before," Ditch finally said, looking away from the bodies of Toole and Bedgley.

"Me, either."

"Did you hear that sound he made?" Ditch said. "That was spooky as hell. Pa told me about something called the 'death rattle.' He said when you hear it, you know the reaper's at the door. He also told me once you hear it, you never forget."

"Best get used to it," Pritchard said, wiping Ditch's blade on the dead deputy's shirt. "I reckon you'll be hearing it again."

Chapter 4

"You have no right to keep us here," Dovie Pritchard said to Burnell Shipley, the mayor of Atherton. "We must leave Atherton and go home."

"I'm afraid I can't allow it." Shipley shook his head. "It's especially unsafe for a woman such as yourself, and your young daughter, to be out on the road. There are reb raiders about. I couldn't call myself a Christian man if I allowed two defenseless gals to go gallivanting off into the night amid these troubles."

"I didn't realize you called yourself a Christian at all," Dovie said.

Mayor Burnell Shipley had doffed his usual wool suit and derby and donned his blue Federal uniform and wide-brimmed military hat. He was a portly man, of less-than-medium-height, in his mid-forties. He sported a florid complexion, a bald head with a comb-over, and elaborately groomed facial hair, of which he was known to be uncommonly proud. He stood on the steps of his hotel, the Atherton Arms, before a growing flock of armed men and townsfolk.

It was clear he was about to speak not as mayor, but as Federal district provost marshal. Shipley was flanked by the Jackson County sheriff, dour-faced Horace Foster, and Atherton's skittish town marshal, Elton Stacy. Several sheriff's deputies and marshals were posted around the hotel's entrance.

"I'm worried about Thomas and Samuel," Dovie insisted. Her daughter, Idelle, held her mother's hand. Concern framed both their faces. "Others are worried about their kin, as well. We must be allowed to leave."

"We're all worried," Shipley said, patting her arm. She instinctively pulled away. "And I promise, tomorrow morning, I'll have some men escort you out to your place. But right now, it's just too dangerous. You and your daughter are welcome to stay the night at the hotel, as my guests, free of charge."

"I thank you kindly," Dovie said, "but your hotel is not the sort of place a married woman or a decent young girl would patronize. If you will not allow us to leave Atherton, I will seek lodging elsewhere."

Shipley raised his eyebrows at Dovie and her daughter. "Too good for the Atherton Arms, are you?"

"Most women are," Dovie said.

"You'll excuse me," Shipley said. "I have important duties to attend to."

"Of course."

Shipley turned away from the Pritchard women to face the crowd. He cleared his throat and raised his hands. The crowd quieted.

"As you've probably all heard," he began in his booming voice, "rebel raiders are on the march in Jackson County. We've received word that several farms and ranches have been attacked."

"What 'n hell do you intend to do about it?" a voice called out from the crowd.

"The telegraph lines are down," Shipley went on, "but I've sent riders to Kansas City to summon Federal troops."

"Kansas City's bettern'n twenty miles away," another man shouted. "It could be a day or more before help arrives."

"That's why," Shipley continued, "as of this moment, I'm declaring martial law. As Federal district provost marshal, I'm taking command of all of Jackson County. I'm going to assign men to protect Atherton's critical resources, to keep them from falling into Confederate hands. I will need volunteers to guard the train depot, the loading docks, the stockyards, the sawmill, and to assist the town marshal in patrolling the streets. My number one job is to keep the town of Atherton safe."

"Of course it is," another angry voice challenged, "because you own the whole damned town!"

"What about the folks living outside of town?" another voice yelled. "Who's going to keep them safe?"

"I would like nothing more than to send out forces to begin checking on the outlying areas," Shipley smoothly responded, "but it's nighttime, if you haven't noticed. We don't know how many Confederate raiders are out there, perhaps lying in ambush. We barely have enough men to secure the town. If we deplete our ranks by sending our menfolk out into the county, in the dark, we run the risk of being overrun here in town if we're attacked. Tomorrow morning, at first light, we can send out a troop of volunteers. But tonight, as much as it pains me, I must keep all available guns here in town."

"Lots of townsfolk have family in the county," still another voice rang out. It belonged to a warehouseman employed at Shipley's Mercantile and General Store. "Especially men like me, who work in town but live outside town limits. You can't expect us to just sit here on our butts in Atherton while our wives and children are left defenseless?"

"You're tellin' us the stockyards," another indignant voice joined in, "and the damned train depot are more important than our families? Is that what you're tellin' us?"

"I'm sorry," Shipley said, "but you all heard me declare martial law. No one will be allowed to leave Atherton until morning. Anyone caught doing so will be shot. My orders are final."

"That's a load of bull," another man hollered. Others clamored in agreement. The outraged crowd was quickly becoming a mob, a mob hostile to the authority of Federal District Provost Marshal Burnell Shipley.

Shipley looked to the sheriff and marshal.

"Last thing we need is a riot," Marshal Stacy said.

"I ain't got enough men to quell one, if it starts," Sheriff Foster said to Shipley. He scanned the crowd. "We may have a problem on our hands, Burnell."

"Ain't no problem," said Eli Gaines. He was one of Foster's junior deputies. In his early twenties, he was tall, anemically thin, stoop shouldered, with a sallow complexion and brown, corroded teeth. He was also known to be the fastest, and most lethal, gunman in Jackson County. Though only a deputy for a couple of years, Gaines had already gunned down three men. Rumor had it, two of them were back-shot, and the third unarmed.

"All you've got to do is plug the biggest loudmouth

in the mob," Gaines drawled in his high-pitched voice, "and the rest of the rabble will wilt and fall into line."

"There's wisdom in what Gaines says," Marshal Stacy said.

"Then do it," Shipley ordered. "Before things get out of hand."

Sheriff Foster nodded, and Gaines flashed his dirt-brown grin in return. He drew one of his two Navy Colts and started down the steps of the Atherton Arms Hotel.

Suddenly a gunshot rang out, instantly silencing the crowd. Everyone looked in the direction from where it came.

Samuel Pritchard rode alone into town, straight down the middle of Main Street. He was leading a second horse with two bodies, wearing gray coats, draped over the saddle. A smoking .44 revolver was in his hand.

"No need to send out a rescue party," Pritchard announced. "There ain't no Confederate raiders."

Chapter 5

"You heard me," Pritchard said, parting the crowd and riding up to the steps of the Atherton Arms. He dismounted and stuck the revolver in his belt along with the other gun.

"There are no reb raiders," he declared again to the assembled townsfolk. "Only Burnell Shipley's men, dressed up like Confederate rebels."

"Samuel," his mother cried out. Dovie and Idelle scurried past the gawkers to his side.

"Pa's dead," Pritchard said, as he took his mother and sister into his arms. "He was murdered by these two men, along with four of their friends. They burned down our house, too."

Dovie looked into the exhausted face of her son and knew immediately his words were true. She and Idelle began to cry. He pressed them both to his chest.

Earlier that night, with Ditch's help, Pritchard had buried his father, using shovels from the barn. They planted Thomas Pritchard at the edge of his property, overlooking the pond. Then they constructed a makeshift cross from scrap lumber and placed it at the head of the grave.

"You want to say any words?" Ditch asked. He knelt and bowed his head, leaning on his shovel. Pritchard knelt next to him.

"Ain't much to say," Pritchard said as tears slowly fell down his dirt-streaked face. "Pa was a good Christian man, Lord, and a good husband and father. He was peaceful by nature. His only mistake was trying not to take sides in a fight that wasn't his to begin with. I know it ain't for us to question your ways, but Pa didn't deserve what he got. He didn't go looking for trouble. He just didn't want to shed the blood of his fellow man."

Pritchard wiped his eyes and stood up. "I'll be takin' a different path, Lord. Amen."

"Amen," Ditch repeated.

Ditch helped Pritchard lift the bodies of Bob Toole and Deputy Glenn Bedgley and lash them over the saddle of one of their horses. Pritchard took the two Remingtons, leaving Ditch the Colt, and mounted the other horse.

Ditch protested when Pritchard refused to allow his friend to accompany him into town.

"Nobody knows you're involved," Pritchard told him. "You already saved my life tonight, twice. I'll never forget it, or how you helped me bury Pa. There isn't any reason for you to get mixed up in what I've got to do, and no point in both of us catching a ball. You'd best get home and check on your own father."

Ditch recognized the logic in his friend's words. With his mother long dead and his only brother off fighting the war, there was only Ditch and his pa, and the meager horse ranch they operated. The boys hadn't heard any more gunshots or seen any more smoke on the horizon, but Ditch had been worried all night that raiders might have visited his home, too.

The two friends shook hands. Ditch grabbed his rifle and departed on foot, through the woods, back to his place. Pritchard steered the horses to Atherton, only a few miles away.

While Pritchard held his sobbing mother and sister, Marshal Stacy, Sheriff Foster, and several deputies examined the carcasses slung over the saddle.

"It's Bob Toole," the marshal said, after lifting the head of one of the bodies. "He's been stabbed. One of his hands has been cut off."

"Who's the other?" the sheriff demanded.

"One of your deputies. Glenn Bedgley. He's been shot and gutted like a hog."

"You son of a bitch," Sheriff Foster said, moving toward Pritchard.

Pritchard pushed his mother and sister aside and drew both revolvers. He pointed one at Shipley, standing above him on the hotel stoop, and the other at the approaching sheriff. All the deputies and marshals drew their own pistols and aimed them at him.

"You murdered a deputy sheriff," Foster said, still approaching Pritchard. "Drop them guns. You're under arrest."

"These men killed my pa," Pritchard said, "and torched my home. I caught them red-handed. They got what was coming to them. You take one more step, Sheriff, and you'll get yours. Your boss Shipley, too."

"I've got a dozen guns on you, boy," Sheriff Foster said, but he stopped advancing. "You've got no chance. This is the last time I'll tell you. Drop them pistols."

"These men murdered my father on Shipley's orders."

"That's your story," he said. "For all we know, you murdered them yourself."

"If I did, would I dress them up in reb gray and freight them back into town?"

"Stand by to fire," Foster said to the deputies and marshals, "on my signal."

"Go ahead and tell 'em to shoot," Pritchard said, raising the pistol pointed at Foster's chest up to his face. "But you'll never hear the shots. You'll be smokin' in hell before I will."

"No!" Dovie shouted, and ran to stand between her son and the lawmen's guns. "I won't let you kill him!"

"Get clear, Mrs. Pritchard," Sheriff Foster said.

"I will not," she said defiantly. "If you cowards are going to gun down a seventeen-year-old boy, you may as well shoot his mother along with him."

"Mama!" Idelle cried out, and joined her mother and brother.

"Get that child away from there," Sheriff Foster demanded. "I don't want to shoot a woman and child, but if I have to, I will."

"Like hell, you will," a voice from the crowd called out. Two dozen rifles and pistols were instantly directed at Sheriff Foster, Marshal Stacy, and their men.

"I don't know if what the boy says is true," a different man's voice said, "but either way, nobody is gonna shoot no woman or child."

"Damned straight!" another man said. "Hell no!" still another said.

Observing from the hotel porch, Burnell Shipley realized things were rapidly getting out of control. The arrival of Samuel Pritchard, towing the bodies of two of the men he'd dispatched to eliminate Thomas

Pritchard, was a wild card he didn't even know was in the deck.

Shipley's false-flag operation, carried out with help from the marshal and sheriff, and the martial law he'd declared as a result, were supposed to get him custody of the sawmill and further cement Union sentiment within the county. The Pritchard Lumber Company was the only utility he didn't have control of, and he needed to gain possession of it quickly. Only a week before, during a business trip to Jefferson City, his connections within the government informed him that a huge lumber contract was soon to be awarded.

Eliminating Thomas Pritchard was potentially going to benefit Shipley in ways other than financial. Shipley always had his eye on Dovie Pritchard, one of the comeliest women in Jackson County. Making her a widow at the same time he commandeered her dead husband's lumber business was killing two birds with one stone.

Shipley's wife had died under what some called "unusual" circumstances a couple of winters back. According to her husband, she sustained a fatal injury when she fell, drunk, down the icy back steps of the Atherton Hotel and fractured her skull. Except Miranda Shipley was known to be a teetotaler, only hotel employees used the back stairs, and there were no witnesses besides her husband. Regardless of what actually befell the hapless woman, the sheriff and town marshal summarily declared her death an accident. Dr. Mauldin had no choice but to sign the death certificate, listing "accidental" as the cause of her demise. That's where the matter ended.

With Pritchard's unexpected entrance, Shipley's plan had gone awry. Currently the town's police force, the sheriff and his deputies, and half the townspeople were boiling over and pointing guns at one another in the town square. If he didn't get a lid on this powder keg, there was going to be mass bloodshed. And with an enraged teenager pointing a .44 at Shipley's own sizable midsection, it was likely some of that spilled blood would be his.

Even if he survived assassination by Pritchard, Shipley knew an incident like the one about to transpire would inevitably result in the dispatch of troops from Kansas City, something he'd lied about sending for earlier. The last thing Burnell Shipley wanted was additional scrutiny from the U.S. Army at a time when he was finally about to gain complete control of the town of Atherton.

"Everybody calm down," Shipley said, in his silkiest and most paternal tone. "There's no need for gunplay. Sheriff Foster, have your men holster their guns. Marshal Stacy, do the same."

"But he murdered Glenn," Sheriff Foster protested. "He should be hanging from a—"

"Young Pritchard deserves a fair trial," Shipley cut off the sheriff, "like any man who's been accused. He has a right to be heard. Holster those weapons."

The sheriff cursed under his breath, but gestured for his men to stand down. Along with the town marshals they sheathed their guns.

"That's mighty generous of you," Pritchard said to Shipley, making no effort to lower his own pistols, "considering you're the man who ordered Pa's killing."

"Son," Shipley said, "you don't know what you're talking about. I did no such thing. We understand you're distraught at the death of your father, as anyone would be, but you're not thinking straight. I am not your enemy, and guns aren't the answer."

"Wrong on both counts," Pritchard said.

"Put your guns down," Shipley said, "and you'll get a fair trial. If what you say is true, you'll be vindicated. I give you my word as mayor of Atherton, and as district provost marshal."

"If I don't?"

"You'll die in the street, tonight. You may get a few of us, but your own death is a certainty. You might even get your mother and sister killed, and some of these good folks shot along with them. Is that what you want? To have innocent people hurt or killed on account of your actions? Do you really want to be gunned down in front of your family?"

Pritchard looked over at Dovie and Idelle. They held each other, in fear and anguish, but stood their ground between him and the lawmen. As badly as he wanted to pull the triggers, and damn the consequences, he couldn't allow them to be harmed.

Pritchard lowered the hammers and dropped the pistols at his feet. Several deputies moved in and roughly grabbed him by both of his thick arms.

"Just as well you gave up," Eli Gaines's whiny voice spoke in Pritchard's ear. "We both know you didn't have the balls."

"Oh yeah?" Pritchard replied. "Whyn't you ask Bob Toole and Glenn Bedgley about that?"

"Talk tough while you can," Gaines said. "Come tomorrow morning, you'll be swinging from a rope like your old man."

Pritchard stared hard into Eli Gaines's eyes, his

own blazing. "I don't remember tellin' anybody Pa
was hanged."

In reply, Gaines showed Pritchard his infected grin.

"Get him over to the jail," Shipley told Marshal Stacy,
"and do it quietly." Stacy passed the order to his men.

"The rest of you folks," Shipley again addressed the
crowd, still in his conciliatory tone, "simmer down and
put away your guns. We'll need cool heads and every
bit of ball and powder we've got before this night is
through. I want all the menfolk to line up and report
to Sheriff Foster. He'll assign you posts around town.
The womenfolk and kids are welcome to take refuge
inside the hotel."

"We'll do as you say, Shipley," one of the men from
the crowd of townspeople spoke up again, "but come
first light I'm leaving town and heading home. Any
man who gets in my way is gonna catch a ball." A
chorus of voices signaled their agreement.

"That's only fair," Shipley said magnanimously. In
truth, his charade about needing to keep the townspeople in Atherton to stave off Confederate raiders
had merely been a ploy to allow the six riders he'd dispatched earlier that day room to operate unhindered
out in county territory with as few witnesses as possible. Samuel Pritchard's arrival nearly spoiled that.

The riders had been given strict orders. Kill Thomas
Pritchard, burn his house, but damage no other of his
assets, and do the same to a couple of other nearby
farms and ranches so it wouldn't look like Pritchard
alone was targeted. They were to hang any men they
killed, to make it look like border ruffians or Confederate raiders. They were to wear reb coats in case they
were seen, and above all, they were not to remove
their masks.

Four of the riders, Eli Gaines and three other county deputies, had sneaked back into town unnoticed before sunset, as ordered. Two of the men he'd sent, Toole and Bedgley, never returned. When Pritchard showed up with the wayward men strapped over a saddle, Shipley learned why.

Toole and Bedgley had jeopardized everything by allowing themselves to be caught and killed by a teenage boy. As far as Shipley was concerned, they got what they deserved, just like Samuel Pritchard said.

As quickly as the people of Atherton fired up, they calmed down. Pritchard's peaceful surrender deflated their ire, and the logic of staying in town until daylight, with reb raiders potentially on the loose, was irrefutable. Reluctantly, and in an orderly fashion, they shuffled off to do as Shipley commanded.

"This ain't over between you and me," Pritchard said to Shipley, as he was escorted past the hotel toward the jail. Dovie and Idelle followed.

"It most certainly isn't," Shipley said as Pritchard was led away.

Chapter 6

Dovie and Idelle trailed behind the marshals as they escorted Pritchard to the jail, but the lawmen refused to allow them to enter. When she pounded on the door, Marshal Stacy told Dovie to take it up with Mayor Shipley. She marched back across the town square to the Atherton Arms with Idelle holding her hand and struggling to keep up.

Dovie stormed through the hotel lobby, ignoring the bustle of townspeople and marshals stationed inside, until she found a friendly face. It was Mrs. Nettles, one of Atherton's only two schoolteachers. Dovie left Idelle seated in the lobby, in Mrs. Nettleses's care, and went directly to Shipley's office.

She opened the door without knocking and found Shipley seated at his desk with Sheriff Foster standing over him. A bottle of whiskey and two glasses were on the desk.

"I want to see my son," Dovie Pritchard said.

"I thought you were too high and mighty to enter my hotel," Shipley said, sipping whiskey and ignoring her question.

"Don't play games with me," she said.

Shipley made a dismissive gesture to the sheriff. Sheriff Foster scowled, downed his drink, but tipped his hat and walked out. He closed the door behind him.

"Marshal Stacy wouldn't let me see Samuel at the jail. He said you had to authorize it."

"That's true," Shipley said.

"Then authorize it. I want to see my son."

Shipley set down his drink and leaned back in his chair, folding his hands across his sizable belly. "I'd like to help you, Mrs. Pritchard, but I can't. Your son's a dangerous criminal. A murderer, in fact. He's going to be hanged in the morning for his crimes."

"Hanged?" Dovie gasped. "You can't mean that?"

"I do indeed," Shipley said smugly. "That's what we do with murderers here in Atherton."

"But you said Samuel would get a fair trial! There're witnesses who heard you say it!"

"No need for a trial," Shipley said. "Your son admitted to killing two men, one of them a deputy sheriff, in front of those very same witnesses you speak of. Besides, as district provost marshal, operating under duly declared martial law, I have the authority to convene a tribunal and dispense justice as I see fit. For your information, I just convened the tribunal with Sheriff Foster, before you arrived. I'll be dispensing the justice tomorrow at dawn."

"You son of a bitch," Dovie said. "You had Thomas killed, just as my son said. Now you're going to kill him, too."

Shipley shrugged. "I most certainly did not have your husband killed," he lied. "He died, it appears, at the hand of Confederate brigands."

"Samuel says differently."

"It makes no difference what he says. I have a duty

to enforce the law, which means hanging your son. He killed two men. He must be punished. Order must be maintained. We're at war, you know."

Dovie put her face in her hands and began to sob. Shipley retrieved a clean glass from his desk and poured three fingers of whiskey into it. Then he topped off his own. She continued to weep.

"Your son doesn't have to hang, you know," Shipley said.

Dovie parted her hands and looked up. Her crystal blue eyes, a feature she passed on to both her son and daughter, were red from crying.

"What did you say?" she asked hesitantly.

"You heard me. Your son doesn't have to perish at the end of a rope."

"I'm listening," Dovie said.

"If Samuel were to escape," he said, "and go off and enlist in the Federal army, perhaps under an assumed name, who'd be the wiser? He'd have to serve in the war, naturally, and it would mean he could never, ever, return to Atherton. But at least he wouldn't get his neck stretched."

"You'd allow that?"

"I could be persuaded."

Dovie was no fool. "What do I have to do?"

"You're a very beautiful woman," Shipley said, his eyes moving up and down her. "But as of tonight, you're a widow. This is hard country for a woman alone, Mrs. Pritchard. If what your son says is true—"

"You know it is," she cut in.

"—you're also without a home. And you, with a young daughter to support. Unfortunately, it would seem you're now without means as well. Since the sawmill is a critical military resource, and in light of the recent Confederate partisan activity in the area, I've had to commandeer it. For the war effort, of course."

"Of course," Dovie said bitterly. "Just say it plain, Burnell. Quit dancing around and tell me what you want?"

"Direct," he said, sitting up and leaning forward in his chair. "That's another thing I've always admired about you. Very well, I want you to marry me. Not right away, of course. It might look bad if you got re-hitched so soon after your husband's demise. Say, in a month or two?"

"In exchange for becoming your wife, my son doesn't die? Is that what I get in return?"

"You'll get more than that. If you haven't noticed, I'm a very rich man. You and your daughter would be well cared for. You'd live here at the hotel, in luxury, and have anything you'd ever want."

"What I want," Dovie said bitterly, "is my husband and home back, and my son safe."

Shipley pushed the fresh glass of whiskey across the desk. "We can't always have everything we want, Mrs. Pritchard," he said. "Sometimes, we have to settle for what we can get."

"All that Samuel said about you was true," Dovie said, more to herself. She looked at the glass of whiskey on the desk in contempt. "You're a murdering bastard."

"Still high and mighty, eh?" Shipley said. "Well, it's a free country. You certainly don't have to accept my offer. I'm sure you and your daughter can find lodging somewhere around Atherton. But you'll need money to pay for rent and food, which means you'd have to find work. I've got a feeling nobody around here is going to hire you."

"You'd see to that, wouldn't you?"

"I could always use another gal down at the Sidewinder," Shipley said.

The Sidewinder, Atherton's main watering hole, like almost every other building and business in town, was owned by Shipley. The establishment featured drinking and gambling downstairs and two floors of "hospitality hostesses," as he called them, in the bedrooms upstairs.

"Idelle is nine or ten years old now, isn't she?" Shipley mused. "Kids grow up fast in these parts. Who knows? In a few years, she could start working at the Sidewinder along with you."

Dovie knew Shipley had her cornered. She could consent to marry the man who orchestrated her husband's death and had stolen their family's assets, and her son could live, or she could refuse, which would condemn her and her daughter to a life of poverty, prostitution, and shame, and her son would die.

"I need to think it over," she said, her voice barely audible.

"Don't think too long," Shipley said, extracting his gold watch from his vest pocket. "Dawn's only a few hours away."

Shipley repocketed his watch. He picked up the whiskey he'd poured for Dovie and extended the glass.

Dovie's shoulders slumped. She accepted the whiskey and began to drink. When the glass was empty, she looked at Shipley with beaten eyes and nodded.

"Is that a *yes*?"

"It is," she said, casting her gaze to the floor.

"I do believe," Shipley said, his grin widening, "we've just had a jailbreak."

"I want to say good-bye to Samuel," Dovie said without looking up.

"I'll allow it," Shipley said. "Think of it as your engagement present."

Chapter 7

Ditch Clemson rubbed his eyes and forced himself awake. He heard voices below and thought he recognized Pritchard's. He gingerly crawled through the mounds of hay, careful not to make any sound, and peered over the edge of the loft.

Ditch was in the upper tier of the livery stable at the edge of Atherton. He'd arrived in town on foot, unnoticed and exhausted, well after midnight. He found deputies and armed townsmen patrolling the streets, but the resourceful youth was easily able to evade them and enter the stable without being seen.

After Ditch parted ways with Pritchard earlier that night at what was left of the Pritchard home, he ran through the woods to his own family's modest ranch. There was plenty of moonlight to guide him, and he was intimately familiar with the woods, having roamed them since he was able to walk. There, to his relief, he found his father unharmed.

Rand Clemson had been outside tending to his small string of horses that afternoon when he heard riders approaching. Since his son had taken his only gun, the Hawken, without his permission, no doubt to go hunting instead of attending school, the rancher had no choice but to hide. He fled to the woods and hid under a pile of brush as the riders stormed in. With pistols in their hands, they dismounted and invaded his home.

He watched in anger as the riders, six of them, wearing masks and reb coats, roped his five horses together and rode off.

Ditch hugged his father and told him what transpired at the Pritchards'.

"Damn it, boy," Rand cursed. "Why did you involve yourself?"

"What was I supposed to do, Pa? Let them murder Samuel right before my eyes?"

Rand looked at his son, taller than him for two seasons. He put his hand on Ditch's shoulder. "Of course not," he said. "You done the right thing. But none of that matters now."

He led his son into the house and began packing what little food they had, and his son's few clothes, into a bedroll.

"What are you doing?" Ditch asked.

"You've got to flee, son. Iffen you don't, you'll be as dead as Samuel in a day or two."

"Who says Samuel's gonna be dead?"

"You just told me he rode into town alone to face down Burnell Shipley," his father answered. "Between the marshal and sheriff, Shipley has two dozen guns. Your friend doesn't have a prayer. Neither do you, I'm afraid."

"Pa, nobody knows about my part in what happened over at the Pritchard place. Samuel surely won't tell."

"You're cooked if he does," Rand Clemson said, not harshly. "If Samuel went into town, and he ain't already dead, he's been captured. There're ways of making the tightest-lipped men talk. I know of what I speak, son. I was about your age during the Blackhawk War."

"Samuel would never give me up."

"I ain't sayin' he would. Even if he don't, folks around here know you and him are tighter than two ticks on a hound's butt."

This was true. Neighbors David Clemson and Samuel Pritchard had been inseparable since they were knee-high. It was Pritchard who gave Davey his nickname, "Ditch," after a particularly spirited stud named Backbreaker threw the ten-year-old into a hog wallow when the stubborn youth tried to do what most men in the county would not: mount and ride the cursed horse.

"The men who killed Samuel's pa, and burned his home, are Union men," Rand Clemson explained to his son. "I ain't, and everybody knows it, especially with a boy fighting for the Confederacy. Neither Burnell Shipley, nor his sheriff, are going to take what Samuel and you did sittin' down. Those riders will be back. I'm sorry, David, but we have no choice. If you want to stay alive, you have to skedaddle."

Ditch knew his father was right.

Rand handed the bedroll to his son, along with a powder horn and a leather purse containing percussion caps and fifty rounds of .54 caliber ball. Ditch began to reload the Hawken.

Rand went to the hearth and removed a stone from the mantel. From the cavity it concealed, he withdrew a small cloth bag.

"Here's nearly forty dollars in gold," he said. "It's all I got. Take it and go. Stay off the roads. If I were you, I'd get on the river and float west to Kansas City. Buy a horse and go south to Arkansas. Your brother Paul's thereabouts, fighting along with Shelby's boys. Maybe you can find him and together you two can head out west? I hear tell there's money to be made out there, iffen you've got a sharp mind and a stout back."

"What about you?"

"Don't worry about me. I'll get along."

"But you've got no stock left," Ditch protested, "and I'm taking all your money and your only gun?"

Ditch suddenly remembered the Navy Colt in his belt, the one Pritchard took from Bob Toole's dismembered hand. "Here." He handed the pistol to this father. "It's got four balls left in it."

"I won't ask how you got it," Rand Clemson said, accepting the weapon. "Now, get away and don't come back. Missouri ain't no place for a young man to stay healthy anymore." He hugged his boy. "I love you, son. Good luck."

Ditch left his home, wiping tears as he went. He wondered, as he watched his father waving to him from the darkness, if he would ever see him again.

Ditch didn't head for the river, as he'd been advised. He took only part of his father's advice, the part about staying off the roads. Ditch Clemson was damned if he was going to Kansas City and spend good money on a horse when he knew exactly where some of the best horses in the county were. Horses that until a few hours ago belonged his father.

Ditch knew the riders who'd stolen his father's horses would take them only one place: the livery stable in Atherton. Sure enough, when Ditch crept into the stable, he found his pa's animals.

By the time Ditch got inside, after dodging a dozen or more marshals and armed townies, he realized there was no way he'd be able to get a horse out of Atherton through the street patrols without being spotted. He planned to snooze during the day, hidden in the stable's hayloft, and leave Atherton after dark the following night. Hopefully the patrols would be abated by then, and his departure would go undetected.

He ate some corn biscuits and jerky, checked his rifle, and covered himself with hay. Within minutes he was fast asleep. He was awakened, an hour before dawn, by the opening of the stable's gate and the sound of voices.

Ditch looked down, and even in the poor light, easily recognized his friend. Pritchard stood more than a head taller than the three men beside him. To Ditch's relief, he appeared unhurt. His hands were shackled, and he was wearing leg-irons. Marshal Stacy and two of his deputies hovered close to him.

"It takes three of you," Pritchard drawled, "to stand guard over me?"

"We ain't stupid," the jittery Stacy said. "You might be only a boy, but you're the size of a horse and damned near as stout. I was at the county fair last summer when I watched you take on every comer in the wrestlin' contest. You never even came close to losing a match."

"You broke my brother's arm," one of the deputy marshals chimed in. "Picked him up and threw him out of the ring like a sack of grain." He was busy lighting a kerosene lantern. The other deputy town marshal began saddling one of the stabled horses.

"Can't say I'm sorry for that," Pritchard said.

Ditch watched as three newcomers entered the stable. To his astonishment, he saw Samuel's mother. She was accompanied by the stern-faced Sheriff Foster and the bloated Burnell Shipley. Shipley was wearing a Union military uniform.

"Mama!" Pritchard said, clearly surprised to see her.

"Does he have to be chained, like an animal?" she asked Marshal Stacy.

"Afraid so," the marshal said. "At least for now."

"Say what you have to," Shipley commanded her. She nodded and moved in to hug her son. Dovie forced a smile and caressed his face.

"What's going on?" Pritchard asked, confused.

"You have to go, Samuel," Dovie said, tears streaking down her own face in stark contrast to her smile. "You must leave Atherton and never come back."

"I ain't going nowhere without you and Idelle."

"Yes," she contradicted him, "you are."

"If I don't?" Pritchard challenged.

"You'll hang," Shipley spoke up. "Today at dawn. Which, by my estimation, is less than an hour away."

"Okay," Pritchard said to his mother. "I'll go. But you and Idelle are coming with me."

"That's not going to happen," Dovie said. "I have to stay here. Idelle and I have been taken in by the Nettleses." She glanced sideways at Shipley. "At least for now."

"You don't have to stay," Pritchard argued. "There's nothing left for us in Atherton. That murderin' bastard Burnell Shipley," he thrust his chin at Atherton's mayor, "saw to that. Let's go, Mama. We can leave together."

"I can't," she said softly.

"Why not?"

"She's the reason you're not swingin' from a rope already, boy," Shipley said.

Pritchard looked from his mother, who suddenly wouldn't look him in the eye, to Shipley's arrogant, satisfied face. Comprehension hit him like a punch in the gut.

"No, Mama," Pritchard pleaded, unable to hide his revulsion. "You can't do it. I just put Pa into the ground last night. What would he think about you takin' up with Shipley? Pa's—"

"—dead!" Dovie snapped, finishing her son's sentence for him. "He's dead and gone. You're my only son, and you're still alive. I'm going to do whatever it takes to see you stay that way."

"I won't let you become Burnell Shipley's whore," Pritchard said. "I don't care what they do to me."

Dovie slapped him across the face. "You're still my little boy," she scolded, her tears falling freely, "and you'll do what you're told. I have Idelle to think of, or didn't you consider her? Do you think Idelle's life is worth any more than yours? Or mine?"

Pritchard was stunned by his mother's outburst, but not so shocked that he couldn't understand her meaning. A man like Burnell Shipley, who thought nothing of murdering his father and forcing his mother to consort with him under penalty of her son's death, wouldn't hesitate to kill Idelle to accomplish his ends, or kill Dovie herself, if he couldn't have her. Pritchard faced the fact that he had no more choice regarding his fate than his mother did.

"These men are going to release you," she said, regaining her composure. She brusquely wiped away her tears on a forearm. "You're going to get on a horse and ride. Keep riding and never come back to Atherton."

"Or Jackson County," Sheriff Foster added. "You ever set foot across the county line, you'll be shot on sight. I'll be glad to do it."

"You're a bright young fellow," Shipley said. "I shouldn't have to tell you what's going to happen to your mother and sister if you ever decide to grace Jackson County with your presence again. You can figure that out for yourself."

Shipley lit a cigar and turned to the marshal. "Cut him loose and send him on his way."

Veins bulged in Pritchard's neck and forehead as his shackles and leg-irons were unlocked. Sheriff Foster, Marshal Stacy, and both town marshals drew their pistols. The deputy marshal who'd saddled the horse handed over the reins, doing so gingerly, with his gun leveled, as if Pritchard were a rattler about to strike.

"My men will escort you out," Marshal Stacy said. "Don't come back."

"Good-bye, Mama," Pritchard said. "Tell Idelle I'm sorry for not saying good-bye."

"Go, Samuel," she said. "If you love your sister and me, you'll never come back."

"I won't be back," Pritchard said. "I hope God forgives you for what you've done, Mama, because I can't."

Pritchard glared at Shipley as he rode out. The last thing he heard was the fading sound of his mother's sobs.

Chapter 8

From the loft's window, Ditch watched the two marshals mount and escort Pritchard off. He waited until Dovie Pritchard, Burnell Shipley, Sheriff Foster, and Marshal Stacy extinguished the lantern and departed, before grabbing his rifle and bedroll and scampering down.

The livery stables were situated at the edge of town. Ditch made his way, again unseen, back into the woods. He began paralleling the road, following the horses on foot.

The first glint of the coming dawn crept over the horizon. It wasn't difficult to keep the riders in sight. He knew there was a sharp curve farther down the road. Ditch raced ahead through the woods, hoping to intercept Pritchard and the marshals.

"This is as far as we go," one of the town marshals said to Pritchard when they'd rounded a curve a couple of miles from Atherton.

"And as far as you go," Eli Gaines said, emerging from the woods to block Pritchard's path. He leveled both his revolvers, the hammers back, at Pritchard. Two more sheriff's deputies appeared behind him, their guns also at the ready.

The town marshals gave Gaines a nod, then wordlessly turned their horses and headed back toward town.

"Get your hands behind you," Gaines ordered. Pritchard had no choice but to comply. The gangly deputy put a pistol barrel against his belly as the other two deputies shackled his hands behind his back.

"You didn't really think Burnell Shipley was going to spend the rest of his life lookin' over his shoulder, did you?" Gaines said in his high-pitched voice.

"I reckon not," Pritchard answered.

"Even if Burnell didn't want you dead," Gaines said, "I damn sure wasn't going to let you go off and join the Union army. My older brother, Reuben, is off fightin' for the South."

Pritchard vaguely remembered Deputy Gaines had an older brother who was just as gangly, ugly, and mean as Eli. Everyone thought he'd grown up and moved on, but no one could have guessed a Gaines boy would join up to fight for the Confederacy.

"Does Burnell know you've got a brother fighting for the South? Seems to me, as the head Union man in this county, he might take offense."

"Pa sure took offense," Gaines said, "before he died. Having his oldest son run off to fight for the South is likely what killed him."

"Maybe Burnell will feel the same way?"

"What he don't know," Gaines said, "won't hurt him. Me, either."

Gaines and the county deputies had obviously been lying in wait to waylay Pritchard on Shipley's orders.

He realized, with bitterness, that his mother would never know his fate. She would honor the pact she'd made to preserve his life, never learning that Shipley had crawfished on his end of the deal. Dovie Pritchard would marry the repugnant mayor, taking comfort in the false knowledge her sacrifice had been her son's salvation. His insides roiled.

"Let's get moving," Gaines ordered. The two deputies brought out three horses, which had been tied out of sight in the woods. One of the them took the reins of Pritchard's horse as the three lawmen mounted up.

"Where're we going?" Pritchard asked.

"Down to the river," Gaines said.

"The river Jordan," one of the other deputies said with a smirk.

The quartet rode for another mile before Gaines led them off the road into the heavy woods. The Missouri River was only a hundred yards away.

When they reached the riverbank, Gaines stopped. He dismounted and signaled for the deputies to follow suit.

"Get him off his horse," Gaines said. One of the deputies, Boudroy, a heavyset man in his thirties with a full beard, shoved Pritchard from the saddle. He fell, with his hands bound behind him, heavily to the soft earth.

Gaines produced a short shovel from his saddle and tossed it to the other deputy, a thin, dirty-looking, man named Merle Crittenden. "Start digging."

"Why don't we have him do it?" Crittenden complained, pointing the shovel at Pritchard. "He looks stout enough to dig a forty-foot well in a single afternoon."

"Deputy Gaines is too frightened to let me have my

hands free," Pritchard said, sitting up. "He's afraid I'd kick his bony ass."

"I ain't afraid of no such thing," Gaines scoffed.

"Sure, you are," Pritchard argued. "I don't blame you. If I was a weed-skinny varmint like you, I'd be afraid myself. Without those guns, I'll bet you're terrified of your own shadow."

Boudroy and Crittenden looked uneasily at each other. They knew Eli Gaines was prone to dark moods, mean as a snake, and nearly as fast with those two Navy Colts he was never without. They preferred not to witness any insult to the hair-trigger deputy. He was unpredictable as hell, and might hold it against them later that they'd heard the Pritchard boy chide him.

Crittenden busied himself digging and pretended not to hear any more of the conversation. Boudroy, with his pistol in his hand but the hammer forward, stood over Pritchard.

"Keep bumping your gums, Pritchard," Gaines said. "It'll make what's coming to you that much easier for me."

"How hard can pulling a trigger be?" Pritchard said.

"It's a better end than you deserve," Gaines said. "It beats dancing at the end of a rope, like your pa, which is how you was gonna go out iffen your ma hadn't agreed to bend over and take it from Burn Shipley."

"Ha!" Boudroy guffawed. "I'll bet ole Burnell is helping her over a fence right now!"

Pritchard rolled onto his back and kicked the burly deputy standing over him in the groin. When the lawman sagged to his knees and reflexively began to vomit, Pritchard piston-kicked him again, squarely in the face. Deputy Boudroy flew backwards and landed ten feet away, unconscious. Blood and puke smeared his face around his shattered jaw and broken teeth. Pritchard wriggled to his knees.

Gaines rolled his eyes, shook his head, and drew one of his revolvers, casually pointing it at Pritchard.

"Still want him to do your digging for you?" he asked Crittenden.

"No, thanks," the deputy replied, looking over at the laid-out Boudroy. "I'll dig this grave myself."

"I'd be glad to help," Pritchard offered. "It's no bother."

"I'll bet you would," Gaines said.

Crittenden had dug a trench wide enough for a man, and two feet deep, when he clambered out of the hole and wiped his sweaty brow. "There're too many roots," he complained. "I can't get any deeper without a pickax."

"That ought to be deep enough," Gaines said. "We only want to cover him up, not sink him to China. Besides, we should be gettin' back to town before we're missed."

Boudroy began to stir, and sat up. He groaned, spat a mouthful of blood and teeth, vomited again, and held his jaw in place with both hands.

"Good morning, Deputy," Pritchard said.

"Jesus, Boudroy," Gaines said, "you're a holy mess."

"Let me do it," Boudroy mumbled through his split and busted mouth. He got shakily to his feet and picked up the revolver he'd dropped when Pritchard kicked him.

"Not a chance," Gaines said. "You couldn't hit the side of a barn in your condition. Get on your horse before you fall again. This'll only take a minute."

Gaines moved off five paces from the kneeling Pritchard and cocked his revolver. Crittenden dropped the shovel and dashed hastily out of the line of fire. Gaines made an elaborate production of raising his gun over his head, then lowered it directly at Pritchard.

"You got any last words, Samuel Pritchard?"

"I'll see you in hell," Pritchard said, as he stared without expression into the cold, black eye of the revolver's barrel. His last, tortured thoughts were of his mother and sister in Shipley's filthy hands.

"You surely will," Gaines said as he shot Pritchard in the forehead.

Chapter 9

Ditch watched helplessly as his best friend was executed with a pistol shot to the head. He was out of breath from running through the woods, trying to keep up with the quartet of horses on the road. He'd snuck as close as he dared to the river's edge, where the three deputies held Pritchard. He was near enough to observe the group, but not so near he could hear what was being said, or get a clear shot with the Hawken through the heavy brush.

He saw the muzzle blast and smoke from Gaines's revolver and heard the report a split second later. Pritchard fell forward on his face and didn't move. Ditch hung his head.

Ditch could barely bring himself to look up, through tear-filled eyes, as Gaines and Crittenden unshackled Pritchard's limp hands and roughly dragged him into the shallow grave. He desperately wanted to rise from where he was concealed, cock the Hawken, and charge, but realized it was futile. He knew he could get only one of the murderous lawmen with the single-shot rifle, at best, before the other two cut him down.

Gaines languidly rolled a cigarette. By the time he

was finished smoking it, Crittenden had scraped dirt over Pritchard and covered him up. He brushed leaves and twigs over the mound, blending it in with the surrounding terrain as best he could.

The emaciated deputy tossed his cigarette butt onto the mound. He and Crittenden mounted up, joined the bloodied Boudroy, and rode off.

Once the trio had gone, Ditch walked with stooped shoulders over to the mound. He dropped his bedroll and rifle. Then he knelt at his friend's grave and began to cry as he slowly scooped the dirt away. Gaines's cigarette butt was still smoldering.

He wasn't even sure why he began uncovering Pritchard's body. His grieving mind angrily contemplated stealing a couple of horses from the Atherton stable, returning to the grave, and freighting the body back into town, as Pritchard had done with the two dead deputies. He wanted Pritchard's mother to know she'd been cheated by Shipley, and her devil's bargain with the corrupt mayor hadn't saved her son.

He discarded the thought as quickly as it came. Such an act wouldn't bring Pritchard back, and would rouse Shipley against him. Worse, the venal mayor would undoubtedly go after his father.

For now, he simply wanted Pritchard out of the shallow, unmarked hole. He thought he might rebury him alongside his pa, near the pond at what was once their family's home. He figured he owed his lifelong friend that much.

Pritchard wasn't buried deep. Ditch was easily able to scoop away the loose earth. In less than a minute, most of the large, upper body was exposed. He found his friend lying faceup, his head turned to one side.

There was a jagged, bloody, circular bullet hole at his hairline over his right eye.

Ditch was uncovering his legs when Pritchard moaned. The sound startled him so badly he fell back onto his rump. With eyes like saucers and a pounding heart, he scuttled away from the open grave.

An instant later, Ditch watched in amazement as Pritchard moaned again. Dirt erupted from his nostrils and mouth, and his head lolled from side to side. Samuel was alive!

Ditch scrambled to the grave, cradled his friend's head, and gently lifted him to a seated position. As Pritchard coughed and sputtered for air, Ditch examined his wounds.

The .36 caliber ball, fired from Deputy Eli Gaines's 1851 Navy Colt, had entered the crown of Pritchard's forehead at a downward angle because he was on his knees. The projectile skirted the skull beneath the skin and exited the back of his head behind his left ear. What looked like a through-and-through headshot was actually only a grazing wound, albeit under the scalp. The impact rendered Pritchard unconscious, and the graphic appearance of entrance and exit wounds on opposite sides of his head led his would-be murderers to conclude he was dead.

"Can you hear me, Samuel?" Ditch asked excitedly. Pritchard's eyes were caked over with dirt.

"Not so loud," Pritchard croaked. "My head hurts."

Ditch hugged his friend, as his tears turned to laughter. "I'm gonna call you Lazarus from now on!"

"My noggin feels like somebody drove a railroad spike through it."

"Can you stand?"

"I think so."

Ditch helped the shaky Pritchard to his feet and led him to the river. Pritchard dunked his head, washing away dirt and blood, while Ditch unfolded his bedroll and began tearing his only clean shirt into bandages.

After Pritchard washed up and drank some water, Ditch carefully bandaged his head. He placed him against a tree and covered him with the bedroll. As Pritchard rested, he refilled the hole with dirt, doing his best to replace the scattered leaves and branches that were left by Deputy Crittenden to camouflage the grave. He even placed Deputy Gaines's cigarette butt back on the mound.

"We've got to get out of here," Ditch said, shouldering his rifle and bedroll. "We don't want to be around if any of Shipley's men come back to inspect their handiwork. Can you move?"

"I'm pretty woozy," Pritchard said, "but I guess I'll have to."

"Only if you want to stay alive," Ditch said.

Chapter 10

"It's nearly nine o'clock," Dovie said to Shipley. "You promised to take me out to our place at first light. I must attend to Thomas's body."

Dovie stood on the hotel steps. Shipley was seated, along with Sheriff Foster, in a pair of rocking chairs on the hotel porch. They were sipping coffee, smoking cigars, and surveying the town. Shipley was still wearing his Union uniform.

"And you will," Shipley said to her, "as soon as it's safe to travel. Sheriff Foster sent out a patrol to make sure the roads are free of Confederate raiders. Isn't that right, Sheriff?"

"That's true," Sheriff Foster said. He pushed back his hat and squinted at three riders, coming toward them down the main street. "Speak of the devil. Here comes the patrol now."

Deputies Gaines, Crittenden, and Boudroy, his neckerchief wrapped under his chin and tied on top of his head to keep his busted jaw in place, rode up.

"Roads are all clear," Gaines drawled his report to the sheriff. "No sign of reb raiders."

"What the hell happened to Boudroy?" Foster asked.

"He let himself get kicked," Gaines chuckled, displaying his decayed teeth, "by a big, angry, horse." Boudroy scowled back at him. Crittenden looked sheepish.

"Get him over to Doc Mauldin's," Foster said. "Then bring yourselves back here. You two are going to escort Mrs. Pritchard out to her place. Find some men to go along with you to bury her husband."

"But we ain't had our breakfast yet," Deputy Crittenden whined.

"Your breakfast can wait," Foster said. "Get moving. I want you back here, and ready to go, in five minutes."

"C'mon, Merle," Gaines said to Crittenden. He spat a gob of tobacco juice at Dovie's feet. The three deputies rode off toward the offices of Atherton's only physician.

"Digging two graves in one day," Crittenden bellyached when they were out of earshot, "and on an empty stomach, to boot. Sheriff Foster sure can be a son of a bitch sometimes."

"You can bet things'll be different," Gaines said, "when I'm sheriff of this county."

"Counting your chickens before they're hatched, ain't ya?" Crittenden chuckled.

"Laugh while you can," Gaines said, turning in the saddle and looking over his shoulder at his Sheriff Foster, growing smaller in the distance. "You may not be laughing so loud when I'm wearing the sheriff's star. Hell," he continued, swiveling back around to stare the mirth off Crittenden's face, "when I'm sheriff, you may not be laughing at all."

* * *

Ditch made his way around to the back of the schoolhouse, staying low. It was daytime, and he had to exert extra care not to be seen. He carefully peered through the rear window and saw the familiar rows of young children seated in their chairs. Alice Nettles, one of the town's only two schoolteachers, was at the chalkboard explaining a math problem. Her husband, Rodney Nettles, taught the older children in the room next door. He'd been Pritchard and Ditch's teacher for the past few years.

Ditch was looking for Idelle Pritchard. While eavesdropping from his hiding place in the hayloft at the Atherton stables, he overhead Dovie Pritchard tell Samuel that she and Idelle were staying at the Nettleses's place. Ditch crept silently away from the schoolhouse and made his way across the yard to the house, situated next door.

He found Idelle sitting on the back porch. She was wearing a rust-colored dress and had her long, blond hair in a ponytail. Her crystal blue eyes were red from lack of sleep and crying. She was aimlessly drawing circles in the dirt with a stick. Ditch didn't know it, but Dovie left Idelle in Atherton while she went out to inspect what was left of her home and care for her husband's remains.

"Hey Idelle," Ditch whispered from behind the cover of the woodpile. "Over here!"

She dropped the stick and looked up. "Ditch!" she cried out, and ran over to him.

"Hush!" he cautioned. "Don't call out my name, for heaven's sakes!"

As Samuel's best friend, nine-year-old Idelle Pritchard had known Ditch Clemson her entire life and had a crush on him for most of it. Though he wasn't tall and muscular, like her blond-haired, blue-eyed brother, Ditch possessed an agile, wiry build, and had dark brown, wavy hair and even darker eyes. She thought he was the handsomest fellow she'd ever seen.

"Why're you hiding?" she asked. Ditch grabbed her wrist and pulled her down behind the woodpile.

"Best you don't ask," he answered. "All you need to know is if I get found, I'm done."

"Why aren't you in school?" she said.

"Why aren't you?" he countered.

"Mrs. Nettles let me have the day off," she said softly, "on account of Pa being dead."

"I know," he said. "I helped your brother bury him. I'm powerful sorry, Idelle."

She nodded, and for a moment it looked like she might begin crying again.

"I need your help," Ditch said. He didn't have time for her tears. "Samuel does, too."

"Do you know where he is?" she said, perking up.

"I do," Ditch admitted, "but he's hurt. He's hiding out, like me. If he's found—"

"—they'll hang him," Idelle finished. "I know. I heard some marshals talking. How bad is he hurt?"

"Bad enough. I need some whiskey and a sheet to make more bandages. I also need some food."

"Pa told me whiskey is bad for you," Idelle said.

"It ain't to drink, Idelle. I need it to clean up Samuel's wounds."

Worry lighted the girl's face. "Please tell me where he is," she pleaded, "and what happened to him?"

"I can't," Ditch insisted. "All I can tell you, is that some very dangerous folks have reason to believe he's dead. I want to keep it that way."

"But he isn't dead," Idelle protested. "Mama said

he had to go away, to keep from getting hanged for killing the men who killed Pa. She said he weren't never coming back."

"You're right," Ditch said. "He's alive. But if the men who believe he's dead discover he ain't, they'll come after him, sure as hell. You and your mama, too. Now do you understand why he's hiding?"

Idelle nodded. "What do you want me to do?"

"Get the things I asked for and stash them behind this woodpile. I'll be back after dark to pick 'em up. Can you manage that?"

"I think so," she said.

"This ain't no game," Ditch said sternly. "If you can't get it done, say so. I don't want you to get in trouble doing this."

"Samuel needs my help," Idelle said. She looked into Ditch's eyes. "You do, too. I'll get it done."

"Thank you," Ditch said. He kissed her on the forehead. "Remember, no matter what happens, you must never, ever, tell anyone we spoke. Not even your mother. Far as you know, your brother just rode away."

"I won't tell Mama," Idelle said. She stared at the ground in shame. "I can't. She's gonna be takin' up with Burnell Shipley. She doesn't think I know, but I do. It makes me sick in my stomach to think about it."

"Don't be so hard on your ma," Ditch said, lifting her chin. "She's only doing it for you and Samuel."

She nodded and produced a weak smile. She couldn't help it, looking into Ditch's eyes.

"I've got to get back to Samuel," Ditch said. "He's in a bad way. Wait here until I'm gone, before you come out. It'd go poorly for all of us, especially him, if we were seen together."

"When are you and Samuel coming back?"

"Don't know if Samuel ever is," Ditch answered. "He has powerful strong feelings against this place. Can't say I blame him. But I'll be back someday, you can count on it. I just don't know when."

"You promise you'll be coming back?"

"Sure," Ditch said. "Atherton is my home. My pa is here, and so's our ranch. Sooner or later, I'll be back."

"I'll wait for you," Idelle said.

"You don't have to," Ditch said, oblivious to her intent. The gap in their ages notwithstanding, he'd known her since she was born and always thought of her as a little sister.

"I know I don't," she said. "But I will."

"Suit yourself," he said. "Good-bye, Idelle."

Idelle sighed, rubbed her forehead where Ditch kissed her, and wistfully watched him make his way silently back into the woods.

Chapter 11

Idelle Pritchard strolled past the Sidewinder, across the street from the Atherton Arms Hotel, swinging her basket nonchalantly. She wore a bonnet and blended in with the many other pedestrians walking on either side of Atherton's main thoroughfare.

Idelle bided her time until late afternoon, after school let out, knowing that was when the downtown streets would fill with folks buying sundries, children just released from class, and townsmen finishing their workday and heading over to the Sidewinder for a whiskey or beer. For what she had planned, Idelle wanted the streets crowded.

Idelle knew where she could get the whiskey, food, and bedsheets Ditch wanted all in one place, and it wasn't from Shipley's Mercantile and General Store. While the store carried each of those items, she had no money, and stealing them was out of the question. The shopkeeper, Mr. Manning, had the eyes of a prairie hawk.

The place Idelle planned to obtain the items Ditch and her brother so desperately needed was the Atherton

Arms Hotel. To get them, however, she needed to create a distraction.

Idelle pilfered several matches from the tobacco drawer in Rodney Nettleses's rolltop desk. As she sidled past the Sidewinder and the array of horses, buckboards, and freight wagons parked in front, she discreetly lit a match and tossed it into one of the larger cargo rigs.

The wagon she chose was loaded with grain, wood, hay bales, and groceries. Idelle didn't stick around to see the blaze start, instead choosing to head purposefully across the street to the hotel. She went inside, selected a chair in a corner of the lobby, sat down, and pretended to examine her fingernails.

In less than a minute, she heard men shouting and the sound of many running feet. She also smelled smoke. Idelle waited patiently until everyone in the lobby, including the hotel's bartender, the desk clerk, and several maids, as well as a number of guests, ran out through the front doors. One of the men was Burnell Shipley, who waddled from his office behind a mob of guests.

Once alone in the lobby, Idelle wasted no time. She went directly behind the bar and took two bottles of brown liquid labeled OLD CROW. From there, she slipped into the hotel kitchen and stuffed a slab of dried beef, and as many jars of fruit preserves as she could carry, into the basket. She exited the hotel through the rear kitchen door and snatched a white sheet off the clothesline as she passed.

Idelle took a moment to cover her plunder in the basket with the sheet and then removed her bonnet and placed it on top to conceal the booty. The basket was very heavy, but she carried it in the crook of her elbow and struggled to pretend it wasn't. She steadily made her way around the hotel to the street.

When she reached the plank sidewalk and began walking rapidly toward the Nettleses's place, she couldn't resist looking behind her. Idelle saw a dozen men fighting the fire, which engulfed the wagon. Several of them were trying to unhitch the panicked team of horses, while others filled buckets of water from nearby troughs in an attempt to douse the flames. A large crowd of onlookers beheld the spectacle, and smoke filled the late-afternoon air.

"What's in the basket, little girl?" a high, scratchy voice demanded. Idelle looked up to find her path on the sidewalk blocked by Eli Gaines. She had never met the deputy, but recognized him as one of Sheriff Foster's minions. He was at least five years older than Samuel, and all she knew of him was that he had horrific teeth and was disliked by everyone who knew him. Gaines leered down at her, like a menacing scarecrow.

"Excuse me," Idelle said, attempting to step around the skeletal figure. He sidestepped, blocking her path again.

"You're young, all right," he said, rubbing his scraggly chin whiskers, "but damn, if you ain't got your mama's looks already started. How old are you, anyways?"

"I'll be ten in a month," she declared indignantly. "Not that it's any of your business."

"How's about I carry your basket for you?" He reached out a lanky arm. Idelle pulled the basket out of reach.

"My parents told me not to talk to strangers," Idelle said.

"Why, I ain't no stranger," Gaines said. "For your information, little lady, I was acquainted with your pa, rest his soul, and your brother, before he suddenly left town. In fact, you might be interested to know I was one of the last people to visit 'em both. Before they departed, I mean."

He laughed as he spoke, a dry, cackling laugh, though Idelle didn't know what he found so funny. She knew only that she wanted to get away from the creepy lawman as quickly as possible.

"I have to go," she said. "Will you let me pass?"

"My pleasure, ma'am," Gaines said, removing his hat with a flourish and stepping aside with an elaborate bow. His collar-length hair was as greasy as his smile.

"Please send my regards again to your ma," he said. "I just got back from escorting her out to your place. Too bad, about your house burning down."

"Good day," Idelle said, brushing past the deputy.

"I'll be keeping my eye on you," Gaines called after her. He stared at her as she walked away, his foul grin widening even more, if that was possible.

"Yes, indeed, Idelle Pritchard," he said to himself. "I'm going to be watchin' you grow up. You can count on that."

Chapter 12

"Stay quiet," Ditch whispered to Pritchard. "Something is spookin' the horses. Wait here, while I check it out."

Ditch and Pritchard had spent the better part of the last two days hiding in an abandoned cropper's shack. They'd been forced to take refuge after only a day on horseback, when Pritchard took a turn for the worse.

Ditch found the parcel left for him by Idelle, behind the woodpile at the Nettleses's place, when he returned after dark. Silently thanking her, he tucked the burlap bag under his arm and made his way to the Atherton stables.

He hid, once again, in the loft, until the stable attendant left for the night. Once he'd gone, Ditch scampered down and saddled and bridled a pair of horses.

He chose the two finest mounts in the stable, both of which belonged to his father. One was a spirited brown quarter horse named Snake. The other, a two-year-old, chestnut-colored Morgan eighteen hands tall, was called Rusty. Ditch saddle-broke and trained them himself.

He stuffed the groceries in the saddlebags and helped himself to some grain and a couple of stable blankets. He'd just mounted Snake, and taken Rusty's reins, when Marshal Stacy walked in carrying a lantern. Ditch couldn't know it, but the town marshal had a fondness for his own horse, which was boarded at the stable. He'd brought a pair of apples as a treat for the animal.

"Hold it, right there," Stacy ordered when he saw Ditch. He drew his revolver. "Get your hands up." Ditch did as he was told.

"You may not know it, boy," the marshal said, "but horse thievery is a hanging offense."

"It ain't thievery when the horses belong to you," Ditch said. "These two are wearing my pa's brand."

Marshal Stacy held up the lantern and squinted. "I know you. You're Rand Clemson's boy, Davey."

"That's right. These horses are mine."

"Like hell," Stacy said. "They were brought in by county deputies. They've been commandeered for the war effort, on Mayor Shipley's orders. They're now owned by the U.S. government. Get off that horse. I ain't gonna tell you again."

"All right," Ditch said. "Don't get your britches in a bunch. I'm a-comin' down."

But instead of easing himself to the ground, the athletic youth suddenly leaped from the saddle. He tackled the overweight, middle-aged town marshal, knocking the pistol and lantern from his hands and sending both of them crashing to the straw-covered ground. Ditch, as intended, landed on top.

Before the terrified marshal could shout an alarm, Ditch furiously fist-beat him into unconsciousness. Once he was sure Stacy was out cold, and he'd caught his breath, he extinguished the lantern. Then he took the lawman's revolver, an Army Colt .44, and his hat, before remounting Snake. He rode out of Atherton unnoticed, leading Rusty, and was back at Pritchard's side in less than an hour.

Ditch left his friend concealed in a stand of trees, wrapped in his bedroll with the Hawken rifle for company, before going into town. Unfortunately, he was only a mile from where he'd risen from the grave. Dizzy and with blurred vision, Pritchard wasn't strong enough to walk far, and Ditch wasn't strong enough to carry his extra-large friend without help.

By the time Ditch got back, he found Pritchard wracked with fever. He explained what transpired at the livery stable as he disinfected the gunshot wounds with whiskey. The urgent need to put as much distance between themselves and the Atherton posse that was soon to be on their trail went unspoken.

Pritchard stifled howls of agony as Ditch poured whiskey on his head and replaced his makeshift bandages with strips of clean bedsheet, courtesy of Idelle and the Atherton Arms Hotel. With his friend's help, and now wearing the marshal's hat, Pritchard was able to mount Rusty. The two boys headed off into the night.

They wouldn't get far. They rode south all night, staying off the roads, but by sunup, Pritchard had become delirious and had fallen off his horse. Ditch was able to get him remounted, but only just. He knew if the barely conscious Pritchard fell off again, he'd never get him back in the saddle.

Ditch found a rickety cropper's shack at the edge of a vast field of corn, on a plot of land twenty miles south of Atherton. That was far too close for his liking, but he had no choice. Pritchard simply couldn't go on.

Ditch led Pritchard into the shack, got some water, peach preserves, and a bit of whiskey into him, and wrapped his trembling friend in the blankets he'd pilfered from the stable. Then he grained the horses and tied them out of sight behind the crude hut.

By afternoon it started to rain. It was a heavy late-October downpour. It was cold in the shack, but both boys knew a fire was out of the question. Ditch gnawed on dried beef, kept watch over Pritchard as he fitfully dozed, and made sure the Hawken rifle remained handy.

Not long after dark, Ditch thought he heard a sharp noise outside and the horses whinny and stomp. He couldn't be sure, due to the sound of rainfall on the leaky, thatched roof. He cautioned Pritchard to be quiet, picked up the Hawken rifle, and went out to investigate.

Soon came the report of a scuffle, then a *thud*. The door to the shack flew open, and Ditch was shoved roughly inside to the floor. He was missing his hat, and blood trickled from his hairline. Two soggy men, both wearing Union blue, held revolvers on him. One was holding his Hawken, the other a lantern.

"Got you, you horse-stealin' little son of a bitch," the one with Ditch's rifle announced triumphantly. "You'll be hangin' from a tree come mornin'."

"Who do we have here?" the other asked, pointing his pistol at the form lying under the blankets.

"He ain't nobody," Ditch said, from his hands and knees. "Just a fellow I met on the road. Pay him no mind. He's sick."

"Come out from under those blankets," the shorter of the Union men ordered.

Ditch recognized him. It was Deputy Merle Crittenden. The taller man with him, holding the Hawken, was a Jackson County deputy also, although Ditch couldn't remember his name. The deputies were obviously part of the posse searching for him, and wearing Union colors to prevent being mistaken for rebels if they encountered Union forces.

"You heard me," Crittenden commanded. "Come out from under there, where we can see you."

"Sure thing," replied a weak voice from underneath the blanket.

The blankets were tossed aside and Pritchard came out shooting. His first shot, fired from Marshal Stacy's Colt .44, took the deputy holding the Hawken through the right eye. As soon as he fired, he rolled. Deputy Crittenden's return shot struck empty blankets.

Pritchard's second shot hit Crittenden square through the middle, and his third hit the Jackson County deputy only an inch higher than the first. Crittenden dropped his pistol and lantern, fell back against the wall, and slid slowly to the ground.

"You sure got spry in a hurry," Ditch remarked, regaining his feet. "Thanks for saving my life."

"Don't mention it," Pritchard said, as he stood up. "I reckon I owed you. In fact, I think I'm still down a few lives to you."

"We'll call it even," Ditch said, righting the lantern. He picked up his rifle and the deputies' pistols.

Crittenden held both hands to his blood-soaked gut. He blinked up at Pritchard through the cloud of gun smoke that filled the tiny shack.

"You're dead," he gasped, disbelief accenting the agony in his face. "I watched you die! I buried you myself!"

"Evidently," Pritchard said, "you didn't dig a deep enough hole." He cocked the revolver a fourth time and shot Crittenden in the forehead.

Ditch saw his friend's eyes in the lantern's glow just before he fired the coup de grâce into the gut-shot deputy's brain. Pritchard's countenance darkened as he pulled the trigger, almost as if a shadow had fallen over him. It was an expression Ditch had never before seen on his friend's face, and it shook him.

"When I was on my knees in front of my own grave, looking up into the barrel of a pistol," Pritchard explained, reading the worry on his friend, "I was a dead man."

Ditch dared not interrupt. It was as if Pritchard was speaking in a trance.

"When you pulled me out of that hole," he went on, "and I realized I wasn't dead, do you know what my first thought was?"

"No," Ditch said, his voice barely a whisper. "What were you thinkin'?"

"I was thinking,'" Pritchard continued, looking down at the revolver in his hand and the dead man at his feet, "never again will I let a man point a gun at me without him paying with his life. Not if I can do something about it. I swear it."

"We'd best git," Ditch said, not knowing what else to say. "These boys didn't come alone, and you can bet the rest of their posse ain't far behind. They might have heard the shots, even in this rain. Can you ride?"

"I'll have to," Pritchard said, stuffing the Colt in his belt.

Ditch and Pritchard hurriedly packed up, saddled their horses, and rode off into the night, but not before taking the guns, food, water, ammunition, and money belonging to the deputies. Ditch released the deputies' horses, minus their saddles and bridles, after first dragging the deputies' bodies off into the cornfield.

Ditch and Pritchard spent the next ten, long, arduous days and nights riding south. They traveled by night and hid out and slept by day. They avoided roads and foraged for food as they went. Pritchard's fever abated, and his strength gradually returned. The holes in his scalp began to scab and heal.

On the morning of the sixth day of their journey, Ditch wished Pritchard a happy eighteenth birthday. They each had a sip of whiskey to commemorate the occasion. On the eleventh day the Ozark Mountains loomed ahead, and they knew for sure they'd departed Missouri.

Chapter 13

"Halt, or be fired upon!" a deep voice called out from the forest. The *click*s of twenty or more hammers being drawn back echoed through the heavy fog.

Pritchard and Ditch stopped in their tracks. They were on foot, leading their horses to drink from a stream, when the challenge was issued. It was just after sunrise, and the early-morning fog permitted only a few yards' visibility.

"Put up your hands!" the voice commanded further. "Iffen either of you move so much as a hair, you're done for."

The boys slowly raised their hands. Men in gray uniforms and kepis materialized from the woods. Almost all were bearing Fayetteville rifled muskets, most with bayonets affixed, except one who was armed with a dragoon revolver and saber.

Their horses were taken, and they were searched. The Confederate troops relieved them of their pistols and the Hawken.

"They've got food and water," said a sergeant, rummaging through their saddlebags. "Whiskey, too, and almost forty dollars in gold." He held the bag of coins and a bottle aloft.

"I'll take custody of that," the officer said, taking the bag of gold coins and tucking it inside his uniform. The enlisted soldiers circled and began passing the whiskey among themselves. The bottle was only half-full. Ditch used the other half, and the other bottle, cleaning Pritchard's head wounds three times a day.

"That's my property," Ditch protested, as his money was confiscated.

"Who are you, and what's your business?" the officer demanded.

"My name's Dave Clemson," Ditch spoke up. "This here's—"

"—Joe Atherton," Pritchard broke in.

"—my friend Joe Atherton," Ditch repeated, though he looked quizzically at Pritchard. "We've come from Missouri to find my brother Paul. He's fighting with the Fifth Regiment of Shelby's Iron Brigade. We're lookin' to join up."

The officer, wearing the insignia of a lieutenant, appraised them. "How old are you boys?"

"Twenty," Ditch lied.

"And I'm Abraham Lincoln," the lieutenant said. "Neither of you look more than a month off your mama's teat. You have to be in long britches before you can fight in a war." Several of the soldiers snickered.

"I killed one Union man getting here," Ditch said, red-faced at the insinuation he wasn't man enough to serve, "and Joe here sent three of the bastards to hell. Them revolvers you just took offen us? Every one of 'em was plucked from a dead Union man. We can carry our end."

"Mule fritters," the sergeant grunted. "You boys are

lying. You stole them horses, all right, but you two ain't never killed no four Union men."

"Hell if we didn't," Pritchard said. He removed his hat, and the bandage underneath, to reveal the circular scar at his hairline above his right eye.

"That's a ball hole, all right," the lieutenant whistled, "if ever I saw one." The enlisted men leaned in to examine the still-angry wound. "Why aren't you dead, boy?"

"I've still got a few more Union men to kill," Pritchard said.

The lieutenant frowned. "Well, boys," he said, "you've just been captured by a platoon of Upton Hays's Eleventh. The outfit you seek is further south. Come on along, and I'll introduce you to our commander. Maybe he'll find some use for you."

"Are we prisoners?" Ditch asked.

"You're guests, for now. Depending on the colonel, that could change for better or worse."

Ditch and Pritchard were led through the foggy forest by the soldiers. Before long, they began to smell decomposing flesh. Soon the scent became overwhelming.

They entered a clearing. As the sun rose, the fog began to dissipate, and the scene before them unfolded. Dozens of horses, and countless men in both blue and gray uniforms, lay dead in the tall grass of a large meadow.

The soldiers spread out and kept their weapons ready. They crossed the meadow of dead men and animals unmolested, and within a quarter mile of reentering the forest again were challenged by a sentry supported by a line of riflemen.

Once the password was accepted, the soldiers and their "guests" were allowed to pass the pickets and enter a bivouac area where dozens of tents, and several hundred more Confederate soldiers, milled about. A sizable herd of horses was rope-corralled at one end of the camp. The scent of decomposing flesh from the meadow blended with the odor of cooking food.

Four enlisted men remained with the lieutenant, who went directly to one of the larger tents. The sergeant and the other soldiers took Snake and Rusty in the opposite direction, toward the corral.

"Those horses belong to us," Ditch said. "And that's my daddy's rifle." The lieutenant ignored the comment. He parted the tent flap and saluted.

Seated at a folding table covered by a detailed map, surrounded by several other Confederate officers, sat a thin, bearded, long-haired man in a braided uniform with colonel's insignia on the sleeves. He was smoking a pipe. He casually returned the lieutenant's salute.

"Good morning, Colonel," the junior officer announced. "Lieutenant Gabel, back from the morning patrol. No sign of enemy about, sir."

"They're out there, all right," came the reply. "Even if we can't see them. Better than an entire brigade to our regiment, I'm afraid. Who are these two men?"

"Boys," the junior officer corrected. "Found them on patrol. They claim to be Missourians. Said they were twenty years old. Don't know if either claim is true. They were in possession of a Hawken rifle and several serviceable revolvers, as well as two excellent mounts."

The colonel stood and approached the boys. "They sure breed 'em big in Missouri," he commented, appraising Pritchard.

"They claim to have killed four Union soldiers,"

the lieutenant went on, "and were traveling south to join up with one's brother, allegedly assigned to Shelby's Fifth."

"Ain't no 'claim' about it," Ditch said. "It's the honest truth."

"I sincerely doubt that," the lieutenant said.

"I'm sure gettin' tired of being called a liar," Ditch said, turning to face Gabel. "Do it again, and you'll be eating your teeth for breakfast."

"Young man, if you even attempt—"

"At ease," the colonel cut them both off. He addressed Ditch. "Why don't you tell me your story yourself, son?"

"Except for our ages," Ditch began, "which I admit we lied about, everything else we said was true. We're both only eighteen."

This was only partly factual. While Pritchard's birthday came and went on the trail to Arkansas, Ditch wouldn't turn eighteen until December. Ditch didn't want Pritchard to get any more dispensation than he did, so he fudged his age once more.

"Go on," the colonel said.

"Union men, dressed like rebs, burned down Joe's house and hung his pa from a sycamore tree. We killed two of 'em. The other four got away."

"How exactly did you accomplish this?" the colonel asked.

"I shot one with my pa's Hawken rifle, and Sam—er, Joe—stuck the other with my skinning knife."

"Are you skilled with that Hawken?" the colonel asked.

"I'm a fair hand," Ditch said. "But Joe here is a

plumb sharpshooter. He was one of the best shots in the county."

The colonel gestured to Pritchard with his pipe. "How did you acquire that unique wound on your forehead?"

"Got another just like it on the back of my head," Pritchard said drily.

"Union men captured him," Ditch explained. "They shackled him, took him to the river, put him on his knees, and headshot him. Then they buried him."

"They buried him?" the colonel said, his eyebrows lifting.

"That's right," Pritchard said.

"Evidently," the colonel said, "they didn't do a very effective job of it."

"Ditch," Pritchard said, "I mean Davey, dug me up. I guess I wasn't expired yet. Then he went into town, stole back a couple of the horses the Union men stole from his pa, and we lit out for Arkansas."

"You said you killed four men? When did you kill the other two?"

"We killed a couple of the posse who came riding after us."

"He did it," Ditch said, motioning to Pritchard with his thumb. "With a revolver."

"That's quite a tale," the colonel remarked, drawing on his pipe.

"It ain't a tale," Ditch said. "It's the truth."

"What were your plans, once you arrived in Arkansas?"

"We aim to find his brother Paul," Pritchard said, "and become Confederate cavalrymen."

"So," the colonel said, "you two are horsemen, are you?"

"As good as any you'll find," Ditch said.

"I've got all the horsemen I need," the colonel said abruptly. "And I'm not in the habit of putting lying young whelps on good mounts and sending them off into battle alongside men who've earned the right to be called Confederate cavalrymen." He turned on his heel and went back into the tent.

Ditch and Pritchard exchanged glances.

"Lieutenant Gabel," the colonel said as he resumed his seat. "Put these youngsters in uniform and assign them to burial detail. When all the graves are dug, assign them to the mess. Give them no access to weapons and ensure they are fully informed about what happens around here to deserters."

"Yes, sir," the lieutenant acknowledged with another salute.

"What about our horses?" Ditch said.

"Your horses are now the property of the Confederate States of America," the colonel said. "They will be assigned to cavalrymen who will know how to use them. Dismissed."

"You've got no right!" Ditch protested.

"Get moving," Lieutenant Gabel ordered. The soldiers prodded Ditch and Pritchard from the tent with bayonets and herded them across the camp. They passed the mess tent without being offered food, and were handed shovels by an ancient corporal with a filthy beard and no teeth. A dozen or so disheveled Union prisoners bearing shovels, also being steered by a squad of bayonet-bearing graycoats, joined them.

"They called us liars," Ditch said aloud, elbowing Pritchard, "and took our horses, guns, and property. Now they're going to make us dig graves. You sure this ain't the Union army?"

Chapter 14

Pritchard and Ditch waited in line for food with the rest of the prisoners. It was noon, overcast, chilly, and the gray reb tunics they wore offered far less protection against the Arkansas November than their coats, which had been confiscated.

They were marched back out to the meadow of dead horses and men they crossed on the way into camp and ordered to find Confederate uniform shirts and caps that fit them from among the scattered corpses. Ditch had no problem locating a reasonably clean tunic in his size, but Pritchard had to examine more than a score of bodies before he found a fit, and even then, he was barely able to wriggle into it. Both of their tunics were damp from being in the field, were adorned with ball holes, and were liberally splattered with dried blood.

They spent their morning working alongside Union prisoners. Instead of digging individual graves, they dug a large trench. The work detail was guarded by a dozen Confederate regulars and supervised by a tall, burly sergeant with two Remington revolvers in his belt and a bullwhip in his meaty fist.

"I don't know about you," Ditch whispered as they dug, "but I didn't leave Missouri just to dig holes in Arkansas. First chance I get, I'm bustin' Snake outa that corral, grabbin' my rifle, and getting the hell out of here."

"I'm with you," Pritchard said. "But haven't you forgotten what that uppity lieutenant told us they do around here to deserters? He said first sign of us skedaddling, we'd catch a ball. I've been shot once already, Ditch. It ain't no fun."

"You've gotta be in the army to desert," Ditch said. "We ain't exactly Confederate soldiers. We're wearing dead men's coats and digging holes at gunpoint alongside Union prisoners. Far as I'm concerned, it ain't desertion; it's escape."

"Did you see that map in the colonel's tent?" Pritchard asked.

"I did," Ditch said, "but I didn't pay it any mind."

"There were little pins with flags stuck in them," Pritchard explained. "The flags represented different Confederate and Union units. There was a big gray one with a star on it, which I took to represent where we are, north of Fort Smith. The good news is, Shelby's Fifth looks to be in southern Arkansas, near someplace called Washington."

"The bad news?" Ditch said.

"There's a helluva lot of blue pins surrounding the big gray pin with the star."

"All we have to do," Ditch said, "is get out of here and get down to Washington, wherever that is."

"Easier said than done."

They dug silently for an hour before Ditch spoke again. "What's with the alias? Joe Atherton?"

"Samuel Pritchard is no more. Far as anybody knows,

he was headshot and buried down by the river a mile outside of Atherton. Nobody's going to hunt for somebody who's already dead and buried."

"I see your point."

There was a loud *crack*, and a bolt of agony, like a knife cut, flashed across Pritchard's broad back. He twitched so hard he dropped his shovel and fell to all fours in the trench. A diagonal tear appeared along the length of his tunic, and a line of blood began to form beneath it on his skin.

"More digging," the sergeant said, coiling his whip, "and less talk. Unless you want another taste of the lash."

Pritchard cursed and started to rise. A dozen soldiers lowered their rifles, their bayonets pointing at him. Ditch raised his hands and stepped in front of them.

"Don't," Ditch said to his friend. "They're lookin' for a reason."

"You're brave as hell with my back turned and a squad of guns behind you," Pritchard said to the sergeant. "Wonder how tough you are without 'em?"

"Get back to work," the sergeant ordered, "or you'll find out."

Ditch helped Pritchard stand and handed him his shovel. The husky sergeant laughed and motioned for his men to return their rifles to port arms.

"That's a nasty gash," Ditch said, examining Pritchard's back.

"It hurts worse than it looks," Pritchard said.

The duo dug until noon, when they were ordered to cease. They were then marched, behind the Union prisoners, back through the picket lines to the camp where they lined up for chow at the mess tent. It was clear that all the others within the camp had already been fed. The midday meal looked to be cornmeal, bacon, molasses, and hoecake. There was a boiling pan of coffee on the field stove, as well.

Ditch, Pritchard, and the Union prisoners were ushered past the appetizing buffet to an iron cauldron suspended over a small fire. There, they were handed tin bowls with no utensils. It was only when a scoop of gruel, composed of cornmeal and water, was plopped into their bowl, that they discovered they weren't getting what the regular soldiers ate.

"What's the matter, boys?" the sergeant asked when he saw the dismayed expressions on Pritchard and Ditch's faces. "Don't like the cuisine?"

"Horses get fed better," Pritchard said.

"Best eat up," the sergeant chuckled. "You'll need your strength for digging this afternoon."

"No, thanks," Pritchard said, tossing his gruel to the ground. "I'd rather go hungry."

"Pick that up," the sergeant said, his laughter twisting into a scowl, "and eat it. Right now."

"Eat it yourself," Pritchard said. The crowd of soldiers finishing their meal and loitering near the mess tent suddenly quieted. Everyone nearby, including the prisoners and their guards, gave ground to the big sergeant and the much bigger gravedigger.

"I gave you an order," the sergeant said, unlimbering his bullwhip. "Pick it up, boy. You'd best obey."

"I ain't your boy," Pritchard said, his voice cold and flat. "And you'd best not try to smack me again with that whip. This time, I don't have my back turned."

Ditch, nervously watching his friend confront the sergeant, once again saw a curtain of darkness overcome Pritchard's face. The last time he'd seen that look in Pritchard's eyes was in a Missouri cropper's shack, a split second before he gunned down two armed men.

If ever imminent death could be captured and held within the glint in a man's gaze, Ditch thought, Samuel Pritchard, now Joe Atherton, was that man. He realized, with some alarm, that Pritchard hadn't displayed the lethal glare when he was carving up Glenn Bedgley for killing his pa. Pritchard's shadow, as he'd come to think of it, had shown itself only since he'd emerged from the grave.

Ditch wasn't a particularly religious sort, nor superstitious, but he couldn't help thinking his friend Samuel, whom he'd known as a friend and brother his entire life, had changed. It was as if he'd brought something back with him when he returned from the dead. Whatever it was, it was now on display for all to see.

"Don't," Ditch cautioned Pritchard. "Let it go."

"I'll not be grained like a horse," Pritchard said, his voice monotone, "nor whipped like a dog."

"I decide," the sergeant smirked, "who gets a taste of my lash. And, boy, you've earned one."

The sergeant cracked the whip, aiming for Pritchard's face. Had the metal tip struck its intended target, he would have lost an eye.

Moving faster than Ditch thought he could, Pritchard snatched the tail of the whip. With one powerful jerk of his massive shoulders, he pulled the startled, and now off-balance, sergeant stumbling toward him. Then he threw as hard a right as he'd ever thrown. Pritchard's huge fist struck the noncommissioned officer squarely in the center of his face.

The sergeant's head snapped violently back. He

flew rearward, instantly unconscious. On the way to the ground his head struck the iron cauldron, resulting in a sharp crunching sound. Once down, he began to convulse.

As the sergeant jerked and trembled, and blood trickled from his ears and nose, he emitted a gurgling, coughing noise from deep within his throat. Ditch had heard the sound once before.

Pritchard tossed the bullwhip away. No one else moved, or said anything, until a corporal knelt and examined the sergeant.

"He's in a bad way," the corporal announced.

"Sarge is dying," a soldier exclaimed. "He's done for, sure as hell. That sound he's making? That's the death rattle." Others murmured their assent. They'd heard it before, too.

"I warned him," Pritchard said.

"You son of a bitch," exclaimed another soldier, turning on Pritchard. He drew a revolver from a flap holster, cocked it, and was leveling the weapon to fire when Ditch seized the pan of boiling coffee from the stove and hurled it into the gunman's face.

The soldier shrieked in agony. When he instinctively brought both of his hands to his blistered face, with his cocked revolver still in his grasp, it discharged, searing his face yet again with the side blast from the weapon's cylinder gap. He fell to his knees, next to the dying sergeant, bloodied, blinded, and howling in pain.

"What's going on here?" Lieutenant Gabel demanded. He pushed his way through the crowd, as Pritchard and Ditch were swarmed and held by a mob of Confederate troops. The burned soldier continued to writhe and holler.

"This man attacked Sergeant Stein," the corporal declared, pointing to Pritchard. "His friend attacked Private DeSaltier."

"He's got it the other way around," Ditch said.

"Get the injured men to the surgeon's tent," Gabel ordered. "And for God's sake, tie those two prisoners up." The soldiers scrambled to comply.

"I reckon we ain't guests anymore," Pritchard said to Ditch.

The lieutenant approached Pritchard and Ditch, once they were restrained. "You two certainly didn't waste any time causing mayhem," he said.

"We were just returning the hospitality," Pritchard said.

"You realize, of course, you'll both be shot for this."

"Beats diggin' graves," Ditch said. He spit at the lieutenant's feet.

"Been shot before," Pritchard shrugged.

"Get these men out of my sight," Lieutenant Gabel said.

"Looks like that's another one I owe you," Pritchard said to Ditch, as they were dragged away. "Thanks for saving me. Again."

"Gettin' to be a habit," Ditch grumbled. "And you're welcome."

Chapter 15

"Evidently," Ditch said to Pritchard as they were marched past the mess tent, "they ain't givin' us a last meal."

"Sure they are," Pritchard countered. "They're gonna feed us lead."

The pair spent the remainder of the day under guard, chained to one of the corral posts. At sunset they were once more offered corn gruel, which Pritchard again refused to eat, and given blankets.

"Wouldn't want you two to freeze to death before you're properly shot," the guard issuing the blankets remarked.

"That'd be a shame," Pritchard said, pouring out his gruel and tossing the tin bowl at the guard's feet.

Later that evening, Lieutenant Gabel returned. With him was an old man wearing a clerical collar and carrying a Bible. Pritchard and Ditch looked up at them.

"There's an officer present," a guard said, prodding them with his boot. "On your feet."

"Or what?" Ditch said. "You're gonna shoot us?"

The guards started to prod the seated men with

their bayonets, but Gabel halted them with a wave of his hand. "You may remain seated."

"Thank you kindly," Pritchard said sarcastically.

"I've just come from your court-martial," Lieutenant Gabel began.

"Too bad we weren't invited," Ditch said.

"Your presence would have made no difference," Gabel said. "Sergeant Stein died less than an hour after you attacked him. Private DeSaltier is now blind in one eye."

"I didn't attack Sergeant Stein," Pritchard said. "He attacked me. I gave him fair warning to leave me be."

"Don't expect me to express regret over the private's lost eye, neither," Ditch said. "One less eye will make it harder for him to back-shoot unarmed men."

"I'm not interested in your excuses. I came here to inform you that you've been lawfully tried and duly sentenced under military law. You've both been sentenced to death."

"What a surprise," Pritchard said.

"Astounding," Ditch said with a grunt.

"The sentence will be carried out tomorrow at dawn," Gabel said. "This is Pastor McKinley. He's here to minister to your souls. He'll unburden you of your sins, if either of you have a mind to repent."

"If we repent," Ditch grinned, "will we get a reprieve?"

"Of course not," Lieutenant Gabel said.

"Then what's the point?" Ditch asked.

"What sins have we committed?" Pritchard asked.

"The only sin we're guilty of," Ditch answered, "is being foolish enough to think this horse-stealing bunch of peckerwoods pretending to be Confederate soldiers were honorable men."

"Are you refusing the ministrations of God?" Gabel asked.

"If this is my last night on earth," Pritchard said, "I'll not spend it listening to an old gasbag lecture me about my wicked ways, when all I ever did was do unto others, like the Good Book says. I only did harm to those who harmed me first. You and that Bible-thumper can both go straight to hell."

"And you, Mr. Clemson?"

"Joe speaks for me, too."

Lieutenant Gabel nodded to the pastor, who took his leave. "I'd be lying," he said, with a satisfied smile, "if I told you I wasn't looking forward to commanding tomorrow's firing squad. I will see you gentlemen at sunrise. Pleasant dreams."

It was cold that night, dipping below freezing. Pritchard and Ditch huddled under their blankets and shivered, getting little sleep. Their only consolation was Ditch could see Snake and Rusty in the corral among the other horses. Their saddles, and even the Hawken rifle, were visible in a pile of tack stacked along the fence line.

Just before dawn, Pritchard and Ditch were roused from their frigid slumber by Lieutenant Gabel and six sleepy-eyed soldiers. The soldiers unchained them from the corral, leg-ironed them to each other, and marched them across camp. They were forced to walk in step with each other, due to the irons. Soldiers making their morning toilet stopped their tasks and stared at the condemned men as they were paraded to the sentry line.

Once clear of the camp, Pritchard and Ditch were prodded over the meadow of dead soldiers and horses where they'd spent the previous day digging the burial trench. It was bitterly cold, and the mountain fog was even thicker than it had been the morning before.

Pritchard and Ditch were placed with their backs to the edge of the trench, which was now filled with dozens of bodies, both rebel and Union. Lieutenant Gabel marked off ten paces and arranged the six soldiers in a line.

"Looks like we dug our own grave," Ditch commented, glancing over his shoulder into the trench.

"Somebody else dug my last one," Pritchard replied.

"Detail," the lieutenant said in his deepest command voice. He raised his saber. "Prepare to fire!"

"Excuse me," one of the soldiers said. "Begging your pardon, sir, but I can barely see them two boys through all this fog. With your permission, could we move a little closer?"

"For your information, Private," Lieutenant Gabel said, lowering his saber, "regulations clearly state the prescribed distance for a military firing squad is ten paces." He made no attempt to conceal his irritation at being interrupted.

"I'm sure they do," the private said, "but I'm guessin' whoever wrote them regulations never had to conduct a firing squad in the Ozark Mountains in November. This pea soup is so thick, I can barely see the front sight of my own rifle. Iffen I don't get closer, the only thing I'm gonna be shootin' is Arkansas mist." The other members of the firing squad nodded in agreement.

"Very well," Gabel relented. "Detail," he loudly commanded, again raising his saber, "move forward five paces on my command!" He waited several seconds for effect. "Move!" The line advanced five steps. Pritchard and Ditch were now vaguely in view.

"He surely likes the sound of his own voice," Pritchard remarked.

"Probably got a future in politics," Ditch said.

"Sir." The same private spoke up again, this time in a hushed tone. "With all due respect," he glanced nervously about, "we're way out ahead of our lines, and this area is crawlin' with Union troops. A feller can't see five feet in front of his nose in this fog, but he can hear just fine. Would the lieutenant mind keepin' his voice down?"

"Proper military protocols will be observed," Lieutenant Gabel said, making no effort to lower the volume of his speech. "Get back in line, Private."

The private complied, muttering under his breath.

"Detail," Lieutenant Gabel commanded for the third time, once more raising his saber. "Prepare to fire!"

"Do you have any last words, Atherton?" Gabel asked, as his men readied their Fayetteville muskets.

"No last words," Pritchard said. "Only regrets. I regret I didn't get a chance to put a ball into your pea brain."

"How about you, Clemson? Any final words?"

"Yeah," Ditch said. "Kiss my Missouri ass."

"Ready!" the lieutenant said, in his loudest and most official command voice. The firing squad conducted a half turn, brought their rifles to port arms, and cocked the hammers back.

"Aim!" Gabel commanded, in his parade-ground voice. The rifles were raised.

"Fire!"

The sound of gunfire erupted.

Chapter 16

The thunderous report of hundreds of rifles echoed across the meadow. A carpet of thick gray smoke was added to the already heavy morning fog, reducing visibility from yards to feet. Pritchard and Ditch heard the sound of a bugle. The footsteps and battle cry of an entire Union brigade closed in behind them.

Lieutenant Gabel and four of the firing squad were hit and fell to the ground. The fifth went to a knee and fired his rifle into the fog before he, too, was felled. The sixth member of the firing squad dropped his rifle and ran back toward his regiment's lines.

At the sound of the first shots, Pritchard elbowed Ditch backward into the trench. They landed heavily among the pile of dead.

"Don't move," Pritchard whispered to Ditch. "Play dead."

Pritchard and Ditch lay motionless among the rancid bodies for long minutes as countless men and horses moved past them in waves. Twice men in Union uniforms fell into the trench, obviously unable to see the large hole due to the fog and smoke. Both cursed and immediately climbed out to rejoin their comrades in the attack on the Confederate camp. Soon the sounds of even more gunfire, the clash of steel, and the fierce and agonizing screams of men in battle were emanating from within the rebel post across the meadow.

"Now's our chance," Ditch said, once the fighting shifted to the camp. "We've got to get going before this fog lifts."

"Right behind you," Pritchard said.

They had to move together, since they were still connected by leg-irons. They clambered out of the trench and belly-crawled through the grass toward the firing squad.

They found Lieutenant Gabel lying faceup with a gunshot wound in his chest. His eyes were closed, and he didn't move. Ditch and Pritchard began searching his pockets for the key to the irons.

Ditch found the key and grinned when Pritchard located his father's bag of gold coins, tucked away in the officer's inside breast pocket.

"Thieving bastard," he said, taking the purse from Pritchard.

Gabel suddenly opened his eyes and grabbed for Pritchard's wrist. The officer's lips parted to release a shout. With his other hand, he went for the butt of one of the Remington revolvers in his belt.

Pritchard clamped one giant hand over the lieutenant's mouth, stifling the bellow before it began. He beat the officer to the draw for the revolver with the other.

"Looks like I've got no regrets at all now," Pritchard said, remembering his nearly last words. He snatched the revolver, cocked it, and put the muzzle against the officer's head while Ditch occupied himself unlocking their irons.

"Go ahead," Lieutenant Gabel said through a mouthful of blood. "Finish me, you coward."

"Who's calling who a coward?" Pritchard said. "Ain't you the feller who marched us out here, unarmed and in chains, to be shot?"

Ditch looked to his friend's face. He was gratified to note the lethal shadow had not yet overtaken Pritchard's features.

"Do it," Lieutenant Gabel insisted.

"Not today," Pritchard said, releasing the hammer. "I ain't going to shoot you. I believe I'll leave you in this field to die slow, without my assistance. You can go to your end knowing that while Ditch and I may not be Confederate officers, nor gentlemen, we're better men than you."

"That's it," Ditch said, removing the chain from Pritchard's ankle. Ditch helped himself to Gabel's other revolver.

Pritchard and Ditch both stood up, but started to go in different directions.

"You're heading the wrong way," Pritchard admonished. "That's the way back to camp."

"I know," Ditch said. "I'm going back for my pa's horse and rifle."

"Are you loco?" Pritchard asked. "They're fighting a battle back there, or can't you hear?"

"I ain't leaving without what's mine. Go on ahead, I'll catch up."

"I ain't going to let you go back into that reb camp alone," Pritchard said.

"No use in both of us getting killed," Ditch argued.

"I've got an idea," Pritchard said, jumping back into the trench. He came up a minute later with a Union coat and cap. "Put these on," he ordered Ditch, "and grab one of those rifles."

While Ditch picked up one of the rifles belonging to their execution squad and ensured it was still charged, Pritchard recovered the leg-irons and draped them, unlocked, over his wrists. Then he took Ditch's revolver and tucked his Confederate tunic over both pistols in his belt.

"I'm your prisoner," Pritchard said. "You're going to march me back into that camp, pretty as you please."

"And you called me loco?" Ditch said.

Pritchard started to walk toward the Confederate camp. His hands were folded before him, near his concealed revolvers, though ostensibly restrained in irons. Ditch walked dutifully behind him, the bayonet of his Fayetteville musket in Pritchard's back.

They passed the picket, where dead men lay all around them. The vast majority of the bodies were clad in Confederate gray.

In the camp, still shrouded in fog and a heavy blanket of gun smoke, the firing had grown sporadic. Dead and wounded men, many moaning and crying, covered the ground. Pritchard and Ditch had to step over a number of corpses to navigate their way towards the corral, which was fortunately near the edge of the camp. What was left of the fighting was now deeper within the interior of the post.

Pritchard and Ditch entered the corral. Several of the horses had been struck by gunfire and lay dead or wounded in the rope pen. To Ditch's relief, Snake and Rusty were both unharmed.

Ditch shouldered his rifle, Pritchard dropped his chains, and they quickly located their saddles. Ditch was further relieved to find his pa's Hawken rifle, still in its scabbard. They also found their coats and hats among a similar pile of confiscated clothing. They hurriedly began to saddle their horses.

"You there," a voice called out. "What are you doing in that corral?"

Pritchard and Ditch turned to find a Union captain pointing a pistol at them. He was outside the corral, with a very tall sergeant. The sergeant's rifle was also directed their way.

"Private Clemson, sir," Ditch spoke up. "This here's my prisoner."

"I didn't ask your name," the captain said. "I asked you what you were doing."

"The medical officer ordered me to take this prisoner," Ditch lied, "round up a coupla good horses, and meet him in the field to search for our wounded."

"Interesting," the captain said. "Especially since I am the medical officer. Drop that rifle and get your hands in the air. Both of you."

Ditch shrugged off his rifle, shaking his head in defeat. Pritchard, however, in one lightning-fast movement, lifted his tunic, drew one of the Remingtons, and shot the sergeant in the neck.

He dropped to one knee as the captain fired, his hasty revolver shot sailing over Pritchard's head. Pritchard fired the .44 twice more, both shots striking the captain in the upper chest. He fell next to the sergeant and didn't move again.

Ditch thought he saw a remnant of Pritchard's now-familiar death-shadow fade from his countenance as his friend slowly stood up. Smoke filtered from the barrel of the Remington.

"You're getting pretty good with those things," Ditch commented.

"Gettin' plenty of practice," was all Pritchard said.

Ditch hastily finished saddling Snake, then cinched the strap on Rusty's saddle. Pritchard was busy collecting the ammunition belt and holster from the dead captain and stripping the uniform tunic from the dead sergeant.

"Let's get out of here," Ditch said, "before any more soldiers try to waylay us."

"Union, or Confederate soldiers?"

"Does it matter?" Ditch answered.

"From now on, in our travels," Pritchard explained, holding up the blue coat for Ditch to inspect, "I'm carrying both colors."

"Not a bad idea," Ditch agreed. They mounted and rode off into the fog.

Chapter 17

"Idelle is not moving into the hotel, and that's final."

"I thought you'd want to keep her near you," Shipley said.

"I do," Dovie said, "but not at the expense of having her reside in the Atherton Arms and exposed to the sort of characters who frequent this establishment."

Shipley and Dovie were seated at a table in the hotel restaurant. She was drinking tea and he was drinking bourbon. She'd reluctantly relented to begin allowing him to be seen with her in public. She'd put if off as long as she could.

"I believe," Shipley said, around his mustache and cigar, "you're confusing the Atherton Arms with the Sidewinder, across the street. While the Sidewinder's clientele is admittedly of a coarser nature, the Atherton Arms is highly reputable." He chuckled. "I happen to know the owner of both establishments quite well."

"Don't insult my intelligence," Dovie said. "The Sidewinder is merely the more honest of the two businesses, that's all. It doesn't pretend to be anything but a drovers' saloon, gambling hall, and whorehouse. Here at the Atherton, the rooms are more expensive, there's linen and doilies on the tables, and you're served by folks who've bathed since their last payday. But just like the Sidewinder, the Atherton's got liquor and gambling downstairs and women on their backs upstairs. Neither is a suitable place to raise a young girl."

"You're a well-informed woman, Mrs. Pritchard."

"One doesn't need to be well informed to know what services the Atherton Arms and Sidewinder provide," she said. "One only needs a working pair of eyes."

More than a month had transpired since Thomas Pritchard's death. Dovie and Idelle had been guests of Alice and Rodney Nettles since his killing, but Dovie was under growing pressure from Burnell Shipley to take up residence with him at the Atherton Arms, as she'd agreed.

It had been a profitable month for Shipley. The Atherton sawmill, formerly the Pritchard Lumber Company, received the government order he'd been alerted to, and with a substantial down payment from the U.S. Army. The lumber demand had become so great, Shipley had to purchase a third steam-driven saw, hire a dozen more men, and the operation still struggled to fill the order.

Since armies marched on their bellies, business was also booming at the Atherton stockyards. The army bought beef and horses as fast as the drovers could herd them into town. The railroad couldn't ship out the lumber and livestock to Kansas City fast enough.

These enterprises, fueled by the war and coupled with Shipley's primary financial endeavors, liquor, gambling, and prostitution, had in very short order made Atherton a boomtown, and Mayor Burnell Shipley an even wealthier man.

"What do you propose to do with Idelle?" Shipley said.

"I want her to stay at the Nettleses' place," she said, "permanently. I will reside with you here at the Atherton Arms, as promised, but she will live with them. I expect you to pay a suitable stipend to the Nettleses for her care."

"I'll agree to that," Shipley said.

"Thank you," she said, rising. "If you'll excuse me, I must attend to my daughter."

Shipley put down his cigar and stood. "When can I expect you to be taking up residence here at the Atherton?" he asked. "I believe a 'month or two' after your husband's funeral was the length of time discussed?"

"I will not be moving in until we're married," she said.

"I'm a patient man," Shipley said. "But my patience has limits. Did you have a date in mind for the nuptials?"

"You may announce our engagement at Christmas," Dovie said without emotion. "I will marry you no earlier than Valentine's Day."

"And your wifely duties?" he asked.

"After the ceremony, of course."

"Of course," Shipley said, his grin widening. "But Valentine's Day is more than two months away. How do you expect me to satiate my masculine urges until then?"

"I suggest you go across the street to the Sidewinder,"

Dovie said. "You claim to know the owner. Perhaps he'll give you a discount?"

"Oh, Mrs. Pritchard," Shipley said to himself once she left the hotel. "I do look forward to our wedding day." He extinguished his cigar in the remains of his drink. "And especially our wedding night."

Chapter 18

It took Pritchard and Ditch almost three weeks to make the nearly two-hundred-mile journey south to Washington, Arkansas. They hadn't forgotten how easily they'd been captured. As a result, they took their time and were extremely cautious in their movements.

Arkansas had declared itself a Confederate state, but most of the northern region was still infested with Union forces. Pritchard and Ditch hoped to see fewer bluecoats the farther south they rode.

They crossed the Arkansas River east of Fort Smith to avoid the Union troops posted there. Traveling by night, they took cover in woods or thickets during the day, and avoided detection by steering clear of roads and towns.

They were able to skirt the larger columns of Union troops they encountered by sticking to the forests and adhering strictly to their nighttime-travel routine. When they began to observe more Confederate units than Union ones, by mutual agreement, they decided not to announce themselves until they spotted rebel cavalry. Ditch's brother was supposedly assigned to such a unit, and the last thing they wanted was a repeat of their encounter with the reb infantry regiment back in the Ozarks.

Pritchard and Ditch found late autumn in Arkansas mild, compared to Missouri, and noticed the weather got milder as they progressed south. There was fresh water in the numerous streams, ponds, and lakes, still-green grass for the horses, and plentiful game. They had no trouble bagging deer, turkey, and rabbit, taking turns hunting with the Hawken.

Each morning they would find a remote place along their route to make camp. The location was carefully selected. It had to be hidden and defensible, and was typically within a stand of trees or in heavy brush. While one of them tended to the horses, the other would take the Hawken and scout the vicinity. Pritchard and Ditch took pains to ensure there was no one in the area before discharging a weapon or building a fire.

After obtaining their daily meat, they would clean, cook, and eat it. Once they'd filled their bellies, they would take turns sleeping and keeping watch until sunset. Ditch filled his daylight hours, when not resting, caring for the horses. Pritchard spent his time while awake cleaning the two Remington revolvers and the Hawken rifle. Once darkness fell, they would once again mount up, point their horses south, and ride on.

Pritchard preferred the Remington revolvers over the Colts. The Remingtons were sturdier and felt more solid in his hand. But the main reason he preferred the Remingtons were the safety notches milled between the charging holes. These meant he could load with six shots and not merely five. He also liked how quickly the Remington could be reloaded. With a spare charged cylinder, he could have an empty Remington reloaded in a few seconds.

When not cleaning the revolvers, Pritchard practiced drawing from his belt and dry-firing them. He repeated this routine for over an hour each day. He would wedge one of Ditch's gold coins into a tree at head level and pace off ten steps. Then he would repeatedly draw, cock, and fire. Even though the guns were empty, he always ensured the front sight split the coin before squeezing the trigger. He worked both of his large, muscular hands equally, until there was no difference in the speed and dexterity with which he could draw and fire with either.

"Don't you ever get tired of pretending to shoot those guns?" Ditch asked once, after their meal, as Pritchard conducted his daily practice regimen.

"No more than I get tired of living," Pritchard said, without taking his eyes off the coin.

It was at a trading post near Oden, halfway to their destination, that Ditch and Pritchard met their first trouble since escaping the Confederate camp. They spotted a large cabin on the Ouachita River, with a slat corral and hog wallow behind it, bearing a sign that read TRADING POST & GENERAL STORE. They found the building by following the scent of smoked pork and observed the store from hiding for the better part of a day before deciding to approach.

Both Pritchard and Ditch's only clothes were becoming threadbare, and neither had shaved in almost three weeks. There were a few items, such as a razor, new clothes, salt, medicinal whiskey, another knife, powder, and other necessities they thought they might try to obtain, as well as grain for the horses. They had money, hadn't seen soldiers from either army in two days, and convinced themselves patronizing the store was worth the risk.

Pritchard checked his revolvers, ensuring they were both charged with six balls each. He also made certain they were tucked loosely in his belt under his unbuttoned coat. Ditch readied the Hawken and patted his knife. They tied Rusty and Snake to the hitching post, next to two horses and a mule, and went inside.

The trading post's interior was dim and warm and smelled of cooked bacon and charred wood. Behind the counter, cutting meat with a large blade, stood a squat, bearded man with thick forearms. Across the room, seated at a table with a bottle in front of him, was a very tall, heavyset, man wearing a long wool coat and a top hat. Despite the coat and hat he appeared disheveled, as if he'd been sleeping in the rough like Pritchard and Ditch were.

Seated on the dirt floor next to him, tied with a rope around one ankle, was a young girl. She was clad in only a crudely sewn burlap dress, wore no shoes, and appeared cold and malnourished. She looked to Pritchard to be perhaps thirteen or fourteen years old, though she was too thin for him to tell, and he unconsciously thought of Idelle. The girl stared at the wall with vacant eyes, and it was only after his own eyes adjusted to the darker interior of the cabin that he realized what he could see of the girl's unwashed body was covered in welts and bruises. The other end of the rope was tied to the man in the top hat's chair.

"What can I do for you two gentlemen?" the man behind the counter asked without looking up.

Pritchard noticed a shotgun leaning against a chair behind him.

"Need some powder, salt, and whiskey," Ditch said. "A knife if you got one, a razor, and we'd also like to see what you have in the way of garments suitable for two traveling men."

"You fellers seem a mite young," the proprietor said. "Before I start setting out goods, I'll need to see the color of your money."

Without thinking, Ditch foolishly produced the bag of gold coins and displayed them all for the proprietor to see. He instantly stopped cutting meat and looked up. Across the room, the man in the top hat's eyebrows lifted. He swiveled in his chair to face Pritchard and Ditch.

"I have everything you want," the proprietor said. "Give me a minute to set you up. While you're waiting, you boys care for a drink? Best whiskey in three counties."

"No thank you," Pritchard said, before Ditch could answer.

"How about some food? Got pork stew, made yesterday."

"How much?"

"Five cents a bowl. I'll throw in the corn bread for free."

"We'll take two bowls," Ditch said.

"Coming right up." The proprietor vanished through a raggedy curtain to a room behind the counter, presumably the kitchen.

"Hello, pilgrims," the man in the top hat said. "Couldn't help overhearing you're traveling men, like myself. Where did you say you were heading?"

"Didn't say," Ditch said.

"My name's Calverson," the man said, standing and extending his hand. "I'm a prospector by trade. What is you boys' occupation?" When he stood his coat parted, and the double-action Starr revolver holstered at his waist became visible.

"Didn't say," Ditch repeated. Neither he nor Pritchard shook Calverson's offered hand.

"Tell me, Mr. Calverson," Pritchard said. "Why is that young lady on a tether?"

"Her?" he said. "That there's Missy. That's what I call her, anyway. Don't know her given name. She belongs to me."

"How'd that come to be?"

"Won her in a card game in Hot Springs, a couple of weeks back. Real accommodating young girl, if you know what I mean. Which reminds me, if either of you fellows are in a sporting mood, I could be persuaded to allow you a poke for say, two dollars each. She looks a bit rough, but trust me, she's a young, spirited gal. She'll let you have her front, back, and sideways, if that's your inclination. Worth every penny of two dollars, I can assure you."

"Seems to me," Pritchard said, "the need to keep her tethered would suggest she's not as accommodating as you advertise."

"She'll be as accommodating as you want," Calverson said. "You'll get your two dollars' worth, I can promise you that."

"Sounds like you know from personal experience?"

"Can't very well recommend something I haven't tried myself, can I?"

"I thought you said you were a prospector," Pritchard said. "Sounds to me like you're a pimp."

"A man does what he has to," Calverson said, his expression hardening. "How old are you boys, anyway?"

"Old enough," Pritchard said. Ditch watched apprehensively as the familiar shadow began to fall over his friend's eyes.

"Here's your stew," the shopkeeper announced, entering with a wooden tray and two bowls.

"Fetch another bowl," Pritchard told him, "for the lady."

"Now, hold on a minute," Calverson said. "I don't recall Missy saying she was hungry."

"She's hungry, all right," Pritchard said. "She looks like she hasn't eaten in a week."

"I suppose I could let you feed her," Calverson said, scratching his chin, "if that would entertain you. But it'll cost you."

"How much?"

"Two dollars."

"You're going to charge me two dollars to feed a starving child a nickel's worth of hog soup?"

"You have to pay for the pleasure of her company," Calverson said. "Whether you dance with her, poke her, or feed her. It's all the same to me. Two dollars is the going rate."

"I'll make you a better offer," Pritchard said. "How about you untie her, allow her to sit at the table like a human being, and eat a bowl of hot stew? In exchange, I'll let you keep on breathing."

"That's your idea of a better offer?" Calverson said, taking a step back and grimacing.

"It is," Pritchard said. "A real bargain, too."

"You think you're pretty funny, don't you, boy?" Calverson said. His hand slowly began to stray from his chin, down his vest, to his belt.

"No," Pritchard said. "Not funny. Just fast."

Calverson went for his gun.

Before he cleared leather, Pritchard had one of the Remington .44s out and the hammer back. He drilled Calverson neatly through the sternum. The pimp staggered, shakily withdrew the Starr, and tried to raise it. Pritchard fired again, and a hole appeared in the center of Calverson's forehead. He dropped his gun and collapsed.

Pritchard spun to face the proprietor, who was reaching for the shotgun behind the counter. He needn't have worried. The shopkeeper's hand stopped when the barrel of Ditch's Hawken rifle pressed against his neck.

"The lady's waitin' for her stew," Ditch said.

Chapter 19

Pritchard and Ditch rode up to the church at dawn. They would have preferred to be under cover in deep woods by daybreak, but were forced to deviate from their customary nocturnal travel routine on account of the girl.

After Pritchard shot Calverson, he untied her. Ditch noted the death-shadow, which had befallen his friend once again, faded almost as fast as it appeared.

With a blank expression on her face and no resistance, as if accustomed to being led places by strange men, the girl let Pritchard lead her to a seat at the table. He placed a bowl of stew and corn bread before her. She wordlessly began devouring the food.

"I didn't see nuthin'," the proprietor said. His hands were over his head and shaking. Ditch's Hawken rifle was still against his neck.

"I don't care if you did," Pritchard said. "He drew first."

Pritchard walked behind the counter and took the shotgun, broke it open, and removed the shells. "Put your hands down," he said, "and fetch the merchandise we asked for."

The proprietor scurried to the back room.

"Best accompany him, Ditch," Pritchard said, "in case he's got another gun stashed back there." Ditch nodded and followed.

The girl wolfed down her bowl of stew, and Pritchard handed her another. If she seemed bothered by the death of Calverson, she didn't show it. In fact, she showed no emotion at all. By the time she inhaled the second bowl of stew, the proprietor, with Ditch on his tail, returned.

Pritchard and Ditch each selected a pair of durable britches made of coarse cloth, wool shirts, socks, a pair of blankets, a bone-handled knife, a razor, a hatchet, a pan, a quantity of salt, grain, gunpowder, and a bottle of whiskey. Ditch even found a box of .54 caliber balls for his Hawken rifle, and some .44s for Pritchard.

"Will that be all?" the proprietor asked, anxious to get Pritchard and Ditch out of his trading post.

"You got clothes suitable for the girl?" Pritchard asked.

"I do."

"Fetch 'em. Shoes and a coat, too."

While the shopkeeper again went into the back room, Pritchard searched Calverson's body. He found six dollars and a tobacco tin. He removed the wool coat and gun belt from the big corpse and picked up the Starr revolver. It was rare for Pritchard to find a man who wore a large enough size to fit him. He donned the coat and offered the pistol to Ditch.

"Don't like pistols much," Ditch said, shaking his head. "If it's all the same to you, I'll stick with my rifle."

"Suit yourself."

The shopkeeper brought out woolen underclothes, shoes, a coat, and a plain frock dress.

"Put these on," Pritchard said to the girl. She nodded and walked into the back room to change.

"How much do we owe you?"

"Eighteen dollars," the shopkeeper said.

"Give him ten," Pritchard told Ditch. "Here's six more," he said, handing over the money he'd taken from Calverson's body.

"You're two dollars short," the proprietor complained.

"I'll make you an offer," Pritchard said. "I'll let you keep the mule and one of the horses that belonged to Mr. Calverson. Providing, of course, you bury him and keep your mouth shut. That should make you a handsome profit."

"I don't want his mule or his lame horse," the proprietor said, greed overtaking his fear. "And I sure as hell don't want to bury nobody I didn't kill. I'll take the full eighteen dollars, if you please?"

"Let me make you an even better offer," Pritchard said, drawing his .44 again. "How about I plug you? You can join Mr. Calverson in the sawdust, and we'll ride out with your merchandise and our sixteen dollars still in our pockets."

"Sixteen dollars and the two animals sounds more than fair," the proprietor quickly agreed.

"Figured you'd recognize a bargain," Pritchard said, "when you saw one." He returned his gun to his belt.

The girl came out, dressed in her new clothes.

"You look real nice," Ditch complimented her. She stared silently back at him.

"Does she talk?" Pritchard asked.

"They've been here almost a week, sleeping down by the river. Calverson's been renting her out to trappers, traders, saddle tramps and such, who pass through.

I ain't never heard her speak a word. She hollers when whipped, and cries out, so I know she can."

"And you just stood by and let him do it?" Pritchard asked.

"Ain't none of my business," the proprietor said.

"You got a better bargain from me today than you know," Pritchard said. "I ought to shoot you on general principle."

"Take it easy," Ditch admonished.

The proprietor gulped and tried not to sweat so profusely. He failed.

"Is there a religious congregation around here?" Pritchard finally asked.

"Nearest church is ten miles south, in Mount Ida."

"C'mon." Pritchard motioned to the girl. "You're coming with us." She dutifully obeyed, as if she had no will of her own. Ditch collected their sundries, and the trio went outside to pack the saddlebags.

Ditch selected the better of the two horses Calverson owned, which wasn't a particularly good animal, and put the girl up in the saddle.

"I know your face," Pritchard called out to the trading-post proprietor as he swung into his own saddle, "and I know where you sleep. Bury that dead fool, forget us, and I'll forget you. If you send a posse after us, once I gun them, I'll be back to kill you graveyard dead."

"You don't have to worry about me," the proprietor said.

"Wish I could say the same."

Pritchard, Ditch, and the girl crossed the Ouachita River at dusk, over a rickety wooden bridge, and spent the remainder of the night as they did most nights, riding cautiously south. Ditch held the reins of the girl's horse. She slumped in the saddle, dozing. A little after midnight, they saw the silhouettes of rooftops ahead and knew they'd reached Mount Ida.

They tied the horses to a tree in a thicket, on a hill overlooking the town, and settled in to a fireless camp.

Pritchard carried the girl from her saddle while Ditch laid out the blankets. He gently placed her in the makeshift bed. She was fast asleep.

"I reckon a person can experience something so hard on 'em," Ditch remarked, "it takes all their words clean away."

"I reckon so," Pritchard said, covering her up.

"Something I've been wanting to ask you," Ditch said.

"Go ahead."

"Do you think it's changing us?"

"Is what changing us?"

"The killing," Ditch said. "You've put down seven men to my one, and truth be told, you finished off the only one I shot. Don't take offense, but it seems to me killing's getting easier for you."

"That's because it is," Pritchard said. He sat down and put his back against a tree. Ditch retrieved the bottle of whiskey from the saddlebags and sat cross-legged opposite him.

"Does it feel wrong to you?" Ditch asked. He uncorked the bottle. "Don't get me wrong; I don't regret what we've done. Everybody we did in had it comin'. But when I think about it, sometimes, it sorta feels wrong."

"Killing ain't about right or wrong," Pritchard said. "It's about them or us."

"I ain't so sure," Ditch said. "It wasn't them or us

back at that trading post. We could have bought our sundries and left. We didn't have to involve ourselves in Calverson's business with that girl, but we did."

"You mean, I did," Pritchard said.

"It's the same thing. I back your play, no matter what."

"When you put it that way," Pritchard said, "I guess it is about right or wrong. Just seemed wrong to me, a man keeping a little girl on a tether, like a dog."

"Are we still good men, Samuel?"

"What's a good man these days, Ditch? My pa was a good man. He was the best man I ever knew. He was honest, and fair, and he never tried to take undue advantage of anyone."

"He was a damned honorable man," Ditch agreed, "and then some."

"You know what his noble intentions got him?" Pritchard said. "Beaten, shot, and strung up like gutted venison. His wife was made to take up with the man who killed him, his daughter has to grow up watching it, and his only son was skull-shot and buried like a fevered hog."

"I know," Ditch said. "I'm sorry for what befell your family." He took a slug, winced, and handed the bottle to Pritchard.

"The difference between me and Pa," Pritchard went on, "is he saw folks as he wanted them to be. He always looked for the good in them. I used to be like that, too. Now I see folks as they are. I don't try to look into their hearts. I watch their hands, instead. It's a man's hands, not his heart, that'll kill you."

"Speaking of hands," Ditch said, "you sure are gettin' fast with those pistols."

"I aim to get a lot faster," Pritchard said.

"Just don't let your guns get ahead of you," Ditch said. "Don't let 'em change who you are."

"I ain't sure I know anymore," Pritchard said. He took a drink of whiskey. "I was dead, buried, and resurrected, remember? Hell, you're the fella who dug me up."

"I remember," Ditch said, thinking of the shadow Pritchard brought out of the grave with him. He took another swig.

At sunrise, Pritchard and Ditch fed the girl breakfast and gave her a ten-dollar gold coin. They mounted up and rode into Mount Ida. They stopped at the church, which was the tallest building in town.

When they reached the church, Ditch helped the girl off her horse while Pritchard knocked at the pastor's cottage. A middle-aged woman in an apron answered the door with flour on her hands.

"Good morning, ma'am," Pritchard said. "My name's Joe Atherton. Me and my friend found this young lady on the road, in a terrible state. I believe, on account of she doesn't speak, that she's suffered greatly. We were afraid worse men than us might find her alone and take advantage, so we brought her here. We didn't know what else to do."

"You did the right thing," the woman said. She put her arms around the girl. "Let me get my husband. He's the minister here. He'll want to speak with you."

"That won't be necessary," Pritchard said, tipping his hat. "We have to be ridin' on."

"Do you know her name?"

"We don't," Pritchard said. He and Ditch swung back into their saddles.

The girl suddenly left the woman's embrace and ran over to Pritchard, stepping in front of his horse.

"Caroline," she said, in a voice almost too soft to hear. "My name is Caroline."

Chapter 20

When Pritchard and Ditch rode into Washington, Arkansas, they were relieved to discover a Confederate hospital had been set up there. They walked Snake and Rusty up to a sentry, keeping their hands in view, and inquired if any cavalrymen attached to Shelby's Missouri Iron Brigade might be located within one of the tents.

The sentry called for his sergeant. A noncommissioned officer arrived, and Ditch again explained he was seeking his brother.

"There's plenty of fellows here assigned to Shelby," the sergeant said. "I can have one of my men escort you into where they're convalescing, but you'll have to leave your arms outside."

Pritchard put his revolvers in his saddlebags, and Ditch hung the Hawken over the pommel of his saddle, before tying their horses to a tree. They were led into a vast tent by an orderly wearing a blood-soaked apron. They beheld rows and rows of men lying on cots.

There was an overwhelming scent of blood and infection permeating the place. The sounds of men in grievous pain could be heard everywhere. Pritchard and Ditch followed the orderly past many horribly wounded soldiers. The vast majority were missing at least one limb.

"This here's Major Turner," the orderly said, as he introduced them to a bearded man missing his left arm at the elbow and left leg below the knee. He was smoking a corncob pipe and was propped up in his cot. "These two fellows are looking for someone from your regiment."

The orderly took his leave. "Who're you looking for?" Turner asked.

"My older brother," Ditch said. "His name is Paul Clemson."

"Pony Clemson," Turner said, appraising Ditch. "Damned, if you ain't the spittin' image of him."

"You know him?" Ditch exclaimed, ecstatic to hear the nickname only someone who was acquainted with his brother would know.

"I know him well. He's one of the best horse wranglers in the Confederate army."

"Horses are his calling," Ditch said, "that's a fact. Do you know where I can find him?"

"He's with B Company, Fifth Regiment. They're called Witherspoon's Rangers. Captain Jedediah Witherspoon, that's their commander. They just got back into Arkansas from raising hell up in Missouri."

"We raised a little hell in Missouri ourselves," Pritchard said.

"B Company is probably somewhere between here and Murfreesboro by now, on their way to Hot Springs. They've been ordered back to Kansas, to cause more mischief for the army of Mr. Lincoln. I'm only telling you boys this because it's common knowledge, and because you, young man, are clearly Pony's brother."

"I thank you," Ditch said.

"You boys plan to join the outfit?"

"We do," Ditch said. "If they'll have us."

"Can you boys ride and shoot?"

"As good as any man they've got," Ditch answered.

"They'll have you, all right. Good luck, boys. Tell 'em Major Turner, from Tennessee, sends his regards."

Pritchard and Ditch retrieved their horses and guns and started back the way they'd come. Murfreesboro was only thirty miles north of Washington, and there was still plenty of daylight left. They hoped to meet up with Paul's unit no later than the following afternoon.

As it turned out, it was shortly after dawn the next morning when they located the company of partisan rangers they were looking for.

The sun was just coming up as Pritchard and Ditch crested the steep ridge over Prairie Creek, a few miles south of Murfreesboro. They dismounted and took cover in some brush, because down below they could see several companies of Union infantry advancing through the woods toward a contingent of Confederate horsemen bivouacked at the creek.

The topography was such that Pritchard and Ditch could easily see the advancing Union forces, due to their overhead vantage point. But it was clear that the reb cavalry hadn't yet detected them, as evidenced by their seeming lack of awareness. The Confederates were mustered in clumps, tending to their horses and morning toilet, and many were not yet fully dressed and armed. There was a campfire going and an iron pot on a tripod over it.

"Those rebs are fixin' to get ambushed," Pritchard

said, stating the obvious. "They don't have a clue about what's coming at 'em through those woods."

"Paul might be down there with 'em," Ditch said, concern spreading over his features. "We've got to do something."

"Give me the Hawken," Pritchard said. "Then get ready to ride."

"Those blue bellies look to be at least five hundred yards out," Ditch said, handing the Hawken to Pritchard. "Ain't no way you're going to hit any of them, unless out of sheer luck."

"Ain't aiming for the blue bellies," Pritchard said, lying prone and shouldering the rifle. He cocked the hammer back. "Get ahold of Rusty," he said. "I don't want the shot to spook him and leave me stranded afoot." Ditch grabbed the big Morgan's reins.

Pritchard exhaled, paused, and fired. Almost a full second after the shot, a faint metallic *clang* was heard. A blue cloud of gun smoke hovered over them.

"You hit the cooking pot in the reb camp!" Ditch laughed. "That ought to wake those fools up!"

"It'll also let the blue bellies know we're up here," Pritchard said, tossing the rifle to Ditch and jumping on Rusty. "Let's go!"

Sure enough, as they galloped down the hill, dozens of Union guns fired on them. The distance prevented accurate shooting, but the sheer volume of fire resulted in numerous balls whistling past the two horsemen as they rode pell-mell for the rebel camp.

Within the camp, the alarm was sounded. In no time, the Confederate soldiers took up arms, hastily cleared camp, and mounted. Soon, approximately one hundred horses bearing Confederate cavalrymen were racing east, away from Prairie Creek, and the Union troops behind them.

Pritchard and Ditch took an intersecting path, spurring their horses at maximum gallop, as they rode between the Union attackers and the fleeing rebel raiders. They continued to push the animals at full sprint until the Union balls stopped whistling at them. They closed in on the rebel horsemen ahead.

Just as they caught up to the rebel cavalry, a mile from the creek, the Confederates turned sharply northward and, as one, slowed to a trot. As Pritchard and Ditch entered their formation from the rear, a dozen or more rebs pivoted their mounts sharply and came about, their revolvers leveled, to face the newcomers.

"Whoa!" Ditch protested, his hands in the air along with Pritchard's. "Don't shoot. We're friendlies."

"Then why are you riding up on us?" a reb cavalryman demanded.

"What's going on here?" Another rebel cavalryman rode up. He was tall, bearded, and wore a slouch hat with the right side pinned up by a star and feather. "What's the holdup?"

"Caught these two ridin' up on us, Cap'n," the soldier reported. "They might've been the ones who fired on us from that hill."

"We didn't fire on you," Ditch said. "We fired on your breakfast. It was the only way to warn you of the Union soldiers coming at you through the woods."

"You made the shot from on top of that hill?" the captain asked, his eyebrows lifting.

"He did," Ditch pointed to Pritchard, "with this here Hawken rifle."

"What do you two boys want?"

"To join up."

"Bring 'em along," said the captain. "I want some distance between us and that Union infantry. We'll sort this out later. Keep an eye on 'em, though."

They rode until noon, with Ditch and Pritchard riding at the back of the column, surrounded by several rebel guerrillas. This frustrated Ditch, because he couldn't determine if his brother was among any of the riders ahead.

The company stopped at a copse of trees with a small creek running through it and dismounted. When Ditch and Pritchard came out of their saddles, they were immediately covered again by several revolvers.

The captain approached, with a stocky, bandy-legged sergeant at his heels. "What're your names?" he asked.

"Davey!" a voice cried out, before either Ditch or Pritchard could answer. Paul Clemson, wearing reb gray, emerged from the crowd of soldiers. He and Ditch embraced.

"You know this man?" the captain asked.

"I surely do, Cap'n," Paul said. "This here's my little brother, Davey. Everybody calls him Ditch. And this fellow," he started toward Pritchard, "is—"

"Joe Atherton," Ditch blurted, cutting Paul off before he could finish his sentence. He gave his older brother a *play along, I'll tell you later* glare and stepped between Paul and Pritchard before the two could embrace.

"I met Joe on the road," Ditch went on. "His family was murdered in Missouri by Union men. He saved my life, more'n once. He wants to join up, too."

Paul, who'd known Pritchard since he was born, went along with the charade. He shook Pritchard's hand and said, "Nice to meet you, Joe. Thanks for saving my little brother's worthless life."

"Can your brother handle horses as good as you?" the captain asked Paul.

"Better," came the reply. "He was the best breaker in Jackson County."

"And what about you?" the captain asked Pritchard. "You're big as a tree and look twice as stout. You got any skills I can use?"

"I can kill," Pritchard said. "Is that enough skill for you?"

"He made that shot from up on that hill, to warn your unit," Ditch offered. "He's one helluva sharpshooter, with either a rifle or a pistol."

"That was at least a four-hundred-yard shot," said the sergeant.

"If Pony Clemson says you're a horseman," the captain said to Ditch, "that's good enough for me. Pony's the best there is, and I need all the wranglers I can get. But as far as your marksmanship," he said to Pritchard, "I'm ridin' with the best riflemen and pistoleers in the Confederacy. Unless you can prove your friend's bold claim, you'll have to ride on."

Pritchard walked over to Ditch's horse and retrieved the Hawken, ignoring the half-dozen revolvers leveled at him.

"Put me to the test," he said as he began to reload the rifle.

"Lower your guns," the captain said. "Sergeant Murphy, have someone ride a target out as far as he'll let you."

The squat sergeant took a canteen and handed it to a reb soldier, who mounted his horse.

"Three hundred yards ought to do," Pritchard said.

"Which direction?" the rider asked.

"Don't matter," said Pritchard. "Sun's overhead."

"Can you even see a target that small at three hundred yards?" Sergeant Murphy said.

"Been shooting squirrels farther than that since I was a kid," Pritchard said. "Last I checked, canteens don't move."

The rider hung the canteen on a branch at head level, as close to three hundred yards as one could guess. Then he pulled his horse back and waved his kerchief.

"Hell," another soldier said, "you can't hardly see the horse and rider from this far away."

"I can see a tiny bit of metal, glinting in the sunlight," another remarked.

Pritchard finished loading the Hawken and replaced the rod. Then he knelt and scooped up a handful of Arkansas dirt, letting it filter into the breeze. Finally, he lay prone and thumbed back the hammer.

"At your command, Captain," Pritchard said.

"Fire when ready."

The captain no sooner uttered the words than Pritchard fired. The rifle boomed. Nearly a second later, a faint *tink* was heard. Pritchard slowly stood up. In the distance, the rider gathered the canteen and galloped back across the prairie.

The reb rider pulled his horse up to the company, holding the canteen aloft for all to see. There was a neat hole in front and back. The men whistled their approval.

"Waste of a good canteen," the rider said.

"I didn't think he'd hit it," Sergeant Murphy said.

"You ever shoot anything besides a squirrel?" the captain asked.

"I have," Pritchard answered. "But not with this rifle."

"We've killed eight men since we've been riding together," Ditch said. "I done in one of them with that Hawken rifle, and Joe killed the other seven: five with pistols, one with a knife, and one with his bare hands."

"Is this true?" the captain asked Pritchard.

In answer Pritchard took off his hat, revealing the bullet scar on his forehead. The silence that ensued among the rebel soldiers reflected their awe.

"Most men don't walk away from a headshot," the captain said.

"I ain't most men."

"What do you think, Sergeant Murphy?" the captain asked. "Shall we take on the big one, too?"

"He's right good with that old Hawken, there's no doubt," the sergeant said. "I can only imagine what kind of hell he could raise with a Sharps or a Whitworth in his hands. But we're mounted guerrillas, Cap'n, not infantry sharpshooters. We do most of our fighting on horseback, up close, where precision rifle shooting ain't worth a damn. It's pistoleers we need."

Pritchard nodded to Ditch. Ditch suddenly snatched the canteen from the reb soldier's hand and tossed it into the air. With lightning speed, Pritchard lifted his coat, drew one of the Remingtons from his belt, and fan-fired it three times. Each shot struck the canteen before it hit the ground.

"He'll do," Sergeant Murphy said.

Chapter 21

"Do you boys swear allegiance to the Confederate States of America, and further swear to lay down your lives, if necessary, to defend her?"

Pritchard and Ditch put their left hands on Sergeant Murphy's Bible and raised their right hands.

"I do," Ditch said.

"I do," Pritchard said.

"Congratulations, boys," Sergeant Murphy said. "You're in the Confederate army." He shook their hands. "Welcome to B Company, Fifth Regiment, of Shelby's Iron Brigade. We're known as Witherspoon's Rangers."

It was night, and the company was bivouacked on the western bank of Millwood Lake. They'd ridden all day and encountered no other Union forces.

"My name is Captain Jedediah Witherspoon," the captain said to them. "All you need to know about me is that I rode into Lawrence with Bill Quantrill and Bloody Bill Anderson. Iffen you boys were lookin' to fight like proper soldiers, lined up in ranks on the field of battle with bayonets a-gleamin', you'll be disappointed. Iffen you came to kill Union men, you came to the right place. Tomorrow we ride for the Oklahoma Territory. From there, it's back to Kansas."

Supper was salted pork, beans, and biscuits. Pritchard and Ditch sat with Paul, away from the others, as they ate under a tree. There was a cold wind coming off the lake.

"We're partisan rangers," Paul explained to Pritchard and Ditch. "Our standing orders, if that's what you want to call them, are to travel about at the Cap'n's discretion and create as much havoc as we can for the Union. We just came down from Missouri, where we killed more Union folks than I could count. We also burned a helluva lot of farms, robbed two banks and a train, and tore up some railroad tracks near Springfield."

"You fight in any big battles?"

"Only when we can't avoid it," Paul said. "We're guerrilla fighters. We're supposed to be fast and nimble, and besides, they've got cavalry units attached to the regular army for that. There ain't a man in this outfit, 'cept maybe the cap'n and Sergeant Murphy, who've been trained and drilled as regular soldiers. Every rider in this company joined up and signed on the same way you did."

"The captain said you were his horse wrangler?" Pritchard said.

"That's my secondary job. Yours, too, Ditch. Most everybody's got one. Some guys hunt for food, others do the patching up when someone is wounded, others do the cooking. My contribution is to break in the horses we commandeer."

"Commandeer?" Ditch said. "Ain't that a fancy word for stealin'?"

"That's what some would call it," Paul said. "Others, like Cap'n Witherspoon, would say we're only takin' what we need to support the war effort."

"What do the folks who own what you 'commandeer' have to say?" Pritchard asked.

"Nothin'," Paul said around a mouth full of beans, "iffen they want to stay aboveground. Sometimes we eat lean, like tonight, and other times, it's beef and whiskey. All depends on what booty we've commandeered."

"Sounds like you're nothin' but a band of brigands," Ditch said.

"Keep your voice down," Paul said, glancing nervously around. None of the other dining guerrillas paid them any notice.

"There're times I'd agree with you," he went on. "We engage Union troops sometimes, but it's always hit and run. Mostly, we attack civilian forces, supposedly sided with the Union. I'd be lyin' to you if I said that was always the case. When we're on a spree, some of the fellows ain't particular who gets shot or what happens to the women and kids."

"I don't stand for that," Pritchard said. "Rape, or the killing of those who ain't fighting, isn't soldiering and it ain't right."

"If you want to stay healthy," Paul said, "you'll stand for whatever goes and keep your mouth shut. I ain't any prouder of some of what we've done than you are, but you voluntarily signed on with Cap'n Witherspoon's company. You came lookin' for us, remember? You took an oath, and now you're ridin' with hard men. Best remember that."

"You don't . . . ?" Ditch asked. "You've never . . . ?"

"Of course not," Paul said. "I ain't never touched a woman didn't want me to, nor shot an unarmed man. But I'm ridin' with those that will gladly do both. So are you. Cap'n Witherspoon already told you he stormed into Kansas with Quantrill and Bloody Bill. You know what them boys did to the town of Lawrence?"

"They say," Ditch said, "women and children were executed right along with unarmed men."

"They weren't lying," Paul said. "That's the way of this war. Iffen you ain't the raiders, you're the ones bein' raided. I don't like it any more than you boys, but that's how it is."

The trio ate in silence for a while, as Pritchard and Ditch absorbed Paul's words.

"How come," Paul finally said, lowering his voice even more, "you're going by an alias, Samuel?"

"Samuel Pritchard is dead and buried," Pritchard said. He and Ditch explained what had transpired back in Missouri, and on their journey to Arkansas.

"If word ever gets back to Atherton that Samuel's still alive," Ditch finished, "his ma and sister are skinned and cooked."

"I'm powerful sorry for what happened to you and your family," Paul said. "Your secret's safe with me. All the same, Joe, it might be just as well everybody believes you're dead. Especially if you ever decide to go back to Missouri."

"I've thought of that," Pritchard said.

The next morning, Company B broke camp and rode west. Two days later, their column of nearly one hundred Confederate rangers entered Oklahoma

Territory. At Broken Bow they turned north and headed for Kansas.

Witherspoon's Rangers spent the next ten days riding the prairies northward. They foraged as they went and lived on buffalo and beans. They avoided towns, and on the fifth day encountered a large Chickasaw war party. The captain ordered the Confederate flag hoisted up on a rifle barrel. The Indians let them pass unmolested.

On the eighth day, Ditch asked his brother if the company had a destination, or were just aimlessly riding north.

"The cap'n always has a destination," Paul answered.

"Where're we going?"

"Cap'n will tell us when we get there," Paul said. "Best shut up and ride."

On the evening of the tenth day, Sergeant Murphy announced they'd left the Oklahoma Territory and entered Kansas, which was Union country. Fires were prohibited, and everyone was told to ready their arms, and themselves, for action.

The following morning, B Company met dawn at the outskirts of Independence, Kansas.

Captain Witherspoon divided the company into two columns, one led by him and the other by Sergeant Murphy. On his signal, a pistol shot, the company rode down the main street at full gallop, firing their revolvers and screeching rebel yells at the top of their voices.

The left flank, commanded by Witherspoon, was to take control of all interests on that side of the street; the right flank, led by Murphy, the opposite side. The objectives were the telegraph office, marshal's office, bank, general store, livery stable, and eventually, as Paul explained to Pritchard and Ditch, the saloon.

Ditch was assigned to his brother, to assist in acquiring horses from the livery. Pritchard was assigned to a group of guerrillas designated to secure the marshal's office and general store.

There was sporadic gunfire from a few shops and houses as the they descended on the town. Pritchard saw a ranger next to him get shot out of his saddle, a bullet tearing through his jaw. He was trampled by his own comrade's horses as the rebel columns continued their charge.

An elderly man in a shopkeeper's apron and glasses emerged from the general store and aimed a shotgun at Pritchard. He fired his pistol reflexively, and the man teetered. Before Pritchard could shoot again, the shopkeeper was struck several more times by pistol shots from other Confederate rangers and fell dead.

Frightened people were running and screaming, and the sound of gunfire was everywhere. A cloud of blue smoke filled the streets of Independence.

Pritchard reached the marshal's office and dismounted, along with two other rangers. As he ran up the steps, a Remington .44 in each hand, he was met at the door by a deputy town marshal wielding an Army Colt.

Both fired at each other from point-blank range. The deputy's pistol misfired and produced only a hollow *click*. Pritchard's shot hit the deputy through his nose. He stepped over the body and into the office.

There were no other deputies inside, and only two men locked in the jail. One looked, and smelled, like a tramp. The other prisoner was well fed and clean. The tramp appeared hungover. His roommate looked scared.

"Stay here," one of the other rangers told Pritchard, "and hold. We'll head on down to the general store."

Pritchard nodded. As the rangers left, he went to the door and beheld the carnage unfolding before him.

What little resistance being offered by the townsfolk had all but ceased. The telegraph office was on fire, and the general store and bank were being swarmed by his fellow rangers. He could see the bodies of eight or ten townsmen littered along the street and sidewalk. A freight wagon had been "commandeered," as Paul would say, and a mob of rebel horsemen were busily loading items from the store into the wagon's bed.

Down the street, he could see Paul and Ditch leading a string of roped horses.

Pritchard bent down and took the Army Colt from the deputy marshal he'd shot. The man looked to have been in his early thirties, and had rough, calloused hands. The weapon was fouled with a significant accumulation of powder residue, and its cylinder would barely turn. Pritchard wondered if the deputy marshal hadn't been anything more than a simple farmer before pinning on his star. Pritchard set the useless revolver on the marshal's desk.

The gunfire stopped. The remaining townsfolk, a few old men, young boys, and a large collection of women and small children, were lined up at gunpoint along the wooden sidewalks. They huddled together, their terrified faces looking up at the disheveled men on horseback who'd invaded their town.

"I'm Captain Jed Witherspoon," the captain announced. "General Shelby sends his regards. This town and all it contains, including you, are now the property of the Confederate States of America."

The captain continued his address. "Which one of you is the mayor?"

"He's lying dead in front of his store," an old man answered. Pritchard realized, with some chagrin, that it had been one of his balls that contributed to his death.

"Where's your town marshal?"

No one answered.

"I'll ask only once more," Captain Witherspoon said. "Where's your town marshal?"

"He's in here," a voice behind Pritchard said. He turned around to find the tramp had spoken. "He took off his tin star and gun and locked himself in his own jail when he saw you fellers ridin' in." One look at the prisoner told Pritchard the tramp's words were true.

"Bring him out," the captain commanded.

A ranger went past Pritchard, took the key from a nail on the wall, and opened the jail door. At first, the marshal refused to come out. It was only at gunpoint that he relented. He was marched into the street before Captain Witherspoon, who was still on his horse.

"So, you hid out in your own jail," Witherspoon asked, "while your fellow citizens died fighting? That's rather cowardly conduct, considering you're the one sworn to protect these good people from the likes of men such as myself."

"Please," the man pleaded. He was a tall, heavy, middle-aged man with sideburns. "I don't want any trouble."

"Then you're in luck," Witherspoon said. He drew his pistol and shot the marshal in the head. "Your troubles are over." Several women on the sidewalk covered their children's eyes. Others began to sob.

"We're going to rest here for a while," the captain went on, "and be on our way. We'll be helping ourselves to whatever we decide is needed for the war effort. Do as you're told, and we won't have to shoot any more of you."

Pritchard shook his head and turned back to the tramp, standing in the jail cell's open doorway.

"You didn't have to speak up," Pritchard said. "You could have let him hide out and pretend to be a prisoner, like you. You got that man killed for nothing."

"Weren't nuthin'," the tramp said, grinning. "I didn't like him. That's somethin'."

"What are you locked up for, anyway?"

"Had my way with a Creek squaw," the tramp said, stepping out of the cell. "Marshal said it was unlawful. Called it 'rape.' Far as I can tell, iffen they can't say *no* in English, it ain't no rape."

Pritchard blocked the tramp's path. "Get back in your cell."

"Ain't you going to let me out?" the tramp asked, looking up at Pritchard towering over him.

"Nope," Pritchard said.

"Why not? The marshal's dead, and from what I hear, so is Mayor Bromley. He's the justice of the peace around here. Without no lawman or judge, I can't be tried, can I? Why not let me go free?"

"Because I don't like you," Pritchard said.

The tramp suddenly lunged for the revolver on the marshal's desk. Pritchard let him reach the Colt and bring it up before drawing and shooting him twice through the middle. The tramp died with the inoperative revolver still in his hand.

"What's the shootin' about?" Sergeant Murphy said, entering the marshal's office with another ranger.

"He was one of the deputies," Pritchard lied, motioning with his pistol to the dead tramp. "He was hiding out with the marshal. Grabbed that gun and tried to make a break for it."

"Nicely done," Murphy said, kicking the tramp's corpse. "I'm beginning to like you, Joe."

Chapter 22

"We lost four men," Sergeant Murphy began, "killed outright. Got six more wounded. Four of them can ride. The other two won't likely make it through the night."

Most of Witherspoon's Rangers not on watch were inside Whistler's, Independence's main saloon. Captain Witherspoon was seated at a table before an unopened bottle of whiskey, receiving the after-action report.

It was dusk, and the men were standing around inside the tavern, anxiously awaiting word from their commander to begin drinking. Pritchard was loitering in the back of the saloon, awaiting the arrival of Ditch and Paul, who were at the livery tending to the company's horses.

"How many of theirs killed?"

"Twenty-one men, two women, and a child."

No mention of wounded was made. Pritchard didn't know it yet, but Witherspoon's Rangers, as a partisan guerrilla force, didn't take prisoners.

"Horses?" Witherspoon asked.

"We lost nine," the sergeant said.

"What did we take in?"

"It's a solid haul, Cap'n," Murphy said. "Got thirty good horses and plenty of ammunition, powder, and grain from the general store."

"The bank?"

"More'n thirty thousand," the sergeant said. "Over twenty in gold, the rest in Union paper."

"Where're all the townsfolk?"

"We put 'em all in the church, like usual," the sergeant said. "Maybe two hundred of them, mostly women and kids."

Pritchard watched the hungry eyes of the men as the sergeant mentioned the women.

"Has the watch been set?"

"Yes, sir. The town of Independence is secure."

"Very well," Captain Witherspoon said, uncorking the bottle, "those not on watch later tonight may commence their recreation. Advise the men we pull out at dawn. Any ranger unfit to ride will be left behind."

Rebel yells filled the saloon and echoed across the vacant streets of Independence, Kansas. Confederate rangers vaulted the bar and began distributing bottles, which were quickly passed out among the men.

Pritchard picked up his rifle and walked out unnoticed through the saloon's rear door. He made a stop at the jail for more ammunition, then collected Rusty and made his way through the empty street toward the church.

The rifle was an 1859 Sharps, which he found in the marshal's office and "commandeered." It had been well cared for, and Pritchard found it clean and in excellent working order. There were several boxes of .52 caliber paper cartridges for the weapon inside the marshal's desk.

Pritchard spent the afternoon cleaning and reloading his Remingtons, and disassembling and cleaning the Army Colt .44 that would have killed him had its owner maintained it. Once he was finished, and the Colt was reassembled, he loaded it with five balls and strapped on the belt and holster worn by the deputy marshal he left lying on the steps. Then he helped himself to as much powder, cap, and .44 caliber ball as he could carry.

Shortly before dark, all the rangers who weren't standing guard mustered inside Whistler's Saloon. After hearing the after-action report, and watching the rangers begin their drunken revelry, Pritchard knew what would transpire next.

He also knew what he had to do.

Pritchard led Rusty to the edge of town where the church was located. It was a beautiful structure, two stories tall, with a belfry topped by a cross. He tied the Morgan to a tree in the woods behind it and approached the ranger standing guard at the front door.

"I'm your relief," Pritchard announced as he walked up. "You'd better head on down to the saloon before all the whiskey's gone."

"Don't have to tell me twice," the elated ranger said. He went off toward town as fast as he could walk.

Once the sentry was out of sight, Pritchard opened the church doors and entered. More than two hundred frightened faces looked up at him. Most of them were women.

The church was lit with lanterns, and Pritchard surveyed the congregation. There were only a handful of males, and those who weren't children were old or infirm. He expected as much, since most towns in the territory were devoid of able-bodied men of fighting age due to the war.

"Who's in charge here?" Pritchard asked.

"I am." An ancient man stepped forward. He was bent over with rheumatism, and one of his eyes was white with cataract. "I'm Pastor Milburn Greer."

"They'll be coming soon," Pritchard said, "for the women. You haven't got much time. Just long enough for those boys to get a good drunk going."

"You're one of them," an older woman snapped. "You'll be joining them in the raping. The killing, too."

"No, ma'am," Pritchard said, "I will not. I have killed, sure enough, but only when I had to, and only armed men who were trying to do the same to me."

"Then why did you come down here to the church?" another woman asked. She was quite pretty, and about his mother's age.

"To stave them off," Pritchard said, "iffen I can."

"Why should we believe you?" yet another woman asked. She was about Pritchard's age, and was holding an infant.

"You don't have to believe me," Pritchard said. "All you have to do is wait a few more minutes, and about seventy-five drunk and horny rebel guerrillas will come marching down the street and put truth to my words."

"We could run and hide in the woods," still another woman offered.

"You wouldn't get far," Pritchard countered. "A group this large would be easily tracked."

The women looked at one another. "What choice do we have?" one asked.

"All right," the pretty woman said. "What do you want us to do?"

"Is there a cyclone cellar in this church?"

"There is," the pastor answered. Evidently his hearing was better than his vision. "Biggest one in town."

"Will it hold everyone?"

"It'll be tight, but we can cram 'em all in."

"Then do it," Pritchard ordered. Someone opened a floor-hatch at the rear of the church, and the older woman began to herd everyone down. "No matter what you hear above," Pritchard admonished, "do not come up out of that cellar until I say so."

"We understand."

Pritchard addressed the pastor. "How do I get up to the belfry?"

"I'll show you the ladder," the pastor said. "What, exactly, do you propose to do with my bell tower?"

"Same thing you do with it," Pritchard said, opening the Sharps's action and inserting a paper cartridge into the breech. "Lead sinners into the arms of Jesus."

Chapter 23

Pritchard fired as the mob approached. The reb guerrillas paraded down the street, hooting and laughing. Most carried bottles. It was nearly a full moon, and he could easily make out his targets.

The shot shattered a bottle carried by one of the lead guerrillas. The mob stopped.

"That's far enough," Pritchard called down from the belfry. He opened the rifle's breech, reloaded another paper cartridge, and replaced the percussion cap.

"What the hell are you doing up there, Atherton?" the reb who'd had the bottle shot out of his hand yelled from the street. "You could've killed me."

"And I will," Pritchard said, "if any of you come one step closer. My next shot hits meat."

"What's got into you, Joe?" another reb said. "We're just comin' down to visit the ladies, that's all. Ain't like your ma or sister's in that church."

"She may as well be," Pritchard said, his thoughts momentarily drifting to Dovie and Idelle. He couldn't help but imagine they were hiding in the cellar below. "What you aim to do is wrong, and you know it. Go on back to the saloon and leave the womenfolk be."

"You go to hell!" a drunken voice replied.

"It's one thing to shoot Union men who are shootin' at you," Pritchard said. "That's war. It's another to molest their women and kids. That ain't what soldiers do."

"We ain't regular soldiers," a different reb challenged. "We're guerrilla fighters. We don't have to follow no rules. We take what we want. Besides, we ain't gonna do nuthin' to them gals their men wouldn't be doin' iffen they was around!" The company burst into laughter.

"Nobody's doin' nuthin' to these women," Pritchard said. "You'd best take my word on that."

"We don't give a damn about your word," the ranger said, drawing his pistol. Others drew as well. "Who the hell are you to be tellin' us what to do with our peckers? You ain't been ridin' with us but a couple of weeks. Come down from that bell tower, boy, and I'll kick your Missouri ass!"

"Ain't gonna do it," Pritchard said. "Last warning. Go back to the saloon. Leave the women be."

In response, ten or fifteen rangers fired their pistols at the belfry.

No bell rung, however. Before the mob arrived, Pritchard had taken the liberty of removing the heavy bell from its mount. He set it aside on the roof and tied one end of the bell rope, which led all the way down to the church, to a post before tossing it over the side.

Pritchard took aim with the Sharps, as pistol shots struck the heavy wooden belfry all around him. He fired, and the ranger who'd threatened to kick his ass fell dead with a bullet through his head. Pritchard levered open the action and had another cartridge in the breech, and a cap on the nipple, in an instant. His next shot dropped another reb with a .52 caliber bullet to the skull.

Pritchard commenced systematically firing. The men of B Company, Witherspoon's Rangers, most of them well on their way to being blind drunk, foolishly stood like a herd of cattle in the street and fired their revolvers up at him.

Pritchard had fair light, high ground, excellent cover, a superb rifle, more than one hundred cartridges in his coat pocket, along with that many percussion caps, and multiple targets of opportunity bunched up below him like ducks in a barrel. Confederate guerrillas dropped left and right.

More than twenty rebs lay dead in the street before the mob collectively decided to break and run. Pritchard didn't let up as they scattered. He methodically fired, reloaded, and fired, again and again. Another ten men were shot down running away.

Pritchard paused and opened the action to let it cool. He liked the Sharps, which he considered a vast improvement over the Hawken. The weapon had power, balance, ease of reloading, and seemed to fit his hands as if made for him.

Not all of Witherspoon's men fled. He noticed a guerrilla taking aim at him from behind a trough. He snapped another cartridge and cap on the weapon, took aim, and pulled the trigger, just as the reb fired. The pistol shot whanged harmlessly on the belfry's roof, but Pritchard's rifle shot hit his intended target squarely in the chest.

Pritchard reloaded and waited. As expected, Captain Witherspoon soon came walking down the street with Sergeant Murphy beside him. He was surrounded by what was left of his furious men.

"Private Atherton," the captain called out. He shook his head as he stepped over the bodies of his rangers. "What is your problem, son? You just wiped out damn near half my men."

"Their choice, Cap'n," Pritchard replied, "not mine. I told them to leave the womenfolk be, or I'd take it personal. They chose to ignore my warning."

"It would seem," the captain continued, still counting dead bodies, "that your sense of chivalry is only exceeded by your marksmanship."

"I hit what I aim at, sir."

"This won't do," Captain Witherspoon said, putting his hands on his hips. "I'm afraid I'm going to have to hang you for this, Atherton."

"I'm getting powerful tired," Pritchard said, shouldering the Sharps and taking aim, "of hearing men in uniform threaten to hang, or shoot, me."

"There's simply no way around it, son. Military discipline must be maintained. Come on down from that belfry."

"I believe I will oblige you to come up here and get me," Pritchard said.

"I was afraid you'd say that," Witherspoon said. "You realize, of course, your noble intentions, however misplaced, were for naught. Because now, instead of hanging only you, I'm going to have to burn that church to the ground. I'm certain the fair maidens you were so hell-bent on protecting, if given the choice, would have rather endured the rough affections of my men, and live, than die in the flames of their house of worship along with you and your noble intentions."

The captain motioned to his men. Several began lighting torches.

"You'd do that?" Pritchard said. "Roast innocent women and children?"

"Without a second's hesitation," Witherspoon said. "You heard me tell how I rode into Lawrence with Bloody Bill and Quantrill, didn't you?"

"Roast in hell," Pritchard said as he fired. His shot blew the top of Witherspoon's head off.

Pritchard began his rapid-firing sequence again, aiming first for the men with torches. He got three before they got near the church. Then he took aim at anyone else in reb gray.

Some stood and fought, others took cover and returned fire, and still others simply ran. To Pritchard, it made no difference. He focused all his attention on loading, priming, and aiming the Sharps. One by one, Confederate guerrillas fell. Before long, another twenty-five men had joined their brethren lying dead on the main street of Independence, Kansas.

Except for Sergeant Murphy and two rangers, what was left of B Company, Shelby's 5th, ran for their horses and rode out of town.

While Pritchard was firing down on the soldiers, Murphy and his two followers lit torches and stormed the church, setting it ablaze. The sergeant and his men stood at the bottom of the belfry ladder as the church began to burn. He yelled up at Pritchard, a revolver in each hand.

"Get out of that perch!" Murphy shouted. "Come down and fight, Atherton, you gutless son of a bitch!"

"I'm right here, Sergeant," Pritchard said from behind him.

When Pritchard saw Murphy and the two Confederate guerrillas enter the church, he slung the Sharps, grabbed the bell rope he'd thrown over the side of the roof, and slid to the ground. He entered the church, a Remington in each hand, and found Murphy and the two partisan rangers still looking up the ladder.

The three rebs whirled to face Pritchard, but not fast enough. He fired three times, and all went down. Sergeant Murphy weakly tried to raise his pistol from flat on his back, and Pritchard shot him between the eyes.

Pritchard ran through the church, which was quickly becoming consumed, and threw open the cellar doors. He was met with terrified faces.

"Everybody out!" he shouted. He began to usher people out of the cellar.

"Samuel!"

Ditch and Paul came running into the church. They, too, began to help escort the residents of Independence, Kansas, from the cellar. Within a few minutes, everyone was outside. Pritchard, Ditch, and Paul stood with the congregation and watched the church burn.

"Where were you boys when the fireworks were going off?" Pritchard asked, coughing.

"We were watching your shooting gallery from safely down the street," Paul said. "We were afraid to get any closer, for fear you'd shoot us by mistake."

"A wise move," Pritchard said. "Any reb guerrillas left around?"

"None that I can see," Ditch said. "About the time you killed more'n half of 'em, and unhinged the top of their commanding officer's head, the rest decided to skedaddle. Can't say as I blame 'em." He noticed the remnant of Pritchard's death-shadow still lingering on his friend's face.

Pastor Greer approached Pritchard. "You did it, son. You delivered us."

"I'm sorry for the loss of your church," Pritchard

said. "For what it's worth, the money taken from your town's bank is spread out on a card table down at the saloon. Maybe you can rebuild it?"

"Don't worry on it too much," the pastor said, beholding the inferno. "This was God's will."

"Iffen you say so," Pritchard said.

"What now?" Paul asked.

"Yeah," Ditch chimed in. "What do we do now?"

"I don't know about you fellers," Pritchard said, "but I'm done soldiering. I've got no stomach for killin' women and children. Besides, it seems to me, it don't make no difference whether it's Union blue or Confederate gray we soldier for. Both armies are lookin' to kill us. I'm leavin' Kansas a civilian."

"Where will you go?" Ditch said.

"Reckon I'll head further south," Pritchard said, "and seek my fortune in Texas."

"You want some company?" Ditch asked.

PART TWO
RANGER

Chapter 24

Central Texas, May 1869

Pritchard crawled on his belly slowly to avoid disturbing the dry, sandy, dirt. There wasn't much wind, and he didn't want to create a telltale puff of dust that would reveal his movement and location. He kept one gloved hand hooded over the top of the spyglass's lens to prevent a glint that might also give away his position.

Down below, at the creek, he counted over thirty armed men. The group was composed of a mix of white outlaws, Mexican bandits, and Comanche warriors. He noted a couple of Henry rifles and a few Spencer repeaters, but most were armed with single-shot, trapdoor Springfields left over from the war.

Pritchard knew the odds he and his fellow Rangers faced were fair, at best. He was with a company of seventeen other Texas Rangers, each one armed with a Henry repeating rifle and at least two revolvers. They had the sun at their backs, and for now, at least, the element of surprise. He wasn't overly concerned. Pritchard had faced worse odds, many times before.

Pritchard and the Clemson brothers left Kansas in late November 1863, bound for Texas. They brought with them a string of fifty-three top-quality Confederate horses, formerly belonging to B Company, 5th Regiment, of Shelby's Iron Brigade. They also had over two thousand dollars in Union cash and gold taken from the bodies of Captain Witherspoon and his partisan guerrillas.

They sold the animals in Fort Worth, in January of 1864, to a horse buyer for the Union army, for $160 per head. By Texas standards, that made them rich. They then rode west in search of available ranch land, and found it near a lake in Taylor County, just south of what would someday become Abilene. Pritchard, Ditch, and Paul Clemson bought twenty thousand acres of Texas dirt for five thousand dollars. They called the property the SD&P Ranch.

They spent the remainder of the winter and the spring of 1864 building a ranch house, erecting a corral, digging a well, and preparing for the coming summer. When it arrived, they rode into Fort Worth and bought four hundred head of cattle. It took Pritchard, Ditch, and Paul almost two weeks to herd them back to the ranch.

By summer's end, rustlers and the Comanche had depleted their herd by a third. The SD&P's cattle were too spread out for only three watchmen, and the thieves too persistent. Despite their constant patrols and endless vigilance, their livestock continued to dwindle.

It was on a hot September afternoon when Pritchard and Paul finally met up with one of the crews of cattle thieves who'd been plaguing them. The rustlers had become so brazen, since facing no challenge, that they'd moved to within only a few miles of the ranch house to ply their illicit trade.

Ditch had remained at the house to do chores, and Pritchard and Paul had ridden out to check the stock. They smelled smoke and followed the scent. When they crested a shallow rise, they found five men over a campfire altering the SD&P brand on some of their cows to BB&B.

The rustlers went for their pistols. Pritchard spurred Rusty and charged. He shot two of them down with his own pistols before Paul even got his carbine clear of its saddle scabbard.

Pritchard rode right through them, with Rusty jumping the campfire, and shot another at point-blank range. Paul shot a fourth with his Spencer, and the fifth rustler dropped his pistol and raised his hands.

It would be the first of many encounters with rustlers, Indians, and outlaws the three Missourians would experience in Texas. But it would be Pritchard's last before becoming a Texas Ranger.

Paul and Pritchard tied up the surviving rustler, loaded his dead companions onto their horses, and rode them all into the nearby town of Bristow. It was their intent to turn their prisoner, and the bodies, over to the marshal there.

They'd contemplated hanging the rustler, but the town was closer than the nearest tree. When they got to Bristow they were surprised to find a large crowd of people assembled in the street in front of the marshal's office.

The marshal, a hard-faced old cuss named Bud Logan, stood in front of the jail with a shotgun across his bony chest. Standing next to him was a tall, lean, man with a mustache. Pritchard had never seen him before. He was wearing a star on his chest, a wide-brimmed Stetson Boss of the Plains hat, and a brace of Colt .44s.

"You boys are gonna wish you hadn't come into town today," their prisoner said to Pritchard and Paul as they rode in. He laughed. "This is my lucky day, that's for sure."

"Shut up," Paul told him.

The crowd turned to gawk at the convoy of dead bodies, with one live prisoner, being led into town by Pritchard and Paul.

"Howdy, fellas," the captive rustler called out to the crowd. Pritchard noticed that while most of the mob was composed of regular townsfolk, at the front of the pack stood a clump of about a dozen hard cases, all wearing pistols and spoiling for a fight.

"What gives?" the marshal called out to Pritchard and Paul as they reined their horses to a stop.

"Caught these five boys rebranding our cows," Paul answered. "Four of 'em put up a fight. I'd ask you the same question, Marshal?"

"Got Wade Boone in my jail for back-shootin' a clerk during a bank robbery in Waco," the marshal replied. "This Texas Ranger is here to take him back to Waco for trial. Seems some of Wade's friends aren't particularly pleased about that."

The Boone spread, or Triple B, known by the BB&B brand, was the ranch north of the SD&P. Old Man Boone had long been suspected of not only being one of the busiest rustlers around, but of selling his rustled beef and stolen horses to the Comanche,

Comancheros, and the Mexican government. His two adult sons, Wade and Wesley, were notorious trouble-makers. When not out thieving cattle or horses, they spent their time in gambling halls, saloons, and whore-houses. That Wade was suspected of bank robbery and murder didn't surprise Pritchard or Paul in the least.

"Iffen you don't mind," Pritchard said, "we'd be obliged if you'd allow us to deposit this rustler in your jail, so we can get on about our business."

"Nobody's goin' into that jail," one of the men at the front of the crowd said. Pritchard recognized him as the foreman at Boone's Triple B Ranch, and the men surrounding him as cowhands employed there. "As a matter of fact, somebody's coming out. Turn Wade loose, Marshal Logan."

"Ain't gonna," the marshal said.

"Then we'll march in and get him," the ranch fore-man said. "And don't think no withered old town marshal, nor one lonely, stinkin' Ranger is gonna stop us, neither."

"Well, come on, then," Marshal Logan said, level-ing the shotgun at the spokesman. "See what's a-waitin' for you."

The onlookers and townsfolk who'd been watching the unfolding drama began to move back. Within sec-onds, there were only the two lawmen standing in front of the jail, with a dozen fuming cowboys facing them, each one primed to draw. Everybody else had moved to a position of cover behind a barrel, trough, or post to observe the drama from relative safety.

Pritchard dismounted, gesturing for Paul to keep their prisoner covered with his carbine from horse-back. He slowly walked through the throng of cowboys, a full head taller than any of them, until he turned to stand shoulder to shoulder with Marshal Logan and the Ranger in front of the jail.

"What do you think you're doing, Atherton?" the foreman said. "Are you taking sides with them lawmen?"

"Might as well," Pritchard said. "I already killed three of you thievin' Triple B hands today, and it's still early."

"You son of a bitch," the foreman said. He and the two men on either side of him went for their guns.

In the blink of an eye, Pritchard drew and fired three times. He felled the trio of gunmen with three headshots. Marshal Logan started to pull the shotgun's trigger, and the Ranger had drawn both his revolvers, but both checked their trigger fingers after witnessing Pritchard's display of blazingly fast, and deadly accurate, gunmanship.

"Anybody else?" Pritchard asked what was left of the pack. Nobody answered him, nor dared move. His smoking guns, and the look in his eye, froze them in place.

"Git on outa here!" Marshal Logan ordered. "Take your friends' miserable carcasses back to your boss, and tell him Bristow is off-limits to the Boone spread. I see anybody from the Triple B walking the streets from here on out, I'll shoot 'em on sight."

The BB&B cowboys grudgingly picked up their three dead comrades from the street and took the reins of the horses carrying their four other dead hands. Paul nudged his prisoner off his mount and let them take that animal, as well. The cowboys grudgingly moved off.

"Into the jail," Paul said, prodding the no-longer-laughing rustler with his Spencer.

While Marshal Logan locked their prisoner in the cell with Wade Boone, the Ranger turned to Pritchard and Paul.

"That was the finest piece of pistoleering I've ever seen, and I've seen gunplay from New Orleans to the Dakota Territory," he said. "I'm Tom Franchard, of the Texas Rangers. What's your name, son?"

"Joe Atherton," Pritchard said, adhering to his alias. "This here is Paul Clemson." They shook hands. "We own a spread not far from here. A spread the Boone family has been plundering."

"I'm not surprised. I tracked Wade here from Waco. I was hoping to bag him before he got home, to avoid exactly this kind of showdown."

"Why didn't you boys just hang him when you caught him rustling?" Marshal Logan asked, motioning to their now-despondent prisoner. "Might've saved us both some trouble. Nobody on this side of the law would have cared a whit."

"There weren't no trees around," Paul said.

"I won't make that mistake again," Pritchard said.

"Tell me," Franchard asked, "how old are you boys?"

"I'm eighteen," Pritchard said. "Paul's twenty-one."

"Where'd you learn to shoot like that?"

"Necessity," Pritchard said, "and the war." He removed his hat and revealed the bullet-hole scar on his forehead.

"Have you ever considered a career with the Texas Rangers?" Franchard asked.

Five violent, eventful, years had come and gone since Pritchard parted ways with Ditch and Paul Clemson and cast his lot with the Texas Rangers.

He bid his friends good-bye, refusing to take payment for his share of the ranch, and accompanied Ranger Thomas Franchard to Waco with Wade Boone in tow. As expected in cattle country, the Triple B rustler Pritchard and Paul deposited in Bristow's jail was tried and hanged within days of their departure.

"Ranching was never the life for me," Pritchard told Ditch, as they shook hands before he left. "I'm better with guns than horses and cows."

"I know," Ditch said, thinking of the death-shadow that hung over his friend. "Good luck to you."

Also, as expected, Ranger Franchard and Pritchard were ambushed en route to Waco by a party of Triple B hands, forty miles east of Bristow. Ten cowboys came charging at them on horseback while they were breaking morning camp. They whooped and hollered and fired their pistols, hoping to convince the Ranger and his young sidekick to abandon their prisoner and flee for their lives.

That was before Pritchard unlimbered the Sharps from his saddle, Franchard his Henry, and both men cut loose. The two riders who fled moments later, with their tails between their legs, left eight of their friends lying dead in the Texas dust behind them.

Five days later, Pritchard, Franchard, and Wade Boone arrived in Waco. On the sixth day, the good citizens of that town held a brief trial. On the morning of the seventh day, Wade Boone had his neck stretched in the town square. That was also the day Samuel Pritchard, otherwise known as Joe Atherton, was sworn in as a Texas Ranger.

In the ensuing five years, Pritchard fought Indians, battled renegades, hunted outlaws, faced off with bandits, and traveled from New Mexico to the Oklahoma

Territory in the service of the Republic of Texas. Though one of the youngest Rangers to ever pin on a cinco-peso star, he soon became a legend within the ranks of lawmen and outlaws alike as "Smokin' Joe" Atherton. He earned the moniker, it was said, because if you were foolish enough to cross him you'd end up smoking in hell.

No one knew the true number of men Ranger Smokin' Joe Atherton had sent to boot hill, but anyone who'd ever seen the huge Ranger shoot didn't doubt the figure, however exaggerated it might have been.

During that same period, Tom Franchard had been promoted twice; from ranger, to sergeant, to captain. He now commanded his own Ranger detachment. He always made certain, wherever he went, and with each new promotion or assignment, to take young Ranger Joe Atherton along with him.

"How many, Joe?" Franchard asked, his voice a whisper.

"About thirty, I reckon," Pritchard said, handing the spyglass to the senior Ranger. "Maybe thirty-five. See for yourself."

Franchard scooched down next to Pritchard and squinted through the lens. "I count at least thirty, all right," he said. "The women look to be unhurt."

"For now," Pritchard said. "Those Comancheros have been ridin' 'em too hard to get in much rapin'. I'm guessing that's about to change."

"It's likely why they took the women down into that wash," Franchard said.

The night before, a band of Comancheros who had been terrorizing the territory raided the fledgling town of San Angelo, in the Concho Valley. They killed several men and made off with eleven females. The oldest was in her forties, and the youngest not yet ten years old. By chance, Captain Franchard's contingent of Texas Rangers was passing through the valley on the way back from Fort Stockton after action against the Comanche, and took up the hunt.

"What do you think?" Franchard asked Pritchard.

"I think it's going to be messy," Pritchard said, "but we've got no choice. If we split our forces and try to head them off at the other end, they'll spot us for sure. Even if they don't, we'll lose the rest of the day. But if we let them get out of that wash, they'll scatter, and we'll never get those hostages back alive."

"I agree. How do you want to play it?"

"Only one way to play it," Pritchard said. "Straight at 'em, hell-bent for leather."

Chapter 25

Dovie walked down the sidewalk with her head high, exuding a confidence she didn't feel. She felt the many scornful eyes on her, but ignored them, as she always did when out in public in Atherton.

It was spring, and more than five years had passed since she took Burnell Shipley's name during a Valentine's Day ceremony performed in the lobby of the Atherton Arms Hotel. It was a day she loathed to remember.

Since the wedding, Atherton had become a boomtown. Dovie's new husband, as he'd once boasted, had indeed become the wealthiest and most powerful man in not only Jackson County, but the entire region.

After the surrender, Burnell convinced the railroad companies it would be in their mutual financial interests to build a special rail line from Atherton to Kansas City. This gave the once-small town direct access to all the many benefits of the postwar expansion.

By then, America's great westward migration was in full swing. While the country's never-ending demand for beef and lumber fueled the massive tide of humanity west toward the promise of California,

Atherton, Missouri, under Burnell Shipley's greedy stewardship, became one of the midcontinental hubs to provide both.

Burnell built up Atherton as the migrants and carpetbaggers flocked in. He erected another hotel, and two more saloons, in addition to expanding the stockyards and lumber enterprise. He traveled once a month to Jefferson City to meet with a sympathetic, and easily bribed, senator, and spent at least two weeks each month in Kansas City, allegedly conducting business.

Dovie suspected her husband did indeed conduct some business in Kansas City, but knew that most of his transactions were conducted at the city's saloons, poker tables, and bordellos.

She didn't care what her husband did, and in truth, was grateful for the times he was away. Succumbing to his occasional marital demands when he was in Atherton was beyond revolting. Dovie consoled herself, while suffering in the midst of Burnell's grunting throes, with the knowledge that her daughter was growing up safe and healthy, and her son, wherever he was, was still alive. She'd kept her word, and honored her end of the bargain. In that small thing, and the safety of her children it wrought, she took her only comfort.

Dovie walked through the bustling streets, aware that men who didn't know her still stopped and stared. She was an uncommonly beautiful woman, and despite the burden of shame she'd borne since Thomas's death, maintained her youthful and healthy appearance.

Dovie reached the Nettleses' modest home, next to the schoolhouse. Before she could knock, the door was flung open, and Idelle rushed out to greet her. Her first vision of her daughter was always like a tonic, and she hugged her child every day as if seeing her for the first time in years.

Idelle was now fifteen, and like her mother before her, had blossomed into a breathtakingly beautiful young woman. Her long blond hair flowed over her shoulders, and her crystal blue eyes, a family trait, sparkled along with her smile.

"Hello, Mama. Are you ready to go?"

"As always." She held up the basket. "I brought your favorite. Fried chicken and peach pie."

It was Dovie and Idelle's custom each Saturday, when the weather permitted, to have a picnic lunch on the schoolhouse lawn. It was close enough to town to be an easy walk for Dovie, and private enough, since not a school day, for them to enjoy each other's company without interruption in the seclusion of the schoolyard.

Idelle grabbed a blanket, took her mother's hand, and they retreated to the rear of the schoolhouse. In another moment they had the blanket spread and the food laid out.

As always before dining, they joined hands in prayer. Dovie led the invocation.

"We thank thee, Lord," she began, "for thy bounty. Bless the memory of Thomas, who is at your side, and keep watch over Samuel, wherever he may be. In your grace, amen."

"Amen," Idelle repeated.

They began to eat, chatting and reveling in the delicious food, unseasonably warm spring day, and the joy of each other's companionship. Both Dovie and Idelle looked forward all week to their Saturdays together.

Since her father's death Idelle resided, at Dovie's

insistence, at the Nettleses' home. Dovie held Burnell to his promise of a generous stipend, one hundred dollars per month, for Idelle's board and care. She also strictly forbade her daughter from ever going into town without her, or entering the Atherton Arms Hotel.

As she grew, Idelle began assisting Alice Nettles in her teaching duties. As Atherton's population grew, so did her responsibilities. By the time she was fourteen, Idelle was handling the kinder classes all by herself and receiving university-level instruction from Alice's husband, Rodney.

Dovie was so proud of Idelle, and the confident young woman she'd become. Every minute she spent with her daughter made enduring the torment of being Burnell Shipley's wife bearable. If only she could see Samuel, and be reassured he was happy and well, she would be satisfied.

But Dovie knew seeing her son again was not in the cards. His life had only been spared by her sacrifice and his promise never to return. Should Samuel come back to Atherton, as much as she longed to see him, it would be his end. The end of her and Idelle in all likelihood, too.

So Dovie was forced to console herself with imagining that Samuel was safe somewhere, far from Atherton, perhaps living near the ocean in California. In her dreams she always envisioned him with a beautiful young wife and children, happy in the loving embrace of a new family to replace the one he'd lost.

Dovie's reverie was shattered by the clop of hooves. Two riders approached from around the schoolhouse. Dovie looked up to find Eli Gaines and another deputy named Bernard Moss, a slovenly man with a long beard, pull their mounts to a stop at the edge of their picnic blanket.

"Afternoon, ladies," Gaines drawled in his high-pitched voice. He had a wad of tobacco in his distended jaw. Neither he nor Deputy Moss made any effort to conceal their leers as they ogled the two women.

"What do you want?" Dovie demanded.

"Just stopped by to check in on you," Gaines said. "As a lawman, I'm responsible for your safety. I'd expect you'd be a little more appreciative of my concern for your well-being."

"We're fine," Dovie said. "If you'll excuse us?"

"You know," Gaines went on, ignoring Dovie's plea for him to depart, "I've been keeping my eye on you, Idelle. You're gettin' to be quite a growed-up woman." He turned his head and spat without taking his eyes off Idelle. "Ain't gonna be too long before you'll be of age to get hitched."

Dovie stood. "Hold your tongue," she said. "I'll not sit idly by and have the likes of you slobber over my daughter."

"Not good enough for her, am I?"

"As a matter of fact, you're not. You're swine."

"Hear that, Eli?" Moss laughed. "She called you a pig."

"Not very neighborly of her, is it?" Gaines said.

"You two animals aren't fit to breathe the same air as Idelle, much less talk to her. Get out of here and leave us be, before I—"

"Before you what, Mrs. Shipley?" Gaines interrupted her. "Tell your husband?" He spat again and laughed. "Your husband is in Kansas City, puttin' chips on the table and whores on their backs. And my boss, the honorable Sheriff Horace Foster, is there gettin' his wick dipped right along with him. Which leaves me, as chief deputy, the man currently in charge of Jackson County. So, if I want to talk to your daughter, I'll damn well do it. What do you think of that?"

"Forgive me, Deputy," Dovie said, casting her eyes downward. "I apologize for being so disrespectful."

"Mama!" Idelle protested. "You don't have to take that from him!"

"Quiet, Idelle," Dovie commanded. "We're being impolite. Would you gentlemen care for some peach pie?" Dovie asked, reaching into the basket.

"Why, sure," Gaines said, pleased to have submitted Dovie. "That's more like it. I expect in the future, you'll remember your place and show me a little more respect." He began to dismount.

"Of course, Deputy Gaines," Dovie said demurely.

Dovie came out of the basket not with pie, but with a sterling silver fork from the Atherton Arms Hotel. She struck out and jabbed Gaines's horse in the flank. The horse reared and began to buck violently, tossing the skeletal deputy from the stirrups. He landed in the grass with a *thud*, as his hat flew off and his horse ran away.

Idelle couldn't keep from laughing, but Dovie's face remained hard and flat. She held the fork like a weapon as Gaines slowly got up. He was furious. His face was crimson, and his anemic body trembled with rage. He started to draw one of his pistols.

"Take it easy, Eli," Moss said, afraid of what the enraged deputy was about to do. He was fully aware of

Gaines's well-deserved homicidal reputation. "There's folks watching."

"Shut up," Gaines told him. He took a step toward Dovie, who shielded Idelle behind her.

"Go ahead," Dovie said. "Shoot me. Gun down an unarmed woman, like the coward you are."

"Wouldn't be the first Pritchard I've shot," Gaines said.

"Eli," Deputy Moss said, nervously glancing around. "Think about what you're doing."

"What did you say?" Dovie asked.

Gaines's rage suddenly dissipated. He grinned and holstered his revolver. "Nothin' worth repeating," he said.

"Let's get out of here," Moss said. "I'll fetch your horse."

"You do that," Gaines said as the deputy rode off. He picked up his hat and began to dust himself off.

"That was a pretty good trick," he said, "offerin' me pie and then spookin' my horse. Hope you both got a good laugh out of it."

"I surely did," Idelle blurted.

"Enjoy it while you can," he said. "Because pretty soon, Mrs. Shipley, what Ole Burnell is doin' to you, I'm gonna be doin' to your precious Idelle. We'll see how loud you laugh about that."

"Over my dead body," Dovie said.

"Funny you mention that," Gaines said. "Especially in light of what befell the previous Mrs. Shipley. I was in town the night she had her 'accident.' I remember it was a rather peculiar affair. Almost looked like she fell down those stairs twice."

Deputy Moss rode back with Gaines's horse in tow. Gaines put on his hat and mounted.

"You ladies have a fine afternoon," he said as they rode off. "I'll be seeing you around, Idelle. You can be sure of that."

"Hope you enjoyed the pie," Idelle called out after him.

Chapter 26

"All right, boys," Captain Franchard addressed his Rangers. "I ain't gonna lie to you. There's more'n thirty Comancheros down in that gulch. Could be as many as forty. Them ain't favorable odds."

"When have we ever faced a square deck?" a Ranger chuckled.

"They're holding eleven women and girls," Franchard continued. "After they've had their way with those poor gals, they're gonna sell what's left of 'em to the Comanche. That don't sit well with me. I'm fixin' to ride down there and kill every one of them sons of bitches. Any of you Texans want to join me?"

Seventeen Rangers grinned as one. "What are we waitin' for?" Pritchard asked.

"That's what I thought," Franchard said. "Mount up, boys. You care to lead us, Atherton?"

"Might as well," another Ranger chuckled, playfully punching Pritchard in the shoulder. "Smokin' Joe is the biggest target we've got. He might draw some of the lead offen the rest of us." The others laughed.

"Be glad to, Captain," Pritchard said with a smile, tipping his hat to his compadres.

"Aim careful," Franchard cautioned as the Rangers climbed into their saddles. "I don't want none of them womenfolk hit."

Pritchard guided Rusty to the head of the column and drew his Henry carbine from its scabbard.

"Follow me, boys!" he yelled, and spurred the big Morgan.

Eighteen experienced, battle-hardened, Texas Rangers bore down into the wash at full gallop. The Comancheros were dismounted and bunched up, their attention focused on something on the ground the Rangers couldn't see. The captive women were bound and seated in a group, twenty feet away from them.

When the Comancheros saw and heard the column of horsemen bearing down on them, they broke and went for their rifles and pistols.

The Rangers closed in, with Pritchard at the head of the pack. The Comancheros panicked. Typically the raiders, they weren't accustomed to being raided themselves. They fired wildly at the mounted gunmen descending upon them with little effect.

The Rangers were savvy-enough guerrilla fighters to know that accuracy from horseback, whether from a rifle or pistol, was nearly impossible unless at point-blank range. Despite the bullets flying in their direction, they held their fire to a man until Pritchard led them right into the Comancheros' makeshift camp.

Steering Rusty with his knees, the reins in his teeth, Pritchard fired his Henry rifle again and again, levering the action as fast as he could. He shot a Mexican in the face, a half-breed through the lungs, and a white pistolero with a Spencer rifle in the neck. All around him, his fellow Rangers did the same, engaging targets as they rode over them.

The hostages huddled together, shrieking in terror, as the Rangers stormed the camp. Several Comancheros who didn't fall, overwhelmed by the sheer firepower of the Texans' furious charge, chose to abandon the fight. They dropped their weapons and tried to flee.

A small group of Rangers, Pritchard among them, dismounted and ran to the women, taking positions to defend them. Other Rangers rode after the fleeing Comancheros.

After emptying his carbine, Pritchard tossed it aside and continued to fight at close quarters with his pistols against those Comancheros hardy enough to continue the combat. He put two more down before the fighting ended.

It was over in minutes.

The silence that ensued when the gunfire ceased was deafening. All you could hear were the sound of women sobbing, and hoofbeats as Rangers rode down the Comancheros fleeing on foot.

Pritchard holstered his pistols and drew his knife. He began cutting the leather bonds restraining the women. They were filthy, and their bare feet were bloody and raw from being dragged along behind their captors.

"Report!" Captain Franchard called out.

"One Ranger wounded, not badly," a voice called out. "Two horses shot. All the hostages appear to be safe."

"Reload," Franchard ordered, "and stand ready."

It was standard Ranger practice to immediately reload and prepare for counterattack in the wake of any skirmish. It was this sort of discipline that distinguished the Texas Rangers from many other frontier guerrilla outfits. Most, if not all, of the men in Franchard's command had fought for the Confederacy, and many were experienced Indian fighters as well. They knew first-hand how quickly a seeming victory could be turned against them into a lethal rout.

"Thank you," a woman exclaimed. She stood shakily and stumbled into Pritchard's arms. She looked to be in her early twenties, and despite the exhaustion and fear in her eyes, was quite comely.

"Easy," he said, lowering her back to a sitting position.

"Get these women some water," Franchard commanded, "and round up all those renegade horses." Rangers scrambled to comply.

"Over here, Cap'n," a Ranger called out from across the camp. "Somethin' you'd better see."

Franchard and Pritchard walked past more than two dozen dead Comancheros to where a couple of Rangers stood staring at something on the ground. It was evidently what the Comancheros had been focusing on just before the Rangers rode in.

"Jesus, God, Almighty," Franchard said under his breath.

Lying before them, staked out on the ground, was what was left of a young woman. She was naked and had clearly been attacked by multiple rapists, if not raped by every Comanchero in the camp. The Rangers couldn't tell if she'd been bludgeoned, or cut, to death, so severe, and so many, were her wounds.

"Some Comancheros believe the value of their captives is higher if they haven't been tainted," Franchard explained, removing his hat and wiping his brow. "But sometimes they'll pick one out and use her to slake their urges. After the last one has had his way, they'll kill her, since they know she ain't got any value left. Just like the rape, each one partakes in the killing, so they're all equal party to it. They usually do it in front of the other women, to remove any notion of resistance. Makes for a docile herd of captives."

"Bastards," a Ranger said.

"Get something over her," Franchard said. "I don't want the womenfolk to see her."

"They already saw," another Ranger said, as he gently laid a blanket over the woman's body.

The group of Rangers who'd pursued the fleeing Comancheros came riding back into camp, herding six men on foot at gunpoint. It was three whites, two Mexicans, and a Comanche.

Captain Franchard issued more orders. "Put the women up on those Comanchero horses and take them out of this gulch. Make camp on the ridge, get a fire going, tend to their wounds, and get them fed. Keep a solid watch. Five men will stay here with me for a detail. We'll join you up at the crest by nightfall."

Pritchard and four other Rangers elected to remain with Captain Franchard. The rest of the detachment, led by Sergeant Finley, helped the women onto horseback. After collecting the remaining horses and weapons from the dead Comancheros, they headed off to the place where they'd begun their fateful charge.

Captain Franchard turned to the six Comanchero prisoners, on their knees before him.

"You boys are going to dig," the captain said, pointing to a stack of shovels left behind by his Rangers. "Two holes. One small hole for that poor, Christian, woman, and one big hole, for you and your filthy brethren."

"Kiss my ass, Ranger," one of the white Comancheros said. "You're gonna shoot me anyways. Don't see no point to workin' for you none, before you do it. I'll take my bullet now, iffen you please, and you can dig your own damned holes."

"Who said anything about a bullet?" Franchard said as he kicked the man in the teeth. "Tie him up," he ordered. "Bind his feet, too."

Pritchard and two Rangers covered the other five prisoners with their pistols, as the remaining two Rangers lashed the once-defiant and now-semiconscious prisoner's hands behind his back. They also hobbled his legs.

As they did this, Captain Franchard went to his saddlebag and extracted a bottle of whiskey. He poured half the bottle's contents onto the bound Comanchero, which woke him from his stupor. Then he lit a match and tossed it on the soaking man.

The Comanchero burst into flames, howling and thrashing. Franchard let him cook for half a minute, before he began kicking dirt on him. He nodded to the other Rangers to assist in extinguishing the flaming prisoner. When they finished, the Comanchero was still alive, still conscious, and charred beyond recognition. He lay on his back, twitching and gasping in agony.

"Your friend was right," Captain Franchard said to the other prisoners. "Your miserable lives are indeed going to end this day. He may take all night to expire, I don't rightly know. All I know for sure is that his journey to perdition is gonna be a painful one. Iffen you boys want to die by a bullet, quick and painless, and have your remains put into the ground, you'll earn it by digging. Otherwise, you'll burn like your compadre and get left aboveground to feed the coyotes and buzzards, just like him. I've got three more bottles of whiskey, and it makes no nevermind to me."

The five remaining Comancheros hastily grabbed shovels and began to dig.

Chapter 27

Captain Franchard and his Rangers returned the ten surviving captives safely to their homes in San Angelo. Thanks to the technological wizardry of the telegraph, by the time they reached Fort Worth, more than a week later, word of their dramatic battle with the Comancheros and the rescue of the hostage women had spread far and wide.

When they rode into Fort Worth, filthy and battle-worn from weeks on the bloody trail, the Rangers were surprised to be met by cheering crowds, glad-handing politicians, and reporters from as far away as Chicago, New Orleans, and Kansas City. Everyone wanted a glimpse of the heroic, outnumbered, Sons of Texas who'd charged into a Comanchero camp, guns a-blazing, and rescued the cherished womanhood of the Lone Star State.

In the days that followed, they were swarmed by inquisitive townsfolk and newsmen alike. Each Ranger became a celebrity. Captain Franchard, who looked every bit the grizzled, veteran, mustachioed, lawman of legend, was cited by the governor for his extraordinary leadership and unfailing courage. The other

Rangers in the detachment were individually singled out for their unique characteristics and contribution to the historic victory.

America's appetite for all things relating to the western frontier was already insatiable, particularly back East, and few topics within the popular culture were devoured so voraciously as the subject of the Texas Rangers. Every newspaper across the nation heralded the story of the "Rescue of the Captive Women of San Angelo by the Fearless Texas Rangers!"

Ironically, it was Ranger Joe Atherton, the Ranger who least sought the spotlight, who ended up garnering the most attention.

Described by one breathless reporter as ". . . six and a half feet tall, with the powerful physique of a lumberjack, blond-haired, blue-eyed Texas Ranger Joe Atherton is the living embodiment of an ancient Viking warrior come back to life. Not yet twenty-four years old, and bearing an ominous bullet scar on his forehead, it has been reported to this journalist by those in good standing to know that this young man, whose origins and past remain a mystery, is a veteran of the late troubles on the side of the Confederacy. It has also been reported, again, by those in authority with privilege to such information, that Ranger Atherton is the fastest, most lethal pistoleer in all the Texas Rangers, with countless outlaws, renegades, rustlers, and road agents having fallen to the thunderous justice of his brace of revolvers."

A photograph of all eighteen of Captain Franchard's Texas Rangers was taken on the steps of the Fort Worth town hall and published in every newspaper across America. Pritchard, as the tallest, stood in the back alongside Captain Franchard.

The Rangers remained in Fort Worth, resting their horses, buying new duds, and having drinks and steaks bought for them by virtually anyone they met. Pritchard did his best to keep a low profile, but due to his celebrity, height, youth, and good looks, found himself more often than not hounded by reporters, gawkers, inquisitive citizens, and not the least of all, attractive young women.

Pritchard would politely decline the unwanted company, and ended up spending more than one afternoon hiding out with Rusty in the livery to escape the annoyance of pestering fans. He cleaned and oiled his guns, practiced with them, cared for his horse, and counted the days and hours until his Ranger unit would ride out of bustling Fort Worth and get back to the familiar anonymity of the dusty trail.

Captain Franchard explained to his men that as distasteful as being in town was, he had orders to temporarily remain in Fort Worth. Their overlords in the Texas Rangers relished the excellent publicity Franchard's men had brought upon their organization and hoped to parlay it into political influence and greater funding from Austin.

The entire detachment was boarded at Fort Worth's finest hotel, which made it that much more difficult for Pritchard to lay low and remain unbothered. He was walking back to the hotel from the livery, just before supper, when a distinguished-looking man wearing a bowler and a pressed suit approached him in the lobby.

"Are you Ranger Atherton?" the man asked.

"I am," Pritchard said. "No disrespect intended, but I'm done talking to reporters."

"I am not a reporter," the man said. "My name is Benjamin Woodruff. I am an attorney from Austin."

"Good for you," Pritchard said. "Is there something I can do for you?"

"Actually," Woodruff said, "I represent someone who very much wants to speak with you."

"I'm sorry to disappoint you," Pritchard said, "but I'm plumb talked out. I just want to be left alone."

"I understand your desire for privacy," Woodruff went on. "My client desires the same. I beg you, please indulge her? She has traveled quite a distance for the opportunity to converse with you."

"I'd rather not," Pritchard said.

"I would be happy to compensate you for your time."

"I don't want your client's money," Pritchard said. "Frankly, Mr. Woodruff, I'm tired of being gawked at. I never wanted to be famous. If you'll excuse me?" He tipped his Stetson and began to walk past the attorney.

"My client is aware of your preference for anonymity," Woodruff said, sidestepping to block Pritchard's path. "She distinctly remembers you wanted no thanks when she last saw you."

"Last saw me?" Pritchard said, puzzled.

"Allow me to introduce my client," Woodruff said, stepping aside.

A stunning auburn-haired woman, perhaps twenty years old, walked toward them from across the lobby. She had huge, deep brown eyes and was wearing an elegant, and undoubtedly very expensive, emerald-colored dress that did a poor job of concealing the contours of her extraordinary figure. While there was something vaguely familiar about her, Pritchard was certain if he'd seen so beautiful a woman before he would have remembered.

"Good evening, ma'am," Pritchard said as he removed his hat. "I don't believe I've had the pleasure?"

"We met once before," the woman spoke. "On the Ouachita River. You saved me, just like those women of San Angelo I read about in the newspaper. My name is Caroline."

Chapter 28

A dumbstruck Pritchard sat across from Caroline at a candlelit table in a private dining room reserved in the Fort Worth Grand Hotel by Mr. Woodruff. He found it nearly impossible to believe the gorgeous young woman seated before him was the filthy, starved, abused waif he'd discovered tied to a chair in an Arkansas trading post, five years before. He found it even harder to keep from staring into her alluring brown eyes.

"I'm afraid you have me on my heels," Pritchard said. "You don't look a thing like the Caroline I remember."

"Thanks to you," she said, "I am no longer that girl. After you left me in the care of the pastor and his wife, I became very sick. No doubt it had something to do with what I had . . . experienced. I was at death's door. Desperate, and not knowing what else to do, they took me to Hot Springs. It was the nearest town with a real doctor. By chance, a famous Texas surgeon named Dr. Jonathon Biggs happened to be visiting relatives there. Like you, he saved my life."

"I'm indebted to him," Pritchard said.

"As it turned out, Dr. Biggs and his wife took a liking to me. They had no children of their own, and adopted me as their daughter. After what I had gone through, to be taken into the hearts and home of such kind and loving people was beyond anything I could have dreamed of. My name is now Caroline Biggs."

She looked down at her folded hands. "When I was in the hands of that evil man, Calverson, he . . . and other men . . . did things to me. When it was happening, I used to close my eyes and pretend I was a princess in a fairy tale. I imagined all the bad things that were befalling me were only occurring so that when a handsome prince came to rescue me, it would make the happy ending that much more wonderful. And then you showed up. You rescued me."

"I'm no prince," Pritchard said. He didn't know what else to say. He wasn't thirsty, but suddenly found his throat dry, and tight, and the room oddly warm.

"Since that time, I have resided in Austin," Caroline continued, "attending the finest schools, and in truth, living a fairy-tale existence. My adopted parents are quite wealthy, and I haven't wanted for anything. But I never forgot the orphan I once was, or the tall, brave, young man who came to my rescue and made my fairy tale come true."

She produced a gold coin and placed it on the table between them. Pritchard recognized it as the ten-dollar gold piece he and Ditch gave her when they deposited her at the church in Mount Ida, Arkansas.

"I still have the blanket and the clothes you bought for me, as well," she said, staring at the coin and smiling. "Although, I must admit, they no longer fit."

"They no longer suit you," Pritchard said. "How did you find me?"

"Last week, I happened to glance at a newspaper headline regaling the Texas Rangers. These Rangers, at great peril to their own lives, apparently rescued a group of captive women from a band of slave traders. Naturally, given the circumstances of my own history, I was keenly interested. I read the article."

She looked up from the coin, directly into Pritchard's eyes. Her own were brimming with tears. "You can only imagine how I felt when I saw your photograph and read your name. It was the same name you gave the pastor's wife at the church, that morning in Arkansas, on the day of my salvation."

Pritchard felt his face flush.

"After that, I devoured every news account of the raid I could find. One of them described you as the 'fastest, most accurate, and deadly pistoleer in the Texas Rangers.' Then I remembered how quickly you gunned down Calverson, even though he drew on you first. Any doubt I may have had about your identity vanished."

"I'm sorry you had to witness that," Pritchard said.

"I'm not," she said, brushing away her tears. "Though it's probably not Christian of me to admit, I take great satisfaction in the memory of his death. I sincerely hope Mr. Calverson is, as your namesake implies, 'smokin' in hell.'"

"You read about that, too, huh?" Pritchard said, rolling his eyes.

"Of course. 'Smokin' Joe,' they call you. I believe it's an appropriate title."

"That nickname wasn't my choice," Pritchard grunted.

"I'm sure it wasn't. I spoke to my father. Once I explained that I'd discovered your identity and where-abouts, he agreed to allow me to take the stagecoach to Fort Worth as long as I was accompanied by Mr. Woodruff. He handles my family's legal affairs, and had business up here. I hope you'll forgive me for being so insistent on this meeting, but I simply had to see you in person."

"There's nothing to forgive," Pritchard said.

Caroline Biggs stood. Pritchard immediately followed suit, as etiquette dictated. Caroline walked over to him, put her hands on his broad chest, and looked up at the tall Missourian.

"Thank you," she said.

"No thanks are necessary," Pritchard stuttered, "I was only—"

Pritchard's words were cut off in midsentence, as Caroline Biggs suddenly threw her arms around his neck, pulled him down to her, and kissed him.

Chapter 29

Pritchard soon discovered firsthand what the phrase *what a difference a day makes* truly meant.

The day before meeting Caroline Biggs in the Fort Worth Grand Hotel, he felt like a fish out of water. He disliked being stuck in Fort Worth, corralled by the bustling city and surrounded by so many people. He badgered Captain Franchard on a daily basis, inquiring when their detachment was going to leave the claustrophobic town and get back to ranging the Texas countryside in search of outlaws.

Franchard would placate his youngest and most valued Ranger by reminding him that not every duty assigned to a Texas Ranger was of their choice or liking. He would further explain the need for what their commanding officers called *public relations*, and finish his lecture by pointing out that his fellow Rangers seemed quite content to remain in Fort Worth, sleeping on feather beds instead of the cold prairie, slugging down free whiskey, and regaling gullible townsfolk with exaggerated tales of their derring-do.

Pritchard would glumly nod, walk away, and then the very next day would again be back at Captain

Franchard's door, first thing in the morning, asking when their detachment was going to move out.

This ritual went on each day. Pritchard's visit to Franchard had become so regular, the captain was surprised one morning when Ranger Atherton didn't interrupt his breakfast with his daily entreaty to depart Fort Worth.

Looking across the lobby at the Grand Hotel, Franchard noticed Pritchard escorting a remarkably beautiful young woman down the stairs toward the dining room. They walked arm in arm, seemingly oblivious to anyone or anything around them except each other. Grinning to himself under his mustache, Franchard approached the pair as they were being seated.

"Good morning, Ranger Atherton," Franchard said. Pritchard stood up.

"Good morning, sir," Pritchard said. "Captain Franchard, may I present Miss Caroline Biggs, of Austin."

"Pleased to make your acquaintance, ma'am," the veteran Ranger said. "I apologize for the interruption," he continued, "but since I didn't see you this morning, Joe, I thought I'd give you an update on your daily query as to when the company will be pulling out of Fort Worth, especially on account of how badly you've been pestering me lately to get back on the trail."

"Uh," Pritchard stammered, "there's no hurry, Cap'n. I understand the need to follow orders. I fully recognize that our higher-ups in the Texas Rangers believe it's in our best interest to be posted in town, and I stand ready to do my duty here in Fort Worth."

"I suspected you might feel that way," Captain

Franchard said, giving Caroline a wink. "Carry on, Ranger." He tipped his hat and walked away.

It didn't take long for the press to catch wind of the romance blossoming between the oversized blond Texas Ranger with the mysterious scar and the gorgeous young lady from Austin. The statuesque couple appeared to have "stepped from the pages of an Arthurian folktale," as one reporter put it, and were bird-dogged by newsmen and curious onlookers wherever they went.

Pritchard and Caroline didn't seem to notice. They were inseparable over the next several days, which didn't make reporting on the progress of their relationship any more difficult. And after Mr. Benjamin Woodruff, the young lady's chaperone and attorney, gave an interview to a spellbound group of reporters detailing the extraordinary circumstances of how Ranger Atherton had rescued Ms. Biggs, years before as a child, from the clutches of yet another slaver, the press went absolutely wild. The story was picked up by every newspaper from California to New York, with a corresponding photograph of the couple, of course.

Pritchard ensured, during each of the two photographs taken of him, one with his Ranger company, and the other with Caroline, that he wore his ten-gallon Stetson. And he was careful to lower his head, not difficult to do as a result of his height, just enough so the wide brim covered most of his face.

Some of his fellow Rangers playfully chided him, after viewing the newspapers featuring the photographs, for being so tall his face got lost in the clouds. That Pritchard may have deliberately shadowed his features with his hat during the photography was not lost on Captain Franchard.

One morning, desperate for time alone with Caroline without the prying eyes of others, Pritchard rented a buckboard and they escaped Fort Worth for the countryside. He brought a basket of food from the hotel kitchen, and they set out before dawn before anyone, save the livery attendant, noticed.

The first days of summer were upon them. They watched the sun come up, holding hands as Pritchard guided the buckboard out of town. They drove for more than an hour, until he found a creek surrounded by a lush stand of shade trees. He brought the buckboard to a halt and spread out a blanket.

They saw no evidence of others as far as the eye could see, but Pritchard nonetheless kept his Henry rifle handy. Breakfast was biscuits, blueberry tart, and clear, cool water from the stream.

"This place is so beautiful, Joe," Caroline said after they'd breakfasted. "It's the perfect spot."

"The perfect spot for what?" Pritchard said, lying on his back and patting his satisfied belly.

"For this," she said, rolling on top of him.

Despite her cumbersome dress and petticoat, and his boots and belted pistols, they were both soon naked and entwined in each other. They passed the rest of the morning in a maelstrom of passion, as they repeatedly slaked the desperate yearning that had been building to an almost unbearable ache since they'd first laid eyes on each other at Fort Worth's Grand Hotel.

At times soft and gentle, and at others awkwardly, or like ravenous animals, they thrashed, moaned, giggled, and cried out. When they finally collapsed, gasping and spent, their clothes and breakfast scattered on the blanket around them, it was approaching noon.

"Is it lunchtime, yet?" Pritchard asked.

"Is that all you have to say?" Caroline laughed, playfully punching him in the shoulder.

"No," Pritchard said. He stared up at the Texas sky, a hesitant look in his eye. "I've got something else to say to you."

"What would that be?"

"My name isn't Joe Atherton," he said. "It's Samuel Pritchard. I want you to know who I am—who I really am—before I ask you to marry me."

"I'm listening," Caroline said, resting her chin on his chest and looking into his blue eyes.

Pritchard told her. He explained his past, the scar on his forehead, and why he'd taken the alias. As he spoke, she held his face in her hands.

"You deserve to know the truth," Pritchard finished, "before making your decision. It's only right."

"There's something you should know about me, as well," Caroline said, "before you seek my hand in marriage. It may give you pause to ask me to be your wife."

She looked away and placed her cheek against his chest. "I can't bear you children, Samuel."

It was the first time Caroline had spoken his true name. "Because of what happened," she began, her voice barely a whisper, "before you rescued me, I'm barren. The surgery my father performed saved my life, but rendered me unable to conceive. I must, in good faith, tell you this, because a man has a right to a wife who will bear him offspring and provide him a family. This I cannot do."

He felt her tears trickle down his chest onto his stomach. He reached down and turned her face back to meet his.

"You're all the family I want," Pritchard said, "or need. I'm askin' you, Caroline, will you marry me?"

"Are you sure?" she asked, anguish in her voice. "You say that now, but someday, you might have regrets. You may want children of your own."

"I want you," Pritchard said. "Just you. I asked you a question. I'm waiting for an answer."

"Yes," she said, her tears of sorrow becoming tears of joy. "I'd be honored to marry you."

Chapter 30

When Pritchard and Caroline returned to the Fort Worth Grand Hotel late that afternoon, Benjamin Woodruff was not a happy man. He was most displeased that Caroline, whom he reminded was his ward, had chosen to run off for the day without divulging her destination or whereabouts.

His mood lightened considerably when she told him she and Pritchard were engaged.

While Caroline and Woodruff went off to the telegraph office to wire her parents the good news, Pritchard sought out Captain Franchard. He found the grizzled Ranger inside the saloon across from the hotel, nursing a whiskey and holding court until supper, as had been his custom each day since arriving in Fort Worth.

"Captain Franchard," Pritchard said, removing his hat. "I'd like to have a word with you, if you please?"

"Sure," Franchard said, gesturing to an empty seat. "Sit down. You're making me nervous, standing there with your hat in your hand. You look like you just swallowed a frog. What's on your mind?"

"I'd like to request a leave of absence," Pritchard said.

"We've been ridin' together more'n five years, Joe. This is the first time you've ever asked for so much as a day off. Lord knows you're entitled. You mind if I ask why?"

"I'm going to Austin," he said. "To get married."

"I see," Franchard said. "No doubt to that pretty young lass I met in your company?"

"Miss Caroline Biggs." Pritchard nodded. "That is correct."

"Can't say I blame you. And after the wedding?"

"I'm thinking about turning in my star," Pritchard said, "and resigning from the Rangers."

"Rangerin' ain't exactly conducive to a successful marriage," Franchard said, "that's a fact. I can attest to it personally. You sure this is what you want to do?"

"I'm positive," Pritchard said. "She's the one."

"I don't mean the wedding," Franchard said. "I meant givin' up the Texas Rangers."

"I've got to think on it," Pritchard said. "It's why I'm asking for a leave of absence instead of turning in my star right now. I'd like to make my decision after the honeymoon."

"Fair enough. You've been one of the most reliable Rangers I've ever had the privilege to ride with, and I'd sorely hate to lose you. But if ever a Ranger was owed some time off to settle his affairs, it's you. I'll wire headquarters in Austin and see what I can do about your request."

"Thank you, Cap'n."

"Meantime," Franchard poured two shots of whiskey and handed one to Pritchard, "please accept my congratulations. Here's to you, the lovely Miss

Biggs, and a long life of happiness to you both on the trail ahead."

The Rangers drank.

Two sullen cowhands sat at table in the far corner of the saloon and watched a giant young Ranger speaking to a weathered old one. They'd already consumed most of a bottle of rye whiskey.

"You sure it's him?" Wesley Boone asked.

"I'm sure," the other cowhand, a hard-bitten fellow named Jim Collins, said around his cigarette. "That great, big, tall feller with the scar on his head ain't somebody you're likely to forget. He's the one, all right. Him and that old Ranger buffaloed us when we tried to bust Wade out of jail in Bristow. Came ridin' in with four of our hands slung over the saddle like beaver pelts. Then I watched him gun three more Triple B hands down, quicker than a rattler bites. Killed eight more of our boys when we tried to waylay 'em on the trail to Waco. You weren't around then, bein' locked up in Yuma and all."

"Pa's gonna want to hear about this," Wesley said. "He'll know what to do."

"I already know what to do," Collins said. "Wait outside, and when them two lawmen come out we'll blast 'em straight to hell."

"Don't be a fool," Wesley said. "You just told me those two buried fifteen of our hands. You think we're gonna take 'em ourselves? Besides, this whole town is crawling with Rangers. Even if we got lucky and plugged that pair of lawmen before they got us,

we'd be captured or shot before we got out of town.
You itchin' to hang?"

"Nope."

"Then shut up. We'll keep an eye on 'em and bide
our time. Ain't gonna be hard to find 'em, since they're
all stayin' at that fancy hotel across the square on account of being the big heroes of Texas. I'll get a wire to
Pa in Bristow. You go tell the other hands to be ready
and to keep quiet. I don't want none of 'em getting too
drunk and drawing attention to us while we're here
in town. We'll wait to hear what Pa has to say. Then
we'll see about them Rangers who strung up Wade."

Pritchard's request for a leave of absence from the
Texas Rangers was granted. The wedding was to be
held in two weeks, in the capital. Their engagement
was announced in both the Fort Worth and Austin
newspapers.

Pritchard bought a diamond and gold wedding ring,
for five hundred dollars, from a jeweler in Fort Worth.
All he owned was his horse, saddle, guns, and a few
clothes, and he'd saved every penny of his Ranger pay
over the last five years. This savings included his share
of countless reward bounties on various outlaws
he'd brought to justice, dead or alive. As a result, he
had accumulated a sum of over ten thousand dollars.
The money and ring, a surprise for Caroline on her
wedding day, were secreted inside his saddle, in a
pocket under the lining. It was his plan to use the
money to buy a cottage for he and Caroline, in Austin,
near her parents.

The smiling couple, along with Mr. Woodruff and
three other passengers, boarded a stage on a warm

July morning to begin the three-day journey to Austin. Caroline's trunk and Pritchard's saddle were packed on top with the other passengers' luggage. Rusty was tethered to the rear of the coach.

Pritchard's fellow Rangers were there to see him off, as well as a large crowd of onlookers and well-wishers. Captain Franchard shook Pritchard's hand, kissed Caroline's, and the entire Ranger detachment escorted the stage out of town, whoopin' and hollerin', Texas style.

Two people who were not at the stage's raucous send-off were Wesley Boone and Jim Collins. They, along with the other hands from the Triple B who'd been dallying in Fort Worth, had already left town the night before.

Chapter 31

The stage rolled into its first stop, sixty miles south of Fort Worth, at sundown. The shotgun messenger blew his bugle a half mile out, as was customary. This was to alert the station manager and his family, if he had one living with him at the remote outpost, of the coach's impending arrival.

Pritchard got out first, to assist Caroline and the other female passenger in disembarking, and to help the driver and shotgun messenger with the luggage. He noticed the corral, some distance from the adobe building that served as the station house, was chock-full of horses; at least thirty, to his count. He'd never before seen so many animals at a single coach station, but gave it little thought as he handed down luggage from the roof of the stage.

The driver herded the passengers, led by Mr. Woodruff, into the station house. Accompanying Caroline and her chaperone was a middle-aged farmer and his matronly wife, en route to Austin to visit her sister, and a sour-faced surveyor going to the capital to file claims. By the time Pritchard and the shotgun messenger retrieved the luggage, everyone else had already gone inside.

As soon as Pritchard entered, ducking through the doorway due to his height, the first thing he realized was the station house was packed with people. The second thing he felt was the barrel of a pistol against his neck.

The luggage was torn from his grasp, and rough hands grabbed his arms. Both his pistols were taken. As Pritchard's eyes adjusted to the dim interior, he realized men, many of them, were holding Caroline, the driver, shotgun messenger, and the other passengers at gunpoint. He presumed another man, tied to a chair in the corner, was the station agent.

The men had obviously been waiting, cramped inside the station, for the stage to arrive. He suddenly realized why so many horses were in the corral. He surmised their saddles and bridles had been stashed behind the station house.

A kerosene lantern was lit, and the room filled with light. "Good evening, Ranger Atherton," one of the men croaked.

The speaker was short, bowlegged, and bent with age. The face under his ten-gallon hat was lined, and Pritchard saw no teeth in his mouth when he spoke. Pritchard looked slowly from face to face, burning the features of each gunman into his memory.

"Do I know you?" Pritchard asked.

"We haven't formally met," the man said. "My name is Winston Boone. This here," he motioned with his pistol to a younger man beside him who bore resemblance, "is my boy Wesley. You already met my older son, Wade, when you strung him up in Waco, five years back."

Pritchard's heart sank as he realized this was no ordinary stage robbery. He glanced at Caroline, across the room, and read the fear in her eyes. She, too, recognized what was transpiring as no mere theft and that these men were not common highwaymen.

"I understand," Pritchard began, "iffen you hold a grudge against me. These good folks got nothing to do with what's between us. Let them go. We can settle our differences without them."

"Are you askin' me to grant mercy?" Boone said.

"I am," Pritchard said.

"Why, sure," the old cowboy said. "I'll be glad to. I'll grant these folks the same mercy you showed Wade." A round of filthy laughter echoed throughout the station house.

"Read about your upcoming nuptials in the newspaper," Boone went on. He walked over to Caroline. "Actually," he said, "I had somebody read the paper to me. Can't read, myself. Never saw no point to it. Fine-looking woman, your fiancée."

He grabbed her cheeks in one calloused hand, and ran the barrel of his revolver over her breasts. "Nice figure, too. You're a lucky man, Ranger."

Caroline spit into his face. Boone smiled, wiped his face on his forearm, and turned back to Pritchard.

"Newspaper said your wedding was gonna be the 'social event of the season,' down in Austin. Even said the governor might attend, on account of the bride's pa is a wealthy doctor and the groom is a bona fide Texas hero."

"Let them go," Pritchard repeated. "Do as you will with me, but these people don't deserve to suffer harm on my account. Let them be on their way."

"Don't you worry none, Ranger," Boone said. "I'm going to send them on their way, all right."

"All the way to hell," Wesley said. More hard laughter ensued.

"But before they depart," Winston Boone continued, "I thought we might have a little wedding celebration right here in this station. At least a honeymoon, anyways. And you're gonna watch, Ranger. Put her on the table, boys," he ordered, "and line up. Who's first?"

Cowhands carried Caroline, thrashing and fighting, to the big table in the center of the room, still covered with dishes and utensils. The cowboys began to whoop and holler. Pritchard started forward, enraged. Several revolvers, with their hammers back, jabbed into his gut, halting him.

"Leave her be!" Benjamin Woodruff shouted, breaking free of the man restraining him and lurching toward Caroline. He'd almost reached her when a single gunshot rang out. Wesley Boone shot the attorney in the back. He slumped to the floor.

The farmer's wife began to cry. Everyone paused for an instant, to stare at Woodruff's lifeless body.

Caroline seized that moment to grab a steak knife from the table. She thrust it, hilt deep, into the neck of the cowboy who'd been holding her. He screamed, and when he let go of her to clutch his throat, she dashed across the room to Pritchard.

Several of the cowboys, distracted and still gawking at the attorney lying dead at their feet, were startled by Caroline's actions and instinctively fired. A hail of bullets tore into her and Pritchard, just as they embraced.

Both went to the dirt floor. Pritchard felt the searing agony of multiple bullets entering his body, but could think of nothing but catching Caroline.

He landed on his back, with her limp form draping over his.

"So much for the honeymoon," Winston Boone shrugged.

The station house air smelled of gun smoke. Pritchard looked up at the ceiling, as his vision rapidly faded. He felt Caroline's warm body against him. He tried to put his arms around her, but found he couldn't lift them. He could hear the farmer's wife sobbing, and Winston Boone giving orders.

"Saddle up our horses," he said. "And get them other passengers outside. How's Toby?"

"Toby's done for," he heard Wesley answer. "He just don't know it yet. She stuck him good. Can't you hear him a-hackin' and a-sputterin'?"

Pritchard couldn't see the man dying from the throat wound Caroline had inflicted, but he could hear him. The all-too-familiar sound of the death rattle, as the cowboy's life dwindled, was unmistakable.

"His own damned fault for lettin' the spitfire stick him," Winston Boone said. "Once he's finished, get his carcass on a horse."

Pritchard heard men scrambling to comply, and sensed the hostages being herded from the station house. His vison had completely gone, and darkness was all he could see. He felt Caroline being pulled off him.

"She's dead," Wesley announced, "and the Ranger's gettin' there." Pritchard heard a revolver's hammer click back. "You want me to finish him?"

"Nope," Winston told his son. "That'd be doing him a favor. He'll bleed out before too long. Leave him be, to contemplate. I want him to spend his last minutes ruminating on the wedding he ain't gonna attend."

"Whatever you say, Pa."

The last thing Pritchard heard, before slipping into unconsciousness, was the sound of gunshots outside the station house.

Chapter 32

"You surely are one hard man to kill," a familiar voice said.

Pritchard slowly opened his eyes. He found himself in pain, lying in bed, in an unfamiliar room. He also found himself staring into the worried face of Ditch Clemson.

"How . . . long?"

"Ten days," Ditch said. "The next stage passing through that station found you just this side of perdition. You refused to die, like the stubborn Missouri mule you are. You were shot three times, Samuel. When they got you here to Waco, your life was hangin' by a thread. Some famous doctor from Austin came up and put you under his knife. They say he saved your life. You've been conked out, recovering, ever since."

"The other passengers?" Pritchard asked, already knowing the answer.

"Dead," Ditch said. "Driver, shotgun messenger, and station agent, too. They were all shot and left to rot where they fell."

Pritchard lowered his head.

"I'm awful sorry about your fiancée," Ditch said solemnly.

Pritchard closed his eyes, tears squeezing from the corners. The image of his beloved Caroline, shot to pieces in his arms, flooded his memory.

"It was—"

"Winston Boone," Ditch finished for him, "and his boys from the Triple B. I know. They left a trail a blind man could follow. Twenty horses, at least."

"Closer to thirty," Pritchard said. "Where're they going?"

"They abandoned their spread. It looks like the whole outfit is headed south to Mexico. Captain Franchard and a detachment of Rangers is ridin' after 'em."

"How'd you find out?"

"The Triple B spread is just north of ours, remember? When the Rangers came through, looking for Old Man Boone and his outfit, they stopped by the ranch to water their mounts."

Pritchard struggled to sit up.

"Take it easy," Ditch said. "You don't want to start those stitches a-leakin'. That doctor is a mean old cuss. He wasn't going to let me in to see you. I had to insist. Practically had to threaten him. He saved you, all right, but he sure don't act like he's very fond of you."

"He has every right to be angry with me," Pritchard said. "He's Caroline's father."

"Oh, hell," was all Ditch said.

"I hate to ask you," Pritchard said, wincing as the words came out, "but can you loan me a few dollars? I need a horse and a gun. Everything I had was taken from me at that coach station."

Ditch knew his friend wasn't referring to merely his property.

"You can barely sit yourself up," Ditch said. "What do you plan on doing with a horse and a gun?"

"What I have to," Pritchard said.

"It's being done. I already told you, Captain Franchard and a company of Rangers are out scouring the Texas countryside for those Triple B boys."

"They'll never catch 'em before they get into Mexico," Pritchard said, slowly swinging his legs over the side of the bed. "Rangers have to stop at the Rio Grande. I don't."

"You're planning on going into Mexico, all by yourself? After thirty armed men? In your condition?"

"That's right," Pritchard said.

"You're crazy," Ditch said. "That's too many guns to go up against, even for you."

"I took on more than that once, in Independence, Kansas. An entire company of Confederate guerrillas, if I recall. Besides, Old Man Boone and his Triple B hands don't know I'm comin' after 'em. They think I'm dead."

"True enough," Ditch had to admit.

"Are you going to loan me the money for a horse and gun," Pritchard said, "or not?"

"Do I have a choice?" Ditch said. "Seems you forget that you own one third of the SD&P Ranch. Which is rolling, by the way. These past few years, while you've been away rangerin', me and Paul have been selling all the horse and beef stock we can muster to the army and the railroads like whiskey to Irishmen. They can't buy it fast enough, and pay top dollar. We're gettin' plumb rich. Could sure use you at the ranch, once you get healthy again."

"I'm happy for your success, Ditch. For Paul, too. But we both know I ain't a rancher, and I've got business in Mexico."

"I didn't really think I could talk you out of it," Ditch said, shaking his head, "but I had to try."

"I appreciate your concern," Pritchard said, gingerly testing his weight on his feet, "but this is something that's got to be done. You know it, too."

"I reckon so. That's why I brung you a fine horse. One big enough to haul your heavy carcass around. A good saddle, too. I also brung you these."

Ditch opened a saddlebag he brought with him and produced two brand-new Remington revolvers. "I bought these pistols for you in Dallas. A gunsmith there makes them up special. They're the same as your ball-and-powder guns, except they've been converted to fire .44 cartridges, same as your Henry rifle."

"They stole my Henry along with my pistols," Pritchard said. "All my money, too."

"I know," Ditch said. "I took the liberty of bringing you a new Henry, too. Don't need a Gypsy fortune-teller to know what's on your mind."

"I'm obliged," Pritchard said. "I'll pay you back. You know I'm good for it."

"You ain't givin' me a penny," Ditch said. "There's only one thing I want in trade for that horse and those guns, and it ain't negotiable."

"What would that be?"

"I'm going with you."

"This ain't your fight."

"Hell, if it ain't," Ditch said. "You're my brother, Samuel. Them bastards shot my brother and killed my brother's bride-to-be. They're gonna pay for that."

"You sure about this, Ditch? You'd best know, I ain't

going after 'em as Joe Atherton. A Texas Ranger has to follow the law and must stop at the U.S. border. I'm going into Mexico as Samuel Pritchard. And I damn sure ain't bringing any of 'em back for a trial by jury. I'm the only judge, jury, and executioner Winston Boone and his Triple B boys are ever going to face. I aim to send every one of them cowardly, back-shootin' sons of bitches straight to hell, or die tryin'."

"Just like old times," Ditch said. "Wouldn't have it any other way."

Chapter 33

It took a week for Pritchard and Ditch to ride the 350 miles from Waco to the border town of Del Rio, Texas. The first couple of days, Pritchard was so weak Ditch thought he was going to fall out of the saddle. His complexion was sallow, his lean body was hunched over, and he spoke little, as if saving all his energy to remain atop his horse.

At Pritchard's insistence, however, the duo pushed hard, riding all day with little rest. At Ditch's insistence, they made camp each day by sunset, ate a hearty meal, and slept the entire night. It was a far different journey from the one they'd made during the war, when they were forced to travel by night and sleep by day to survive. By the third day, Pritchard had strengthened considerably, and by the end of the week he was sitting in the saddle almost like his old self.

Ditch carefully watched his brooding friend. On several occasions, as they rode the trail in silence, he thought he saw Pritchard's death-shadow descend for a brief instant, before rapidly flickering away. He'd only previously witnessed the lethal specter on Pritchard's features during violent, life-or-death actions he was forced to undertake to save his, Ditch's, or someone else's life. That the dark cowl fell over him while simply riding, without being triggered by a deadly threat or the need to kill, was cause for concern.

Five days into their journey, a band of six Comanche braves on horseback began paralleling them from a distance. After a few hours of shadowing the two riders and their packhorse, the braves slowly began to close in. When they got to within two hundred yards, Pritchard stopped his horse, pulled his Henry rifle from the saddle scabbard, and stared at them. Ditch followed suit. After a long, tense moment, the Comanche turned their horses around and rode off. Ditch couldn't help but wonder, as he watched the death veil again fade from Pritchard's face, if the superstitious Indians had seen it, too, and its appearance was the reason they'd elected to depart.

The horse Ditch brought Pritchard was a palomino, eighteen hands tall, named Biscuit. Though not his beloved Rusty, Biscuit was a strong horse of reliable temperament, and he could tell his friend was pleased with the choice.

Each night, while Ditch started the fire, made the fixings for supper, and tended to their three horses, Pritchard practiced with his pistols. Just as he had years before, he unloaded his guns and wedged a coin into a tree's bark at head level. Then he would draw, aim, and fire, over and over again, with each hand, for hours at a time.

The first night's practice, Ditch could tell the pain from Pritchard's healing wounds was hindering his movement. He was still lightning fast, but there was an awkwardness, almost a hesitancy, to his draw.

By the end of the week, after hours of training, no

such impediment remained. Pritchard was faster than Ditch had ever seen him draw before, and quicker than he thought a mortal man could be.

On the evening of the sixth day, Pritchard kept his revolvers loaded. His first shot blew the coin from the tree, and the remaining eleven bullets, all fired in scant seconds, cut out a hole in the tree the size of a whiskey glass where the coin had been.

The following morning, Pritchard and Ditch entered the border town of Del Rio. As the two riders led their packhorse down the main street, a lone figure stepped out to block their path.

"Howdy, Joe," Captain Franchard said. "Hello, Ditch." Ditch nodded his greeting, having met the Ranger captain at his ranch when they were searching for Winston Boone.

"What're you doin' here?" Pritchard asked.

"Tie up your ponies, come into the saloon, and I'll tell you."

Once they were seated, Franchard ordered a bottle and three glasses. Pritchard noticed the captain wasn't wearing his cinco-peso star. It was the first time he'd seen the tough old Ranger without it.

"We followed Boone's trail down here to Del Rio," Franchard explained. "It wasn't hard to do. Thirty men on horseback leave plenty of sign. But we never got closer than two days behind them."

"They had a solid head start," Pritchard said.

"They crossed into Mexico a couple of days ago," Franchard went on. "That's when I sent my Rangers back to Fort Worth and wired Austin, requesting a leave of absence."

"A leave of absence?" Pritchard said.

"Figured I'm due a vacation. I hear Mexico's nice this time of year."

"How'd you know I was coming?" Pritchard asked.

"You've been ridin' with me as a Texas Ranger for five years," Franchard said. "A fella can learn a thing or two about another fella in that time."

"Iffen you want to come with me, Cap'n, I can't stop you. I couldn't stop Ditch. But I'll tell you the same thing I told him; I ain't makin' any arrests, nor takin' prisoners. This ain't no posse. It's a war party. You ain't obliged to come along, if you ain't comfortable with that."

"First off," Franchard began, "once we cross the Mexico line, it ain't *Captain*. It's *Tom*. Second thing, is that what befell you at the hands of Winston Boone and his tribe was set in motion because you once stood with me when you weren't obliged to. I didn't forget that. Third, why don't you boys take a walk with me down to the livery?"

Franchard stood, grabbed the bottle and three glasses, and headed out of the saloon. Pritchard and Ditch shrugged to each other and followed after him.

They watched the tall Ranger captain's back all the way down the main street to the livery stable. He went in, nodded to the attendant, and then set down the bottle and glasses and began digging through a large stack of hay.

Pritchard and Ditch looked at each other again, puzzled. Franchard uncovered three wooden crates. One of them was small, and the two other considerably larger.

"Take a look, boys," Franchard said. "I brung along some supplies for our Mexican vacation."

Pritchard and Ditch knelt and examined the crates. The smaller one contained five hundred rounds of .44 caliber ammunition. The larger crates contained dynamite.

Pritchard and Ditch accepted the glasses handed to them by Franchard. He poured three generous shots of whiskey. They clinked glasses and drank.

"Still think I'm interested in takin' prisoners?" Franchard asked, wiping his mustache on his sleeve.

Chapter 34

"That's three of 'em, all right," Pritchard said.

"You're positive?" Ditch asked.

In response, Pritchard just looked at his friend and said nothing.

"Just askin'," Ditch said sheepishly.

A trio of Triple B hands were seated in a small cantina, speaking with two Mexican men. It was after dark, and Pritchard, Ditch, and Tom Franchard watched them enter from a different cantina across the street. Ditch was carrying his Henry rifle, and Franchard a double-barreled coach gun.

Pritchard had wanted to cross the Rio Grande and enter Mexico immediately, to continue the pursuit, but was talked out of it by Franchard. He explained to Pritchard and Ditch that their best bet was to remain in Del Rio for a few days and wait until a few Triple B hands returned.

Franchard informed them that Winston Boone made his money by rustling horses and cattle in Texas, herding them over the Rio Grande, and selling them to the Mexican army. The BB&B outfit would be expected to continue delivering stolen American stock, regardless of what troubles the rustlers had created for themselves in the United States with their attack on the stagecoach station house. If not, the Mexican government wouldn't continue to grant the men of the Triple B the unofficial asylum they enjoyed below the border; sanctuary they now required to escape the hanging justice above it.

Franchard believed that small parties of Triple B hands would be sneaking back into the U.S. to scout for herds of cattle and horses to rustle. When a potential herd was located, which could be at any ranch or stockyard from El Paso to San Antonio, all the way south to Laredo, the scouting party would split up. Part of the crew would remain in Texas to keep an eye on the targeted herd, while the others would return to Mexico to alert Winston and the rest of the hands. The entire outfit would then meet up at a prearranged location on the U.S. side of the border to commit the stock theft.

Franchard claimed it made better sense to wait in Del Rio and capture a member of one of the Triple B's scouting parties. A prisoner could tell them exactly where Winston Boone and the rest of the Triple B hands were hiding out, as opposed to traipsing all over Mexico in search of them.

Pritchard and Ditch couldn't argue with Franchard's logic, especially since Pritchard insisted that the face of each and every one of the Triple B men who were present at the coach station when Caroline was murdered was burned into his memory, like a brand.

"How do you want to play it?" Franchard asked Pritchard.

"You take the front, Tom. Ditch, you cover the rear."

"What about you?"

"I'm going into that cantina to get me a prisoner."

"Alone?" Ditch said. "Don't be a fool. Let one of us come with you."

"Not necessary," Pritchard said.

"Let him go," Franchard said to Ditch. "He'll make out." To Pritchard, he said, "Just be sure to leave one of those hands alive. It wouldn't be a bad idea to keep one of the Mexicans they're parlayin' with this side of perdition, too. Those Mexes brokerin' the deal with 'em in there probably know quite a bit about the area Winston is hiding out in. Could be, they could provide us with valuable tactical intelligence."

"Okay," Pritchard said, adjusting his pistol belt. "Be back out in a minute."

Pritchard waited a moment for Ditch to make his way to the rear door of the cantina. Then he nodded to Franchard, at the front doors, and went inside.

He wasted no time. He knew a white man as big as he was would be noticed immediately, so he strolled directly over to where the three Triple B hands sat drinking tequila at a corner table.

Three sets of eyes widened as the Triple B hands looked up and recognized Pritchard. The two Mexicans looked from their seated companions, who were clearly shocked by the arrival of the newcomer, to the giant man looming over them.

"You're supposed to be dead," one of the incredulous Triple B men said. It was Jim Collins.

"You ain't the first person to tell me that," Pritchard said. Four of the five drew on him.

It was over in a second or two.

The first Triple B hand went for a cross-draw pistol while seated, the second for a revolver in his belt, and Collins tried to stand and draw from a belt holster. In a flash, Pritchard drew both of his pistols and shot the two seated gunmen in the face simultaneously. He shot Collins twice, in the elbow and shoulder of his gun hand. He finished by drilling one of the Mexicans, the one drawing a Navy Colt, through the eye. The other Mexican never went for his gun, opting instead to slowly raise his hands.

Pritchard pivoted, with his revolvers leveled, and scanned the rest of the cantina. No one else moved. Ditch suddenly appeared from behind the bar. Franchard entered through the half doors, his shotgun at the ready. Ditch watched as the death-shadow once again dwindled from his friend's features, and his normally placid countenance returned.

"Bar's closed," Franchard loudly announced. "¡*Vete de aquí!* Get lost!"

Everyone inside the cantina, including the bartender and waitresses, rapidly scurried past Franchard through the front door.

Franchard walked over to the wounded Triple B hand, Collins, lying on the floor in a growing pool of his own blood. His face was twisted in pain, his right arm was useless, and his unfired revolver lay on the ground next to him. Franchard lowered the shotgun until its twin barrels rested against his cheek.

"You," Franchard said, "are going to tell us where Winston Boone and the rest of his boys are hidin'." He slowly raised the shotgun and poked the barrels under the nose of the Mexican, who stood, with his hands still raised, like a statue. "And you," he went on, "are going to tell us about the neighborhood they're hidin' in. ¿*Comprende?*"

Both men nodded.

Chapter 35

The Triple B hand who'd been shot twice by Pritchard, Jim Collins, died less than ten minutes after the gunfight. The bullet that tore into his shoulder ruptured an artery, and he bled out.

Before he expired, he expressed regret to Pritchard for the death of his fiancée. He further claimed he didn't know that Winston Boone, his son Wesley, and the other Triple B hands were planning to rape her and kill everyone at the stagecoach station.

Pritchard said nothing in reply. He reloaded his guns without expression and stared silently out into the street.

Franchard, however, called Collins a liar. He said the only way he could prove his dying words as the truth was to tell them where Boone and the remainder of the BB&B hands were hiding out in Mexico.

Collins told them they were holed up at a ranch, a day's ride south, a couple of miles outside a Mexican town called Zaragosa. Boone had built the place for the specific purpose of storing and transferring American horses and cattle to the Mexican government. Zaragosa had a cantina, which featured a brothel, that serviced the Mexican soldiers who regularly came to take possession of Boone's stolen stock.

The surviving Mexican, who spoke English, said his name was Alejandro Ruiz. He readily admitted to being an intermediary who brokered the transfer of stolen stock, for a fee, between the Mexican government and Winston Boone's rustling outfit. He insisted he knew nothing of the Triple B's attack on Pritchard's woman, which he considered a cowardly and unforgivable act, and the murder of the stagecoach passengers. He offered, in exchange for his life, to guide Pritchard, Ditch, and Franchard to Boone's south-of-the-border hideout.

They departed for Mexico the following morning at dawn. The quartet, along with their heavily laden packhorse, waded the Rio Grande at a shallow crossing a few miles south of Del Rio.

Pritchard made it clear to their guide that at the first inkling of treachery on his part, he would be instantly shot dead, and he, Ditch, and Franchard would find Boone's Mexican ranch themselves. Ruiz signaled his understanding. He hadn't forgotten the speed with which Pritchard had gunned down four men.

It was a full day's ride, as Ruiz had promised, to Zaragosa. By sundown, Pritchard, Ditch, Franchard, and their Mexican guide were overlooking Winston Boone's Mexican spread from the crest of a ridge a quarter mile out.

There was a ranch house, a large bunkhouse, an outhouse, and a barn next to an extensive corral. Ditch pointed out that it was at least as extensive an operation as Winston Boone's spread back in the States. The horse corral contained at least forty horses, but there were no cows in sight.

Ruiz explained the lack of cattle was because the Triple B outfit had only recently arrived in Mexico, evidently forced to flee as a result of the massacre at the stagecoach station. He conjectured that Boone was probably in the process of soliciting livestock orders from the Mexican army. The three men he'd sent back into the U.S., whom Pritchard killed along with Ruiz's partner, were scouting for herds to steal. Ruiz admitted his meeting at the cantina in Del Rio with Collins and his two companions was for the express purpose of guiding them to a ranch in Corpus Christi where a vast herd of cattle was ripe for the plucking.

"You've been to Boone's Mexican ranch before?" Franchard asked him.

"*Sí.* Señor Boone and his son, and a few of his most trusted hands, stay in the ranch house. Sometimes there are Mexican army officers who stay there, too. None of the ordinary hands, whether Boone's or the Mexican soldiers, are allowed inside. They must remain in the bunkhouse. There are many cots within it, and a kitchen."

"I see only two guards standing watch outside," Pritchard said, peering through his spyglass. "The one near the ranch house is in uniform. The one near the bunkhouse looks like a cowhand. There's smoke coming from both chimneys." He handed the glass to Franchard, who confirmed his observations.

"No need for any more watchmen," Franchard commented. "There ain't no herd to guard yet."

"You think Winston and Wesley are down there?" Ditch asked.

"I do," Pritchard said. "I can feel 'em."

"It is going to be cold tonight," Ruiz said. "The men will be drinking and playing cards indoors."

"You honored your word," Pritchard said to Ruiz. "You did what you said you were going to do and led us to the ranch. I'll keep my word, too. I give you back your life. You're free to go." He retrieved Ruiz's revolver from Ditch's saddlebag and extended it to the Mexican.

"I will not leave," Ruiz said. "These men, who I have done business with, I believed were only rustlers of cattle. I have learned from you that they are men who rape and murder. I will not go. I will stay and help you fight them."

"You sure you want to do that?" Ditch asked. "Between the Triple B hands and the Mex soldiers, there must be fifty men down there."

"No matter what you may think of me, Señor Ditch," Ruiz said, "I am a man of honor. I will fight. Besides," he accepted his revolver and looked at Pritchard, "I owe your friend my life."

"It's your funeral," Pritchard said.

"Let's get to it," Franchard said.

They emptied two sets of saddlebags from the packhorse and transferred the cases of dynamite into them. Franchard fixed what he said was an approximately one-minute fuse to each bag. They also packed bottles of whiskey. Then they set out distributing .44 ammunition and loading cartridges into belts, which each man crisscrossed over his chest. They finished by taking a drink of water and checking their guns. Ditch, Franchard, and Ruiz took rifles. Ruiz was forced to borrow Pritchard's, since he didn't have one of his own.

They left their horses tied at the crest and made

their way down to the ranch on foot. There was no moon, for which all were grateful. It was easy going, since they had the lights in the windows of both the ranch house and bunkhouse to guide them.

Ruiz led them at an oblique angle to their destination, using the corral full of horses as cover. They took their time, pausing to stop, watch, and listen at regular intervals. Pritchard was gratified to find Rusty in the corral, and elbowed Ditch when he recognized the big Morgan.

When they were fifty yards from the ranch house, the guard changed. Another Mexican soldier and cowhand came out of the bunkhouse and replaced the two who'd been standing watch.

Franchard held their party in place until the soldier and cowboy lit cigarettes, which they knew would temporarily ruin their night vision. Once they'd fired up, they advanced again. Before the pair of guards finished smoking, they passed the corral.

Franchard and Ditch paired up, taking the saddlebags. Pritchard partnered with Ruiz. Each pair separated and took off in different directions.

Franchard and Ditch went around to the far side of bunkhouse. The Ranger captain stood watch with both rifles while Ditch took the bags and crawled under the wooden foundation.

Pritchard and Ruiz had tougher going. Ditch and Franchard were obscured from view by the bunkhouse, but Pritchard and Ruiz had twenty yards of open space to traverse between the corral and the guards. The bunkhouse's guard, a Triple B hand, sat on the front porch of the large one-level building, lighting a second cigarette with his Henry rifle across his knees.

The Mexican soldier stood his post directly in front of the one-story ranch house's front door.

Ruiz crept along the bunkhouse, beneath the windows, with his knife in his teeth. He made eye contact with Pritchard, who had worked his way behind a trough near the well, twenty feet from the Mexican soldier.

Ruiz whistled, and both men sprang into action. Ruiz rushed the seated cowboy. As the Triple B guard looked up, he was butt-stroked in the face with a Henry rifle before he could cry out. As he fell, unconscious, Ruiz cut his throat.

The Mexican soldier heard the scuffle behind him, across the yard, and turned to investigate. He saw Ruiz pounce on the other guard. He raised his army-issued Spencer repeating carbine, and was drawing the hammer back, when Pritchard grabbed him from behind. Like Ruiz, the powerful Pritchard struck a blow that rendered the soldier unconscious. He finished the guard by stabbing him in the back of the neck.

Ruiz whistled softly again, and Franchard and Ditch came running toward them. There was no sign their actions had alerted anyone inside either the ranch house or bunkhouse. Ruiz tossed Pritchard his Henry carbine back, having confiscated a similar rifle belonging to the guard he'd just killed.

"The fuses are lit," Franchard whispered, as he joined Pritchard and Ruiz. All four quietly levered their Henry rifles. "You all know what to do. Once the bunkhouse blows, I'll take the back of the ranch house, Ditch and Al the sides, and Joe the front. Torch the place, and when they come runnin' out let 'em have it."

The four men scurried to duck behind the trough and stone well. Pritchard, Ditch, and Ruiz watched Franchard set down his rifle, close his eyes, and plug his ears with his thumbs. They all looked at one another, then hastily followed suit.

A tremendous explosion erupted under the bunkhouse, followed by a second, equally thunderous, blast an instant later. The two cases of dynamite detonated almost as one.

The ground shook. Pritchard, Ditch, Franchard, and Ruiz felt the concussion all the way to their bones. They sensed the brief flash, even though their eyes were shut. When they opened them, the entire bunkhouse, and the nearly fifty Triple B hands and Mexican soldiers inside, had been obliterated. Only a large, smoking hole, a mushroom-shaped cloud of dust, and a cascade of falling wood splinters and ash remained.

"Get goin'!" Franchard yelled, awakening the others from their awestruck states. They grabbed their rifles and ran to their assigned places surrounding the ranch house.

Pritchard remained behind the trough, which was in front of the ranch house's front door. No sooner had Franchard, Ditch, and Ruiz vanished into the dust cloud, than the ranch house door flew open and several men began rushing outside.

The first two out were wearing Mexican military uniforms, followed by men in cowboy attire. All were carrying pistols. Pritchard downed three of them with his rifle, working the lever rapidly between shots, before the others were able to retreat inside and close the door. A moment later, he heard shots emanating from the sides and rear of the building. He also smelled smoke.

Pritchard knew that Franchard, Ditch, and Ruiz had thrown whiskey bottles on their respective sides of the ranch house and ignited the flammable beverage. Within a minute or so, he saw flames licking all around the wooden structure.

Then he heard more gunshots. There were many of them, coming from three sides of the ranch house.

Those inside the ranch house, unable to flee through the front door because of Pritchard's deadly accurate rifle fire, had evidently attempted to exit through the side windows and rear door. Instead of escape, they were met with a blazing inferno, and the equally deadly rifles of Ditch, Ruiz, and Franchard.

After a minute of intense shooting, no further shots rang out, and no more attempts to leave the ranch house were made by those inside. The only sounds were the terrified braying of the horses, whinnying and stomping in the corral in the wake of the massive explosion, and the growing roar of the fire as the exterior of the ranch house steadily burned.

"Reload and stand ready." Pritchard heard Franchard call out the familiar Ranger after-action order. He reflexively began to recharge his Henry rifle's fifteen-round tube from the cartridge belt across his chest, and presumed his compatriots were doing the same.

"You outside," a man's coughing voice called from inside the burning ranch house. "What do you want?"

"I want every one of you in that ranch house to come out the front door with your hands in the air," Pritchard answered back.

"If we do that," the voice said, "you'll shoot us."

"That ain't certain," Pritchard said. "But what is certain, is we've got you surrounded and bottled up. If you don't come out, you're going to roast. You can join your friends in the bunkhouse on their way to hell."

"We're coming out."

"Everybody out through the front door," Pritchard barked instructions. "Anyone who drops their hands below their ears gets plugged. *Comprende?*"

"We understand. Don't shoot. We're all coming out."

One by one, ten people emerged from the ranch house. As they came out, Franchard, Ditch, and Ruiz rejoined Pritchard at the front.

The first four men out were Mexican army officers. All appeared wounded. They helped one another along, attempting to keep their hands high, as ordered.

The next four men out of the ranch house were Triple B hands Pritchard recognized from the coach house massacre. Finally, Winston Boon stumbled out, helping his son Wesley, who was also obviously wounded. Old Man Boone looked even smaller and more bow-legged without his ten-gallon hat. All the former residents of the ranch house, Mexican and American alike, wore holstered pistols and appeared to have been drinking. Pritchard, Ditch, Franchard, and Ruiz covered them with their rifles.

Winston Boone, a stupefied expression on his ancient face, looked up at Pritchard.

"You're dead," Boone exclaimed, disbelieving his eyes. "We already done killed you."

"You didn't kill me enough," Pritchard said.

"I told you, Pa," Wesley griped, his voice tight with

pain. "You should've let me finish him off in that stagecoach station. Now lookit what he's done. He's wiped us out."

"You are Americans," one of the Mexican officers said in excellent English to Franchard. "I know you. I have seen you before, in Dallas. You are a Texas Ranger. The Texas Rangers have no right to be in Mexico."

"I'm on vacation," Franchard said.

"I demand you release us at once," the officer continued, emboldened. He suddenly lowered his hands and stood up straight. "This is illegal. I will not stand for this. I am a major in His Excellency's army."

"You're a rustler and a horse thief in a soldier's uniform," Franchard said. "Put your hands back up."

"Rest assured, your government will be made aware of this breach of our country's sovereignty."

"Put your hands up," Franchard said. "Ain't gonna tell you again."

"I will take no more orders from you," the major said. "You have no authority here."

"Maybe not," Franchard said, "but my rifle does." He shot the major dead. Behind the major's body, the ranch house was now fully engulfed in flames.

"Anybody else have a problem with doin' what they're told?" Franchard asked, levering the action on his Henry.

"You can all go to hell, Rangers," Wesley Boone said. He leaned on his father and spat blood.

"You were the first to line up after my fiancée was laid out on that table, weren't you, Wesley?" Pritchard said. He tossed his Henry rifle to Ditch, who caught it.

He used Pritchard's carbine, along with his own, to continue covering the prisoners.

"Go for your pistol, Wesley," Pritchard said. "I'll give you more of a chance than you gave Caroline."

Wesley pushed off from his father and glared at Pritchard with unbridled hatred in his eyes. Then he went for his holstered revolver. He'd barely touched it when Pritchard drew and fired. The bullet entered just below his nose. Wesley spun around and fell on his face. Winston Boone cried out and dropped to his hands and knees.

"My boy," he whimpered. "You killed my boy."

"Your boy shot an unarmed woman in the back," Pritchard said. "He died better than he deserved."

Winston tried to draw his own revolver. Pritchard stepped forward and effortlessly kicked it away. The rest of the prisoners cast uneasy glances at one another.

"I know what you're all thinkin'," Franchard said. "There're eight of you, all armed, and only four of us. Those are pretty fair odds. You might as well go for it. It's the only chance you're gettin' out of us, and a helluva lot more chance than you gave them poor souls at the stagecoach station. Go on," he challenged. "Draw, you yellow bastards."

No one was sure who drew first. Whether a Mexican army officer or a Triple B rustler, as soon as one went for his gun, they all did. Ditch, Franchard, and Ruiz cut loose with their Henry rifles. Pritchard drew both pistols and fired. Seven men fell to the ground without firing a shot.

Most of the downed men died instantly, but a few still twitched and writhed in the dust. Eventually even they ceased moving, and lay still as their death rattles echoed across the Mexican desert. The only one left alive was Winston Boone, loudly grieving his son. It occurred to Ditch that every time he'd heard the now-familiar sound, he'd been in Pritchard's company.

Pritchard ejected the empty .44 cases from his Remingtons, as Winston Boone angrily wailed and sobbed. The others automatically reloaded their Henry rifles. Pritchard inserted fresh cartridges into his revolver's cylinders, holstered the guns, and turned to face the old rustler.

"Get up," Pritchard said. Winston Boone shakily complied.

"You done killed both my boys," Boone said to Pritchard. "Finish me."

"Not a chance," Pritchard said. He drew and fired.

He fired four times. The first shot went into Winston Boone's left elbow, the second into his right, and the next two shots ripped through both knees. Boone shrieked in pain and flopped to the dirt on his back.

"You're going to take a while," Pritchard said, "to meet your end. I'll remind you of what you once said, Winston. 'Leave him be, to contemplate,' you told your son at the coach house, when he wanted to end me quick. I'll be showin' you the same mercy you showed me."

"Kill me," Boone begged.

"So long, Winston Boone. Enjoy your slow ride to hell. I hope the coyote and scorpions enjoy you, because I sure ain't puttin' you into the ground."

Ditch looked on as Pritchard again reloaded and then holstered his pistol. Then he turned and walked away from the crippled, dying, old man, silhouetted against the burning ranch house.

As he handed Pritchard back his Henry carbine, Ditch saw the death-shadow, as he had so many times before, fade once more from his friend's visage.

"What did we just do?" Ditch asked, examining the carnage surrounding him.

"What had to be done," Pritchard answered.

"Hell of a vacation," Franchard said.

Chapter 36

It took two days for Pritchard, Ditch, Ruiz, and Franchard to get across the Rio Grande and back into the United States. That's because instead of riding alone, as they had been when they entered Mexico, they were riding herd over more than fifty horses.

They decided, since all the horses belonging to the Triple B were stolen, that they had as much right to the animals as anyone. Especially since there was no one left alive from the BB&B outfit to dispute their claim.

Before they left the rustlers' ranch, they searched the barn. Among a large stack of stolen saddles, tack, and other pirated goods stashed there, they found Pritchard's saddle and bridle. This was a particularly fortuitous find, because his ten thousand dollars and the wedding ring he'd purchased for his bride were still secreted within the saddle's lining.

Pritchard stared at the ring a moment before wiping his eyes and pocketing it. The others left him alone and busied themselves rounding up the horses.

The trio bridled the animals, most of which were

top-quality mounts, and strung them together. They then lugged the dead bodies into the barn and set it aflame. The agonized moaning of Winston Boone could still be heard as they all rode off.

The quartet pushed hard for the border, stopping only a couple of times to rest and water the horses. They knew the dead Mexican troops, unlike Old Man Boone and his Triple B hands, would soon be missed. When a relief detachment came looking for the delinquent soldiers, the trail left by Pritchard, Ditch, Ruiz, Franchard, and the fifty horses they were leading, would be an easy one to follow.

Two grueling days later, they were back in America. The minute they crossed the Rio Grande, Franchard immediately pinned his cinco-peso Texas Ranger star back on his shirt. After that, he wordlessly reached into his pocket and produced another. He tossed it to Pritchard.

Pritchard stared at the star a moment, as he had the wedding ring. He nodded to Franchard, then pinned the star onto his own shirt.

In Del Rio, they found sixteen Rangers from Franchard's detachment waiting for them.

"I thought I ordered you boys back to Fort Worth," Franchard said.

"I don't believe I recall that order," the Ranger sergeant, a stocky Irishman named Finley, said.

"I'm a bit hard of hearing, Cap'n," said a Ranger.

"I've got a powerful lot of wax in my ears," said another.

Franchard grinned. "How long were you boys going to wait before violating international law and charging into Mexico after us?"

"We thought we'd give you a full week," Sergeant Finley said in his thick Irish brogue, "just to be courteous."

"It's just as well you stuck around," Franchard said. "If any of you boys are ever asked—"

"You were here with us in Del Rio the whole time," Finley cut his commanding officer off. "Getting drunk. So was Joe and your two pals, there. Never left our sight." The other Rangers nodded their assent.

"I appreciate it," Franchard said.

"Did you find those murdering rustlers?" Finley asked. "I don't see any prisoners."

Franchard looked at Pritchard before answering. "We found every damned one of 'em," he said, "and we didn't take any prisoners. By the way, Sergeant, thanks for the dynamite. Came in right handy."

"What dynamite?" Finley asked innocently.

"Would you fellas mind takin' all these horses down to the livery and getting them corralled and fed?" he asked his Rangers. "We ain't hardly ate, nor slept, in days."

"Sure thing, Cap'n. Wouldn't hurt if you boys cleaned up a bit," Finley suggested. "If you don't mind me saying so, you look like you just got back from—"

"—vacation," it was Franchard's turn to interrupt. "Good idea."

Pritchard switched his saddle from Biscuit to Rusty and let the Rangers lead the palomino off with the rest of the herd. Then he, Ditch, Ruiz, and Franchard went to the hotel. Each got a bath, a shave, and a change of clothes before meeting down in the restaurant. Franchard already had a table, a bottle, and four glasses by the time Pritchard, Ditch, and Ruiz arrived.

"I appreciate what you boys did," Pritchard said,

once their steaks were ordered and the drinks were poured. "I won't forget it. I know Caroline's grateful, too, wherever she is."

"Nothing can bring your woman back," Ruiz said in his heavy accent, "but she has been avenged. This is not a small thing, Señor Joe. Her soul can be at peace now. You must take comfort in that."

"To the memory of Caroline Biggs," Ditch said, raising his glass. "No finer woman ever graced the Republic of Texas."

"Damn straight," Captain Franchard said. The others raised their glasses and drank.

"What are you going to do now?" Ditch asked Pritchard.

"With Caroline gone . . . I don't rightly know. I guess I'll stick with rangerin'. What else can I do?"

"There're plenty of other things to do," Ditch said. "Maybe it's time for you to look into a line of work that don't involve killing? Heaven knows, you've seen your share of death. No disrespect, Captain Franchard, but there's more to life than hunting down murderers and outlaws. Why don't you come back to the ranch with me and Alejandro?"

"You and Alejandro?" Pritchard said.

"Señor Ditch has offered me a job on his ranch," Ruiz explained. "I have accepted."

"We've got more work than me and Paul can handle by ourselves," Ditch said. "Folks need horses and beef more than ever. We're raking in money faster than you can imagine. Now that the Triple B is no more, I'm thinking of taking over that spread, too. If I can raise the money, I'm positive I can purchase Old Man Boone's ranch from the county, especially since I have it on good authority it'll soon be unclaimed land."

"I heard that rumor, too," Franchard said.

"Think about it," Ditch continued, "We can double the size of the SD&P. We'll become cattle, horse, and land barons. What do you say, Samuel?"

Ditch winced, realizing he'd just called Pritchard by his true name instead of Joe.

"Your friend's proposition might be worth considering," Franchard said. "You've always got a home in the Texas Rangers. But maybe there is something else out there, *Samuel*, just waitin' for you to find it?"

"You knew?" Pritchard asked.

"Don't worry," the Ranger captain said. "Whatever your name is, your secret's safe with me. Hell, half the Rangers I ever rode with used aliases and were runnin' from one thing or another. It's almost a requirement of the job. Most Rangers got things in their past they ain't proud of."

"You are the best man with a gun I have ever seen," Ruiz spoke up, "and I have known many pistoleros. This I also know; a man does not become as skilled with a revolver as you are by living a life free from trouble. Death follows you, Señor Joe. It stalks you like a puma. You cannot elude it. You must learn to make death your friend, or die. There is no other way."

"Don't listen to that crazy Mexican witch doctor," Ditch said, "and his superstitious mumbo jumbo. Come back to the ranch with us? All you have to do is go back to being who you used to be."

Even as he spoke, Ditch doubted his own words. He was reminded of the death-shadow that hung over his friend; something he himself had witnessed on numerous occasions. He couldn't help believing Ruiz must have sensed it, too.

"I don't know who that is anymore," Pritchard said. "With Caroline, I thought I knew. But I was wrong. That fella was dead and buried a long time ago."

"You're talkin' foolish," Ditch said. "You can be whoever you want."

"No, Ditch," Pritchard said, "Alejandro is right. For me, it's either death or the way of the gun. There just ain't no other path. It's like a brand. I was a fool to think otherwise. My mistake cost Caroline her life."

"You're wrong," Ditch said, not entirely believing Pritchard was. "What happened to her wasn't your fault."

"Sure it was," Pritchard said, not harshly. "I saved her once. But she came back and found me. When she did, my troubles found her. It's just like Alejandro said."

"What about your family?"

"Saving what was left of my family is why I turned my back on them. You should know that better than anybody, Ditch. Do you think I want what happened to my fiancée to happen to Ma and Idelle?"

"Of course not," Ditch said.

"Then you know why I can't go with you. And why I have to remain Joe Atherton."

Ditch only nodded.

"I'm sure you have your reasons for keeping your past hidden," Franchard said. "If they're good enough for you, they're good enough for me and the Texas Rangers."

"Thanks, Cap'n," Pritchard said. "And thanks for the offer, Ditch," he said to his friend. "Maybe someday I'll take you up on it. For now, I'll be stickin' with the Rangers."

"Suit yourself," Ditch said. "Just don't forget who you are."

Pritchard looked from Ditch, to Franchard, to Ruiz, and then into his empty glass.

"I know who I am," he said.

"Who's that?" Ditch asked.

"Smokin' Joe Atherton," Pritchard said.

Part Three
GUNFIGHTER

Chapter 37

Dovie sat in the parlor and sipped her tea, smiling, as her husband's tortured screams echoed throughout their apartment. She knew Burnell's howls could be heard outside their opulent penthouse, in the hotel rooms below, and probably even down in the lobby, restaurant, and bar.

Burnell had been receiving treatment for several years for what the town's physician, Dr. Mauldin, referred to as "an affliction of the blood," but which Dovie knew was really the "sporting pox," as it was more commonly called. Burnell had no doubt contracted it from one of the "hospitality hostesses" he employed, or during one of his frequent trips to Kansas City where his consorting with prostitutes was common knowledge.

Burnell Shipley's stomach had always bothered him, but over the past couple of years his skin had turned gray, his gums began to bleed, his eyesight had gradually begun failing, and he'd developed a tremor in his hands. He often spent as much as thirty minutes in the lavatory at a time, and usually moaned in anguish while relieving himself.

Dr. Mauldin visited weekly and treated his patient with doses of calomel. Shipley usually drank the mercury chloride solution while Mauldin rubbed an ointment made of the compound on the sores that had begun to spread over his obese body. But for the last several months, at least once every few weeks, the doctor was forced to come to their home at the hotel to inject the calomel, with a specially heated, red-hot syringe, directly into Burnell's penis.

It was no mystery to anyone within earshot of the Atherton Arms Hotel which of Dr. Mauldin's visits was merely to administer the calomel syrup orally, and which of his visits was to give Burnell the "blacksmith's rod," as the staff at the hotel mockingly called it behind his back.

Dovie took no comfort in her husband's illness or suffering. In fact, she was burdened by the knowledge that she herself had likely become infected, during the early days of their marriage, when forced to submit to Burnell's humiliating marital desires.

Burnell had been unable to pursue her sexually for the last several years, due to the steadily worsening condition of his health and his contaminated reproductive organs. While this provided Dovie endless relief, she couldn't help but suspect, with increasing dread, the disease was the reason she had avoided becoming pregnant.

Burnell Shipley made no secret of his wish for Dovie to provide him a son. He desired an heir to inherit his sprawling empire. But as the years went by, no pregnancy resulted. Despite Burnell's frequent rages at what he deemed were Dovie's failings as a wife, she was pleased to have failed to fulfill her husband's most fervent demand.

Her apparent inability to conceive, coupled with her own growing symptoms, which included heavy female bleeding, the occasional and random onset of weakness, extremely painful abdominal cramps, and unexplained fevers that beset her without warning, led Dovie to suspect she had indeed become infected.

She was afraid to visit the doctor, for fear he would verify she was barren and inform Burnell. Dovie suffered no delusions about what her husband would do if he became convinced she couldn't bear him a child.

Dovie was aware that Burnell's mind was failing as rapidly as his body. She knew madness was one of the other signs of advanced "sporting pox." One of the many ways his diminishing sanity was manifesting itself, other than his mood swings, fits of rage, and general distemper, was his outlandish belief that Dr. Mauldin was somehow going to eventually "cure" him.

Burnell often spoke, irrationally, of how he was going to impregnate Dovie as soon as he was "healed." Were he to be faced with the truth of either reality— that he would never be cured of the venereal ailment not only afflicting him but slowly killing him, and that Dovie would never bear him a son—there was no telling how he would react.

Or what he would do. The only thing she was certain about was that Burnell Shipley would take the unpleasant realization of their mutual infection and her inability to conceive out on her.

Or on Idelle.

Burnell's screams grew louder, reached a crescendo, and then faded to a wailing sob. There followed a sound of breaking glass and angry shouting. A moment later, Dr. Mauldin quickly emerged from Burnell's room.

The white-haired physician's face was red and covered with a sheen of sweat. He had his coat over one arm and his bag in the other. He wiped his brow with a handkerchief.

"I wouldn't go in there, if I were you," Mauldin said to Dovie.

"I hadn't planned to," she replied.

"He's in a lot of pain," he went on. "Might be better for both of you if you let him drink a bit. It may calm him down."

"My husband drinks all day whether I allow it or not," she said. "His drinking is rarely better for anyone."

"I'd best be going," the doctor said. He started for the door.

"He's dying, isn't he?" Dove asked.

Dr. Mauldin slowly turned around. "He believes he's getting better."

"That's not what I asked you."

The doctor's shoulders slumped. "What he's afflicted with doesn't get better," he said. "It only gets worse. He should know that, but he doesn't want to. Once it starts to affect the eyes and brain, the end is coming. But there's no telling how soon it'll take him. Could be a few months, or it could be a few years."

Dovie lifted her chin. "And the likelihood I've contracted it?"

"It's a disease that hides, Mrs. Shipley," he said. "Sometimes, you don't even know you have it for many years once you've contracted it. After that, it comes and goes. Your husband likely had it most of his life. If you've had marital relations, no matter how long ago,

I'd say it's a fair bet you've got it hiding inside of you, too. I'm sorry."

She closed her eyes and nodded.

"I'll be going now. Call on me when he needs another dose, and I'll be back."

Dovie put on her shawl and went downstairs to the lobby. As she exited the hotel, she encountered Sheriff Horace Foster and his chief deputy, Eli Gaines, entering.

Gaines tipped his hat and grinned at her through his rancid jack-o'-lantern, smile. Though only in his early thirties, a lifetime of poor hygiene and heavy alcohol and tobacco use had decimated the skeletal deputy's teeth and gums.

"Afternoon, Mrs. Shipley," Sheriff Foster said. "How's your husband feeling?"

"Why don't you ask him yourself?" she said curtly.

"That's what we came to do," Foster said. "We heard he was feeling poorly."

"Anyone within a half mile with a pair of ears knows he's feeling poorly," Dovie said. "If you'll excuse me?" She started past them and down the hotel steps.

"I also heard your daughter is almost eighteen years old?" Gaines said.

Dovie stopped, slowly turned around, and faced him.

"My daughter's birthday is no concern of yours, Deputy."

"Chief Deputy," he said. "Be sure and tell Idelle I'll be a-calling on her, real soon."

"No," Dovie said, "you won't."

"We'll see about that," Gaines retorted, his toothless leer spreading across his narrow face. "And please tell your husband, like you, I sincerely hope he gets to feelin' better."

"Go to hell," Dovie said.

"Yes, ma'am," Gaines said through his infected grin.

"Shut up, Gaines," Sheriff Foster said. "Let's go see Burnell."

Dovie left the lawmen on the steps of the hotel and walked through the suffocating Missouri heat across the street, past the Sidewinder, and into Shipley's Mercantile and General Store.

The establishment had expanded, along with Atherton, into a booming retail enterprise that added even more money to Burnell Shipley's sprawling empire. Mr. Manning, who'd run the facility since it opened its doors, was an old skinflint employed by Shipley for his miserly ways and cowardly demeanor. Everyone knew Manning was too frightened to skim from Shipley.

When Dovie entered, Manning, whose bespectacled eyes never missed anything occurring inside his store, wordlessly left the customer he was helping and greeted her.

"Good afternoon, Mrs. Shipley," the old shopkeeper said in his oily voice.

"Did my package arrive yet?" she asked.

"It did. Came on the train with yesterday's delivery. I would have sent it over to you at the hotel, with your regular order, but you told me not to."

"That's right," Dovie said. "It's a Christmas present for Burnell, so I want to keep it a secret. It's also why I'm paying cash, instead of having it charged. You understand?"

"Of course," Manning said. "Christmas presents are one of the few secrets a wife is allowed to keep from her husband. You want me to stash it here until then?"

"That won't be necessary," she said.

"Here it is," Manning said, producing a polished wooden box from under the counter and opening it for Dovie's examination. "All the way from Connecticut."

Inside the case was a pair of ornately engraved Colt Cloverleaf pocket pistols. Chambered in .41 rimfire and featuring a four-shot cylinder, the weapons were compact, powerful, and designed to be concealed rather than worn openly in a belt holster. There were twenty cartridges for the weapons in the felt-lined box.

"Beautiful, ain't they?" Manning said. "A real thoughtful gift, if I may say so. Just the thing for a well-dressed, traveling gentleman. I'm sure your husband will find them useful during his trips to Kansas City."

Whenever Dovie patronized the store, Manning couldn't resist revealing that he knew about Burnell's extracurricular activities, as if he were in her husband's intimate confidence. As far as she was concerned, few in town didn't know. Like the many other indignities she endured as Burnell Shipley's wife, she endured this one with silent indifference.

"They'll certainly come in handy," was all she said as she paid the shopkeeper.

"You sure you don't want me to store them here for you until Christmas?" Manning said. "It's no trouble at all."

"That won't be necessary. I have the perfect place to hide them. Besides," she said, closing the case and tucking it under her arm, "I want the guns to be a surprise. Good day, Mr. Manning."

Chapter 38

*150 miles west of Fort Worth, Texas,
March 1873*

Pritchard waved to Ditch from horseback as he led the single file of mounted Texas Rangers toward the ranch house he himself had helped to build.

More than three years had passed since that fateful summer when Caroline found him. Three years since he kissed her, held her, made love to her, betrothed himself to her, and watched her die.

In that time Samuel Pritchard, who'd once only pretended to be Ranger, gunfighter, and man-killer Smokin' Joe Atherton, had become him.

Pritchard hadn't cut his hair since Caroline's death, and his blond locks fell well below his shoulders. His mane was long enough, even without his ten-gallon Stetson, to easily conceal the bullet scar on the crown of his forehead. He also sported a full beard, which made him look older than his twenty-seven years.

These additions, in concert with his six-and-a-half-foot-tall, muscular, frame, ever-present brace of pistols, hat, boots, and spurs, lent him an appearance that matched his increasingly fearsome reputation. The legend of Texas Ranger Smokin' Joe Atherton, already formidable, had only grown since Caroline's murder. And like most legends, there were more than a few grains of truth contained within its verses.

In the wake of his fiancée's death, Pritchard reassumed his duties as a Texas Ranger with singular vengeance and ruthless efficiency. Now, when encountering outlaws, renegades, rustlers, and gunfighters in the line of duty, he gave only a brief warning, if any at all. More often than not, his notice to an armed lawbreaker was communicated merely through the look in his eyes and the portent of the shadow that hung over him. If the warning wasn't heeded, his pistols did any further speaking for him.

Some claimed Smokin' Joe had accumulated twenty notches; others said it was closer to fifty. Still others pointed out that since no one could say exactly how many men he'd killed during the war, before he became a Texas Ranger, there was no way to know his tally for certain.

The only thing anyone knew for sure about Ranger Smokin' Joe Atherton was that he seldom spoke, rarely drank, and anyone who crossed him did it only once.

When not on the trail with Captain Franchard and his Rangers, Pritchard lived a uniquely Spartan life. He kept to himself, took his meals alone in a small café, and slept in the loft above Fort Worth's main livery stable. He eschewed the whiskey, gambling, and nightlife favored by his fellow Rangers when billeted in town. He practiced religiously with his revolvers each day, and during what little leisure time he found, took long, solo rides in the country on his faithful Morgan, Rusty.

The ten thousand dollars he'd planned to use to buy his bride a home, he deposited in the Wells Fargo Bank of Fort Worth, along with the several thousand dollars he'd accrued in reward money. Most of the bounties were of the dead-or-alive variety, with very few of Pritchard's collections arriving in the *alive* category.

All of Pritchard's fellow Rangers respected him, some feared him, and most understood and accepted his desire to be left alone. Though he avoided socializing, and repeatedly turned down offers to promote to the rank of sergeant, they nonetheless recognized him as their brother at arms. They also noticed the paternal manner with which Captain Franchard regarded his top Ranger.

When special orders were telegraphed from the capital in Austin, and Franchard began to select Rangers for a long-range, and particularly hazardous, assignment, there was no doubt in anyone's mind that Smokin' Joe Atherton would be the first man chosen.

Franchard and his Ranger detachment were destined for the New Mexico Territory, on orders direct from Governor Davis. They were to assist the territorial governor there, a useless Connecticut Yankee named Marsh Giddings, in the tracking and apprehension of one of the most violent bands of outlaws the increasingly lawless region had ever seen: the Stiles Gang.

Major Dalton Stiles was a Missourian, like Pritchard. Also, like Pritchard, he'd been a partisan guerrilla fighting on the side of the Confederacy as a member of a different company of Shelby's Missouri Iron Brigade. That's where their similarities ended.

Whereas Pritchard took life only when his own or others' were threatened, Major Stiles and the freelance group of partisan rangers he commanded killed at whim. And like many such far-ranging guerrilla outfits during the war, acting alone and without restraint by lawful authority or a chain of command, they killed not only Union soldiers, but men, women, and children on both sides as the mood suited them.

They also robbed, raped, and burned. After the surrender, even against the murderously inhuman standards set during the Civil War, Stiles and his partisan rangers were considered bloodthirsty renegades by both the Union, and what was left of the Confederate, authorities. When Stiles and his men tried to rejoin General Shelby after he refused to surrender on his final, defiant, march into Mexico, they were turned away at gunpoint.

In the years since the war, Stiles and the surviving remnants of his partisan rangers didn't abandon their raiding, robbing, and killing. This, in itself, was not particularly unusual. Many Confederate guerrillas, such as the James and Younger gang, continued their wartime activities after the war ended, as outlaws instead of soldiers, without the cover of a flag or uniform. But what singled Stiles and his gang out from other renegade bands of veteran guerrillas was the scale, savagery, and sheer bloodlust of their criminal acts.

All of the crimes committed by Stiles resulted in needless deaths. In the Arizona Territory in 1868, instead of merely robbing the passengers, they tore up the railroad tracks and derailed the train. The ensuing crash killed over twenty people. In 1870, in the New Mexico Territory, they robbed a bank in

Las Cruces. The townspeople, led by the sheriff and two deputies, put up a valiant fight. When it was over and the gun smoke cleared, twenty-two men, three women, and a five-year-old boy lay dead in the streets.

The U.S. Army, composed of too few soldiers in the territory, too thinly spread out, and too busy dealing with the warring Apache, were no more effective against Stiles's highly mobile band of raiders than they'd been during the war. After each bloody raid, Stiles and his horsemen simply vanished into the vast, untamed New Mexico or Arizona territories, where they would remain hidden until reemerging to commit their next murderous crime.

New Mexico Territorial Governor Marsh Giddings, a former civil judge from Michigan with no military or law enforcement experience, was utterly unprepared and completely at a loss as to how to deal with the widespread lawlessness pervading his jurisdiction. He was especially vexed by the Stiles Gang.

After the Magdalena Mine Massacre, as it had come to be known, which occurred in December of 1872, the frustrated Giddings, in desperation, reached out to the Texas governor for help.

On Christmas Eve, just after dawn, twenty members of the Stiles Gang rode into the silver mining town of Magdalena. Instead of robbing the bank, which was heavily fortified because it was stuffed with silver, they converged on the mine. After placing dynamite at the entrance, Major Stiles sent an emissary into the town with a simple demand.

Every citizen was to surrender all their valuables, including everything in the bank, to Stiles's men in the town square by noon. Failure to comply would result in a detonation at the mine's opening, which would turn Magdalena's sole economic engine into its largest grave.

Since almost all the townsmen were working down in the mine, and Stiles's riders had taken the liberty of killing the town marshal and his deputies upon their arrival, the people of Magdalena had little choice but to comply. They dutifully began to pile their money, jewels, and silver in the town square.

By eleven-thirty a.m., Stiles's men had loaded a wagon with the town's treasure. At noon, not wanting a posse of over one hundred enraged miners after them, he ordered the mine blown.

One hundred and twenty-seven men were sealed underground in the blast, turning the Magdalena Silver Mine into a giant tomb. After taking most of the town's horses and livestock, and raping a number of womenfolk, the Stiles Gang rode off, pulling their wagonload of booty behind them.

Governor Giddings wired the Texas governor for help. Captain Franchard and his Ranger detachment, the best in Texas, were dispatched. Their orders were simple: capture or kill Major Dalton Stiles, eradicate his gang, and do so with all due haste.

Captain Tom Franchard, Pritchard, and sixteen other veteran Rangers left Fort Worth on horseback in January of 1873.

It was more than six hundred miles to the New Mexico Territory. Three days into their journey, Franchard and his Rangers made a stop at the SD&P ranch.

Ditch had made good on his intent to acquire the vast BB&B spread, just north of his own ranch, formerly belonging to the late Winston Boone and his now-deceased sons. Ditch and Paul Clemson used the additional grazing land to support several thousand more head of cattle and more than fifty breeding horses. They had also taken on a staff of ten hands, in addition to Foreman Alejandro Ruiz, as well as a full-time cook.

"Been a while," Ditch said as he shook Pritchard's, and then Captain Franchard's, hands.

"Nigh on three years," Pritchard agreed.

Ditch examined his friend. "With that long hair and beard, you look like Goliath stepped right out of the pages of the Bible," he chuckled. "You tryin' to tempt the Comanche into takin' your scalp?"

"If I'm Goliath," Pritchard unleashed one of his rare smiles, "who does that make you?"

"Just because I'm smaller than you," Ditch laughed, "and my name's David?"

Ditch ordered his cook to slaughter a cow, and the Rangers had beefsteak and beer for supper. At dusk, Paul and Ruiz, who'd been out checking stock with their men all day, rode in.

Ruiz shook Franchard's hand, but hugged Pritchard. "It is good to see you, Señor Joe," he said, "even if you do look like a big, yellow, bear."

During the evening meal, Ditch announced that when spring weather was fully set in, in another month or two, he, Paul, Ruiz, and the hands of the SD&P Ranch were going to drive their herd up north, to Kansas.

Texas had an overabundance of cattle, Ditch explained. The going price in San Antonio was currently around one dollar and fifty cents per head. But in Abilene, Kansas, five hundred miles north, where the railroads could launch beef eastward, a fair-sized steer sold for as much as twenty-four dollars.

Ditch planned to take the entire SD&P outfit, along with a herd of over three thousand Texas longhorns, to the railhead in Abilene. He knew in addition to ornery cattle, they'd face harsh weather, warring Indians, bandits, rustlers, ticks, disease, and many other dangers during the drive. He figured they could make close to fifteen miles a day and still keep meat on the cows. That would put as much as seventy-five thousand dollars in their pockets in less than two months' time.

Ditch finished the discussion by once again offering Pritchard the opportunity to rejoin the SD&P Ranch and accompany the outfit on their cattle drive.

"I'd surely like to," Pritchard admitted, "but I can't. Not now, anyway. I'm committed." He nodded to Franchard. The Ranger captain divulged his unit's destination and mission.

"You're goin' into the New Mexico Territory after Dalton Stiles and his boys?" Ditch said. "That ain't just loco," he shook his head, "it's suicide. Iffen Stiles and his gang don't get you, the Apache will. You boys lookin' to get shot, or scalped?"

"You've heard of Stiles and his gang?" Franchard asked.

"Who ain't?" Ditch said. "Everywhere Stiles goes, that madman brings nothin' but mayhem and murder. The damned fool never figured out the war is over. He kills for the plumb joy of killin'."

"That's why he's got to be stopped," Pritchard said.

"He may be a damned fool," Franchard said, "but Major Dalton Stiles is no idiot. So far, he's stayed out of Texas. He's limited his murder and mayhem, as you called it, to the New Mexico and Arizona territories. That ain't no coincidence."

"You can't blame him for that," Ruiz said. "He does not want the Texas Rangers to come after him."

"He's got 'em on his trail now," Captain Franchard said.

Chapter 39

Pritchard ducked his head as he rode through the gritty, red New Mexico dust. The stampede string on his hat was tightly cinched around his chin, and his neckerchief covered his face below his eyes. He was on the easiest trail he'd ever followed, and the hardest one he'd ever ridden. All he and his fellow Texas Rangers had to do to track the Stiles Gang was go from town to town in the New Mexico Territory and meet widows.

After a night's rest and a good breakfast, Pritchard, Captain Franchard, and the Texas Rangers bid Ditch, Paul, Ruiz, and the SD&P Ranch good-bye and continued their trek westward.

Three weeks, two minor skirmishes with Apache war parties, and a freak blizzard later, they found themselves in El Paso. They rested their horses, refitted with ammunition and supplies, and added six Rangers from the El Paso detachment to their unit. Two days later, twenty-four Texas Rangers rode into Las Cruces, in the New Mexico Territory.

The memory of what the Stiles Gang had done almost three years before was still fresh in the townspeople's collective memory. Las Cruces was a small town, and people came out when they saw the string of riders coming down the main street. When they noticed the cinco-peso stars pinned on the Rangers' chests, and learned of their mission, they didn't hide their indifference. After a few glances, most returned indoors.

The mayor, whose brother-in-law was one of the townsmen killed by Stiles and his gang during the bank robbery, remained in the street to greet them.

"Not the friendliest town I ever saw," a Ranger commented.

"We saw you riding in from a distance," the mayor explained. "We was hopin', when somebody finally came around to bring justice, it would be the army. Folks around here don't think twenty-four Rangers is gonna make a dent in Stiles's Gang."

"That's comforting," another Ranger said.

"Don't be too hard on 'em," the mayor said. "A lot of the womenfolk watched their husbands gunned in front of them. Some of them had to bear children sired by the men who did it. That'll leave a mark on a town."

"I reckon it would," Captain Franchard said.

The mayor recognized Pritchard. "You're Smokin' Joe Atherton, ain't you?" he asked, as Pritchard dismounted.

"I'm Atherton," he acknowledged.

"I read about you," the mayor said. "The paper said you're the deadliest gun in Texas. Faster, even, than Bill Hickok."

"Don't believe everything you read," Pritchard said.

"It'll be reassuring for my wife to know the best gun in Texas is going after Dalton Stiles and the murderin' gang of cutthroats who killed her brother. He was a deputy here in town."

"We'll be stayin' the night," Franchard said, "and pullin' out, come morning. We'll need our horses boarded and some grub. I can pay in Texas gold."

"We'll accommodate you," the mayor said.

"I'd also like to have a word with anyone who eyeballed, firsthand, the robbery here a few years back."

"Everybody in town witnessed what happened," the mayor said. "I reckon not many are going to want to talk about it. I'll talk to ya. Saw the whole shootin' match, from right over there in front of the post office."

"Tell me about Stiles," Franchard said. "Whatever you can remember."

"He's a husky man," the mayor began, "of medium height. In his late forties, I'd guess. Has red hair and muttonchop whiskers. He wears one of those widebrimmed, Johnny Reb hats with a feather in it. Rides a big, black horse, too. You can tell he's the one in charge; ain't no doubt about it. Meaner'n hell. Didn't bat an eye when he ordered his men to shoot the sheriff and deputies, my brother-in-law included, after they'd already surrendered."

"What can you tell me about his men?"

"Not much to tell," the mayor said. "There was about forty riders, maybe fifty. All white men. Murderin' saddle trash, they were. Armed to the teeth, every one of 'em. They laughed as they shot our menfolk down. Shot two of our women, too; those who refused to let themselves be soiled during what came . . . after the killin'."

"You don't remember anything special, or unusual, that stood out in your mind about any of Stiles's men?" Franchard asked.

The mayor, a rotund man in his fifties, rubbed his chin. "Come to think of it," he said, "there was one of the gang who stood out. He was a tall, skinny fella with only one eye. Doesn't wear a patch over it, neither, like he's proud of it. Just a black hole and a big ole scar where his left eye should be. I kinda got the feeling he was the second-in-command."

"What made you believe that?" Franchard asked.

"When the rapin' began," the mayor lowered his voice, "he was next in line, right after Stiles. The others made way for him. If I remember right, the rest of the gang called him 'Rube.' That's right; I'm sure I heard someone call him Rube."

Pritchard's ears perked up. He recalled Jackson County Deputy Eli Gaines had an older brother named Reuben; a brother he claimed had run off to join Shelby's Missouri Iron Brigade. Major Dalton Stiles was reputed to have been in command of a detachment of that same brigade. The physical description, with the exception of the missing eye, certainly fit the Gaines family as Pritchard remembered them, and the loss of an eye was a common war injury. Could "Rube," of the Stiles Gang, be Reuben Gaines?

"Anything else you remember about Rube?" Pritchard spoke up, causing Franchard to raise his eyebrows.

"Yes," the mayor said, "now that you mention it. There was one thing about that cruel, skinny, bastard I remember."

"What's that?" Pritchard asked.

"He was fast on the draw. Faster than hell."

Chapter 40

Five cold, dusty days later, Captain Tom Franchard led his Rangers into the town of Magdalena. The first thing they noticed was the lack of menfolk.

They rode in midmorning, and saw plenty of people on the streets going about their daily routines. Only a handful were male, and of those, most were very young boys. The rest were a mixture of old men, both white and Apache, and were engaged in various menial chores.

The second thing the Rangers noticed was the women were armed. Those not wearing pistols had rifles within reach. When the Rangers rode in, the women looked up at them with suspicious expressions. Some appeared fearful. All either put their hands on their holstered sidearms or picked up their long arms.

"Texas Rangers," Captain Franchard called out, raising a hand in greeting. "We come in peace." He halted the column in front of the general store, but gave no signal to dismount.

"What's your business here?" a woman stepped forward and demanded. She was a handsome brunette in

her early forties, with an excellent figure and an old
Colt Dragoon belted around her waist.

"We've come at the request of Governor Giddings,"
Franchard said, "to capture or kill the Stiles Gang."

The woman spat on the ground in front of Franchard's horse. "Little late for that, ain't you?"

"I reckon so," Franchard said. "May I dismount,
ma'am?"

She appraised Franchard and his men for long seconds before answering. "You may," she finally said.

"Captain Tom Franchard," he said, removing his
gloves and extending his hand. He still gave no signal
for the other Rangers to climb down from their saddles.

"My name's Margaret Chase," the woman said, ignoring Franchard's proffered hand. "Folks call me
Maggie. I'm the closest thing to a mayor we have right
now in Magdalena. My husband used to be the mayor,
but he and the rest of the town council are currently
holding court at the bottom of the mine."

"I understand," Franchard said.

"Do you?" Maggie said. "Do you understand it's
been four months since Dalton Stiles and his outfit
rode in and buried damned near every man in town in
that infernal mine? Four months since he took almost
every penny we had? Four months since he stole most of
our horses? Four months since his boys lined up our
women, who'd just watched their husbands, fathers,
sons, and brothers die, and defiled them in the town
square? Four months since we sent word to Fort Wingate
for help and got nothing but a telegram in return? Is
that what you understand, Captain Franchard?"

Franchard lowered his hand and removed his hat.
"I chose my words poorly," he said, "and I apologize.
There ain't no way anybody but those who've suffered

here can know what you folks have been through. I can't do nothin' about what's already happened. All I can do is give you my word as a Texan, a Ranger, and a man that I'll do everything in my power to see Stiles and his men catch a bullet, or swing from a rope, or die tryin'. And these Texas boys I'm a-ridin' with will be following me all the way."

"To hell," Pritchard said, "and then some." The other Rangers nodded their assent.

Maggie silently counted the Rangers. "There ain't nearly enough of you," she remarked, almost to herself. "Where'd you come from?"

"Fort Worth," Franchard said.

She put her hands on her hips and cocked her head. "You boys rode almost seven hundred miles just for the opportunity to get bawled out by me and killed by the Stiles Gang?"

"Yes, ma'am," Franchard said. "And glad to do it."

Maggie shook her head. "I suppose you're tired and hungry," she said. "Have 'em get off their horses and come into the saloon. We use the place for our town hall, now that there's no men to drink in it. I'll see about getting some coffee and grub going." She turned, headed for the saloon, and motioned for Franchard and his men to follow her.

Franchard signaled to his men, who dismounted. "Tell 'em to be on their best behavior," he discreetly addressed Sergeant Finley. "We may be going into a saloon, but there'll be no drinking or other foolishness. Pass the word; any wood needs choppin', water needs totin', or any other chores have to be done, we'll do 'em. Also, I want the men to clean themselves up. Shave and wash at the earliest opportunity. That's an order."

"But, Cap'n," the sergeant grumbled, "we're Rangers, not store clerks or saloonkeepers. We don't need to pretty ourselves up for a bunch of—"

"I wasn't askin', Sergeant Finley," Franchard cut him off. "I don't want my men looking anything like the men who committed murder and rape in this town. Do I make myself clear?"

"Yes, sir," the sergeant said.

The men secured their horses and went into the saloon. Franchard removed two heavy bags from his saddle and brought them in with him. Shortly after entering, women began filing in. Old women, young women, and teens soon filled the establishment. Coffee was poured, and a simple meal consisting of bowls of cornmeal hash and bread was served to the hungry Rangers.

The women eyed the Rangers as they ate. Many of the women were quite pretty. Pritchard noticed more than a few were pregnant.

"We're going to have a population explosion around here, come September," Maggie said, taking a seat at the table where Franchard sat with Pritchard. "Thanks to the Stiles Gang, we've got over twenty pregnant gals in town, and no doctor. But we do have Miss Bina. She's as good as any doctor, I'd wager, when it comes to birthing babies."

"Who's Miss Bina?" Franchard asked.

"She's our midwife. Bina's young, but she knows her business. Her mother was Apache, and her father was a white trapper. They were killed during a Comanchero raid when Bina was a little girl. She splits her time with us, in Magdalena, and with the Apache, in their lodges just north of here. Sort of exists between two worlds, I guess. Learned her trade from midwives in both.

Lucky for her, and us, she wasn't in town when Stiles and his outfit rode in. They kill half-breeds on sight."

"You wouldn't have any idea where Stiles and his crew might be now, would you?" Franchard said.

"All anybody knows," Maggie said, "is they fade into the Indian Nations after a job. They only come out to ply their wicked trade, like they did here in Magdalena last Christmas."

"Why the Nations? Ain't they afraid of the Apache?"

"Not Major Dalton Stiles," Maggie scoffed. "He's protected by superstition. The Apache, and every other tribe in the territories, believe Stiles is a cursed god and his men are demons. The Indians consider him very bad medicine. They steer clear of him and his gang."

"Why is that?"

"Because he and his men take the scalps of their own tribe. They rape and torture their own people. To the Apache, who might be viewed as savages by civilized white society, such behavior is considered barbaric and unholy."

"If you don't mind me sayin' so," Franchard said, "things look a bit lean around here."

"What did you expect?" Maggie said. "The mine's shut down, if you hadn't noticed on your way in. We have no money or livestock, and all we've been living on to get us through the winter is our stores of fruit and vegetable preserves, and what little grain we have left. We can't even leave. Even if we wanted to pack up and pull out of Magdalena, which we don't, we don't have any horses left that are fit to pull a wagon. How long do you think a couple of hundred women and children would survive, marching across the territory, on foot?"

"Not very long," he conceded.

"We'd have about the same chance as you and your Rangers," she said, "of finding Major Dalton Stiles in the Nations. Or of staying alive after you do."

"She's right," Pritchard said, keeping his voice low so no one but Franchard and Maggie could hear him. "Stiles and his men are experienced horseback guerrillas, and they know this territory much better than we do. Skilled as we are, Captain, we could spend twenty years wandering the Nations and never find 'em."

"Even if we did find 'em," Franchard said, "it would only be because Stiles wanted us to. And it would be at a place and time of his choosing. He'd cut us to pieces."

"When I saw only twenty-four of you ride in," Maggie said, "I knew you didn't have a prayer. He has more than fifty men, and each one is a merciless killer. You go after Major Dalton Stiles, Captain Franchard, you'll end up the same as my husband—dead and buried. I'm sorry to have to be the one to tell you, but you and your Rangers are outmatched and outgunned."

"Call me Tom," Franchard said to Maggie as he opened his saddlebags and revealed the stacks of gold coins inside. "And who said anything about going after Major Dalton Stiles?"

Chapter 41

Captain Franchard's plan was bold, clever, and simple. It was also the reason he'd been carrying over twenty thousand dollars in cash and gold, provided by the Republic of Texas and guaranteed by the governor of the New Mexico Territory.

The morning following their arrival in Magdalena, Franchard sent twenty-two Rangers, led by Sergeant Finley, on the two-day ride north into Albuquerque with a shopping list and a mission. There, they bought several dozen horses, over two hundred head of cattle, and four wagons, which they loaded with medical supplies, ammunition, two cases of dynamite, a large roll of barbed wire, and as much food and sundries as they could haul.

Finley and his men didn't wear their cinco-peso stars. They'd been given orders to drink a little and talk a lot in the Albuquerque saloons while on their shopping spree.

They spread rumors around the taverns that they were temporary hired hands who'd been employed by the widows of Magdalena, as they'd become known in the region, to fetch their horses, cows, and sundries. The Rangers bragged that the women weren't destitute, as they'd claimed, and had fooled Major Stiles and his gang of thieves during the Christmas robbery and massacre.

The undercover Rangers claimed the women had hidden the bulk of the town's bountiful silver stores, turning over just enough to make Stiles believe they'd gotten it all, and denied the outlaw guerrillas the mother lode. Their extravagant spending in Albuquerque, and the amount and quality of the merchandise they bought, provided all the proof needed to back up these undercover "hired hands" claims.

Less than a week later, Finley and his men were back in Magdalena, this time herding horses, cows, and four wagonloads of goods. As they rode into town through the center of the main street, the women came out to greet them, this time with smiles instead of scorn.

Captain Franchard and Pritchard spent their time while the other Rangers were away scouting the terrain surrounding Magdalena, conducting a detailed survey of the town's entrance and exit points, and examining every building, alley, and rooftop within the small mining community.

That night, at the saloon/meeting hall, instead of cornmeal hash and bread it was steak and beer for dinner.

"I must admit, Tom," Maggie said, sitting down with Franchard and Pritchard, "even if your plan doesn't work, it's mighty nice to have horses, beef, and a few sundries back in our cupboards again."

"The plan'll work, all right," he said. "If Dalton Stiles is half the guerrilla fighter he's reputed to be, he's got eyes and ears all over the territory. It'll get back to him, soon enough, that you women held out your silver on him."

"That'll get under his saddle," Pritchard said.

"It surely will," Franchard agreed.

"Then what?" Maggie asked. "He'll be furious. He and his gang will come roaring back into Magdalena with blood in their eyes."

"That's kinda the point," Franchard said.

"But you can't stay here and protect us forever. What if Stiles sends only half his men? Then what? After you Rangers leave, the rest will return."

"We're not going let that happen," Franchard reassured her. "We're gonna wipe that vermin out to the last man, Maggie. If Stiles don't send in all his boys, which I believe unlikely, since there's supposedly nothin' but undefended women here, we'll capture a couple of 'em. They'll tell us where the rest are, and we'll hunt 'em down and finish 'em off."

"What makes you think they'll tell you?" she asked.

"The cap'n can be very persuasive," Pritchard said, remembering how Franchard had once convinced a group of captive Comancheros to dig their own graves.

"I wouldn't have said this a week ago," Maggie said, smiling at Franchard, "but I trust you, Tom."

As ordered, the Rangers had cleaned up. All had shaved, including Pritchard, though many, like Franchard, kept their now well-trimmed mustaches. Pritchard had even allowed Maggie to cut his long blond hair while his fellow Rangers were off in Albuquerque.

While Maggie was giving Pritchard his haircut, in a chair in the barbershop, a number of women came to watch, point, and giggle as his Samson-length hair was clipped off. They stopped laughing and silently stared when the tall, broad-shouldered, blue-eyed, chisel-jawed, and now clean-shaven Ranger stepped out of the barber's chair to examine his face in the mirror.

While trimming his hair, Maggie couldn't help but notice the pronounced bullet scar, but said nothing. She wordlessly left enough on top to partly conceal the telltale mark when his hat was off.

"You're a right handsome fella," she smiled, brushing the hair remnants off his back and shoulders. "I must admit, though, you're a mite younger than I took you for without those whiskers."

"It's been a long time since I've seen my own face," Pritchard said, rubbing a hand across his bare jaw. "I forgot what I look like."

Maggie gestured with her thumb at the women gawking at him from outside the shop. "If you forget again, I reckon there's a few gals around here might want the opportunity to tell you, in private and up close."

She was pleased to see him blush, which she took as a sign of his youth and good character. "Tell me," she said, "do you have a gal back in Fort Worth? I've got a feeling there're some in town would like to know." She handed him his hat.

"No, ma'am," he said softly.

"I find that hard to believe," she said. "You are one of the finest-looking specimens of manhood I've ever seen. My late husband excepted, of course."

"I was engaged to be married, once," Pritchard said, staring at the hat in his large hands. "It was a few years ago. The wedding didn't go through."

"How did that fool girl ever let a catch like you get away from her?" Maggie asked with a playful grin.

"She's dead," Pritchard said. Maggie's grin vanished.

"I'm sorry," she said. "I didn't mean to—"

"It's all right," Pritchard cut her off. "You couldn't have known." He shook his head. "Don't know why I told you, just now. You're the first woman I've ever said anything about it to. I guess you sorta remind me of my ma. I apologize for burdening you. Thank you for the haircut."

Later that afternoon, while Maggie walked with Franchard around town, as they'd become accustomed to doing each day, she asked about Pritchard. He told her what little he knew of the young Ranger, what happened to Pritchard's fiancée, and to his surprise, even confessed his guilt at being the indirect cause of her death.

Pritchard, for his part, noticed a change in Captain Franchard since they'd arrived in Magdalena and met Maggie Chase. As he ate his steak at supper and drank his beer, he found himself strangely comforted by his mentor's clearly growing affection for Magdalena's unofficial leader. Tom Franchard was rapidly becoming Maggie Chase's man, and she his woman. He could tell because he'd witnessed such signs before, in his own whirlwind courtship with Caroline Biggs.

Pritchard knew Franchard as the toughest, and finest, man, other than his father and Ditch, he'd ever known. He also knew that of all the countless battles the hardened Ranger captain had fought during his extraordinary career as a Texas Ranger, the impending fight against Major Dalton Stiles and his gang would be his most personal, on account of Maggie Chase.

Pritchard remembered how Franchard had ditched his rank and risked not only his life, but his career and freedom, to help avenge Caroline's murder in Mexico.

He vowed to himself to ensure that Maggie and the rest of the women of Magdalena would suffer no more at the hands of a renegade Confederate guerrilla and outlaw named Dalton Stiles.

The saloon doors opened, and two women entered from the darkness outside. All the other women in the saloon stood up and greeted them warmly.

One of the women was a very old Apache, carrying a bundle. The other was much younger, and carrying a Henry rifle.

The younger woman was of mixed race and couldn't have been older than thirty years of age. Her dark brown hair was pulled into a single braid behind her head. She had mocha-colored skin and coal black eyes. She wore boots and riding breeches, but her blouse was an Apache weave, much like the one worn by the elder woman accompanying her. A revolver and knife were belted across her tiny waist, and another belt of ammunition hung diagonally across her full breasts. Despite the weapons and lack of feminine attire, the woman was extraordinarily beautiful.

While the elder woman began unpacking herbs and medicines from her bundle and distributing it among the townswomen, Maggie led the other newcomer to Franchard and Pritchard's table. Both men hastily stood up.

"May I present Miss Bina," Maggie said, introducing the two Rangers. "She is a true friend to the people of Magdalena."

"Then she's our friend, too," Captain Franchard said, shaking her hand.

"I have heard of you," Bina said, with only a slight accent, when shaking Pritchard's hand. "You are the one named Joe Atherton." When she saw the curious look on his face, she said, "Word travels fast in the Socorro Valley. The Apache call you 'Shadow Man.' I now see why."

"Joe is certainly tall enough to cast a long shadow," Franchard laughed.

"His height is not what the Apache speak of," Bina said.

"What brings you to town?" Maggie asked, as all four sat down. "Not that we ain't always glad to see you. But I've never seen you come after dark or bring your rifle indoors before. Is something wrong?"

"As I said," Bina went on, "word in these parts travels rapidly. I am told the major and his men are crossing El Malpais, the Badlands, as we speak. They are coming back to Magdalena, Maggie."

"That's only three days' ride," Maggie said. "It sounds like your plan worked, Tom."

"I reckon so," Franchard said. "Do you know how many?" he asked Bina.

"Fifty or more," she said. "They say it is the most riders Major Stiles has ever been seen with."

Franchard nodded to himself, stood up, put on his hat, and whistled.

All the Rangers, except the two on watch, one at the east end of town and one at the west, were dining in the saloon. Most of Magdalena's women were in the hall as well. Everyone quieted.

"Listen up, Rangers," Franchard began in his booming voice, though he was aware he was addressing both his troops and the townsfolk. "Sounds like the Stiles Gang took the bait. They're three days out, at most."

Some of the women glanced nervously at one

another. The Rangers sat silently, waiting for their captain to continue.

"We've fought a lot of battles together, men," Franchard went on. "We've taken on holdout renegades, warring Indians, Comancheros, and too many gangs of murderers, outlaws, and rustlers to remember. This battle is going to be different."

The room was silent as the veteran Ranger spoke. "We're facing a well-armed force of hardened ex-military men, all experienced guerrilla fighters, more'n twice our size. We already know they're seasoned killers, and they're being led by a bloodthirsty madman who's the worst killer of 'em all. They're coming back to Magdalena, not just to take the silver they believe they were denied, but to punish the town for holding out."

The nervousness in some of the women began giving way to fear. A few bit nails. Others put their faces in their hands. One began silently praying, Franchard noticed.

"Up till now," he said, "Major Stiles and his fearsome gang of outlaws have enjoyed pretty fair success back-shootin' unarmed bank clerks, killing idle train passengers, burying defenseless miners, and abusing unprotected women."

Franchard paused and scanned the faces riveted on his own. "Their luck's about to change," he said.

"When Major Dalton Stiles and his pack of cowards come ridin' back in, they ain't gonna be greeted by the same women they met during their last visit. They're gonna be welcomed by the finest, bravest, and most determined gals in all of the New Mexico Territory."

A grin spread slowly across Franchard's face. "And they're gonna be meetin' some Texans."

The saloon erupted in rebel yells, as more than twenty Rangers leaped to their feet with their hats and fists in the air.

"It's whiskey tonight," Franchard said when the roars died down, "and work tomorrow. You all know what the plan is, and what we have to do. We begin at dawn."

Chapter 42

When the sun rose over Magdalena the next morning, the Rangers assembled as ordered. Many of them were bleary-eyed, and as they emerged from the various cottages and homes in town they were escorted by smiling women. Up until the previous night, the Texans had been billeted in the livery and the saloon.

Last night, however, except for Pritchard and a couple of married Rangers, every Ranger found alternative lodgings. One of the Rangers who came out of a private domicile, a house that happened to belong to Maggie Chase, was Captain Tom Franchard. Both were grinning when they appeared.

The Rangers were fed a hearty breakfast and commenced their assigned tasks. Under Franchard's command, and Sergeant Finley's gruff supervision, they spent every moment of daylight during the next two days working as if their lives, and the lives of the people of Magdalena, depended on it.

Some Rangers dealt with the livestock. Others, handier with tools, strung barbed wire. Still others cleaned rifles, distributed ammunition, and prepared dynamite. Pritchard reconnoitered the rooftops of each building with his rifle, assessing cover and concealment, gauging distances, checking fields of view, and selecting optimum firing angles.

Rangers took turns standing watch outside the town limits. One stood a post at the east end, and one at the west end, of Magdalena's main street. It was expected Stiles and his men would arrive from the west, through the Badlands, across Magdalena Peak, but Franchard was taking no chances.

Miss Bina, along with several of the townswomen and her elderly Apache helper, spent their time making up the barbershop into a makeshift hospital. She told Franchard that Apache warriors were also standing watch, in the hills surrounding Magdalena. They were much farther out than his own men and would signal when the outlaws were sighted.

"It ain't that I'm not appreciative," Franchard told her after she informed him of the Apache lookouts, "but the Texas Rangers, myself included, and the Apache haven't always enjoyed the most cordial of relationships. As a matter of fact, I've nearly had my scalp lifted a time or two. You'll forgive me if I'm stingy with my trust."

"Do not fear, Captain," Bina said. "You are no longer in Texas. Here, these Apache do not wish to mix in the affairs of white men. But Major Stiles and his raiders, by their deeds, have defiled the Nations. The tribal elders believe the *ga'ans*, or mountain spirits, are displeased that the 'killers of their own tribe' roam Apache land. The Apache will not help you defeat them, for they also believe it is very bad medicine to interfere in another tribe's disputes. But they will watch and listen. When the major approaches, you will know."

"Tell 'em I'm obliged," Franchard said.

Many of the women were tasked with collecting every bucket, pail, tub, basin, and container that could hold water. Each was filled, and strategically placed in front of the buildings in town, in case of fire.

At dusk each day, the men assembled and ate a steak dinner in the saloon. Captain Franchard, Sergeant Finley, and Ranger Atherton usually arrived late, after inspecting the day's work.

"I'm right pleased with what you all have accomplished," Franchard addressed his Rangers and the townsfolk at dinner on the second day. "We're as prepared as we can be for what's comin'. All there is to do now is rest, and stand ready to fight. You all know your assigned posts."

"I want to talk to you about that," Maggie spoke up. "Your notion of putting all the women in the saloon to hide under their skirts doesn't sit too well with us. Most of us can shoot. Maybe not as good as your Rangers, but we're frontier folk, and we can all handle a gun. We can fight." All around her, women nodded and murmured their agreement.

"What do you suggest?" Franchard said.

"Put all the children, the elderly, and those who can't fight in the preserve cellar under the general store," Maggie said. "Have a few armed women with 'em, in case it goes to a last stand. The rest of us can be out with your men, fightin'."

"What if my men are overwhelmed?" Franchard said.

"If that happens, we'll all likely be dead anyway," Maggie said. "There ain't gonna be no surrender. Not this time. We all agreed; we'll not be raped again. It's them or us, Tom. Ain't no other way. And speakin' for myself, if we're gonna lose, I'd rather go down fightin', takin' as many of them as I can with me."

All the women moved to encircle Maggie, their hands on their guns. Their support of her position was unanimous.

"Very well," Franchard said, looking at Maggie with pride. "Any objections if the womenfolk fight alongside you, boys?"

"Hell, no!" the Rangers shouted.

"It's just as well," Pritchard said. "Stiles and his men won't be able to shoot as accurately from horseback; that's a fact. But when they're unhorsed and on the ground, it's a different story. Once afoot, they'll make for the cover of the buildings. Then it won't be one big battle, it'll become dozens of smaller skirmishes, all about town. The barbed wire we strung between the buildings should keep 'em in the open longer than they'd like. When they're out in the open, we've got the advantage. We can't let Stiles's boys get into a place and dug in. Having more guns on the ground, which means a higher volume of fire, would be mighty welcome."

"Then it's agreed," Franchard said. "Sergeant Finley, assign the women to posts and ensure they have weapons and ammunition."

"Yes, sir!"

After supper, having been forbidden to consume alcohol, the Rangers again paired up with their local paramours and drifted off to repose within private residences. Captain Franchard bid his men good night, ensured Sergeant Finley had the watch schedule in place, and then allowed Maggie to lead him away by the hand. The weight of what was to come the following morning was on the faces of every couple.

Pritchard thanked the womenfolk for the excellent

dinner, collected his hat, and left the saloon. He strolled through town to the livery, where he had been lodging, when a lone figure stepped out from the darkness to block his entrance. Both his hands instinctively grasped the walnut-stocked grips of the Remington revolvers belted around his waist.

"Good evening, Ranger Atherton," Bina said. His hands, and his posture, relaxed.

"Good evening, Miss Bina," Pritchard returned the greeting.

"I'm sorry to have startled you."

"No harm done," he said. "What brings you down to the stable?"

"You," she said as she stepped in to kiss him.

Chapter 43

Afterward, when they could catch their breath again, Bina and Pritchard lay naked on the blankets in the livery's loft. She had released her braid. Her long dark hair flowed over his stomach, while her cheek rested against his chest.

"That was unexpected," Pritchard said.

"The Apache do not believe in an afterlife," she said. "We live only for the day. I wanted you, today. Who knows? After Major Stiles comes tomorrow, today may be all we have."

"You're only half-Apache," Pritchard said. "Doesn't your other half contemplate what comes after your death?"

"If death finds me tomorrow," Bina said, "I will know then, will I not?"

"I reckon so. Speaking of your death," Pritchard went on, "why are you still here? You weren't in town when Major Stiles and his gang rode in before. You don't have to be in Magdalena now. You could leave, and they'd be none the wiser. Why not go someplace where you'll be safe?"

"I cannot," she said. "When I was a little girl, I had

a powerful vision. In this vision, I saw myself fighting in the sun alongside the Shadow Man. I did not understand the vision until I met you. Many others of my tribe saw you riding in with the Rangers. They saw the shadow, too. Now you know why I must stay and fight."

"I don't understand," a confused Pritchard said. Bina lifted her head, rested her chin on his chest, and looked into his eyes.

"You are the Shadow Man," she said. "You are cursed. Have you not felt it, circling over you like a vulture?"

"I don't know what you're talkin' about."

"The Shadow of Death," she said. "It looms above you. It feeds not on you, but on what you kill. The shadow also knows you are not who you say you are. It keeps your true spirit captive, to enslave you, so you will continue feeding it."

"That's plumb crazy," Pritchard said.

"Is it?" she asked. "Tell me," she said, "how many men have you killed?"

"I don't—"

"Far more, I suspect," she interrupted him, "than even Captain Franchard or your fellow Rangers know. You feed the shadow well. This is one of the reasons it has chosen you."

Pritchard wasn't sure what to make of what Bina said. She was older than him by a few years and obviously extremely intelligent, as well as breathtakingly beautiful. How could this mysterious woman, who lived between two worlds, know he was not Joe Atherton, but instead Samuel Pritchard? And how could she possibly guess how many men he had killed?"

"Assuming you're right," Pritchard said, "how do I get rid of this 'shadow' you say is bird-dogging me?"

"There is only one way to dispel the curse. You must

return to the place where the shadow befell you and conquer the demon who cursed you. Only then can the shadow be lifted and your spirit again walk free."

"What if I can't go back?" Pritchard said. "What if by going back, I would endanger those I love?"

"Do you not think the shadow knows you cannot return to the one place where it can be defeated?" Bina asked. "This is another of the reasons you were chosen."

Pritchard didn't know what to say. He held the magnificent woman in his arms and tried to absorb the significance of her words. Part of him presumed what she'd told him was superstitious nonsense. But another part, a part gnawing at the back of his mind, couldn't help but harbor the suspicion that what she'd said was true. Bina's statement about who he really was and the shadow that clung to him, in concert with the passion they had just shared, left him doubtful and confused.

Bina suddenly stood up and began to re-braid her hair. Pritchard thought her nude body, in the dim light of the New Mexico moon filtering through the stable's windows, was also a mystical vision.

"I must go," she said, as she finished dressing. "I still have much to do in the infirmary. Tomorrow you, and I, and your shadow will stand together in battle."

"Now that you've told me what my shadow means," Pritchard said, "I'm not sure I want it along."

"Your shadow is not always bad medicine," Bina said. "Tomorrow we will use it to protect the people of Magdalena, and vanquish an even greater evil spirit."

"If you say so," he said.

"Sleep now, Man-Who-Calls-Himself-Joe," she said.

She knelt and kissed him. "Rest, and ready your spirit for the coming fight."

Pritchard propped himself up on his elbows. "You didn't tell me how your vision ended."

She stood back up, smiled at him, and belted on her pistol.

"Good night, Ranger Joe," was all Bina said as she left the stable.

Chapter 44

It was midmorning when the Ranger who'd been assigned the western sentry post came riding into Magdalena at full gallop. He reported to Captain Franchard and Sergeant Finley that two Apache braves had materialized and informed him a column of fifty riders was coming down from the "Lady of the Mountain," or Magdalena Peak, as it was known to the townsfolk. Doubting them, the sentry waited until he could see the column, off in the distance, himself. He estimated they would arrive within the hour.

"Remember your assignments," Franchard called out to the grim-faced Rangers and anxious women as they slung ammunition belts and checked their weapons. "Watch your front sights. Squeeze your triggers, don't jerk 'em, and make every shot count. For this to work, each of you must do your job without fail. Don't fire until you get the signal, and good luck."

As the Rangers and women began to file off to their respective posts, Pritchard felt eyes upon him. He looked up and saw Bina staring at him from across the street. She was in the doorway of the barbershop. She smiled, touched her fingers to her lips, waved, and went inside.

Pritchard, Franchard, and Sergeant Finley went to their places. Forty-five minutes later, Major Dalton Stiles and fifty-one men on fifty-one horses came slowly riding into town in a column of twos.

Stiles, as advertised, wore his feathered rebel campaign hat. He stopped in the center of the street, in the middle of Magdalena. He halted his men with a raised arm and surveyed the silent town. Neither he nor any of his men had yet drawn their weapons.

"We're back," Stiles loudly called out, looking around at the closed doors and shuttered windows. "Not a very friendly welcome, I must say. I know you all can hear me. You might as well come out from your hidey-holes."

"I hear you," Maggie Chase said as she exited the general store. She stood on the wooden sidewalk, a basket looped over one arm.

"Good morning, ma'am," Major Stiles said. "It's a pleasure to see you again. I almost didn't recognize you with your clothes on." The men behind him snickered.

"What do you want?" Maggie said.

"I believe me and my boys are owed an apology," Stiles answered. "I came here today to get it."

"We owe you nothing," Maggie said.

"I'm afraid you're wrong," he countered. "We understand you've got some silver you didn't want to share with us the last time we visited. That wasn't very hospitable."

"You've taken enough from this town."

"We took some," Stiles said, scratching his beard. "But what we take from you today is gonna make what we took last time look like we was bringing candy and flowers. You and the rest of the bitches in this dirt-water town are gonna wish to hell you didn't make us come back."

"You're wrong about that," Maggie said, striking a match. "We invited you."

She lit the clipped fuse of the dynamite stick in her basket and hurled it at the column of horses. Sergeant Finley, a miner by trade before he pinned on a cinco-peso star, and highly skilled with explosives, cut the fuse to last only a few seconds.

The dynamite stick had barely landed at the foot of Stiles's horse when it blew. Maggie ducked back inside the store. Major Stiles, and the rider and horse next to him, were thrown violently off their mounts in the ensuing eruption.

The explosion was the signal the town of Magdalena had been waiting for.

At the same time that twenty more sticks of short-fuse dynamite were thrown from the rooftops of buildings on both sides of the street, a fusillade of gunfire, also from both sides of the street, was unleashed. Rifle shots from every window, doorway, and alley cut loose. An instant later, those who had thrown the dynamite from the roofs began firing their rifles as well. Bullets rained down on the Stiles Gang from each side, and above them. Outlaws and horses began falling right and left.

Over twenty thunderous explosions, in rapid succession, rocked the streets of Magdalena. Most of them went off within the column of riders. Horses and men, sometimes in pieces, were tossed in every direction. Many were killed outright. Others were horribly maimed as the powerful explosives did their work.

Some of the gang members, still able to remain on horseback, tried to flee the blasts and torrent of incoming bullets. They charged through a hail of gunfire in the direction they'd entered, toward the east. When they reached the end of the street they found four wagons blocking the road, and more rifle fire pouring at them from behind the barricade.

Those outlaws not gunned from their horses turned around and charged back the way they'd came, again through a gauntlet of gunfire. By the time they reached the end of town they'd entered, they found a large herd of cattle had been released and was blocking that exit as well. They were trapped, in the open, in Magdalena's main street.

Boxed in and with no way to get out, the remainder of Stiles's men had no choice but to reenter the town and try to ride through the alleys and passageways between buildings, as Pritchard had predicted they would, to make their escape.

The first rider to attempt it steered his terrified horse between the saloon and general store. The barbed wire strung between the buildings felled him and his horse instantly. Several other riders suffered similar fates as they failed to penetrate the spaces between the buildings due to the razor-sharp wire.

All remaining outlaws, those who hadn't been blown up or shot, were now on foot. They ran for their only option left: the sanctuary of the buildings themselves.

Pritchard had tossed his dynamite from the roof above the saloon, then shot as many of Stiles's men as he could with his Henry rifle before the dust cloud from too many detonations, and a fogbank of gun smoke, made accurate shots from distance impossible.

He raced down the stairs from the roof to engage the outlaws in close-quarters combat in the street.

When he reached the ground floor, Pritchard shot a raider twice with his rifle, from the hip, as he tried to enter the saloon. Maggie shot another outlaw entering behind that one with her Dragoon. Pritchard handed her his Henry and ammunition belt and headed out through the saloon doors with a revolver in each hand.

The street was filled with dust, gun smoke, and the sound of men and horses bawling in agony. Pritchard made his way through the carnage across the street.

A bloodied outlaw, trying to stagger to his feet from his knees, raised his pistol. Pritchard shot him in the forehead as he passed. He spotted another, aiming his revolver shakily at him from the ground. Pritchard quick-fired two rounds, one from each pistol, into the outlaw's neck and head.

When he reached the barbershop, Pritchard discovered the door kicked open. He rushed inside.

He found two outlaws, both wounded, holding Bina and her elderly Apache assistant hostage. They were using the women as shields, cowering behind them with their pistol barrels wedged against their captives' heads. Bina's revolver was on the floor at her feet.

"Drop them guns," the man holding Bina ordered Pritchard. He peered from around Bina's shoulder. Pritchard holstered his revolvers and slowly raised his hands. The outlaw had been shot at least once in the torso, and had a nasty barbed-wire gash across his face.

"Take it easy," Pritchard said calmly. "My guns are put away. What do you want?"

"I want a couple of horses," the man continued,

straining to get the words out. "Then me and my partner are going to ride out of town with these here squaws. Iffen you don't do what I say, and get us what we want, we'll plug both of 'em, right now."

"Some water, too," the other outlaw rasped. He appeared to have been gut-shot and could barely stand. Bina had evidently scored hits on both of them before being taken captive.

"Okay," Pritchard said. "I've got what you need."

"Where?" the first outlaw, the one holding Bina, said.

"Right here," Pritchard said as he drew both revolvers.

Pritchard's two .44 bullets, simultaneously fired, took each outlaw in the only portion of their faces they'd uncovered to speak from behind their hostages. Both were dead before they hit the floor.

The elder Apache woman released a torrent of profanity and kicked the outlaw lying dead at her feet. Bina walked over to Pritchard, kissed him, and said, "Thank you, Shadow Man."

Pritchard nodded and headed back out of the barbershop to continue the fight. He needn't have bothered.

The shooting had almost entirely stopped, and the huge dust-and-gun-smoke cloud was slowly dissipating. Rangers were walking among the dead, wounded, and dying men. The only firing left was the merciful dispatching of injured horses. Other Rangers rounded up wounded outlaws.

Captain Franchard stood in the street along with Sergeant Finley.

"Reload and stand ready," Franchard bellowed. Rangers automatically complied.

"Report?" he asked his sergeant.

"All accounted for," Finley said. "One Ranger dead, four wounded. One of the wounded Rangers, an El Paso boy, probably won't last the night. No casualties among the townsfolk, although a couple of women have minor wounds, mostly from glass and shrapnel. All of Major Stiles's men are either dead or wounded."

Franchard nodded. "Once a watch is set, I want our wounded treated first. All prisoners are to be searched, bound, no matter how badly hurt, and placed under guard. Once that's done, round up those loose cows, move the wagons, and get a detail to start hauling these dead horses out of town."

"Yes, sir," Finley said.

"Hello, Joe," Franchard said, as Pritchard approached and Finley went off to implement his captain's orders. "What do you think of our day's work?"

"I think it could have gone a lot worse," he said as he reloaded his revolvers. "Day ain't over, though. Hell, it ain't even noon yet."

Maggie joined them from the barbershop, where she'd been helping with the wounded. "I'm sorry about your men, Tom. Another one just died. Miss Bina did all she could."

"I'm sure she did," he said. "Don't fret too much. All Rangers know there could be a bullet waitin' at the end of every trail. That's just part of bein' a Ranger."

Chapter 45

By noon, the nine surviving members of the Stiles Gang, including Major Dalton Stiles himself, were tied up. They were either seated or lying down, depending on their wounds, on the wooden sidewalk in front of the saloon. The townspeople, Rangers, and Apache warriors assembled in the street before them.

Not long after the smoke cleared from the battle, thirty Apache braves rode into town. Leading them was a very old tribal elder. The Rangers immediately began to take up arms, but Miss Bina walked out and greeted the newcomers as if they were expected.

"Tell your men they have nothing to fear," Bina told Franchard.

Franchard ordered his men to stand down, but remain ready. The Apache dismounted, and the elder joined Bina with Franchard, Sergeant Finley, and Maggie.

"What do they want?" he asked Bina.

She made the introductions. "This is Mangas, our shaman and chief. He wants to bless the town, to dispel the evil spirits you have released here today. This is very important to them, Captain. Major Stiles and his men have defiled Apache land. A cleansing ritual must be conducted, which will ward off any other evil spirits that may try to inhabit their lands in the future. The ceremony will not take long, but you may want to have the people of the town go inside their homes. It may not be something they wish to witness."

"What, exactly, are the Apache going to do?" Franchard asked.

"As part of the ceremony they must scalp all of the outlaws, even those who are still alive. The bodies must then be burned while the religious ritual, which includes a sacred dance, is performed."

"Not exactly a Sunday church meetin'," Franchard said.

"What Stiles's men did here wasn't exactly Christian," Maggie said.

Franchard turned to her. "I've got no objections," he said. "It's up to you and your people, Maggie, how they want the prisoners to die, but die they will. One way is as good as the next, to me."

She turned and addressed the other women of Magdalena. "Anyone object if the men who invaded our home, murdered our menfolk, and raped us are scalped and burned?"

No one spoke up.

"There's your answer, Tom," Maggie said.

"Sounds like we just saved ourselves a burial detail," Sergeant Finley said.

"There's one more thing Chief Mangas asks of you," Bina said.

"What's that?" Franchard said.

"They want to know if they can have the dead horses.

The Apache waste nothing, Captain. They have use for the meat, skin, organs, and bones. Even the teeth."

"Tell 'em to help themselves, with our thanks," Franchard said. "My men will assist them in butchering the animals, and his braves are welcome to borrow our wagons, if they agree to return 'em, to haul the meat back to their people."

Bina translated Franchard's words. The chief nodded.

"If the chief doesn't mind, I have a favor to ask of him," Franchard said.

"What is it?"

"What do they do with the scalps?"

"Since they did not make the kills," Bina said, "they cannot keep the scalps. They only take them during the cleansing ritual. Typically, the scalps are burned in a separate fire, but only to dispose of them. Once removed, they are no longer a part of the ceremony. Why do you ask?"

"I have use for 'em," Franchard said.

Bina spoke in Apache to Mangas. He nodded again.

"The scalps are yours," she said.

The Apache warriors began collecting wood from the stockpiles at each building and assembling a large pyre in the middle of the town square. Franchard signaled to Sergeant Finley, and the Rangers began to help.

Major Stiles, his left leg, arm, and the left side of his face shredded by the dynamite blast that disintegrated his horse beneath him, sat with his surviving men and listened to the exchange between Franchard, Chief Mangas, and the women of Magdalena.

"Hold on," Stiles called out. "You can't give us

over to them redskin bastards. That ain't no way for a soldier to die. It ain't right."

"It's right as hell," Franchard said. "And you ain't a soldier, Stiles. You never were. You're a murderer, robber, rapist, outlaw, and coward who got whupped by a passel of widows and a handful of Texans."

"Did you boys really come all the way from Texas, just for us?" Stiles asked.

"We surely did," Franchard said.

"What the hell for? We never messed with Texas."

"A wise policy," Franchard said, "but it won't do you any good today." He started to walk away.

"Hey, Ranger," Stiles shouted, pain and desperation creeping into his voice. "You ain't really gonna let them savages take our scalps and burn us alive, are you?"

"That's the plan," Franchard said.

"You can't," Stiles said. "We're white men. It ain't Christian to let us die like that."

"After what you and your men did to us," Maggie said, "you're going to claim Christian mercy?"

"I wasn't talkin' to you, bitch," Stiles said.

"I've got one more favor to ask Chief Mangas," Franchard said to Bina.

"What's that?" she said.

"Can she," Franchard pointed to Maggie, "light the fire?"

Bina translated the question to the Apache elder and received another nod in return.

"Probably would have been better off for you, Major," Franchard said with a grin, "iffen you'd died outright, like most of your boys." Stiles lowered his head. "Once them Apache commence to workin' on you, I'm bettin' you're going to wish you'd never messed with New Mexico, neither."

"Please," one of the other wounded outlaws suddenly called out, "don't burn us alive? I've seen men burn. I'm beggin' you? Just shoot us or hang us. Please?"

One of the women stepped forward. "I recognize you," she said to him. She was a pretty young woman with light-colored hair. "I remember begging you not to rape me. This, on the same day you buried my pa and my husband, down in that mine. Did you show me any mercy when me or any of the other womenfolk begged?"

"Please?" he whimpered again.

She spat on him. "There's your mercy," she said.

"Don't beg for nuthin' from these whores and cowards," another captive outlaw said. He was a tall, skinny man in his late thirties, with a scar and a hole where his left eye should have been. He was uninjured, having only been knocked off his horse and rendered temporarily unconscious during one of the blasts.

"They have no choice but to let them redskins scalp and roast us," he went on, "because they ain't got the guts to do it themselves. Ain't a one of 'em got the balls to stand and face me, and they know it. So quit begging and don't give the bastards any satisfaction."

"You're Reuben Gaines," Pritchard said, "ain't you?"

Gaines looked up at Pritchard. "I am. Do I know you, Ranger?"

"I knew your little brother, Eli," Pritchard said, removing his hat. "He gave me this." He pointed to the scar on his forehead.

"Looks like he headshot you. Didn't do a very thorough job of it, apparently."

"He had me tied up, like you are now," Pritchard said. "Then he executed and buried me."

"Evidently," Gaines said, "given that you're still

standin' before me, I'd have to say my little brother
Elijah screwed up your burial, too. If I recall, he was
prone to lunkheaded behaviors. He is a Union man,
after all. So was most of my family, if you can believe it.
I was the black sheep, fightin' for the South. What's
Elijah doing now?"

"It's been nigh on ten years since I've been back,"
Pritchard said. "When he shot me, he was a Jackson
County deputy sheriff."

"That figures," Gaines said. "All of Burnell Shipley's
boys were Union men. Elijah was always long on pistol-
shootin', but short on brains."

"What about you?"

"The brains part is arguable," Gaines said, "but I'm
much better than Elijah ever was with a pistol."

"We'll see about that. Still think none of us are
willin' to face you?"

"Ain't a one of you, yourself included, has the sand
to take me on by himself."

"Untie him," Pritchard ordered. "Give him a pistol.
His own gun, if you can find it. I wouldn't want it said
I took undue advantage."

"Wait a minute," Maggie said. "He's trying to get
you to kill him, Joe. He's the coward. The fraidycat
doesn't want to suffer a scalping and die by fire. He
wants a quick death. Don't fall for it. No point risking
your life. He's already dead."

"Better take her advice," Gaines said, "and let the
redskins kill me. There ain't no risk about it; if you cut
me loose and give me a pistol, you'll end up facedown
in the street. That's a certifiable fact."

"Cut him loose," Pritchard repeated. Sergeant Finley
looked to Franchard. The Ranger captain looked at
Pritchard, then signaled for his men to comply.

One of the Rangers covered Gaines with his rifle, while another cut his bonds. A third went over to the large pile of weapons collected from Stiles's men after the fight.

"It's that Army Colt .44 with the bone handle," Gaines said, standing up and rubbing his wrists.

"Make sure it's loaded," Pritchard directed as a Ranger retrieved the weapon.

"One cartridge," Gaines said, "is all I'm gonna need."

Pritchard stepped back and allowed Gaines to be escorted ten paces away from him. All the other Rangers, women, and Apache retreated to the sidewalks on either side of the street.

Gaines was still wearing his holster and gun belt. The Ranger who'd fetched his Colt inserted the revolver into his holster and quickly moved off.

The two men faced each other. One was tall and thin, the other much taller, and broad.

"Blow his head off," Stiles yelled to Gaines. "Put one right between his eyes," another captive outlaw shouted.

Gaines was hunched in a crouch, his entire body tense, and held his right hand poised above the grip of his revolver. Pritchard stood relaxed, with his hands loosely at his sides.

"You sure look familiar," Gaines said. "Seems if I'd ever met someone as big as you, I'd remember, but I don't. You claim you know Elijah; are you from Missouri, too?"

"I am. A town called Atherton."

"That's my hometown." Gaines's only eye narrowed. "Your father didn't happen to own a sawmill there, did he?"

"He did," Pritchard said.

"Why, hell," Gaines said, "I remember you. You were just a runt when I left."

"Things change."

"They surely do," Gaines said, and went for his gun.

Faster than the eye could track, Pritchard drew his right-hand gun and fired. The .44 bullet tore straight through the elbow of Gaines's gun hand, just as the tip of his pistol's barrel cleared the top of the holster. Gaines uttered an involuntary yelp, and his revolver dropped to the ground from his now-useless hand.

Pritchard fired five more rounds in rapid succession, dancing Gaines's revolver down the street. He then drew his other revolver, left-handed, with similarly blinding speed, and skittered Gaines's Colt even farther with six more shots.

Everyone watching, including Rangers, townsfolk, captive outlaws, and Apache braves, stared at Pritchard, wide-eyed, in silence.

Gaines cradled his shattered arm as his gun ricocheted away. "Finish it," he croaked. "Kill me, you yellow bastard."

"Sorry," Pritchard said with a shrug. He held up his empty revolvers. "Can't help you, Rube. Out of bullets." He turned to Sergeant Finley. "Tie him back up and make sure you bandage his arm. We wouldn't want him to bleed out before the festivities tonight."

As Gaines was returned to the saloon porch, and his hands were rebound, Pritchard ejected the spent cases from his revolvers and reloaded them with fresh cartridges from the loops on his belt.

Franchard picked up Pritchard's hat and handed it to him.

"The first time I saw you shoot," Franchard said, "you gunned down three men after all of 'em had drawn on you first. At the time, I didn't think you could get any faster." He shook his head. "I'm here to tell you, I was wrong."

The Apache chief approached Bina, after she'd finished tending to Gaines's wound, and spoke to her in his native tongue. He pointed at Pritchard as he spoke.

After their brief conversation ended, Bina walked up to Pritchard.

"What did the old man say?" Pritchard asked her.

"He said the shadow over you is strong. He told me to tell you that if you don't break its curse soon, it will grow so strong it will consume you. Then you, and the shadow, will become one. When that happens, you will no longer have a spirit of your own. He said he and his warriors will pray for you tonight, at the ceremony."

"Tell him I'm grateful," Pritchard said. "What about you? Are you going to pray for me tonight, too?"

"No," she said. "I've got something more potent in my medicine bag."

"What's that?"

"I'm going to bed with you."

Chapter 46

The remainder of the day was spent doing communal work. One group of Rangers, Apache braves, and townswomen busied themselves building a large-enough stack of combustible material to consume over fifty bodies; more than forty of which were laid out in a row near the growing mound of fuel. Wood was collected from every pile in town, as well as old planks, fresh lumber, and heaps of straw. Before long, the unlit pyre was the size of a small house.

Another group was occupied with butchering twenty-one dead horses and the grim task of collecting the various parts of the Stiles Gang that had been blown off their owners during the initial blasts. The group loaded the fresh horse meat into the four wagons for the Apache, the human flesh was tossed on the woodpile, and the streets of Magdalena were cleaned up.

A third group slaughtered two cows, butchered them, dug a roasting pit, and prepared the food for supper.

The smallest group dug two single graves in the cemetery at the edge of town. These were for the repose of the two dead Rangers.

On Captain Franchard's orders, a couple of Rangers were tasked with cutting stakes, more than fifty of them, each approximately the length of an Apache spear.

Chief Mangas and two of his braves wearing the colors of apprentice shamans collected blood from each outlaw, whether dead or alive. The blood was obtained from the corpses of the deceased outlaws without protest, but the bound prisoners struggled and howled, cursing the Indians, while they were cut. They had to be restrained with the assistance of burly Rangers. Once the blood from every outlaw was gathered, Mangas poured it into one large bowl. He and his assistants chanted while mixing the blood into a concoction along with herbs from his medicine bag.

The eight surviving members of the Stiles Gang watched, in brooding silence, as the Rangers, braves, and women labored throughout the afternoon. There had originally been nine still alive at the end of the battle, but one of the outlaws expired from his wounds as the afternoon faded into evening.

"Lucky bastard," one of the prisoners remarked, as his fellow outlaw emitted his death rattle.

Just before dusk, the braves assembled in the square. All had stripped to the waist and were wearing paint on their chests and faces. Chief Mangas motioned to Bina.

"It is time," she announced. "Those who do not wish to view the ceremony must leave now. Go inside and do not watch. Those who wish to bear witness must come forward and be marked."

A number of women complied and went inside the buildings. The children had already been herded into the schoolhouse at the far end of town, earlier in the day, to spare them from observing the butchering of horses and collection of bodies.

Rangers and townsfolk, with Franchard and Maggie in the lead, lined up and filed past Chief Mangas. Dipping his fingers into the bowl of liquid concocted with the outlaw's blood, he streaked Apache symbols on the cheeks and foreheads of the men and women.

Bina and Pritchard were the last in line. When it was Pritchard's turn to stand before the chief, Mangas did not paint his face. He gestured for him to remove his hat and shirt.

Pritchard looked to Bina, who nodded her assurance. He removed his Stetson and bib-front shirt. The three bullet-hole scars in his deep, muscular, chest, and diagonal scar across the length of his back, matched the circular scar on his forehead.

Chief Mangas and his two shamans surrounded Pritchard and began to chant. As they chanted, they painted Apache symbols on his chest, back, and arms. The diminutive chief finished by reaching up to the towering Ranger's face. He drew symbols of the moon and stars on each cheek, and the sun on his forehead.

"What's this about?" Pritchard asked Bina.

"They are honoring your shadow, so as not to incur its wrath."

When Mangas finished he looked up to the sky. The last vestige of the sun dipped below the Lady on the Mountain, overlooking Magdalena. He again motioned to Bina.

"Maggie," she said. "It's time to light the fire."

Franchard lit a torch with a match and extended it to Maggie. She gave him a hug, accepted it, and slowly walked toward the gigantic mound.

"No!" one of Stiles's men yelled from the sidewalk, as Maggie ignited the pyre. "Don't do it! You can't burn us alive! Don't kill us like this! We're tied up! We're helpless!"

"Tell that to my husband," Maggie said, tossing the torch and stepping back. In minutes, the town square was aglow with the light from the massive, billowing pyre.

Some of the captive outlaws began to cry. Others began to curse in defiance. Still others simply stared, with vacant expressions, at the mountain of flames.

"Don't we at least get a last meal?" Reuben Gaines called out with a grin.

"You surely do," Franchard answered him. "Barbeque."

The Rangers and women receded as over thirty Apaches, Bina and her elderly assistant included, drew their knives and went to work on the outlaw corpses. They quickly and efficiently scalped the forty-three dead outlaws and tossed the scalps into a pile at Captain Franchard's feet.

Franchard motioned to his Rangers. They assisted the Apache braves in lifting and piling the bodies onto the fire. Once this was done, the Rangers and braves converged, breathing hard from exertion, on the prisoners.

Each prisoner was hog-tied, with their legs bound to their hands behind their backs, and dragged, shrieking and thrashing, to the edge of the now-sizzling inferno. The smell of cooking meat permeated the town. Eight Apache braves, with their bloody knives poised, took positions over the captive outlaws.

Women who had Ranger paramours went into their

men's arms. Maggie stepped into Franchard's. Bina, her knife sheathed but her hands bloody, embraced Pritchard. The other townswomen held one another.

"I'm begging you," Major Stiles said, looking up at Maggie and Franchard. "Please don't let these savages scalp and cook us. If there's a shred of decency left in your hearts, you'll put a bullet to our brains."

"Who's calling who a savage?" Maggie said. "The decency in our hearts you crave so badly, you yourself destroyed. Tell me, Major Stiles; if these Rangers weren't here when you rode in this morning, would you and your boys be showing decency to me now?"

Stiles hung his head and sobbed. Franchard held Maggie tighter, as tears fell from her eyes.

"You're going to burn in hell for what you did to Magdalena," Maggie said, "but not before you burn here on earth. And when you finally get to hell, it'll be without your hair. Good-bye, Major."

She waved to Bina, who spoke in Apache to Mangas.

Mangas raised and lowered his hand, and the Apache braves pounced. Major Dalton Stiles, and what was left of his infamous gang of outlaws, wailed like banshees as they were scalped.

Some of the women closed their eyes. A few also covered their ears.

"The Apache believe their cries salve the spirits of your dead menfolk," Bina declared from Pritchard's arms, over the roar of the fire. "Their spirits hear the screams and are appeased, knowing they have been avenged."

When the fresh scalps were added to the pile at Captain Franchard's feet, the Rangers assisted the Apache braves in hurling the hysterical, howling, and thrashing prisoners onto the fire. By then the pyre was a ravenous inferno, and they had to swing the blubbering outlaws from a distance, due to the intense heat.

As a Ranger and a brave lifted and heaved Major Stiles, his skull exposed, onto the fire, he continued to cry out in pain and fury.

"Witches!" he squealed. "You're a coven of witches!" His agonized cries soon joined the chorus of his men as he burned on the fire.

The piercing screams only got louder as the prisoners were roasted to death atop the dead bodies of their fellow outlaws. It took long minutes for the last, tortured screech to fade.

Chief Mangas began to sing, and he led his braves in a shuffling dance around the fire.

"Magdalena has been cleansed," Bina said to Maggie. "All that's left are the prayers of my people to appease the *ga'ans.* Your work is done."

"Not quite," Franchard said. He called for Sergeant Finley.

The Ranger sergeant released the woman he had been courting all week, an attractive and pregnant redhead, and reported to his captain.

"You know what to do," Franchard said. "Get it done."

"Yes, sir."

The Ranger sergeant, and a detail of ten Rangers carrying the long stakes they had prepared, divided the scalps into two piles. They collected them and the Rangers split up. One group went toward the east end of town, and one group toward the west.

"Where are they taking the scalps?" Maggie asked Franchard. "And why the stakes?"

"They're going to put each scalp on a stake," Franchard said, "and plant half of them at the east end of town, and the other half at the west end. The Romans did the same thing with the heads of their enemies. It sends a particular message to anyone who might come ridin' into Magdalena with bad intentions."

"I like it," Maggie said, pulling Franchard closer. She wiped her eyes and looked up at him.

"Do you think I'm a witch?" she asked.

"Hell, yes," Franchard said. "You put a spell on me."

Chapter 47

Pritchard led Rusty out of the livery while holding Bina's hand and tied the big Morgan to the rail in front of the saloon. It was midmorning in Magdalena, and the scent of burned wood and scorched flesh hung heavily over the town.

After the scalp-and-burn ritual the night before, the Apache declined to stay and dine with the Rangers and townsfolk. They silently hitched up the wagons filled with horseflesh, and rode off into the dark toward the Lady on the Mountain. Bina informed Maggie Chase the wagons would be returned before the next moon.

Everyone met in the saloon for supper. Many had little appetite in the wake of the day's extraordinary events, but the whiskey Franchard allowed his men was readily consumed. As the fire raged well into the night, Rangers and their women, along with everyone but the Rangers on watch, paired up and went off to bed.

At dawn, the Rangers and townsfolk found a smoldering pile of ash where the giant pyre had been the night before. The fire was so large, and had burned so hot, there was nothing left of Major Stiles and his gang but small bits of melted metal from their belts and spurs and fragments of powdered bone.

Captain Franchard assembled his men and spoke at the burial of the two Rangers who'd died fighting for the people of Magdalena. Everyone in town came out for the funeral.

Pritchard spent the night in the livery, in Bina's arms. They spoke little, slept even less, and together watched the first signs of the sun as it clawed its way over the horizon.

Pritchard was still covered in ceremonial Apache blood-paint, so he bathed in the livery trough. By the time he'd dressed, shaved, and saddled Rusty, Bina was already clothed.

"You must go now," she told him. It wasn't a question.

"I reckon so."

"Back to the place you were cursed?"

"Yeah," Pritchard said.

She nodded to herself. "This is a good thing."

"That remains to be seen," he said. "I don't want to leave you."

She put her arms around him. "I like you, Joe," she said, tracing a circle with a finger around the scar on his forehead, "but you must go. I am not for you, and this place is not for you. This we both know."

"You could come with me."

She smiled and shook her head. "I belong here. You do not."

"Is that how your vision ended?" he said. "With me ridin' off alone?"

Bina nodded. "You have many battles left to fight, Shadow Man, in many different places. The time we have shared is almost over. This is how I saw it, and how it must be."

It was Pritchard's turn to nod. "Have breakfast with me," he said, "before I go?"

"Of course."

They met Captain Franchard and Maggie Chase in the saloon. Both had already dined and were enjoying coffee. They motioned for Pritchard and Bina to join them.

"Hell of a yesterday," Franchard said, once they were all seated.

"I'd have to agree," Pritchard said. "Captain," he began, "there's something I have to tell you."

"I already know what it is," Franchard said, taking a sip of coffee. "You're quittin' the Rangers, right? Leavin' today?"

"I told you I'd think it over," Pritchard said, "and I have. I've got unfinished business up north." He unpinned his cinco-peso star and slid it across the table.

"So I heard," Franchard said. "Your conversation with Rube Gaines was very enlightening. Always wondered about that scar on your noggin. Now I know where you got it, and how you earned your last name."

"I figured Atherton was as good a name as any."

"Well," Franchard said, looking over at Maggie, "guess what? You ain't the only Ranger turning in his star. I'll be quittin' the Rangers, too."

Pritchard's eyebrows jumped.

"Don't look so surprised. I was gettin' tired of rangerin'. It took almost thirty years of fightin' battles out of a saddle to finally find a place and somebody worth fightin' for." He reached out and took Maggie's offered hand. "I believe I'll be stayin' in the New Mexico Territory. Gonna make this here town my home."

"I'm happy for you," Pritchard said. "If there was ever a couple of folks who deserved their bite at the apple, it's you two."

"Why don't you stay?" Maggie said. "Most of your Ranger friends are staying. They're going to make Magdalena their home, also."

"Is that true?" Pritchard asked.

"It is," Franchard confirmed. "Sergeant Finley is going to marry that ginger gal he's sweet on, and at least fifteen of the other Rangers have decided this is where they want to settle down. I think the women they're settling down with have something to do with it."

"I reckon so," Pritchard said.

"Finley was a miner," Franchard went on, "before he was a Ranger. He checked out the mine. He says the vein's still rich with silver. He told me it wouldn't take much to blast away the debris covering the entrance. We could dig those men out, bury 'em proper, and get the mine operatin'. Magdalena could have a future again. You're welcome to be part of it."

"I thank you for the offer," Pritchard said, "but I've got to be movin' on." He looked over at Bina, smiling at him, and gave her a smile in return. "It's about time I sorted things out between the feller I am and the feller I used to be. Not to mention, there're some folks got a reckoning comin'."

"I'll bet they do," Franchard said. He pushed the cinco-peso star back across the table.

"Keep it," he said. "At least for now. I'm keepin' mine, for a while, anyways. So are the others who're staying on here in Magdalena. They don't know back in Austin we vanquished Stiles and his gang so soon. Our superiors believe we'll be weeks, if not months, hunting them down throughout the territories. We ain't expected back in Texas until autumn, at the earliest. The boys a deserve a vacation from rangerin', although they've got a lot of work ahead of them puttin' this town back together."

"Why keep the star, if I'm leavin' you and your Ranger company?" Pritchard asked.

"Because it's a long way to Missouri," Franchard said. "Doors will be opened to a Texas Ranger that might be closed on a saddle tramp. Also, if you're settin' out to do what I think you're gonna do, you may need to be Smokin' Joe Atherton a while longer."

Pritchard pinned the star back on his shirt. "Didn't think of that," he said.

"You can resign, along with me and the rest of the boys, come autumn," Franchard said. "Might as well draw your Ranger pay until then. Also, I'm pretty sure you'll run into a few outlaws on your journey who might need your brand of Texas justice."

"I might," Pritchard agreed, "at that."

"What will you do?" asked Maggie.

"I reckon I'll try to catch up with Ditch and his outfit. It's almost May. He's probably on his way up to Kansas with his cows, and could use a hand."

Pritchard stood. Bina, Franchard, and Maggie walked him out of the saloon to his horse.

"I almost forgot," Pritchard said, reaching into his pocket. "Got a present for you, Captain."

"You can't call me *Captain* anymore," Franchard said. He put his arm around Maggie. "It's just *Tom* again."

Pritchard handed the ring he'd bought for Caroline to Franchard. "I figure you'll be able to make use of this."

"I can't accept this," Franchard said. "It cost you five hundred dollars. Besides, it was the ring you were gonna—"

"Those ghosts have been put to rest," Pritchard cut him off. "You helped me bury them. It would mean a lot to me, knowing you and Maggie found use for it."

Franchard accepted the ring. "I'm obliged," he said, showing it to Maggie. "It's beautiful," she told him.

"You can get word to me," Franchard told Pritchard, "at the telegraph office in Albuquerque. Me and some of the boys will be going there at least once a month for supplies. I won't notify Austin of your resignation until you tell me to."

"So long," Pritchard said, climbing into the saddle. "Tell Sergeant Finley and the boys it was an honor ridin' with 'em." He shook hands with Franchard. "You, too, Captain."

"It's Tom," Franchard corrected him.

"Good-bye," Maggie said. "Don't forget where we are."

"I won't," Pritchard said. He looked down at Bina, who was looking up at him.

"Am I ever going to see you again?" she asked.

"Unless you have another vision," Pritchard said, "that ain't for us to say."

Pritchard tipped his hat, pointed Rusty east, and rode out. At the edge of Magdalena he was met with two dozen staked scalps. He ignored them and headed for Kansas.

Part Four
Home

Chapter 48

Oklahoma Territory, July 1873

Ditch sat up with a start and instinctively grabbed for the Henry rifle lying next to him. There was a boot standing on it. He looked up from his bedroll at the men standing over him. Especially the one with the Smith & Wesson revolver pointed directly at his face.

In June, Ditch Clemson, his brother, Paul, Ramrod Alejandro Ruiz, and ten hired hands from the SD&P Ranch headed north from Texas for Abilene, Kansas, with over three thousand head of cattle.

Ditch's first cattle drive had been slower going than he anticipated. He'd hoped for an average of fifteen miles per day, and some days he made that distance. But due to stubborn cows, dust storms, flash rains, attacks by roving bands of Wichita and Cherokee, and difficulties finding adequate water, he usually had to settle for ten. If the herd made twelve miles between sunup and sundown, he felt satisfied.

They'd been on the trail six weeks, and by Ditch's estimation were only twenty miles south of the Kansas border, when he was awakened, not long after midnight, by the sounds of a scuffle in camp. When he awoke, he found Paul, Ruiz, and their cook disarmed and held at gunpoint by five hard-looking men wearing neckerchiefs across the lower portion of their faces. The interlopers were all big hombres, but one was especially big, almost a giant.

"You're Clemson, right?" the one holding the revolver to Ditch's head demanded. "The owner of this outfit?"

"One of them," Ditch said, slowly raising his hands. "What is this?"

"This is us, takin' your beef," the man said, "that's what it is. We surely do appreciate you herdin' 'em up all the way from Texas for us, but we'll take it from here. These cows are still goin' to Kansas, like you planned, but it ain't gonna be your outfit a-takin' 'em."

"What about the rest of my men?" Ditch asked.

"We ain't done nuthin' to 'em, yet," the rustler said. "Far as we know, they're still out ridin' guard over your herd. We're gonna wait right here in camp, until sunrise, when they all come in for breakfast. Then we'll take 'em as easy as we took you."

"You don't have to do this," Ditch said, "If it's money you want, you and your boys are welcome to join up. I could use the help. You can ride into Abilene with us. I'll feed you well, and I pay top wages."

"Hear that?" the ringleader chuckled over his shoulder. "He wants to hire us?" The others with him laughed.

"It's a fair offer," Ditch said.

"That's mighty generous," the leader said, "but I've got a better one. How about we put you and your whole outfit in the dirt? Then we take your herd the last two hundred miles to Abilene by ourselves, sell 'em off, and get rich while you feed the worms? How's that for a fair offer?" The other gunmen laughed again.

"I have an even better idea," the biggest gunman said from beneath his scarf. He held two revolvers loosely in his hands.

"What's that, Bob?" the leader asked.

"How about you and the others drop your guns?"

"Huh?"

"You heard me. Drop 'em."

"What's gotten into you?" the leader said. "Is this some kinda joke?"

"Nope. Drop those pistols, all of you. Won't tell you again."

The leader eyed the other three members of his crew. All were as confused as he was. He suddenly pivoted and brought his revolver from Ditch to the biggest member of his own gang. The other three outlaws followed suit.

The big outlaw fired both pistols twice. All four gunmen fell.

Ditch, Paul, Ruiz, and Knobby, the cook, all stared in bewilderment at the rustler who'd just shot his own gang in the middle of a robbery.

The big rustler pulled down his neckerchief, revealing his face.

"Howdy, Ditch," Pritchard said. "Nice to see you."

"Well, I'll be a son of a bitch," Ditch exclaimed. He stood up and shook Pritchard's hand while Paul and Ruiz checked the downed outlaws.

"What are you doing here?" Ditch asked. "And why the hell were you tryin' to rustle our cows?"

"Picked up your trail a couple of weeks back," Pritchard explained, as he reloaded and holstered his guns. "You don't leave a hard track to follow, with three thousand cows as traveling companions. Ran into these four jaspers a few days ago. They were skulking along, following your herd from a distance. I introduced myself and played like I was a disgruntled hand you'd let go for stealing whiskey from the chuckwagon. They let me join their gang, seein' as I supposedly had insider's knowledge of your outfit and them needing an extra hand to help drive the cows into Abilene once they were taken."

"These four boys are deader than Abe Lincoln," Paul announced. "Headshots, every one of 'em." He and Ruiz each shook Pritchard's hand, and Ditch introduced him to the cook.

"I see you haven't slowed down any," Ruiz said, gesturing to the four dead men, "since we last met."

"I try to stay sharp," Pritchard said.

"You decided to take my offer and join the outfit?" Ditch said.

"I did," Pritchard said. "If you'll still have me?"

"Hell," Ditch said, looking down at the four bodies at his feet, "I'd be a fool not to."

Chapter 49

Dovie threw open the door to the bedroom and stormed inside. There was a maid in the room, filling the water bowl and emptying the chamber pot. When she saw the furious expression on her mistress's face, she hastily made her exit.

Burnell Shipley lay propped up with pillows in bed. His gout and the weakness and tremors in his limbs had left him bedridden for months. His florid face, like most of his skin, was a mass of discolored sores. His eyes had become milky, and he squinted at the doorway.

"Dovie," he called out in his raspy voice, "it that you?"

"You know damned well it is," she said, slamming the door after the maid had gone. "We need to talk."

"What's bothering you now?" Burnell said. He reached for the bottle of brandy that was always stationed on the nightstand near his hand. Keeping the bottle filled was his servant's most important duty.

"Eli Gaines," she said. "That's what. He's not bothering me, he's bothering Idelle. He interrupted her at school today, in the middle of teaching her classes.

He barged into her classroom with another one of Sheriff Foster's thugs, that fat ape, Bernie Moss."

"Your daughter's a pretty girl," Burnell said. "It's natural she draws suitors."

"That filthy deputy is not a suitor," Dovie said. "He's a deranged pig. He'd been drinking, spit tobacco on the schoolhouse floor, and drew his gun and twirled it around in front of the children. Then he announced she was going to marry him, and drunkenly insisted she leave her class immediately to go riding with him. She refused, of course. They eventually left, but only after both of the Nettleses came to her aid and demanded the deputies depart. Gaines actually threatened to shoot Rodney Nettles in front of the children. Idelle was so upset, she came directly down to the hotel to tell me."

"She must have been upset," Burnell said, attempting to pour his glass full to the brim, but sloshing it due to his shaking hands. "I know you forbid her to come to the hotel."

"What are you going to do about this?" Dovie demanded.

"Nothing," Burnell said. "And neither are you. Sheriff Foster's getting old. Doc Mauldin says he's got a bad heart. Eli is the chief deputy. When Foster quits, or dies, he'll take over as sheriff. Idelle could do worse in a husband."

"You can't be serious?" she said. "Gaines is a disgusting, toothless, animal."

"Perhaps," Burnell said, "but he's my animal. He's good at what he does, and I need a man with his unique capabilities. You remember what he did, last spring, when that buffalo skinner was causing trouble at the Sidewinder? Gaines handled that situation quite efficiently."

"He shot an unarmed drunk in the back," Dovie said.

"As I said, Deputy Gaines handled the situation quite efficiently."

"You approve of his marrying Idelle, don't you?"

"If it makes him happy, yes."

"What about Idelle's happiness?"

Burnell emptied his glass in one long slurp and wiped the residue from his cracked lips onto the back of his mottled hand. "Her happiness doesn't matter. Idelle has no more say in marrying Gaines than you had in marrying me."

"Idelle is not marrying Eli Gaines," Dovie said. "If he goes near her again, I'll kill him."

Burnell refilled his glass and laughed. "My first wife used to issue bold statements like that," he said. "Like you, she pretended to have control of her own destiny, too." He gulped more brandy. "Idelle will be marrying Eli Gaines. Get used to it. He's already asked me, and I've given my blessing."

"You're not her father," Dovie snapped. "It wasn't yours to give."

"Nonetheless, it is done. I suggest you convince your daughter to accept what's in her best interest, and yours. I'd hate to have to tell Eli you threatened to kill him. Threatening to kill a law officer is a criminal offense. A hanging, criminal offense."

"I see," Dovie said, suddenly changing her tone. "Then it's already decided? Idelle is to marry Chief Deputy Gaines?"

"She is. Pick a wedding date within the next month or so. There will be no more discussion about it."

"Then I must go to Kansas City for a few days," Dovie said. "I'll need to do some shopping. I'll obviously be taking Idelle with me."

"Anything you need to get, I can have delivered here."

"If Idelle is getting married, she can at least choose her own dress and have it fitted proper. You're not so selfish as to deny her that, are you? I'll not have my daughter wearing something delivered to your store in a box and unwrapped by Mr. Manning's dirty fingers."

"Very well," Burnell said. "Take the train to Kansas City. I'll expect you back within three days. If you're not back within that time, I'll have Gaines and his deputies hunt you both down and bring Idelle back. You, my dear wife, may or may not return to Atherton. I'll leave that up to him."

"We'll depart tomorrow," Dovie said, heading for the door. "Please have word sent to the train station to prepare for our departure."

"Have a nice trip," Burnell said, pouring himself another brandy.

Dovie headed downstairs, but had to stop between floors and steady herself on the railing. The abdominal cramps, blinding headaches, and joint pain she once suffered only occasionally had begun to plague her full-time within the past few weeks. The aching varied in intensity from severe discomfort to bouts of sharp agony, like the ones she was currently experiencing. She knew her condition was worsening steadily and hoped she could conceal the ravages of the disease consuming her, as it had devoured her husband, for a while longer. It was imperative Burnell not find out what she had planned; at least not yet. She only hoped her body wouldn't fail her and, more importantly, her daughter, Idelle.

The waves of pain subsided after a few moments, but left her weak and perspiring. Dovie continued down the stairs on faltering legs and found Idelle where she'd left her, crying alone in the lobby.

"Pack a bag," Dovie told her daughter. "We're leaving tomorrow for Jefferson City."

Chapter 50

Pritchard, Ditch, and Paul walked out of the Wells Fargo Bank together and into the bustling streets of Abilene. Once out, all three grinned and shook hands.

After burying the four rustlers Pritchard had escorted into their camp, the SD&P outfit confiscated their horses and continued the drive to Abilene. Two weeks later they rode in, herding over 3,100 head of cattle.

Their timing couldn't have been better. A number of the Great Plains tribes, including the Arapaho, Cheyenne, and Comanche, took great umbrage at the growing incursions by whites, particularly the cattlemen and the railroads, onto their traditional lands. Due to the infrequent Indian raids on the drovers that resulted, fewer cattle herds had entered Abilene's Great Western Stockyards that summer, and those that did had been significantly delayed. This meant more time on the range and less meat on the cows.

Consequently, beef prices had risen. Ditch sold his entire stock, on the first day they arrived, for just under twenty-five dollars per head. He paid off his hands, giving each a handsome bonus. Then he tasked

Alejandro Ruiz with collecting the flush SD&P cowboys, after a few days' celebration in town, of course, and herding them back to the ranch in Texas.

Ditch, Pritchard, and Paul deposited over seventy-three thousand dollars in the Wells Fargo Bank. They were looking for a café to dine in, to celebrate, when their attention was drawn to a commotion in the streets.

A large crowd had assembled around a wagon that was parked on Cedar Street, in front of the Alamo Saloon. A barker standing in the wagon was addressing an enraptured public. This, in itself, was not an unusual sight, except that this particular sales pitch was punctuated with gunshots.

The trio made their way through the throng of onlookers, which was unsurprisingly composed of mostly cowhands and cattlemen. They found two men at the wagon. The salesman, atop, was small, rotund, and wearing a bowler. He was displaying, for the crowd's admiration, a shiny black revolver.

The fellow with him, standing in the street, sported a wide-brimmed, black hat, had long hair and a sculpted beard, and wore a fancily embroidered suit along with equally fancy hand-carved boots. He also wore twin cross-draw holsters and was firing a pair of pistols at a deck of playing cards set up against a backdrop in the wagon.

". . . the best sidearm to ever grace the frontier," the salesman bellowed to his rapt audience as he held the revolver aloft, like a chalice in a religious ceremony.

"Stronger of frame," he continued, "more accurate, lighter of weight, better of balance, smoother of trigger, and chambered in the .44 caliber cartridge, Colt's new Single Action Army revolver has been adopted by none other than the United States Army! These extraordinary weapons, as you can see demonstrated in the capable hands of none other than famous Union war hero, Indian fighter, and pistoleer, Colonel Dexter Bennington, are the finest, most accurate, one-handed guns ever built!"

As the salesmen made his impassioned speech, Colonel Bennington slowly shot the playing cards, one at a time, from ten paces. He held the pistols at arm's length, with one eye closed, aiming carefully between shots.

"Look at that," Ditch whistled. "A gen-u-wine Yankee war hero and Indian fighter."

"Never heard of him," Pritchard said.

"I have," Paul said. "I heard tell that dandy spent the war in Washington, fightin' off senators' wives. The only Indians he ever shot were in front of a cigar store, and made out of wood."

"While these incredible guns will not be in full production and widely available to the general public for several more months," the peddler continued, "due to the army's demand for them, I happen to have a limited supply of these magnificent weapons right here in my wagon, direct from the Colt factory in Hartford, Connecticut. One of these unparalleled pistols, the finest in the world, can be yours for the meager sum of only twenty dollars. That's right, folks; for a twenty-dollar gold piece, you can get your very own Colt's revolver! For another five dollars, I'll throw in a holster and a box of cartridges to go with it!"

"Twenty dollars for a pistol?" Paul said.

"Must be quite a pistol," Pritchard said.

"Or that salesman is quite a thief," Ditch said.

"Actually," Pritchard said, "he's smart. Selling his guns in a cowtown like Abilene, in the summer, when all the hands are flush with cash, is a shrewd play. Betcha he wouldn't get twenty dollars for 'em in Kansas City in January."

"I reckon not," Ditch agreed.

"Hey," a well-dressed cattleman standing next to Pritchard suddenly exclaimed, "ain't you Joe Atherton?" He elbowed the men with him. "Look fellas, it's Smokin' Joe Atherton! He's a Texas boy, like us! I saw him down in Fort Worth a while back, after he and his Rangers rescued a bunch of kidnapped womenfolk from the Comanche!"

"Sure," another cowhand shouted. "Who could forget him? He's big as a barn!"

Before an astonished Pritchard could say anything, the fellow grabbed his hand and began pumping it.

"Boys!" yet another cowboy shouted to the crowd, "Over here! It's Smokin' Joe Atherton! Right here in Abilene!"

"You're a celebrity," Ditched laughed, as a swarm of cowboys closed in to shake Pritchard's hand.

Within seconds, the crowd had entirely shifted its attention from the sales presentation and marksmanship display they had been viewing to the six-and-a-half-foot-tall Texas Ranger.

The diminutive, and now frustrated, salesman, not about to let his pool of potential customers be lured away, gave a wink and a nod to Colonel Bennington.

The colonel, who had busied himself reloading his pair of Colt revolvers while the crowd flocked around Pritchard, holstered one of them and retrieved an unopened bottle of whiskey from inside the wagon. He tossed the bottle into the sky above where Pritchard was surrounded by admirers, and shot it out of the air.

Glass fragments and whiskey rained down on the

crowd. At the shot, everyone turned angrily back to face the colonel, who was now standing by the wagon with a smug expression on his face.

"Gentlemen," the salesman continued his pitch, "if you will return your attention to the revolver I hold here in my hand, you will notice—"

"You're a bit careless with your shootin'," a cattleman interrupted as he and a number of others, including Ditch, Pritchard, and Paul, removed their hats to shake off the whiskey and glass. "Not to mention, wasteful of good drinkin' stock."

"I shoot where I want," Bennington said, "and hit what I aim at." He glared at the cattlemen. "Do any of you have a problem with that?"

"Pretty bold," Ditch said, "shootin' playin' cards and whiskey bottles. Cards and bottles don't shoot back."

"Maybe you'd like to try shooting against me?"

Ditch opened his coat. "I ain't heeled," he said. "I ain't carryin' a pistol."

"Maybe you should, running your mouth the way you do," Bennington challenged. "Where're you from, boy?"

"That's none of your business," Ditch said. "And I ain't your boy."

"If you were," Bennington said. "I'd peel your britches and turn you over my knee. It doesn't matter where you claim to hail from. You look like Southern trash, to me. All you rebel scum look alike. Smell alike, too."

The crowd rumbled its disapproval. Most were Texans, and the vast majority had fought for the Confederacy.

The salesman noticed the crowd's displeasure and began to glance nervously about. Bennington merely smiled, relishing in taunting the Southerners, and the agitation he had stirred.

Ditch started to step forward, but Paul took his arm. "Let it go," he said. "That blue-bellied popinjay ain't worth your time."

"What did you call me?" Colonel Bennington demanded, his smile vanishing.

"I'm hungry," Paul said, ignoring the colonel's question and turning away. "Let's go get lunch."

"Don't turn your back on me, boy," Bennington said. He drew his other revolver and leveled both at Ditch's and Paul's backs.

"I wouldn't do that," Pritchard said, "if I were you."

"Are you going to stop me?" Bennington said.

The crowd on both sides of Pritchard quickly stepped back, clearing a space between him and the Yankee sharpshooter.

"Iffen you don't stop pointin' your pistols at my friends," Pritchard said flatly, "I'm gonna stop you cold."

"Do you think you can outshoot me?" the colonel grinned.

"I don't know how good I can shoot against cards and bottles," Pritchard admitted, "but I can sure as hell put you in a pine box."

"Is that so?" Bennington asked.

"Certain as sunset," Pritchard said.

Ditch noticed the shadow he'd seen so many times before beginning to descend over Pritchard's features. He knew what was coming next.

The salesman suddenly stepped between them, his hands in the air. "Please, gentlemen," he said, "this isn't necessary."

"Shut up," Bennington ordered the salesman. "It is necessary. I've been insulted. I insist on satisfaction."

"There ain't gonna be no duel at dawn on the moors," Pritchard said. "You're holdin' your pistols, Colonel, and mine are still wearin' leather. Put them guns away, or I'm going to end you. I ain't gonna tell you again."

"You'd best swallow your pride and do as he says," Ditch called out to Bennington. "You have no idea what you're facing."

"This dispute can be settled without blood," the salesman said, seizing upon an idea to both defuse the impending violence about to erupt, and return the crowd's attention to the revolvers he was trying to sell.

"How about a marksmanship contest?" the salesman addressed the crowd. "A test of skill between these two pistoleers? One, a venerated military officer of the North during the recent troubles, and the other, a legendary Texas Ranger and soldier of the South? The winner, as decided by you fair citizens, will get the satisfaction so important to his honor. And as an added prize, a brand-new Colt's revolver!"

The crowd roared their approval.

Bennington holstered his revolvers, utterly confident in his ability to defeat the Ranger. "I accept," he said. "Providing, of course, my opponent isn't too afraid to engage in a fair test of marksmanship?"

"Suits me," Pritchard said.

The salesman started to set up more playing cards, but the crowd booed. "I see you're a Remington man," he remarked to Pritchard. "You'll soon discover the superiority of the Colt revolver."

"It's the man," Pritchard said, "not the gun. And puttin' holes in bits of paper ain't no way to determine who's better with a shootin' iron."

"What do you suggest?" the salesman said.

"Have the colonel and me stand off ten paces, draw, and fire. Whoever's still standin' at the end of the contest, wins." He smiled at Bennington. "Providing, of course, my opponent isn't too afraid to engage in a fair test of marksmanship?"

If the crowd was enthusiastic before, they now went wild.

"Just remember," Bennington admonished the crowd, "it was his idea. Because after I shoot this very large Texan dead, I want to hear no remonstrations."

"I'm uncomfortable with this," the salesman said. "I don't want anyone to get hurt. Certainly not killed."

"You want to sell pistols, don't you?" Bennington asked. "Shut your mouth, put a bullet in that revolver, and fire it in the air. That'll be the signal for us to draw."

"That won't be necessary," Pritchard said. "I'm happy to let the colonel draw first."

Bennington laughed. "You can't be serious?"

Pritchard didn't answer him.

"Very well," Bennington said.

Pritchard paced off ten steps without turning his back on Colonel Bennington. The assembly, which had grown quite large, went silent.

The colonel smoothed his mustache and shook his wrists. He took in a deep breath, exhaled, and stared at Pritchard. Pritchard stood relaxed, with his hands loosely at his sides.

"Anytime you're ready," Pritchard said. Bennington immediately drew the pistol on his right hip.

Pritchard drew and fired, blazingly fast, and shot the colonel through his right wrist. He involuntarily gasped and dropped the revolver. The crowd cheered.

"That should settle it," Pritchard said.

"Not by a mile," an enraged Bennington snarled. He drew his other pistol.

Pritchard, in turn, drew his second gun, just as fast as he'd drawn the first. Another shot rang out, and Bennington dropped his second gun. Both of his wrists were now perforated and shattered. Ditch was relieved to see the shadow lift from Pritchard's face.

"I let you keep your honor today," Pritchard said to Bennington, "and your life. But somebody else will be feedin' you your soup tonight." The congregation howled with laughter.

The colonel stood holding his bloody wrists to his chest, bitter fury seething from every pore.

"I'll get you for this," Bennington hissed.

"I doubt that," Pritchard said. "I suspect it'll be a while before you terrorize any more decks of cards, or whiskey bottles, either."

"I declare Joe Atherton," the salesman said, raising Pritchard's arm and giving Colonel Bennington a disdainful look, "the winner!"

The assembly once again swarmed Pritchard. They patted him on the back, whooping, hollering, and firing their guns into the air.

The salesman made his way through the crowd. "Your prize," he said, handing over a brand-new Colt Single Action Army revolver. The weapon featured a custom five-and-a-half-inch barrel, which differed from the standard barrel length of seven and a half inches, and would at a later date go into regular production as the Artillery Model.

Pritchard hefted the weapon. "Has a good feel to it," he said. "I like the balance." He reached into his pocket and produced a double eagle. "I'll take another, of the same barrel size, if you please. I always carry a pair."

As soon as Pritchard purchased another Colt, dozens of eager men lined up behind him. The delighted salesman sold out his entire wagonload of revolvers within minutes.

"You could make a lot of money," the salesman said to Pritchard, "if you were so inclined. I can use a man like you on the road. Especially now that the colonel's shooting days are over."

"Doing what?" Pritchard asked. "Shootin' cards? No, thanks. I don't shoot for sport."

Chapter 51

The elated mob of cowboys insisted on dragging Pritchard, Ditch, and Paul into the Alamo Saloon for celebratory drinks. That a Texas Ranger, Smokin' Joe Atherton, no less, had outshot and showed up a famous Yankee pistoleer who'd insulted the South, in Kansas, of all places, was too great a victory not to celebrate.

Pritchard and the Clemson brothers never did get to eat their lunch. They spent midday drinking beers and whiskey, none of which they bought, and reveling in the company of Texans. Neither Pritchard, Ditch, nor Paul had the heart to divulge that they weren't really Texans themselves, and hailed originally from Missouri.

They made their exit from the Alamo late in the afternoon. Pritchard made a stop at McInerney's Boot and Saddle Shop and got measured for a custom-fit, two-gun holster rig for his new Colt revolvers. After a much-needed steak-and-potatoes dinner, the trio found themselves back at their hotel. When they walked in, the clerk hailed Pritchard.

"Mr. Atherton," he called out as they entered the lobby. "There's a telegram for you."

Pritchard opened the envelope to discover the telegram was sent by Tom Franchard, from Albuquerque.

His former Ranger captain's telegram alerted Pritchard that if he needed cash, there was a thousand-dollar bounty on a wanted Texas prison escapee named Jack Saunders. Saunders was reputed to be in hiding out in Kansas City under an unknown alias.

Pritchard remembered Jack "Six-Card" Saunders well. He was a high-stakes gambler from El Paso who would find himself a big-money game and then deliberately lose to another player he'd specifically targeted. Through cheating, he'd ensure every other player in the game lost to the mark, as well. When the winner left the gambling establishment, his pockets stuffed with his winnings, Saunders, or one of his men, would be lying in wait to rob him. More often than not, the robbery resulted in the victim's death by gunshot wound to the back.

Franchard and Pritchard had arrested Saunders after he'd fled to San Antonio. He was tried, convicted, and sentenced to twenty years in Huntsville. He should have been hanged for murder, but due to lack of witnesses, the Republic of Texas was only able to pin the robberies on him.

"Looks like I'm going to Kansas City," Pritchard said, showing Ditch and Paul the telegram, "to make some easy money."

"You mind if we come along?" Paul asked.

"It's only a half a day's ride into Atherton from Kansas City," Ditch said, "or a couple of hours by train."

"It'd be good to go home," Paul said, "after all these years. What do you say, Samuel?"

"Way ahead of you," Pritchard said.

Chapter 52

Pritchard stepped off the train and took in Atherton. It had been almost ten years since he'd been run out of town.

He'd spent the last week in Kansas City, with Ditch and Paul, searching the saloons and gambling halls for Jack Saunders. They found him in a riverboat on the Missouri, slinging cards under the name John Barton. Since Saunders knew Pritchard's face, Ditch and Paul sidled up to him at the card table. They made sure their fat wallets, laden with cash, were visible.

They let themselves be cheated all night. Paul and the other four gamblers at the table consistently lost, but Ditch couldn't seem to lose. He alone raked in the pot from hand after hand. By midnight, he was several thousand dollars richer.

Pretending to be drunk, Ditch bid the other gamblers good night and stumbled down the gangplank to the dock. John Barton, claiming to have been cleaned out by Ditch's extraordinary run of good luck, had already made his apologies and bowed out a few minutes prior to Ditch's departure.

When Ditch reached dry land, he found two men with pistols facing him. Though both wore their neckerchiefs over their noses and mouths, one of them was wearing a fancy, ruffled suit suspiciously similar to the one Barton wore during the card game.

"Give me your wallet," Barton demanded.

"Evening, Jack," Pritchard said, stepping from out of the shadows. "It's been a long time. Drop those guns, both of you."

The masked gunman with Saunders spun around and tried to bring his pistol to bear on the tall Ranger. Pritchard drew and fired three times, the shots coming out almost as one. The robber fell off the dock, into the river, and didn't surface.

Saunders instantly dropped his revolver and raised both hands. "Don't kill me, Joe," he begged, recognizing the giant lawman who'd arrested him once before.

"Why would I do that?" Pritchard said. "You're worth a lot of money to me. Dead or alive, of course. I'd rather have you walk under your own steam to jail, but for a thousand dollars I'm happy to drag you."

"Don't shoot," Saunders said, his voice trembling. "I'll walk."

"Figured you would," Pritchard said.

Paul showed up and recovered the two dropped revolvers. Ditch, Paul, and Pritchard marched a despondent Six-Card Saunders to the marshal's office.

"I like these new Colts," Pritchard remarked, as they walked through the streets of Kansas City. "They're fast out of the holster. Point well, too."

"Faster into action than your old Remingtons?" Ditch asked.

"I hate to admit it," Pritchard said, "but I'm afraid so."

"I didn't think you could get any faster," Paul said.

They turned in their prisoner, got a chit for a thousand dollars, and deposited it the next morning, along with the money Ditch "won" at the crooked card game, in the Kansas City office of Wells Fargo.

Then they bought three railroad tickets to Atherton.

Pritchard was largely silent for the short train ride from Kansas City to Atherton. He stared out the window with his hat in his lap, as memories and emotions he'd suppressed for a decade came flooding back.

"Feels kinda strange," Paul remarked, "comin' home, after all these years."

"I've been looking forward to this day," Ditch said, "and dreading it, for over ten years. What about you, Samuel? How do you feel?"

"It's not every day," Pritchard said, "a fellow gets to visit his own grave."

When the train pulled into the station, and other passengers attended to their luggage and began to disembark, Pritchard discreetly checked his revolvers.

"Relax," Paul said. "The war's over."

"Maybe for you," Pritchard said.

It was early afternoon when Pritchard, Ditch, and Paul stepped off the platform into Atherton, Missouri, with their horses in tow. All agreed the town had changed.

The once-tiny burg was now a bustling place, with a modern train station, several more hotels, saloons, and restaurants, and too many new buildings on the main street to count. Atherton was still a small town, but a vibrant one, and had clearly prospered during the postwar years.

The trio led their horses to the livery, in the same spot as the one they all remembered, but now much larger. They paid the attendant to board their horses and turned to one another.

"Well," said Paul, "here we are. Sure doesn't feel like home."

"Ten years is a long time," Ditch said.

"A lifetime," Pritchard said.

"What are you gonna do?" Paul asked Pritchard.

"I'm going to find Idelle and Ma, if they're still around," Pritchard said. "Then I'm going to pay a visit to Burnell Shipley and Eli Gaines. There's going to be blood. I won't take it personally if you boys would rather steer clear of me."

"I've stuck with you this far," Ditch said. "We've been through some bloody times, you and me. I think I'll stick with you today."

"Me, too," Paul said. "I'd like to find time to visit's Pa's grave, though."

"We will," Ditch said. "But we've got a score to settle first."

Several years back, just as the SD&P was beginning to prosper, Ditch sent a wire from Fort Worth to Atherton inquiring at the newspaper office about his father. He'd planned to send money for a stagecoach ticket to Texas and have him join them at the ranch. He and Paul were informed, via a return telegram, that their father had died during an influenza outbreak the previous winter and was buried in the town's cemetery.

"Be honored to have you along," Pritchard said, "but if you boys don't mind, I believe I'll remain Joe Atherton a while longer."

"I understand," Ditch said.

"Sure thing," Paul said.

Their first stop was Shipley's Mercantile and General Store. The sign was still the same, but the store itself, and the warehouse behind it, had been renovated and expanded since they'd left. They found Mr. Manning, who'd gone from old to ancient, behind the counter.

"Good afternoon," Ditch said. "We're looking for someone. We figured as the storekeeper, you'd probably know just about everyone in town. Her name is Idelle Pritchard."

"I know her, all right," Manning said. "What do you want with her?"

"That's our business," Pritchard said. "Where is she?"

"I don't much like your tone," Manning said, squinting up at Pritchard. "Nor your looks. Get out of my store and find somebody else to tell you where she is."

Pritchard grabbed the old clerk by the collar, and with one hand pulled him over the counter. The terrified shopkeeper found himself nose to nose with Pritchard, and his feet off the ground.

"Tell me where she is," Pritchard said, "or I'll tear this place down around your ears."

"Take it easy," Ditch said, looking nervously around at the other customers who were watching.

"She's a-at the s-schoolhouse," Manning stuttered. "She t-teaches school."

"Thank you, kindly," Pritchard said, smiling and tipping his hat. He released the old store clerk, who slunk to the ground on shaky legs, and walked out.

"Are you okay?" Ditch asked, as he and Paul struggled to keep up with Pritchard's determined stride.

"It's been ten years," Pritchard said over his shoulder, "since this town strung up my father, burned my home, stole my family's land and livelihood, tried to murder me, and did who-knows-what to my ma and

sister. I ain't gonna take any guff from anyone in
Atherton. Not today."

Ditch looked anxiously at Paul, who returned the
concerned look. The only consolation Ditch took in
Pritchard's darkening mood was that he had yet to see
the familiar shadow descend upon his friend's face.

They reached the schoolhouse just as the children
were being released from classes for the day. Pritchard,
Ditch, and Paul all recognized their former teachers,
Rodney and Alice Nettles, standing in the schoolyard.

Idelle spotted them as they approached.

At first, she was alarmed. Three men, all apparent
strangers, one very large, were approaching the school
at a fast walk. She watched them with apprehension as
they came closer.

Suddenly, recognition struck her. Idelle dropped
her book and ran into Pritchard's arms. He picked her
up and held her tightly as she let out ten years of
worry, grief, and fear.

"Samuel," she sobbed. "Oh, Samuel. You've come
home."

"I'm here, Idelle," he said. "And I ain't never gonna
leave you again."

She looked up at him with her crystal blue eyes,
brimming with tears. "Promise?"

"I swear it."

After a long minute, she stepped away from Pritchard's embrace, collected herself, and faced Ditch.

"Hello, Idelle," he said, his voice cracking. He could
hardly believe that the stunning young woman standing before him was the same little girl he'd last seen
behind the school's woodpile a decade ago.

"You came back, Ditch," she said, her eyes lighting
up, "just like you promised."

"I didn't forget," he said.

She couldn't resist, and gave him a fierce hug. She thought Ditch was even more handsome, with his dark hair and eyes, than she'd remembered in her dreams.

"You recollect my brother, Paul," he said, flustered and not knowing what else to say.

"Of course," Idelle said, finally detaching herself from Ditch and shaking Paul's hand. "It's good to see you again."

The Nettleses watched the reunion with hesitation. They recognized all three men, having taught them as children, and were uneasy about what their unannounced arrival, after so long an absence, foreboded.

"Where's Mama?" Pritchard asked.

Idelle looked down at her feet. "You know where she is."

"How could I know?" he protested, but knew Idelle was right. "I haven't been back home since the morning after Pa was killed."

"Mama lives at the Atherton Arms Hotel," she said.

"She's Shipley's wife, ain't she?" Pritchard said.

"You know she is," Idelle said. "It's the reason you're not dead."

Ditch watched the shadow creep over Pritchard again. "That ain't the reason," he said softly.

"I'm so glad you're here," Idelle said, oblivious to the silent fury overtaking her brother. "You couldn't have come at a better time. Things are bad. Mama's sick, and I'm supposed to be getting married."

"Married?" Ditch exclaimed. "To who?"

"Burnell is forcing me to marry Eli Gaines. We're supposed to be wed next month."

"Eli Gaines," Pritchard said under his breath.

"Mama doesn't know it yet," she said, "but I was

going to run away. I'm not going to marry that insect and spend my life at his whim."

"No," Pritchard said, "you're not."

"Hell, no," Ditch found himself blurting.

At that moment, three riders came loping into the schoolyard. All were wearing badges. Pritchard didn't recognize any of them.

"They're supposed to be lawmen," Idelle explained, "but they're nothing but Burnell Shipley's private army. The two smaller ones are town marshals. The big, fat, one with the beard is a county deputy. His name is Bernie Moss. He's usually with Gaines. Watch out, Samuel. They're mean, and not afraid to use their guns."

"Got a report of one of you boys roughing up a store clerk in town," one of the marshals said. "You're all under arrest. Turn over your guns."

"Nobody was roughed up," Ditch said. "It's all a misunderstanding. There's no need for an arrest. We'd be happy to go back to the store and apologize, even pay a reparation, if that'll smooth things over."

"The marshal didn't ask you for an explanation," Deputy Moss said, aware he had Idelle for an audience. "He gave you an order. Drop them guns."

"I ain't carrying one," Ditch said, opening his coat.

"Me, either," Paul said, doing the same.

"I am," Pritchard said, stepping away from Idelle, Ditch, and Paul.

"Who're you?"

"My name's Joe Atherton," Pritchard said, raising Idelle's eyebrows. "I'm a Texas Ranger. And I ain't turning my guns over to a bag of guts like you."

"Is that so?" the deputy said, sitting taller in the saddle.

"That's a fact," Pritchard said. "If you want my guns,

Deputy, you're more than welcome to come down off that horse and take 'em."

Moss wasn't prepared for resistance, having bullied the townsfolk for so long without any. He faced a dilemma. He couldn't very well back down in front of the marshals and Idelle, but the huge, muscular, man with the star on his chest and the brace of Colts on his hips didn't seem intimidated and had called his bluff.

This left him with only one option. Deputy Moss leaned over his draft horse, acted like he was merely spitting tobacco juice, and reached for the revolver in the cross-draw holster at his considerable belly.

Pritchard let the deputy get his gun out, far enough for everyone to see that he drew first, then drew his Colt and shot him between the eyes. His massive body fell to the ground with a loud *thud*.

The other two marshals froze, their eyes widened in fear. Idelle's mouth fell open. Both Nettleses gasped. Paul shook his head, and Ditch once again saw the shadow darken Pritchard's brow.

"Either of you want my guns?" Pritchard asked the marshals.

"You can keep 'em," a scared marshal said.

"Thank you," Pritchard said. "Where can I find Eli Gaines?"

"He's in Kansas City," the other marshal said, "with Sheriff Foster. He ain't due back until tomorrow, on the noon train."

"I'll be waitin' at the station," Pritchard said. "Now git. And take your friend with you."

"We can't," the first marshal said. "He's too big for us to lift."

"Then go get a wagon," Pritchard said, "and a few more of Burnell's hired guns. But you'd best tell 'em that if anyone else tries to arrest me, they're gonna end up like the ex-deputy here."

The two marshals rode off at a gallop as Pritchard reloaded and holstered his gun.

"That went well," Paul said, his voice dripping with sarcasm.

"Stand ready," Pritchard said, "because it's about to get worse. I came home to set things right, not have a friendly reunion."

"We'd best get back to the livery," Paul said to his brother, "and get our guns."

"Welcome home," Ditch said.

Chapter 53

Word of the shooting spread throughout Atherton like wildfire in a drought. There had been no shortage of gunplay in Atherton since the war, but it was almost always the marshals or deputies doing the shooting. Those getting shot were usually drunks, saddle tramps, or belligerent mill workers. No one had ever shot back at a deputy or town marshal because they couldn't; the lawmen rarely shot armed men. Certainly no deputy or marshal had been killed since the war. By the time Pritchard, Ditch, Paul, and Idelle walked back across town to the livery, people were staring and scurrying to get themselves off the streets. Doors were closed and windows shuttered.

"Those marshals ain't gonna wait for tomorrow at noon," Ditch said, as they collected guns and ammunition from their saddlebags. Pritchard refilled his empty pistol belt loops with .44 cartridges, while Ditch and Paul belted on their revolvers. Following Pritchard's lead, they'd each bought a new Colt revolver from the wagon vendor in Abilene.

"They surely won't," Paul agreed. "They'll send for

help from the county deputies. When they feel their numbers are sufficient, they'll come for us."

"How many marshals and deputies does Shipley have?" Pritchard asked Idelle.

"Five or six town marshals," Idelle said, "counting Marshal Stacy. Sheriff Foster's got at least ten deputies, but he and Chief Deputy Gaines are out of town."

All three took Henry rifles from their saddle scabbards and ensured the tubes were fully charged with fifteen rounds each. They finished by stuffing their pockets with cartridges.

"How do you want to play this?" Ditch asked Pritchard.

"I'm going to the Atherton Arms, to visit with Burnell and get Ma," he said.

"I'm going with you," Ditch said.

"Paul," Pritchard continued, "you and Idelle take our horses, get back to the schoolhouse, and wait for us. The schoolhouse is built solid and backs up against the woods. Hide the horses there. We shouldn't be too long. If we aren't back in an hour, you and Idelle ride to Kansas City and catch the first train out of Missouri."

"I don't want to go back to the schoolhouse," Idelle protested. "I want to go with you, Samuel."

"Not a chance," Ditch answered before Pritchard could. "I want you safe. Get back to the Nettleses' place, pack what you can't live without, and be ready to ride." She nodded.

Pritchard, Ditch, and Paul shook hands.

"You boys ready to be welcomed home by the town of Atherton?" Pritchard asked.

"Let's make 'em regret what they done to us," Ditch said.

To his surprise and hidden delight, Idelle, without warning, hugged Ditch again. "Be careful," she said. Then, to his utter amazement, she kissed him.

"Get going," Pritchard told her, shaking his head.

Pritchard and Ditch watched as Paul and Idelle mounted, took Rusty's reins, and rode out of the livery.

"You ready for this?" Ditch asked, as he cycled his Henry's lever and topped off the magazine.

"Ready as hell," Pritchard said, levering the action of his own rifle.

They walked out of the livery, toward the town square, with their rifles held across their chests. Despite the fact that it was approaching suppertime, and Atherton should have been bustling with activity, there wasn't a soul to be seen.

The Texas rancher and Texas Ranger scanned both sides of the street as they made their way towards the Atherton Arms Hotel. They felt the countless eyes of the townsfolk upon them, from within the buildings, and searched for those that might be watching from behind a gun.

Suddenly a marshal stepped from around a corner and leveled a rifle. In a flash, Pritchard shouldered his Henry and fired. The lawman fell dead on the sidewalk.

"Looks like they ain't even gonna try to arrest us," Ditch said.

"I wouldn't have it any other way," Pritchard said, levering his rifle.

Another hat and rifle popped up above the mercantile, two stories above them. Ditch fired, levered his carbine, and fired again. The deputy tumbled down to the street, his gun landing next to him.

As they approached the saloon, three men, two with rifles and one with a pistol, came out shooting. Another broke out a tavern window and began shooting from inside.

Pritchard and Ditch separated, taking cover behind a trough and rain barrel. The lawmen fired rapidly and recklessly. None of their rounds struck near either Pritchard or Ditch. Pritchard took careful aim and shot the gunman inside the tavern, through the window. By then, Ditch had already taken out two of the lawmen foolishly shooting from the open. Pritchard dropped the third with a headshot.

"These Atherton lawmen sure don't shoot very well," Ditch commented, as he and Pritchard reloaded.

"How good a shot do you need to be," Pritchard replied, "to shoot unarmed men in the back?"

They resumed their march to the hotel. They'd made another twenty yards when a deputy began shooting with a pistol from an open, upper, window at the Sidewinder Saloon. Both Pritchard and Ditch retuned fire. They were rewarded with a woman's scream from within the room. The lawman slumped forward, his body half in and half out of the window. His revolver clattered to the wooden sidewalk below.

They were met at the steps of the Atherton Arms by yet another town marshal, this one with a Smith & Wesson in each hand. Pritchard's shot hit him first, and Ditch's an instant later. They stepped over his body and entered the lobby. There was no one about inside.

"That's eight," Ditch said as they once again topped

off their rifles. "How many more marshals and deputies you reckon they've got left?"

"Can't be too many more in town," Pritchard said. "Those left are likely stationed upstairs to protect Shipley."

Pritchard handed his rifle to Ditch. "Stay here," he said, taking out his revolvers and inserting a sixth cartridge into each, "and watch our backs. A rifle's too cumbersome inside. I'm going up for Burnell."

"Take your time," Ditch said, accepting the second Henry, "but don't take forever."

Pritchard patted his friend's shoulder and headed upstairs with a Colt revolver in each hand.

A head peeked around the switchback on the second floor. Its owner took a potshot that flew well above Pritchard. He triggered each of his revolvers, and the deputy rolled down the stairs, past him, with two more holes in his face. Pritchard continued his ascent.

At the top floor, which Pritchard knew was the penthouse, he found two lawmen. One was a marshal, holding a shotgun, and the other a deputy, armed with a revolver. Both were in their late thirties or early forties, and looked nervous. Doubtless they'd heard the gunfire drawing closer. Pritchard surmised they were more experienced, given their ages, which was why they'd been assigned to defend the door to Shipley's apartment.

"Drop those guns," Pritchard called out from below them on the stairway, "and you can both walk out of here."

"You go to hell," the deputy said.

"Can't say I didn't give you a chance," Pritchard said. He holstered his left-hand gun, removed his hat, and tossed it above him into the air over the horizon of the stairs.

Both lawmen reflexively fired. The marshal released both barrels, with a resounding *boom*, and the deputy fan-fired his revolver as rapidly as he could, emptying all six shots in a matter of a few seconds.

Pritchard redrew his left-side gun and dashed up the stairs. He fired twice, once with each gun, striking the lawmen in their chests. He shot them both once again, on their way to the floor.

Pritchard holstered his revolvers one at a time, after ejecting the spent cartridge cases and reloading the weapons. He picked up his hat and examined it. None of their shots had even nicked it.

From his position along the wall beside it, Pritchard knocked on the door. "Burnell Shipley," he called out. "May I come in?"

"What do you want?" a muffled voice replied from within.

"I've come all the way from Texas," Pritchard said. "You might at least invite me in. It's the polite thing to do."

"Door's unlocked," the voice said.

Pritchard again holstered one of his guns and turned the knob. It was unlocked. As expected, three shots rang out, and three holes appeared in the center of the door. He pushed the door open, but remained outside.

"That wasn't very neighborly," Pritchard said, as he darted in.

Instead of stopping on the threshold, Pritchard continued to move, redrawing his second gun as he entered. He found Marshal Elton Stacy, older, grayer, and just as skittish as when he'd last seen him, ten years ago. He was standing in the center of the luxurious room, from where he'd fired the three shots into the door, with a smoking pistol. The old marshal got one more shot off, which landed well behind Pritchard, before the crooked lawman was gunned down.

The spacious room was otherwise empty. Keeping an eye on the hallway, Pritchard knelt next to the dying marshal and tipped his hat back with the barrel of one of his pistols.

"You?" Stacy gurgled, through a mouthful of blood, as recognition struck him.

"None other," Pritchard said as the marshal died. "Enjoy hell." He stood up.

"I know you're in there, Burnell," Pritchard announced to the hallway. "Marshal Stacy is dead. So are most of his men. I'm coming down to talk."

"You may as well," a familiar voice called back. "But know that I have a hostage. There's a woman in here with me. If you try anything, I'll shoot her."

"I'm putting away my guns," Pritchard said. "Here I come."

Chapter 54

Pritchard holstered his revolvers and walked down the hallway. He peeked quickly around the corner of the open bedroom door and saw Burnell Shipley sitting in a large bed. His mother, Dovie, was seated at the foot of the bed with her head hung and her hands folded in her lap. Shipley was holding a small, engraved revolver in his shaking hand. The weapon was cocked and pointed at her.

"Don't be afraid," Shipley said. "I won't shoot. Not you, anyway."

Pritchard entered the room and got his first full glimpse of Burnell Shipley in a decade. Shipley was morbidly obese and nearly bald. A few wispy strands of hair were stretched over a pate covered in oozing sores. His eyes were milky, and Pritchard suspected he could see only a few feet. Well enough, unfortunately, to hit Dovie at point-blank range with the gun in his hand.

"Allow me to introduce my wife, Dovie," Shipley said, motioning at her with his revolver. "She bought this fancy little pistol, allegedly as a gift, for me. In truth, I think she intended to shoot me with it. Her mistake was buying it through my store. The man who runs the place for me, Oliver Manning, told me all about it. Marshal Stacy, the man you killed in my parlor just now, found it hidden in her room."

"It's too bad she didn't get a chance to use it," Pritchard said.

Dovie stared at her long-gone son, wide-eyed, with her mouth agape. Pritchard put a finger to his lips and winked.

"My men tell me you're Smokin' Joe Atherton," Shipley went on. "I've heard of you. How could I not, with the same name as this town? Tell me, Joe; why is a famous Texas Ranger in Missouri, shooting all my men?"

"I came for you, Burnell," he said.

"That's ridiculous," Shipley said. "I've never even been to Texas."

"Neither had I," Pritchard said, "until you murdered my father, burned our home, stole our property, and forced my mother to marry you."

Dovie began to cry.

Shipley squinted up at Pritchard, trying to bring the big Ranger into focus. "I don't understand," he said.

"Of course you don't understand," Pritchard said. He removed his hat, revealing the scar. "You were told Deputy Gaines shot me in the head and buried me down by the river. My name isn't Joe Atherton, Burnell. It's Samuel Pritchard."

Realization hit Shipley like a shotgun blast. His face began to flush, and the tremor in his hand worsened.

"I married you," Dovie said, turning to face Shipley. Her tears had been replaced with rage. "Even though you killed my husband and took everything I had, I honored our agreement. I debased myself, all these years, to save my son's life. You lied to me. You tried to murder my boy. You kept me as a slave, pretending he was alive, but believing he was dead."

"That's right," Shipley said smugly, a smile spreading over his cracked lips, "I did all of that and more. If you're expecting an apology, you'll be disappointed."

Dovie suddenly lunged at Shipley, throwing herself on top of him and pummeling him with both fists. Before Pritchard could reach them from across the room, a shot rang out.

Dovie gasped, clutched her abdomen, and slid from the bed to the floor. Pritchard snatched the Cloverleaf revolver from Shipley's hand, at the same time striking a punch to the side of the bloated mayor's head that rendered him senseless.

Dovie lay on the floor, a red stain spreading across her stomach. "Samuel," she said, reaching up to him. Her own face was ashen. "Oh, Samuel."

"Mama," he said. He knelt beside her.

"Finish Burnell," she said, "and it's all Idelle's."

"Stay quiet, Mama," Pritchard said. "Don't talk. Save your strength."

"No!" she said, grabbing his arm. "I'm sick, Samuel. I was dying anyway. I've been infected by Burnell. This way is . . . better."

"No," Pritchard said.

"Yes," she contradicted him. "Hear what I have to say. I went to Jefferson City, to the capital, with Idelle. I made sure the papers were all in order."

"What are you talking about?"

"Burnell owns this town and everything in it. But

I'm his wife. If he dies before me, I inherit everything. When I pass, it all goes to Idelle. The hotels, the stock-yards, the mill, the railroad depot; the entire town. But he must die before I do. Get Dr. Mauldin. Hurry."

He ran out of the apartment to the stairwell and called down to Ditch. "Fetch Dr. Mauldin," he yelled. "Get him up here as fast as you can!" Ditch ran off, a rifle in each hand. Pritchard returned to his mother.

He picked her up, carried her into the parlor, and set her gently on a sofa. "Wait here," he told her. "I'll take care of Burnell."

"What are you going to do?"

"Rest," he said, ignoring her question. "Don't worry."

When Pritchard reentered the bedroom, he found Shipley dazed but conscious. He grabbed the pitcher from the nightstand and threw the water in his face.

A soaking Shipley blinked up at him. "Are you going to kill me now?"

"Sure as I'm standing here," Pritchard said.

"It doesn't matter," Shipley said. "Look at me; I'm already dead. I can't even get out of this bed. But you'd better know you'll be right behind me. Sheriff Foster, Eli Gaines, and a posse of deputies will see you die by nightfall."

"Not likely," Pritchard said. "The next train from Kansas City doesn't arrive before noon tomorrow."

"You're wrong," Shipley said. "As soon as my men reported what happened at the school, I had a telegram sent to the hotel where Foster and Gaines are staying. Kansas City is only twenty miles away from Atherton, or did you forget? They'll be here before dark."

Pritchard heard voices in the parlor. He returned to find Ditch and an out-of-breath Dr. Mauldin. He remembered Atherton's only physician from his youth.

"Samuel Pritchard?" Mauldin said incredulously. "Is that you?"

"Mama's been shot," Pritchard said, ignoring his query, "by Burnell." He led the doctor to Dovie, fading in and out on the sofa. The physician immediately began to examine her.

"I'm so sorry," Ditch said, looking down at Dovie.

"We've got more trouble," Pritchard told Ditch. "Burnell got a telegram off to Foster and Gaines. They're ridin' hard, with a posse, for Atherton as we speak. We've only three or four hours before they get here."

"We'll be ready."

Dr. Mauldin stood up and motioned for Pritchard to join him in the hallway.

"She's been shot through the liver. There's nothing I can do. She doesn't have long."

Ditch watched the shadow fall over Pritchard's features again. "Come with me," Pritchard told the doctor. "Stay with Mama a moment, will you?" he asked Ditch.

Pritchard and Dr. Mauldin entered the bedroom. "Hello, Dr. Mauldin," Burnell said. "Are you here to witness my murder?"

"What?" the confused doctor asked.

"Burnell is about to expire," Pritchard said. "You're going to witness it and sign the death certificate stating the exact time of death and that he died of a heart attack. Your report will indicate that he became deranged and murdered his wife, but perished of heart failure before she passed away."

"I most certainly will not," Dr. Mauldin said. "I will not be a party to murder."

Pritchard reached out, one-handed, and grabbed the doctor by the throat. He squeezed until Mauldin opened his mouth, then he drew a revolver with his other hand and stuck the barrel in, all the way to the back of his throat.

"I applaud the sudden arrival of your ethics," Pritchard said. "But tell me, Doctor, how many times have you signed death certificates stating, 'killed in self-defense' after one of Burnell's marshals or deputies gunned down an unarmed man? Or how many times have you listed 'natural causes' on the document after a hospitality girl at the Sidewinder bled out following one of your operations to relieve her of child?"

Dr. Mauldin's face was turning from red to blue. "If you don't do this, for my mother, you're of no use to me at all," Pritchard said. "I'll end you, right along with Shipley. My mother's dying, I've got a posse on the way, and I'm fresh out of time." He thumbed back the Colt's hammer with a loud *click.* "So are you. What's it going to be, Doc?"

Dr. Mauldin bobbed his head up and down, signaling his cooperation. Pritchard withdrew his revolver, lowered the hammer, and released him. The physician fell to all fours, gasping for air.

"I guess my time's up," Shipley said. "Go ahead and shoot, Ranger."

"Who said I was going to shoot you?" Pritchard said, reaching for a pillow.

Chapter 55

Dovie Pritchard died in her son's arms, a smile on her angelic face despite the pain. She expired shortly after Burnell Shipley's "heart attack."

Her dying words were to ask her son's forgiveness. The last time she'd seen him, when he was seventeen years old and leaving Atherton supposedly forever, he swore he'd never pardon her for what she'd done.

"Of course I forgive you, Mama," he said, brushing her hair from her face. "You ain't done anything to need forgiveness for. I love you."

Dr. Mauldin signed both death certificates, as Pritchard specified, and swore to testify to their veracity if ever required. Which was prudent, on his part, since a grieving Pritchard swore to hunt him down and make the sputtering agony of Burnell Shipley's death seem like a mercy killing if he didn't.

Pritchard sat for a while, cradling his mother's body. Dr. Mauldin left, promising to notify the local undertaker to care for her remains.

"We've got to go, Samuel," Ditch finally said. "It's getting on toward evening. We need to get back to

Paul and Idelle, and come up with a plan for when that posse arrives."

Pritchard nodded and gently released Dovie. He kissed her on the forehead and covered her with a sheet Ditch found in a closet.

Pritchard and Ditch checked their guns and left the hotel by the back stairs. While fairly certain they'd taken out all the deputies and marshals in town, they didn't want to risk gunfire from any holdouts. They selected a route they'd frequented as boys to navigate the woods. It took longer than going through town, but they soon reached their destination.

When they arrived behind the schoolyard they found Rusty, along with Paul and Ditch's horses, hidden in a copse of trees. There was no sign of activity at the schoolhouse. With their rifles at the ready, they left the cover of the forest and crept up to the school.

"Paul?" Ditch called out. "Idelle?" There was no answer.

They crept around the one-level building. When Pritchard and Ditch reached the front, they found the door wide open. They peered inside. Someone was lying on the schoolhouse floor.

"Paul!" Ditch cried out. They rushed in.

Paul Clemson was dead. He'd been shot several times. Empty cartridge cases lay about, but his revolver and rifle were gone. Ditch touched his brother's shoulder and lowered his head.

"They took Idelle," a voice said. Pritchard and Ditch looked up to find Alice Nettles, her eyes red from crying, standing in the doorway.

"Who did?" Pritchard asked.

"Sheriff Foster and Deputy Gaines," she said.

"They were here, along with men I've never seen in town before."

"That's not possible," Ditch said, wiping his eyes. "They couldn't have ridden all the way from Kansas City already."

"They didn't," she said. "I heard them talking. They bragged to Idelle about commandeering a locomotive in Kansas City and forcing the engineer to bring them here at gunpoint."

"That would explain it," Pritchard said. "Was Idelle hurt?"

"No," she said. "At least she wasn't when I last saw her. Paul put up a terrific fight. He shot three of them, but there were just too many."

"Where's your husband?"

"He's in the house, lying down. One of them pistol-whipped him, for no reason at all. He's groggy, but he'll be all right."

"Do you know where they went?" Ditch asked.

"They told me to tell you they'd be at the Sidewinder Saloon, if you wanted to get Idelle back."

"Do they know who I am?" Pritchard said.

"I don't think so," Alice Nettles said. "They know about Ditch, because Sheriff Foster and Deputy Gaines recognized Paul. They think you're a Texas Ranger named Joe Atherton. They're confused as to why you're here, along with the Clemson brothers, causing trouble."

"You'd best get back to your husband," Pritchard said. "Thank you for speaking with us."

"I'm sorry about Paul," she said, starting to cry again. "I remember he was a good boy."

Ditch handed his rifle to Pritchard. He took the elderly schoolteacher in his arms and comforted her.

"Paul was a good brother, too," he said, dropping a few tears himself.

Once they'd collected themselves, and Mrs. Nettles went home, Pritchard handed Ditch back his rifle.

"I have to get Idelle," Pritchard said.

"Wrong," Ditch said, his face hardening. "We have to get Idelle. After that, I'm gonna kill every one of those sons of bitches who had a hand in murdering Paul."

"Wrong yourself," Pritchard said. "We're gonna kill 'em. C'mon. Let's get the horses."

They returned to the stand of trees where their horses were concealed. "You ain't expecting us to ride to the Sidewinder?" Ditch asked. "We'd make pretty easy targets."

"Nope," Pritchard said, opening his saddlebags. "We ain't ridin' anywhere. I need to fetch something."

Ditch busied himself restocking his belt and pockets with .44 ammunition. Pritchard did the same. Both ensured their weapons were filled to capacity before taking a badly needed drink from their canteens.

Pritchard dug once more into Rusty's saddlebag and produced two sticks of dynamite, left over from the explosives used against the Stiles Gang. He cut two three-second, fuses, just like Sergeant Finley taught him, and inserted them into the cylinders. Then he handed them to Ditch.

"Got any matches?" he asked.

"Yep," Ditch said. "How do you want to play this?"

"You with a rifle, from a distance," Pritchard said, "and me with my pistols, close up. The signal will be when I drop my hat. Not when I take my hat off, mind you; when it falls. Make your shots count, Ditch. And if it comes down to a choice between shootin' to save me or Idelle, I want you to—"

"Save Idelle," Ditch interrupted. "Don't worry. I ain't gonna let 'em hurt her."

Pritchard extended his hand. "We've been down a lot of bloody trails together, Ditch. I want you to know, no matter what happens, a fella couldn't ask for a better partner to ride the river with."

"Let's go give 'em hell," Ditch said, shaking Pritchard's hand.

Chapter 56

Pritchard walked down the center of Atherton's main street. He halted between the Atherton Arms Hotel and the Sidewinder Saloon. It was the same place, almost ten years before, where he'd stopped with the bodies of two of his father's killers slung over their saddles. The sun had set. Streetlamps, and the interior lights of the saloon, provided the only illumination.

"Hello, Sheriff Foster," Pritchard called out.

The saloon's half doors swung open. Jackson County Sheriff Horace Foster, along with Chief Deputy Eli Gaines and five other men, stepped outside. Eli stood to the sheriff's right, and the others spread out evenly on either side of them. There was perhaps twenty-five feet of distance between Pritchard, in the middle of the street, and the men on the sidewalk in front of the Sidewinder.

Idelle Pritchard was also in view. She was being held by one of the men. The barrel of an Army Colt revolver, with the hammer back, was pressed against her side. She looked frightened and distraught, but unhurt. He wondered if she'd been told of their mother's death.

Pritchard was comforted to notice all the men, Foster and Gaines included, were armed with only pistols. No one carried a rifle or shotgun. Also encouraging, was that other than the gunman with his revolver on Idelle, none of the others had yet drawn their guns.

"If it ain't Smokin' Joe Atherton," Sheriff Foster said, "come to visit our little town."

Pritchard touched the brim of his hat in greeting.

"You killed a lot of my men," Foster said.

"Hell," Gaines said, "he killed all of 'em. Marshal Stacy and his men, too."

"You seem to have plenty of help," Pritchard said, pointing his chin at the men behind the sheriff and his chief deputy.

"These boys?" Foster said, gesturing with his thumb at the men surrounding him. "They ain't my regular deputies. I hired 'em in Kansas City today after I got Burnell's telegram."

"For your sakes," Pritchard said, "I hope they're reliable."

"We'll find out soon enough," Foster said. "I'm afraid I'm going to have to arrest you, Joe," he went on. "You shot the hell out of this town. You're gonna have to hang for that."

"One of your deputies tried to arrest me earlier today," Pritchard said. "It didn't turn out so well for him."

"This arrest," Foster said, "is going to be different. Because if you don't drop those guns and come along to jail peacefully, the young lady here, Miss Idelle Pritchard, is going to get herself shot."

"That's a mighty cowardly way to make an arrest," Pritchard said, "from behind a woman's petticoats."

"Maybe so," Foster said, "but that's how it is. Give up those guns or she takes a bullet."

"I think I'll keep my guns," Pritchard said. "Go ahead and shoot her."

Idelle's expression switched from fear to indignation. She glared at her brother. He ignored her.

"You really want us to shoot her?" Foster said.

"Help yourself," Pritchard said. "But you'll find your stranglehold on this town gone if you do."

"What are you talking about?"

"Burnell Shipley is dead. He died of a heart attack, shortly after shooting his wife." Pritchard watched the expression on Idelle's face. He could tell she already knew.

"We heard," Foster said. "Doc Mauldin told us. What's it to you?"

"Shipley died before his wife," Pritchard said. "That means she automatically inherited his estate, which is all of Atherton. When she died, that estate transferred to her only living heir, Miss Idelle Pritchard. It's all registered at the capital, in Jefferson City, nice and legal. If you idiots kill her, the state of Missouri inherits this town."

"The hell you say," Foster said.

Pritchard laughed. "I can hear the carpetbaggers now, climbing over themselves to catch the train to Atherton from Jefferson City. Your town, what was once Shipley's empire, will be run by bureaucrats one hundred and fifty miles away. Think you'll still be sheriff after that happens?"

Pritchard could see his words were having an effect on Sheriff Foster. Doubt had overtaken his features.

"Let the woman go," Pritchard said, "or I'll shoot her myself."

"Don't worry, Horace," Gaines said to Foster, also reading the reservation on the older man's face. "I'm going to marry Idelle, remember? Then everything will belong to me. We'll make out just fine."

This fact didn't quell Foster's misgivings. The idea of working for the upstart Gaines had little appeal for the aging lawman.

"It ain't legal to wed a corpse, Deputy Gaines," Pritchard said. "Let her go, or I'll plug her."

"How do you know my name?" Gaines demanded.

"I got acquainted with your brother Reuben," Pritchard said, "down in the New Mexico Territory, just before I killed him."

"You're lyin'," Gaines said.

"Am I?" Pritchard said.

"You seem awfully well informed," Foster said. "How does a Ranger from Texas know so much about the goings-on up here in Missouri?"

"I wasn't born in Texas," Pritchard said, slowly raising his left hand and removing his hat. "I was born and raised right here, in Atherton."

Sheriff Foster was confused. He didn't recognize Pritchard.

Gaines was not. He stepped forward and squinted at Pritchard. His jaw dropped. He couldn't believe his eyes.

"It can't be," Gaines said, astonishment and disbelief fighting for control of his composure. "I shot you myself! I watched you get put into the ground with my own two eyes!"

"When you kill a man," Pritchard said, "you'd best make sure he stays dead."

Pritchard dropped his hat.

Chapter 57

An instant later, an explosion went off in the street, fifty feet to the right of Pritchard. As everyone but Pritchard instinctively turned to see the blast, another detonation went off fifty feet to the left.

Pritchard wasted no time. He drew both revolvers and began firing as dirt and debris descended. He hit Sheriff Foster and two of the hired guns immediately. All three went down.

Pritchard was taking aim at the man holding his pistol on Idelle when a bullet from Ditch's Henry rifle took off the top of the gunman's head.

Bullets whizzed past Pritchard. One after another struck all around where Eli Gaines and the remaining two hired guns stood shooting at him. Eventually, one of the gunmen figured out he was being shot at from the roof of the Atherton Arms, across the street. He raised his gun to fire upward when another of the .44 bullets from Ditch's carbine took him through the throat.

Pritchard put two in the chest of the remaining gunman, as he felt a slap against his thigh. The sting was enough to spoil his aim, and the next shot he fired, at Chief Deputy Eli Gaines, missed by inches. He saw Gaines grab Idelle by the hair and drag her back into the Sidewinder.

Pritchard hobbled to the sidewalk in front of the hotel and took cover behind a post. He was reloading his guns when Ditch appeared, out of breath from running down the stairs.

"Nice timing with that dynamite," Pritchard told him, "and good shootin'."

"Not good enough," Ditch said, examining Pritchard's wounded leg. "Gaines is still breathin', and he's still got Idelle."

Pritchard covered the saloon's entrance with a Henry rifle while Ditch used their neckerchiefs to bandage his friend's leg. Pritchard sustained a deep grazing wound through the meat of his thigh, but the bullet didn't hit any major blood vessels. It would eventually need to be cauterized, but wouldn't take him out of the fight for now.

"Better get around to the rear of the Sidewinder," Pritchard said to Ditch, "before Gaines gets the notion to sneak out the back door with Idelle. Fire a shot to let me know you're in place." Ditch nodded and ran off with his rifle. Less than a minute later, a single shot was heard.

"Eli Gaines," Pritchard shouted at the saloon. "You're all alone and cornered. You've got guns facing you, front and back. Give it up and come on out."

"You go to hell, Samuel Pritchard!" Gaines hollered back from inside the saloon. "You try anything, and I'll plug your little sister. Your bluff about not giving a damn if she gets killed might have worked on old Horace, but it won't work on me. I know you care about her. She's the reason why you came back."

"You're wrong, Eli," Pritchard lied. "When she dies, I become the only living heir to Shipley's estate. All of Atherton becomes mine. That's the reason I came back. I'll tell you the same thing I told Sheriff Foster: go ahead and shoot her. You'd be doing me a favor."

"I don't believe you."

"Do you know how your brother died?" Pritchard asked.

"Suppose you tell me."

"He burned alive," Pritchard said, "howlin' and twitchin' like a frog on a skillet."

"Assuming you're tellin' the truth," Gaines said, "what do I care how he died?"

"Because you're going out the same way," Pritchard said. "You think I'm bluffin' about not caring whether Idelle dies? You won't when I set that saloon on fire."

This time, there was no response from Gaines.

Pritchard limped over to a hay wagon parked nearby and easily lifted out a bale of hay with one hand. He crossed the street and tossed the bale onto the sidewalk, directly in front of the saloon's half doors.

"Hold on a minute," Gaines said, an edge of fear in his voice. "Don't light that hay."

"You called me a liar, Eli. All I have to do is strike a match, and you'll find out who's tellin' the truth. If you still won't believe me, once that building starts to burn, you could always try for the back door and catch a bullet."

Long seconds of silence ensued. "I'm comin' out," Gaines finally said, "to talk. Hold your fire."

"Come on," Pritchard said.

Eli Gaines, walking behind Idelle with one of his revolvers in her back, came out of the saloon. They stepped around the bale of hay and stood on the wooden sidewalk before Pritchard.

Pritchard couldn't tell if it was fear or rage emanating from Idelle's features. Whatever it was, it was visible from across the street.

"I'll make you a deal," Gaines said. "Your gun against mine. Winner takes all. If you win, I die. If I win, you die, and I marry Idelle. Either way, whoever comes out on top runs Atherton. What do you say?"

"Sounds good to me," Pritchard said. "Holster up."

Eli Gaines holstered his gun, pushed Idelle roughly aside, and stepped past her onto the street from the sidewalk. It was the first time since she'd been kidnapped at the schoolhouse that she wasn't surrounded by men with guns.

Jackson County, Missouri's chief deputy squared his narrow shoulders and faced Pritchard with both of his arms dangling over the butts of his twin revolvers.

Pritchard stood opposite the deputy with his rifle in his left hand, using it as a cane to steady himself. His right hand hung loosely at his side.

"You look right healthy for a dead man, Samuel Pritchard," Gaines said through his toothless grin. "I'm about to change that. I'm going to finish what I started ten years ago."

"I ain't bound, this time," Pritchard said. "Whenever you're ready."

Neither man got a chance to draw their guns.

Idelle, standing behind Gaines, suddenly withdrew the Colt Cloverleaf revolver she had concealed inside her dress. She shot the deputy in the back of the head. He fell face-first into the dust.

"Mama gave it to me," she explained as she dropped the engraved pistol. She fell to her knees, sobbing.

"Oh, Mama." Pritchard dropped his rifle and rushed to embrace her.

Ditch came running around the corner. "I heard a shot," he said. Pritchard gestured to Gaines with his chin.

Ditch rolled the deputy over with his boot. Gaines was still alive, though wouldn't be for long. There was an exit wound in the center of his forehead.

His open eyes were rolled back, he was convulsing, and his chest slowly rose and fell. He emitted a wet, rasping, gurgling noise from deep within his throat. Ditch recognized the all-too-familiar sound.

He flashed back, to the first time he'd heard a death rattle. It was ten years prior, also in Samuel Pritchard's company, and not far from where he now stood. Since then, Ditch had heard too many death rattles to count.

Gaines sputtered, clucked for another minute, and died. Ditch looked over at Pritchard, holding his crying sister. Had Idelle not been present, he would have spit on the murderous deputy's corpse. He was relieved to find no trace of the shadow that had haunted his friend since the day he'd pulled him, half-dead, from an unmarked grave, so many years before.

Chapter 58

Pritchard, Ditch, and Idelle stood together in the cemetery long after the pastor and the other mourners departed. Paul Clemson had been buried that morning, next to his parents' adjacent plots.

Dovie Pritchard had been laid to rest a week previously, alongside her husband Thomas, in a plot overlooking the pond on what was once again Pritchard land. There'd been quite a few funerals in Atherton during the past two weeks.

Pritchard and Idelle wired the governor and had gone to Jefferson City to meet with him. Retired Texas Ranger Captain Tom Franchard contacted the governor of the Republic of Texas, who in turn reached out to Missouri's governor and personally vouched for Pritchard's character and service. Once details of Burnell Shipley's reign in Atherton, based on affidavits from Ditch Clemson, the Nettleses, and many other residents, were revealed, no charges were levied against Pritchard, Ditch, or Idelle.

Dovie's dying words came true. She'd carefully ensured, over the years, that all necessary documentation to cement Idelle's status as her legal heir had been properly filed.

Idelle Pritchard, not yet twenty years old, was now the sole owner of two hotels, a saloon, a general store, a railroad depot, the stockyards, docks, a sawmill, and most of the buildings and the property they sat on, in not only the town of Atherton, but Jackson County. Samuel Pritchard, also Dovie's son and heir, could have filed legal papers to become co-owner along with Idelle, but refused.

Idelle's first order of business, after renaming "Shipley's Mercantile" to "Pritchard's Mercantile" and removing Shipley's name from anywhere else in town, was to fire storekeeper Oliver Manning and have him run out of town.

The trio strolled leisurely back into town, with Idelle and Ditch holding hands. Pritchard's leg was healing nicely, and he walked with only a slight limp.

"What now?" Pritchard asked them.

"I sent a telegram to Alejandro," Ditch said, "down in Texas. He's now officially in charge of the SD&P Ranch. I authorized him to purchase another herd of cows, so we'll see him again next spring when he and the boys bring up another load of beef to Abilene." He looked at Idelle, who smiled up at him. "I've decided to stay here in Atherton."

"What's a layabout like you going to do for a living?" Pritchard asked him.

"By coincidence," Ditch said, squeezing Idelle's hand, "I've just been hired by a local businesswoman. I'm going to help run her stockyards."

"That woman must be an imbecile," Pritchard said, "to trust a rustler like you with her livestock. Any other reason you're staying on?"

"Yep," Ditch said, grinning from ear to ear. "I got engaged."

"Don't tell me there are two female imbeciles in Atherton?" Pritchard said.

"Same gal," Ditch said.

"Anybody I know?" Pritchard asked. Idelle punched him in the arm.

"What about you?" Ditch asked. "What are you gonna do, now that you've resigned from the Texas Rangers?"

"I believe I'll be stayin' on in Atherton, myself," Pritchard said. "I've got family here. Not to mention, I just got myself hired by a local businesswoman, too."

"Doing what?" Ditch asked.

Pritchard parted his vest and displayed the star on his chest. It read, ATHERTON MARSHAL.

"It's good to be home," Ditch said.

ACKNOWLEDGMENTS

I wish to express my heartfelt gratitude to the following individuals for their invaluable support in the writing of this novel:

Marc Cameron, a real cowboy (both flesh and steel), retired U.S. Marshal, martial artist, true gentleman, and old-school badass. He's the kind of man I want my son to grow up to be.

My editor, the inimitable Gary Goldstein. If ever there was a fellow who in another life should have been the captain of a pirate ship, it's Gary. I'd pretty much follow him into hell with nothing more than a damp sponge.

My agent, Scott Miller, of Trident Media Group. He's the real deal. I am grateful for his counsel, stewardship, and friendship, and for his steady hand at the tiller.

The Usual Suspects, whose support and encouragement are deeply appreciated.

The Calaveras Crew. Better men to "ride the river with" never existed.

Lastly, and most important, my wife, Denise; daughter, Brynne; and son, Owen: the greatest blessings ever bestowed on a fellow. I am humbled every day. Today, tomorrow, and forever. You know the rest.

TURN THE PAGE FOR AN EXCITING PREVIEW

SAMUEL PRITCHARD
DOESN'T LOOK FOR TROUBLE

It's now 1874, and Samuel Pritchard is once again living under his true name. As Atherton's town marshal, he longs to put his bloody past behind him and finally settle into a peaceful life. But fate has other plans for Pritchard—strangers begin arriving in Atherton. Hard-eyed men wearing guns. Some come alone, others in groups. Besides the fact that every one of them is armed to the teeth, the newcomers share something else in common; they're all gunning for Smokin' Joe Atherton.

IT'S THERE WHEN HE
WAKES UP EVERY MORNING

Someone's placed a bounty on Pritchard's head: $10,000 in gold, payable to whoever can put the legendary pistolero into a pine box. And that someone is Dominic "Cottonmouth" Quincy, a wealthy and politically connected former Union spy, riverboat captain, and the meanest, deadliest cutthroat west of the Mississippi.

THIS DEVIL IS NO ANGEL

Pritchard isn't sure why Cottonmouth Quincy wants him dead—but he's about to find out that the ghosts of boot hill won't stay buried . . .

COTTONMOUTH
THE GUNS OF SAMUEL PRITCHARD
by Sean Lynch

Coming soon, wherever Pinnacle Books are sold.

Chapter 1

Sarpy County, Nebraska,
five miles east of Papillion, March 1874

The reverend reined his wagon to a halt. Four men on horseback were blocking the road ahead. All were wearing town suits and bowlers, and he'd never seen any of them before. They were also wearing revolvers in shoulder holsters that were plainly visible under their open riding jackets.

"Top of the mornin' to you, Reverend Hoskins," the oldest of the riders said. He tipped his hat.

"Do I know you gentleman?" Reverend Hoskins said.

"No," the man said. "But we know you. You're Charles Hoskins, the pastor of the Baptist church in town. We know your family, too. Sitting next to you is your wife, Mary, your daughter, Maura, and your wee little son, Charles Junior."

"How, exactly, do you know all this?" Hoskins asked.

"Why," the man said, "you're famous, Reverend. Your sermons are all the rage. They're right popular with the railroad laborers in these parts. Especially the ones where you call for all the workers to band together, hold out for more money, and strike iffen they don't get what they want from Brody's railroad company. Those sermons are real barn burners, so I'm told."

"Now I know who you are," Hoskins said, making no effort to hide his contempt. "You're Quincy Agency men, aren't you? Cottonmouth Quincy sent you to intimidate me into silence and to stamp down the poor, abused souls being worked like slaves by John Brody."

"It's true," the man confirmed, "we're employed by the Quincy Detective Agency. And as a matter of fact, we did come here to persuade you to temper your sermons to a tone more sympathetic to Mr. Brody's interests. By the way, Mr. Quincy certainly wouldn't appreciate being called 'Cottonmouth' by the likes of you."

"I didn't give him that name," Hoskins retorted. "Quincy earned it himself by slithering around like a serpent, hiding like a thief, peering into keyholes like a rat, and doing John Brody's bidding."

"You surely have a right hostile notion of Mr. Quincy's character," the man said, "for a man of God. I thought all you preachers were supposed to be the forgivin' type?"

"Quincy doesn't need my forgiveness," Hoskins said. "If he wants to save his soul, he needs to repent his wicked ways and stop helping Brody wage war on his poor workers."

"I'll be sure and tell him you said that," the man said. The men with him chuckled.

"Charles," Mary said in a hushed whisper to her husband, "turn us around." The fear was plain on her face and clear in her voice. "We need to leave. Now." She pulled Maura, who was twelve, and Charles Junior, who was six, closer.

"I'll not be buffaloed by Cottonmouth Quincy's hired thugs," Hoskins declared. "You're blocking our way," he said to the riders. "Yield the road and let us pass."

"I don't suppose you're going to voluntarily agree to stop sermonizin' against the railroad," the man said, "and stirrin' up all the workin' folks, are you?"

"I certainly am not."

"Mr. Quincy figured you was gonna say that," the man said, drawing his revolver. He nodded to his men, who also drew theirs.

One of riders guided his horse close enough to the team pulling Hoskins's wagon to seize the harness. Mary stifled a scream and covered both her children's eyes as they huddled together.

"Step down outa that rig, Reverend," the man ordered, "and bring your family with you."

"We will not," Hoskins said. "I'm not afraid of your guns."

"Maybe not," the man said, aiming his Remington at Mary Hoskins and cocking the hammer back, "but I'll wager your wife is."

"All right," Hoskins said, clambering out of the buggy. "Don't shoot." He helped his wife and children disembark.

As soon as the Hoskinses left the wagon, the Quincy men dismounted. One climbed into the driver's seat the reverend vacated.

Hoskins stood protectively in front of his family. It did him no good. The leader holstered his pistol, nodded again, and another of the men clubbed the reverend in the kidney with the butt of his gun. The thin pastor fell gasping to all fours. Mary Hoskins began to cry, along with both of her children.

"Today we're gonna preach you a sermon," the leader said, "and it ain't even Sunday. The topic of this sermon is wrath and retribution. Put your right hand under the wagon wheel."

"What?"

The man kicked Hoskins in the ribs, dropping him from all fours to his stomach. "You heard me, Reverend. Put your hand under the wheel."

"Please," Reverend Hoskins pleaded. "Don't do this."

"Either your hand goes under that wheel, or your daughter's head. Which'll it be?"

The terrified Hoskins hesitated. The leader gave another silent signal, and one of the men roughly snatched twelve-year-old Maura from her mother's arms. Another simultaneously grabbed Mary and Charles Junior by the hair and held them in place.

Maura was dragged, also by her hair, screaming and flailing in terror, and forced to the ground with her head under one of the wagon's rear wheels. The Quincy man in the wagon's seat held up his whip, awaiting the order to start the team of horses.

"No!" Reverend Hoskins said. "Let my daughter go." He crawled to the wagon on his belly and extended his right hand under the front wheel.

The leader gestured to release the girl. Maura Hoskins scrambled to her feet and ran sobbing into her mother's arms. Then the leader nodded a final time, and his man in the wagon cracked the whip.

The wagon lurched forward. Reverend Hoskins cried out in agony as his hand was crushed. His wife sank weeping to her knees, bringing her children with her.

The leader halted the wagon. He walked over to where the reverend lay cradling his mangled hand.

"Are you gonna continue to rile up workers against Mr. Brody and his railroad?"

"N-no," Reverend Hoskins sputtered.

"That's good," the man said. "Because Mr. Quincy gave specific orders about what we're to do if we catch wind of you givin' any more sermons incitin' unrest against the Brody Railroad Company. We'll be back, and what happened today will seem like a church social. We'll burn your church down, Reverend, with you and every one of your flock in it. Then we'll end your wife and daughter in their own beds and shoot your son dead on your doorstep. Do you understand?"

"I understand," Hoskins said.

The Quincy men holstered their revolvers and remounted their horses. "Don't you make us come back," the man admonished, "you hear?"

"I won't," Hoskins said weakly. "You'll have no more trouble from me."

"I reckoned as much," the man said. He shouted, "Cottonmouth Quincy sends his regards," over his shoulder as he and his three companions rode off.

Chapter 2

Atherton, Missouri, April 1874

"I thought I'd find you here," Ditch Clemson said as he entered the marshal's office. His lifelong friend, Marshal Samuel Pritchard, was seated inside at his desk. He was assembling the components of a chair he'd crafted himself.

Ditch put his hands on his hips and shook his head. "It's almost noon," he said, "and the train from Saint Louis is due to arrive any minute."

"So?" Pritchard said without looking up.

"So?" Ditch mimicked, making no effort to conceal the exasperation in his voice. "You know that European feller, Count Strobl, is gonna be on the train."

"So?" Pritchard repeated.

"All the newspapers are writin' about how Strobl got himself kicked out of his own country on account of dueling. He's reputed to be exiled royalty and one of the deadliest shots east of the Mississippi."

"Why should I care?" Pritchard asked.

"You should care," Ditch said, "because he's been bragging to every reporter who'll listen that he's gunning for you."

"Keep your shirt on," Pritchard said, looking up from the partially assembled chair. "Why would this Strobl fella be on the prod for me? I don't know him from General Lee."

"Evidently, he knows you," Ditch said, "at least by reputation. You're tellin' me you ain't a little worried?"

"Nah," Pritchard said. "What's worryin' get you? Anyhow, I'm almost finished puttin' the last leg on my chair. I'll be along in a minute."

"Sometimes a little worryin' can keep you alive. What am I supposed to tell your sister, Idelle, after you get shot to pieces sittin' at your desk, covered in saw-dust, fiddlin' with a wooden chair?"

"You worry too much," Pritchard grinned, fitting the final leg into the seat. He placed the chair on the floor, sat in it, and smiled in satisfaction. "After all we've been through together, do you reckon I'm gonna let a fancy-pants, foreign duelist put a hole in me?"

Pritchard stood to his full six-and-a-half-foot height and smiled down at his medium-sized friend. "Be-sides," he said, "I have no choice but to make my own office chair. The old one is too small. The only way I can get furniture big enough to fit me is to make it myself."

"I just don't want to see you get shot again," Ditch said, looking up at the towering marshal. "Neither does Idelle. She is the mayor, after all. She's insisting on going to the station herself to meet this Count Strobl. She plans to ask him not to provoke you. She doesn't want to see anybody get hurt."

"Sometimes," Pritchard said, "people get hurt. That's a fact. Occasionally it can be prevented, other times it can't. More often than not, it's their own damned fault. Idelle ought to know that as well as anyone. You, too."

"I reckon so," Ditch agreed.

Samuel Pritchard and David "Ditch" Clemson had grown up as friends, neighbors, and blood brothers in rural Atherton. Teenagers when the Civil War began, they fled as partners after Pritchard's father was murdered, his family's property and lumber business were stolen, and his mother was forced to marry the man who'd orchestrated it all: Atherton's corrupt mayor, Burnell Shipley. Young Pritchard was shot in the head, presumed dead, and buried in an unmarked grave.

That was when his fiercely loyal friend, Ditch Clemson, dug him up and found him still clinging to life.

After his resurrection, and bearing a telltale gunshot scar on his forehead over his right eye, Pritchard assumed the alias "Joe Atherton" to protect what was left of his family. Departing Missouri, the boys enlisted in the Confederate army as guerrillas in Arkansas. After a series of harrowing escapades, Pritchard and Ditch, no longer boys, survived the war and parted ways.

Ditch, a skilled horseman, had grown weary of war and killing. He went farther south and sought his fortune in Texas. Within a few years he flourished as a rancher and cattleman.

Pritchard chose a different path, also in Texas; he joined the Texas Rangers. Over the next ten years he blazed a trail, in gun smoke and blood, throughout the Republic of Texas and the New Mexico and Arizona territories. "Smokin' Joe" Atherton, as he became known, earned his nickname for his propensity to send those who challenged him to "smoke in hell." He also earned a well-deserved reputation as the fastest, and most lethal, gunman on the frontier.

The previous summer, fate brought Pritchard and Ditch together once more. The duo joined forces on a cattle drive and ended up back in their hometown. There they courageously faced down Burnell Shipley and his crew of murderous lawmen, but not before Pritchard's mother was killed and his younger sister, Idelle, was taken hostage. The two heroic young Missourians, neither yet thirty years old, eliminated the mayor, cleaned out his crooked gunmen, rescued Idelle, and freed the town of Atherton from the yoke of abuse and corruption that had characterized Burnell Shipley's decades-long reign.

In the nine months since their epic battle in the streets of Atherton, the town, finally out from under the shadow of Shipley's iron-fisted rule, once again prospered. Ditch and Idelle, fulfilling her childhood wish, got engaged.

Ironically, with Burnell Shipley's death and the passing of their mother, Idelle and Samuel Pritchard inherited the vast wealth of Atherton's lucrative lumber, cattle, and merchandising enterprises once controlled exclusively by Shipley.

Pritchard, however, refused any part of the abundant inheritance. He left his share of the money, and the running of Atherton, in his younger sister's capable hands, comforted by the knowledge that Ditch, his most trusted friend, was at her side. As a result of Pritchard's reticence, Idelle found herself in the unique and unexpected position of being the wealthiest person in Jackson County, Missouri. And until the special elections coming up in June, she was also the acting mayor of Atherton.

Pritchard contented himself with putting to rest the alias Smokin' Joe Atherton, and the role of Ranger, gunfighter, and man-killer that had made him a legend under that infamous title.

Meanwhile Ditch, at Idelle's insistence, announced his candidacy for mayor to fill the vacancy created by Burnell Shipley's abrupt demise. She knew he had the temperament, business acumen, and ethical foundation to lead Atherton out of the trauma the community had endured throughout the war and at Shipley's filthy hands.

At Ditch's, Idelle's, and the town council's prodding, Pritchard had taken on the job of town marshal. He had also, reluctantly, allowed himself to be nominated as a candidate for Jackson County sheriff and grudgingly accepted the position of acting sheriff until the election.

"Are you comin' with me to the train station," Ditch asked impatiently, "or ain't ya?"

Pritchard brushed off the sawdust from his button-front shirt and belted on his pair of .45 Colt revolvers. He topped his blond hair, which was closely cropped at the sides and back but long enough on top to mostly cover the bullet-hole scar on his forehead, with his Stetson.

"Let's go welcome the count," he said to Ditch, gesturing toward the door. "I'd hate to keep royalty waiting."

Chapter 3

It was overcast, chilly, and threatening rain when Pritchard and Ditch reached the depot. A sizable crowd, larger than the usual group of townspeople meeting the afternoon train, had assembled at the station. Both men surmised the extra gaggle of spectators were connected to the impending confrontation between the mysterious European passenger and Atherton's town marshal. The train slowly came to a halt in a cloud of hissing steam.

Idelle waved to them from across the station. When they met, she gave her brother and fiancé a hug. Like Pritchard, she had blond hair and crystal blue eyes. But unlike her colossal, rawboned, and muscular brother, Idelle was petite and delicate of feature.

"There's talk all over town of a showdown," she said, glancing around at the people milling excitedly about. "All these folks have come to watch you and that Count Strobl fellow shoot each other to pieces."

"They'll likely be disappointed," Pritchard said.

"Please be careful," Idelle said. "I read in the *Kansas City Enterprise* that Count Strobl has already killed four men in duels since coming to America; one of them with a sword. They say he killed over a dozen more in Europe."

"Hell," Ditch grunted, "Samuel's killed more'n that in one afternoon." Pritchard elbowed his friend.

"This isn't a joke," Idelle said. "According to the article, Strobl's a professional duelist. Which means somebody's put up money to have you killed."

"You're jumping to conclusions," Pritchard said calmly. "Maybe this Strobl feller's just passin' through?"

"Who are you kidding?" Idelle said. "Atherton's only a small town on the rail line to Kansas City from Saint Louis. There's no reason for him to get off the train here, other than you. And why would he brag to all those reporters about wanting to challenge you if he wasn't on the prod?"

"I don't know the answers to those questions," Pritchard said to his sister, "but gettin' worked up over things that ain't yet occurred makes no sense. Give me a chance to meet this Count Strobl. Who knows? Maybe he's a swell feller."

"And maybe he'll shoot you on sight," Idelle said drily.

"Folks are unloading," Ditch remarked, pointing to the passenger cars. They scanned the people as they got off. The crowd's eyes were on Marshal Pritchard, over a full head taller than anyone else at the station, as the passengers began to disembark. Pritchard's, Ditch's, and Idelle's eyes searched for the mysterious Count Strobl.

"Who is she?" Ditch whistled, as a woman stepped off the train.

A number of women had already disembarked, but this particular female stood out dramatically from the rest. She looked to be in her early to mid-thirties, was of slightly less than average height, and possessed a remarkably beautiful face. In addition to extraordinary green eyes, she had pale skin, freckles, flaming red hair tucked under her bonnet, and a strikingly buxom figure.

Another feature that distinguished this woman from others in the crowd was the elegant, and clearly expensive, dress, hat, and matching parasol she sported. Such elaborate feminine attire might have been commonplace in New Orleans or Saint Louis, but was in stark contrast to what women in Atherton typically wore. In addition to its cost, the woman's dress was very formfitting and exposed a great deal of her prominent bust.

The woman seemed aware that many of the men, and more than a few jealous women, had taken notice of her.

"Never seen her before," Pritchard said.

"Would have remembered if I had," Ditch said. "I can't tell if she's on the outside of that dress tryin' to get in, or the inside tryin' to get out."

"Put your jaws back into place," Idelle said, pinching Ditch until he winced. "You two clods act like you've never seen a girl before."

"I've seen plenty of girls," Pritchard said, "but none like her. She's built like a burlap bag full of bobcats."

The red-haired woman's gaze stopped when it met Pritchard's. She stared at him through emerald eyes. After a moment's evaluation, she turned abruptly on her heels and headed toward the luggage car.

"Wonder what brings someone like her to Atherton?" Ditch said.

"Never you mind, Ditch Clemson," Idelle said.

Connect with
U(s)

Visit us online at
KensingtonBooks.com
to read more from your favorite authors, see books
by series, view reading group guides, and more.

Join us on social media

for sneak peeks, chances to win books and prize packs,
and to share your thoughts with other readers.

facebook.com/kensingtonpublishing
twitter.com/kensingtonbooks

Tell us what you think!

To share your thoughts, submit a review,
or sign up for our eNewsletters, please visit:
KensingtonBooks.com/TellUs.